Tree-House Comix Proudly Presents

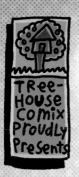

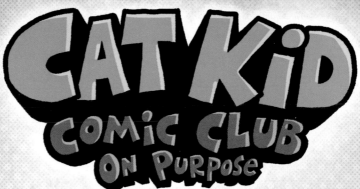

CAT KID COMIC CLUB
ON PURPOSE

WORDS, ILLUSTRATIONS, AND ARTWORK BY

DAV PILKEY

WITH DIGITAL COLOR BY JOSE GARIBALDI

graphix
AN IMPRINT OF
SCHOLASTIC

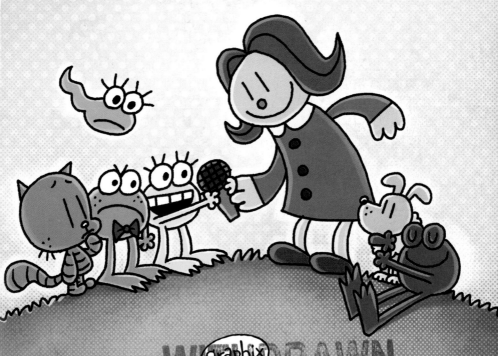

TO JEFF, JULIE, WILL,
AND GRANT KINNEY

Library of Congress Control Number 2021949401

978-1-338-80194-1 (POB)   978-1-338-80195-8 (Library)

10 9 8 7 6 5 4 3 2 1   22 23 24 25 26

Printed in the U.S.A.   44
First edition, April 2022

Illustrations, 3-D models, photography, and hand lettering by Dav Pilkey.

ALL mini comics colored by Dav Pilkey using pencil, watercolors, acrylic paints, markers, colored pencils, crayons, and gouache. 3-D models built out of recycled plastic lids, clay, paper, wood, wire, tape, glue, broken toys, balloons, and other throwaway items.

Digital Color by Jose Garibaldi | Flatting by Aaron Polk

Editor: Ken Geist | Editorial Team: Megan Peace and Jonah Newman
Book design by Dav Pilkey and Phil Falco
Creative Director: Phil Falco
Publisher: David Saylor

CHAPTERS & COMICS

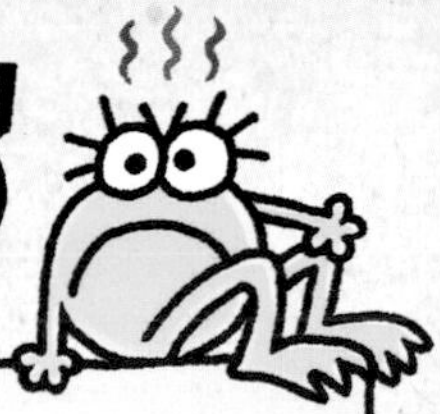

Find out who you are
and do it on purpose.

−Dolly Parton

Chapter 1

Weekend Woes

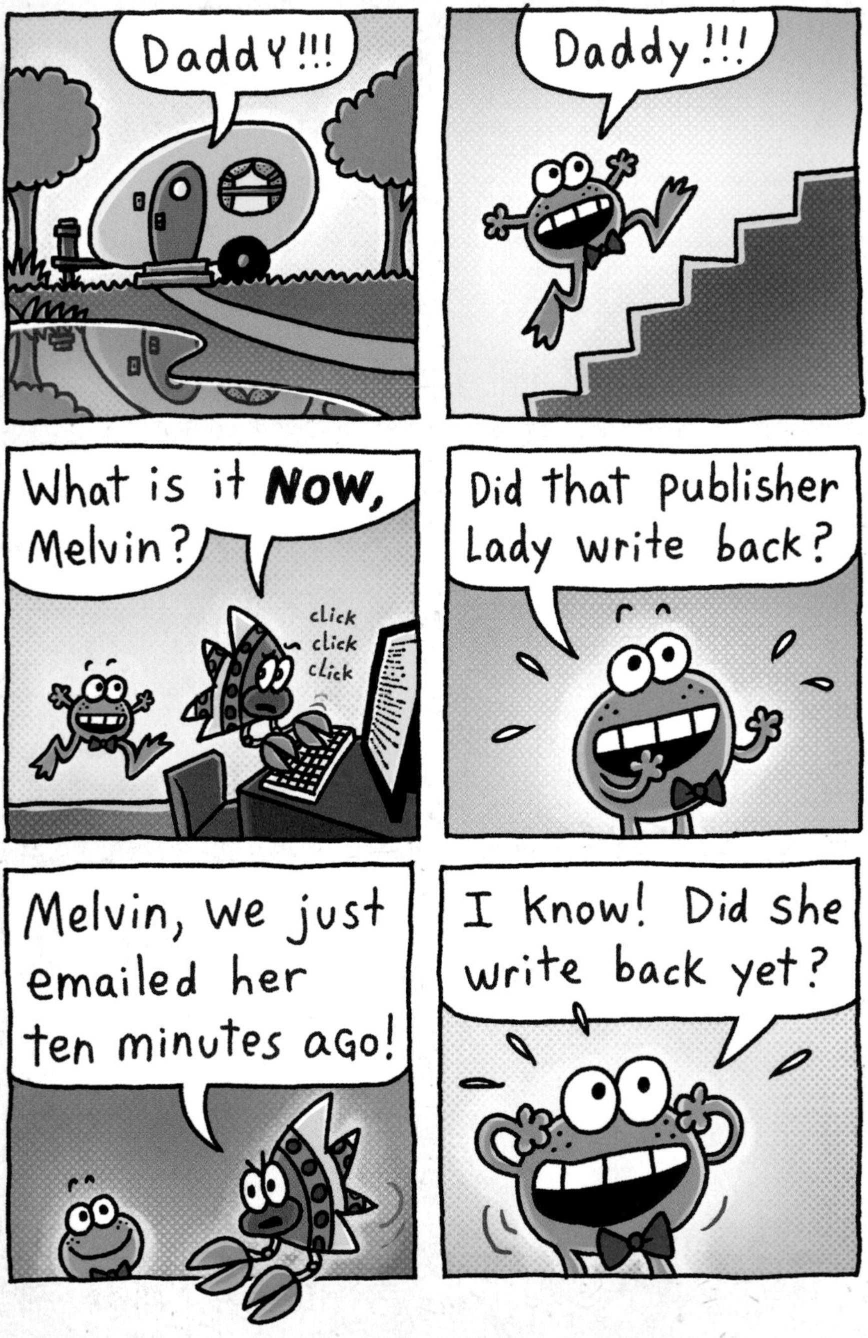
DADDY!!!
Daddy!!!
What is it NOW, Melvin?
click click click
Did that publisher Lady write back?
Melvin, we just emailed her ten minutes AGO!
I know! Did she write back yet?

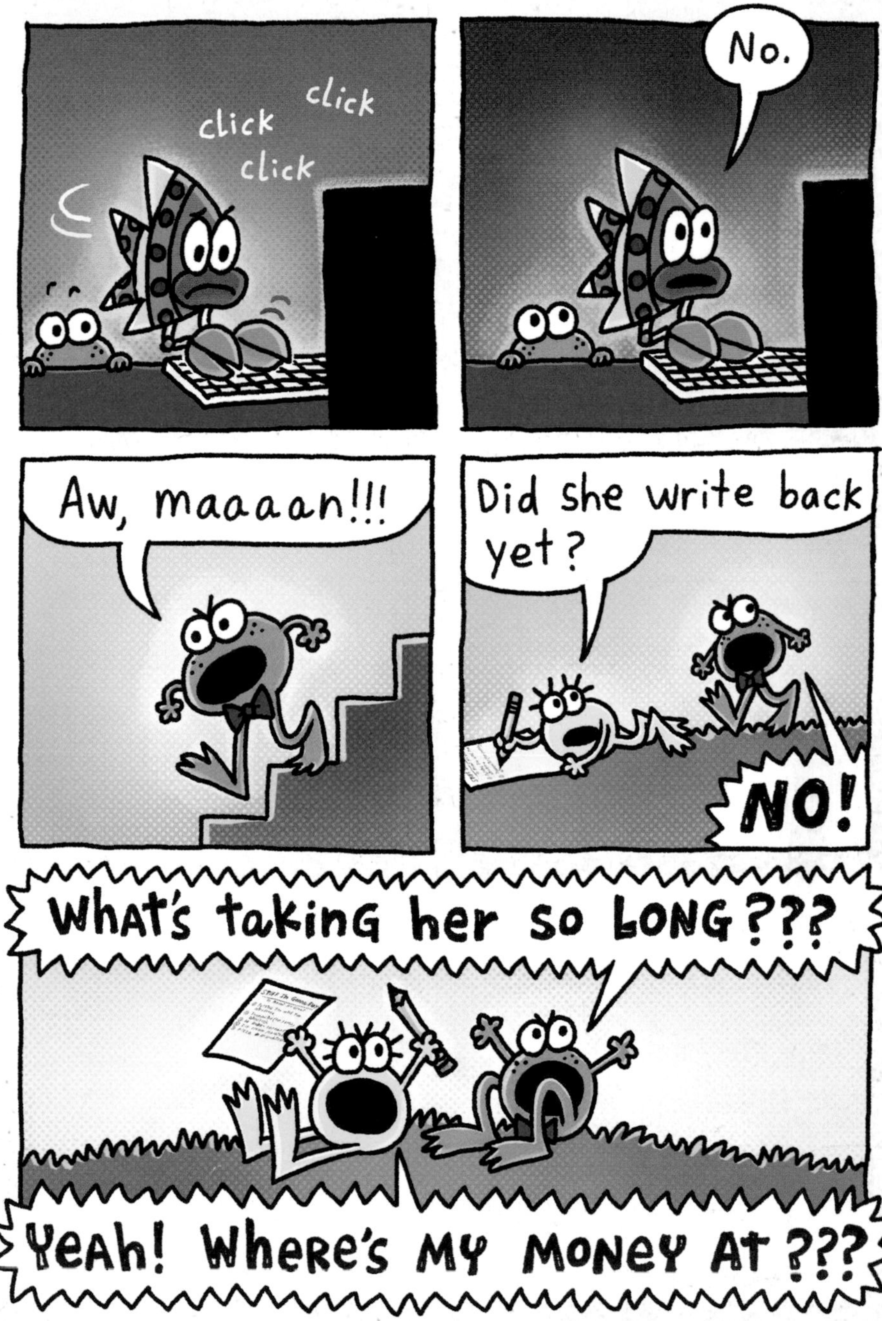
click
click
click
No.
Aw, maaaan!!!
Did she write back yet?
NO!
What's taking her so LONG???
Yeah! Where's my money at???

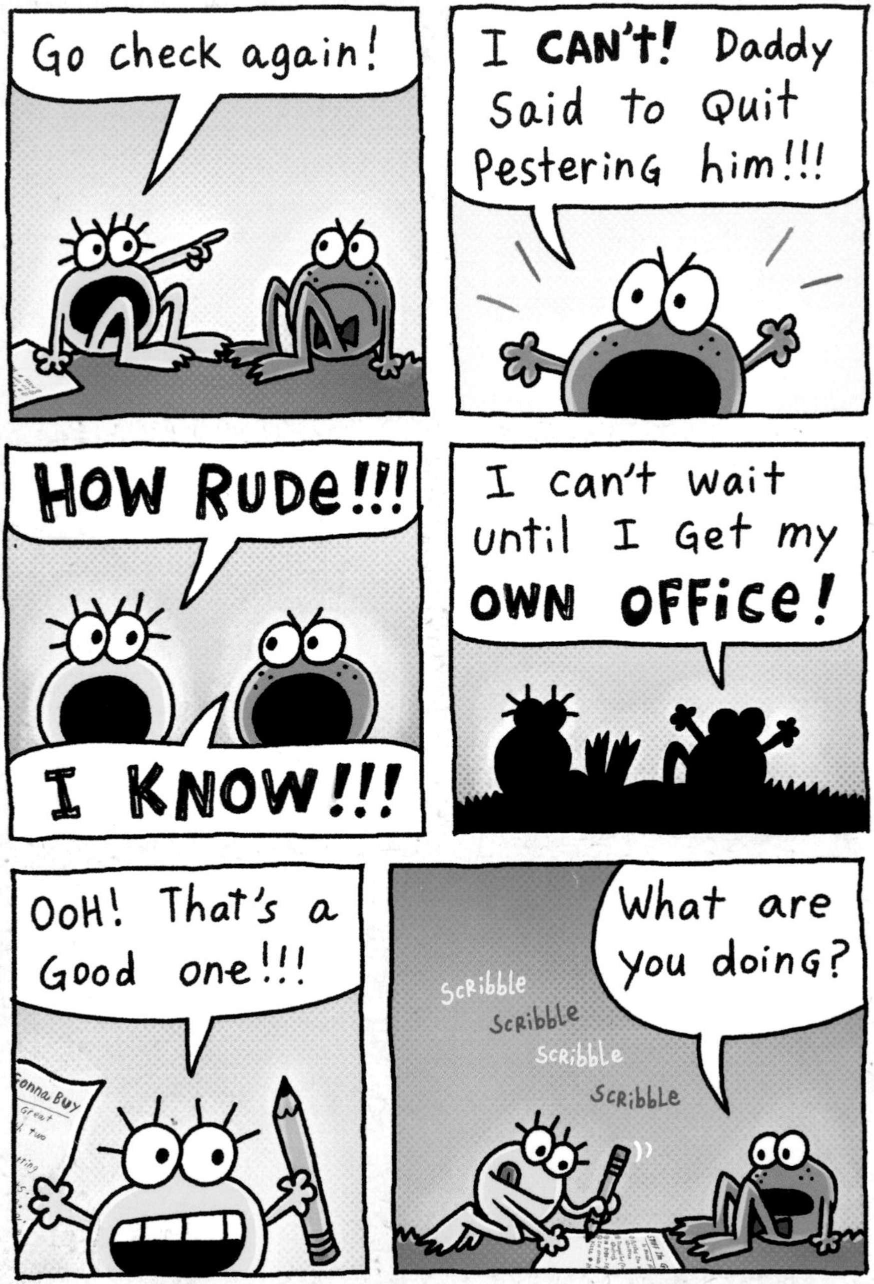
Go check again!
I CAN'T! Daddy Said to Quit Pestering him!!!
HOW RUDE!!!
I KNOW!!!
I can't wait until I Get my OWN OFFICE!
OOH! That's a Good one!!!
Gonna Buy
Great
What are you doinG?
SCRIBBLE
SCRIBBLE
SCRIBBLE
SCRIBBLE

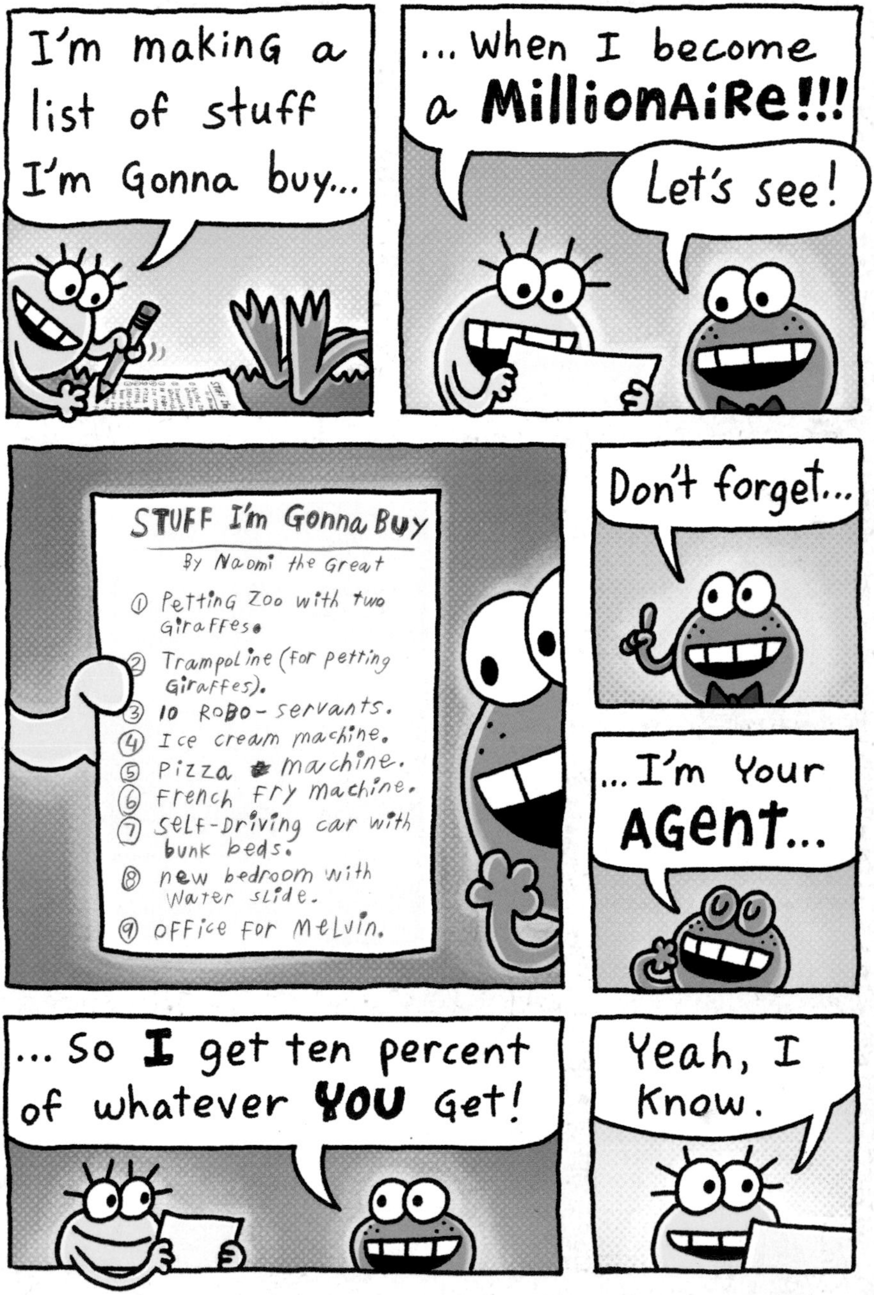
I'm making a list of stuff I'm Gonna buy...
... When I become a MILLIONAIRE!!!
Let's see!
STUFF I'm Gonna BUY
By Naomi the Great
① Petting Zoo with two Giraffes.
② Trampoline (for petting Giraffes).
③ 10 ROBO-servants.
④ Ice cream machine.
⑤ Pizza machine.
⑥ French Fry machine.
⑦ Self-Driving car with bunk beds.
⑧ new bedroom with Water slide.
⑨ office for Melvin.
Don't forget...
... I'm Your AGENT...
... So I get ten percent of whatever YOU Get!
Yeah, I Know.

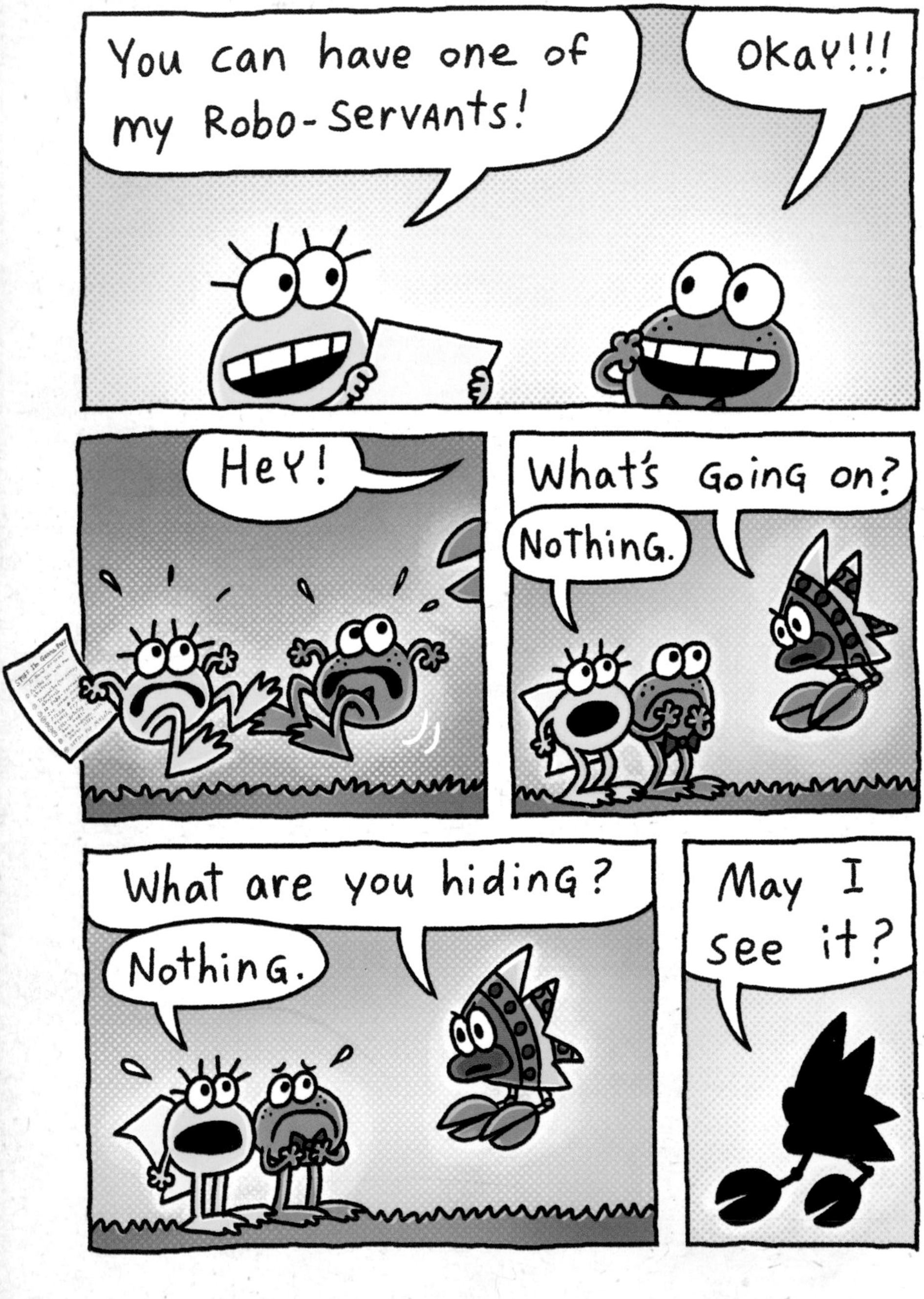
You can have one of my Robo-Servants!
OKAY!!!
HEY!
What's Going on?
Nothing.
What are you hiding?
Nothing.
May I see it?

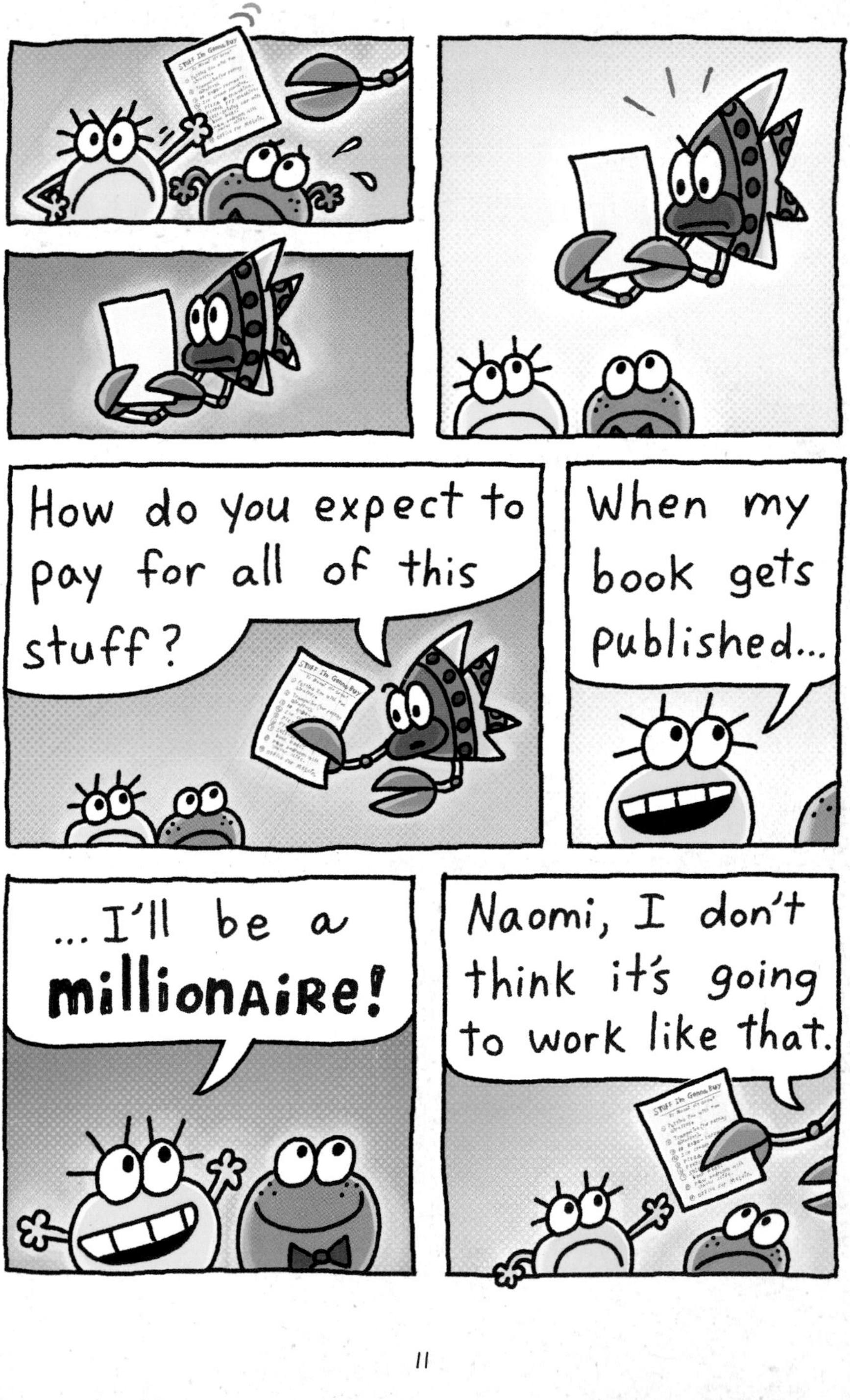
How do you expect to pay for all of this stuff?
When my book gets published...
...I'll be a millionAiRe!
Naomi, I don't think it's going to work like that.

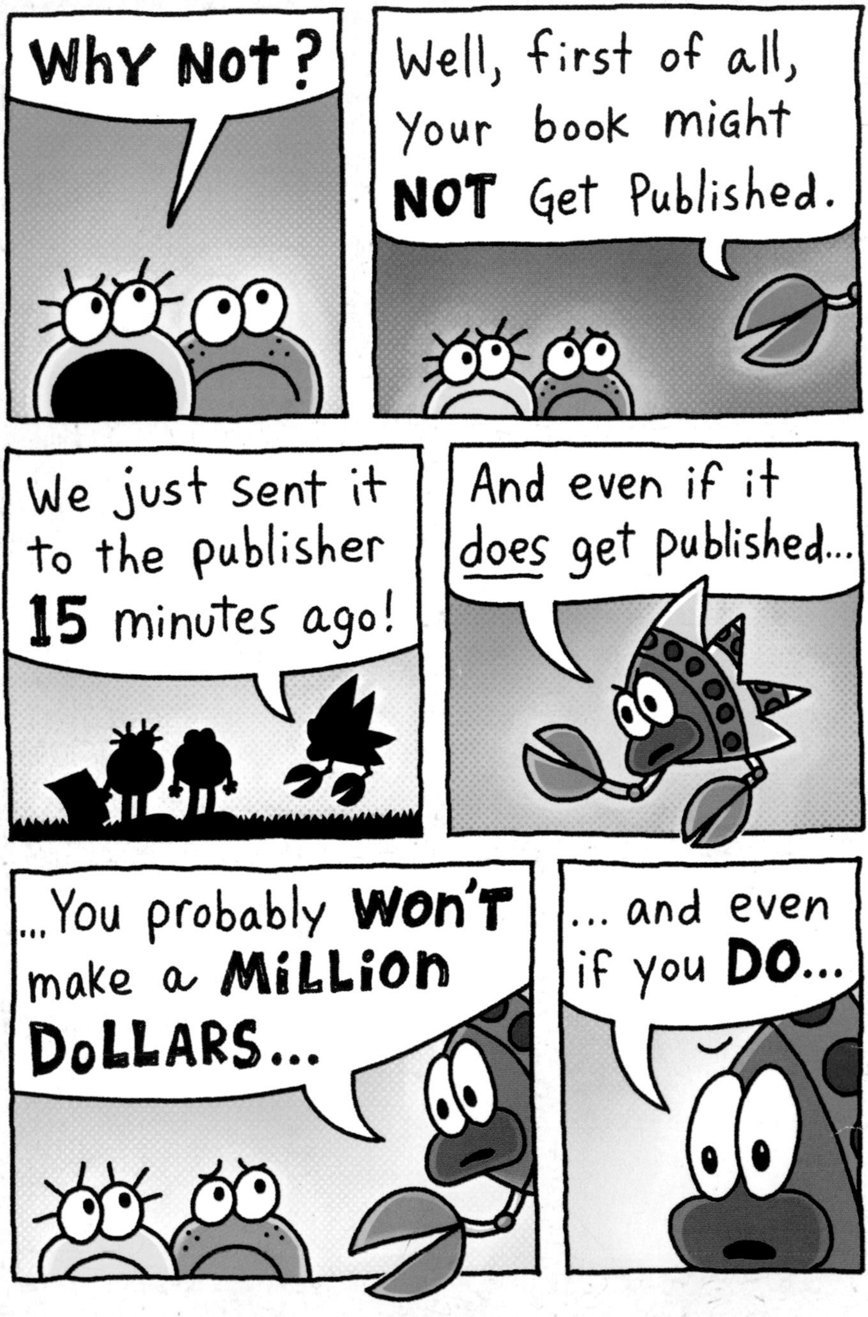
WHY NOT?
Well, first of all, your book might NOT get published.
We just sent it to the publisher 15 minutes ago!
And even if it does get published...
...You probably WON'T make a MILLION DOLLARS...
... and even if you DO...

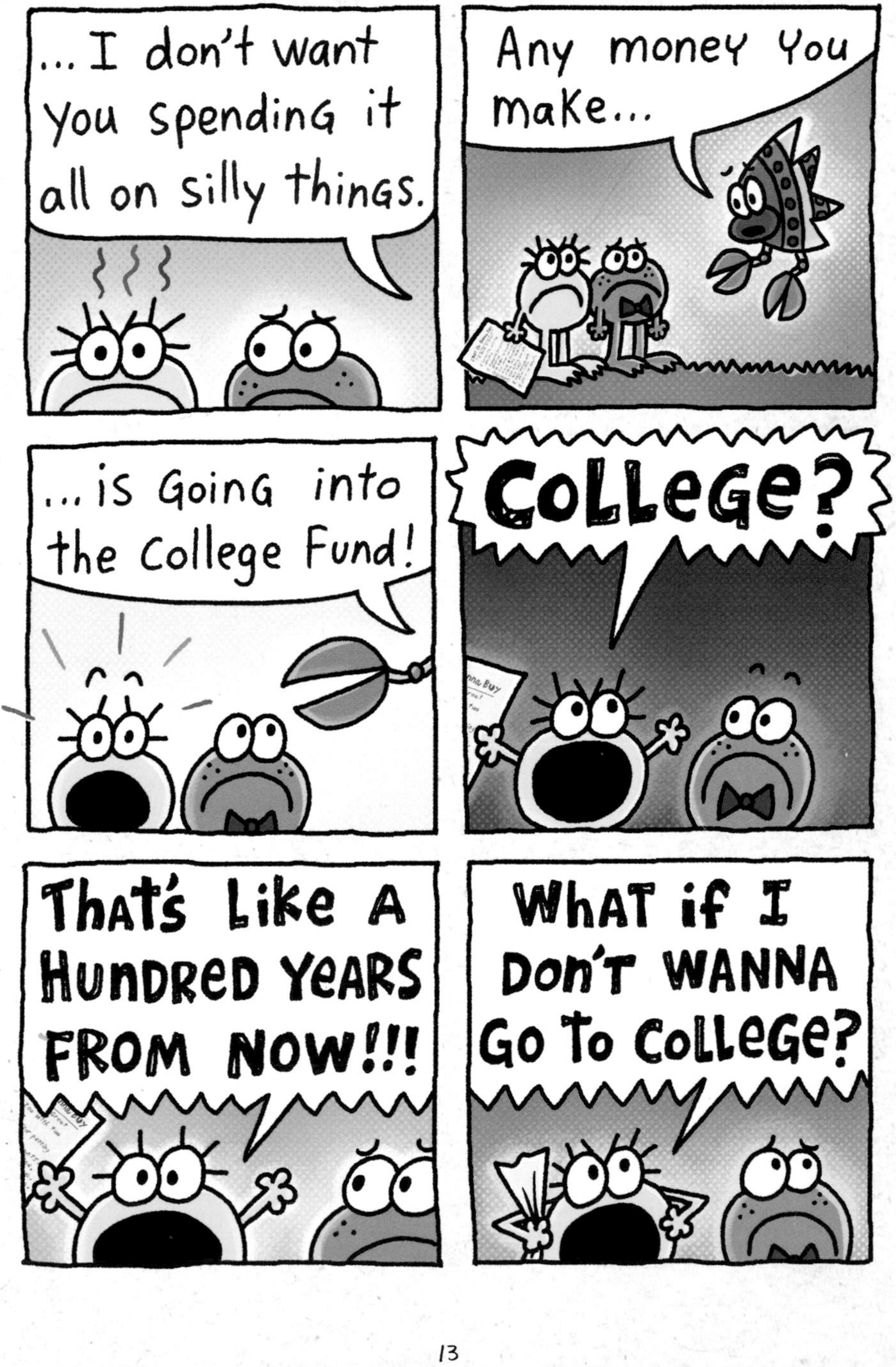
...I don't want you spending it all on silly things.
Any money you make...
...is going into the College Fund!
COLLEGE?
THAT'S LIKE A HUNDRED YEARS FROM NOW!!!
WHAT IF I DON'T WANNA GO TO COLLEGE?

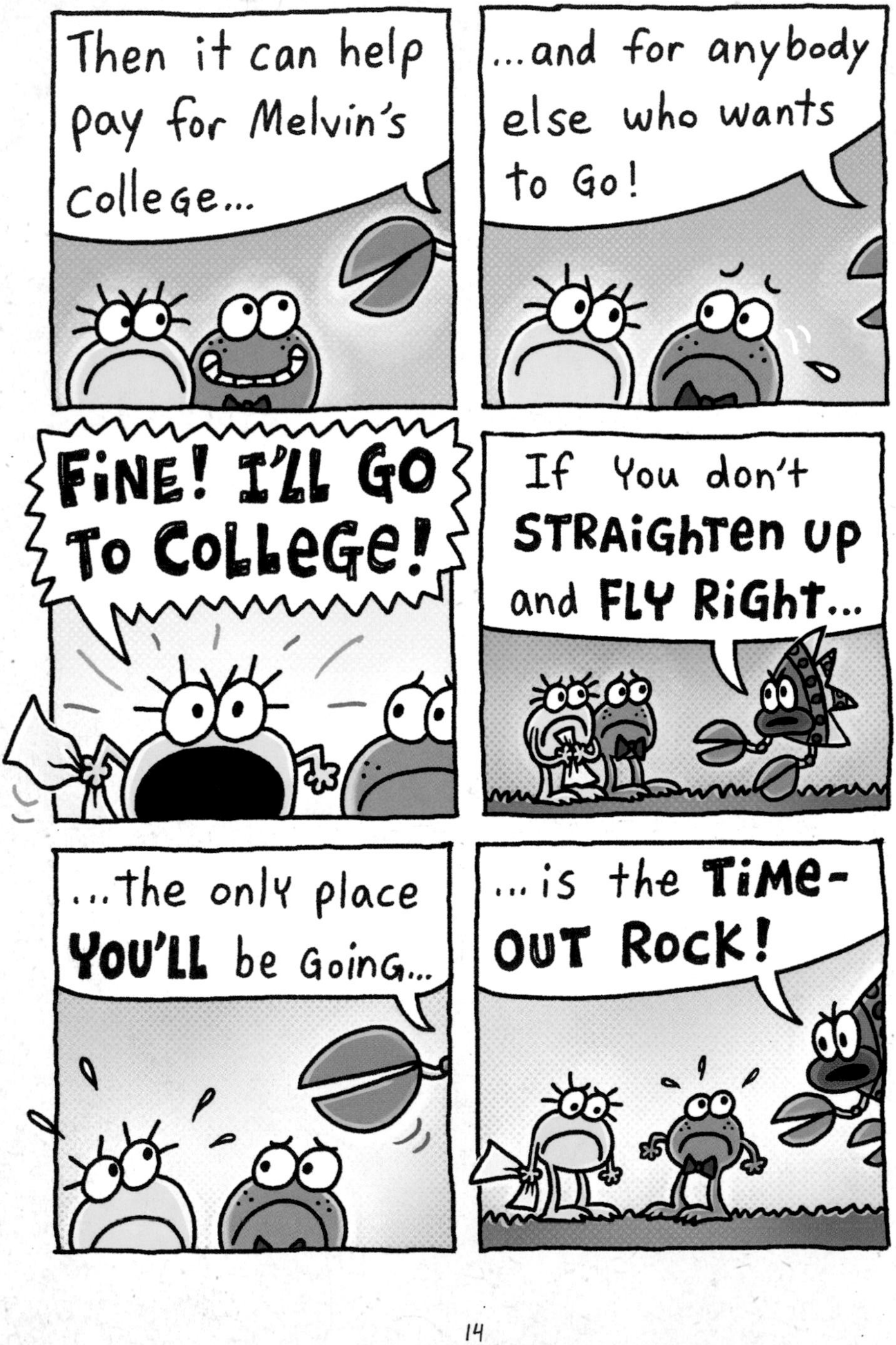
Then it can help pay for Melvin's college...
...and for anybody else who wants to go!
FINE! I'LL GO TO COLLEGE!
If you don't STRAIGHTEN UP and FLY RIGHT...
...the only place YOU'LL be going...
...is the TIME-OUT ROCK!

CHAPTER 2

Bedtime Worries

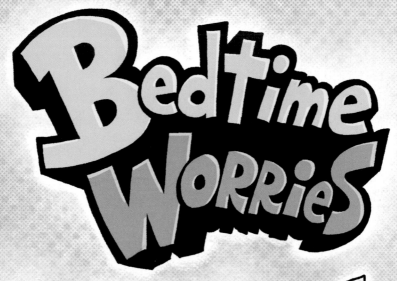

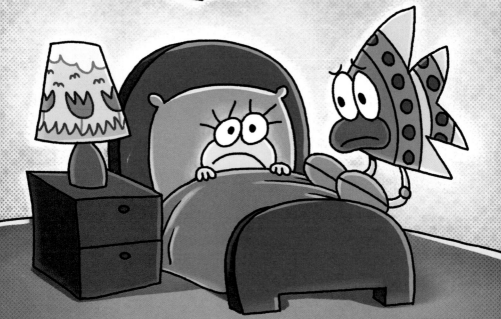

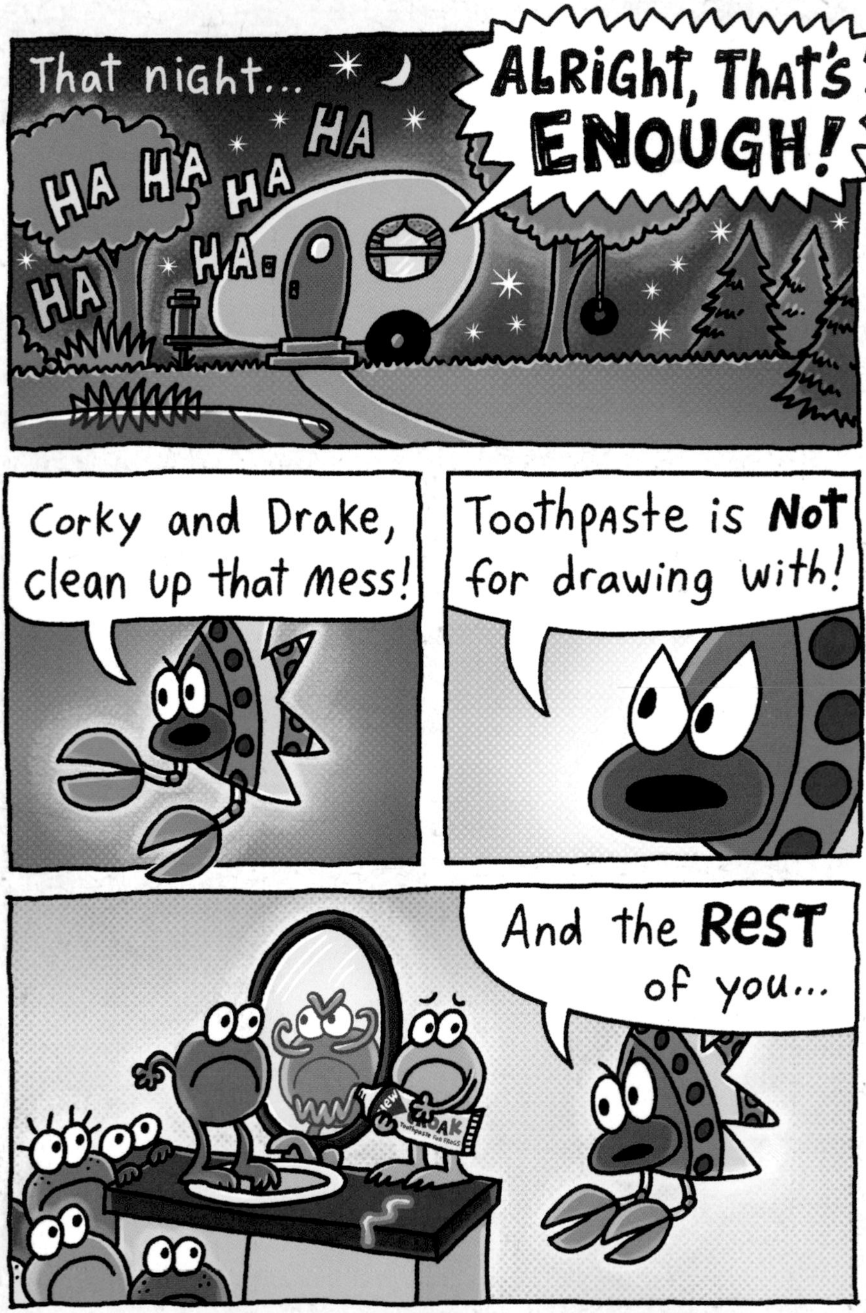
That night...
HA HA HA HA HA HA HA
ALRIGHT, THAT'S ENOUGH!
Corky and Drake, clean up that mess!
Toothpaste is NOT for drawing with!
And the REST of you...

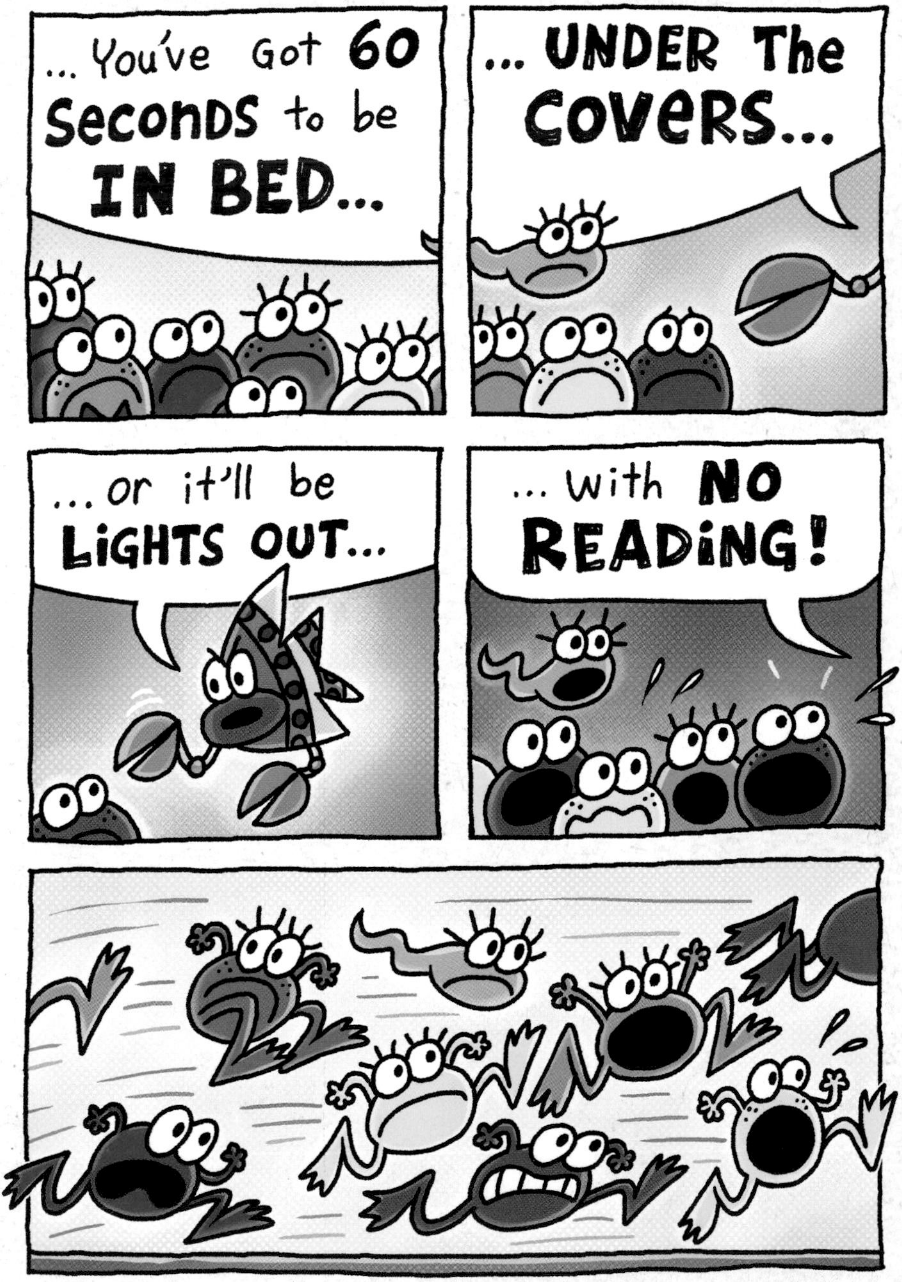
... You've Got 60 SecondS to be IN BED...
... UNDER The COVERS...
... or it'll be LiGHTS OUT...
... with NO READiNG!

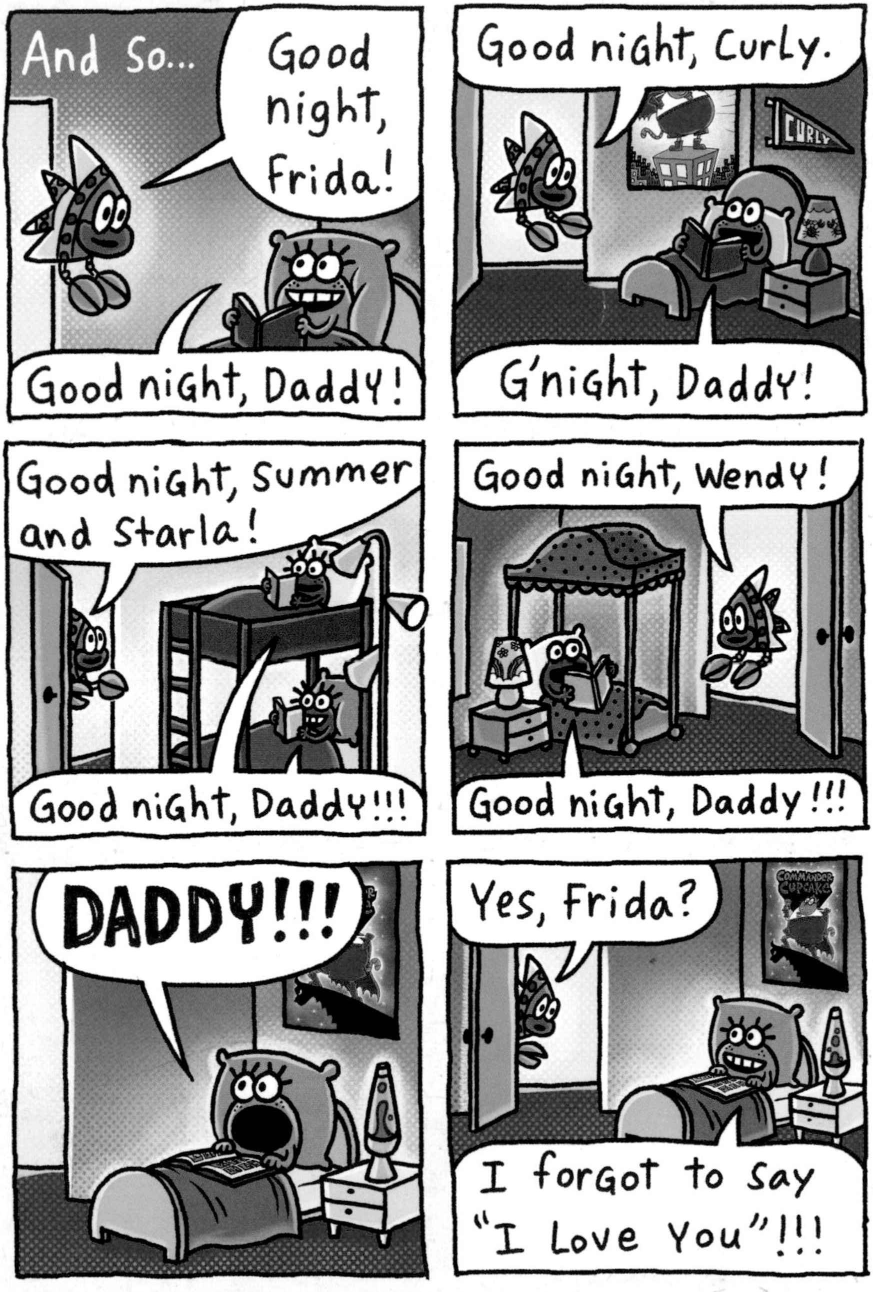
And So...
Good night, Frida!
Good night, Daddy!
Good night, Curly.
G'night, Daddy!
CURLY
Good night, Summer and Starla!
Good night, Daddy!!!
Good night, Wendy!
Good night, Daddy!!!
DADDY!!!
Yes, Frida?
COMMANDER CUPCAKE
I forgot to say "I Love You"!!!

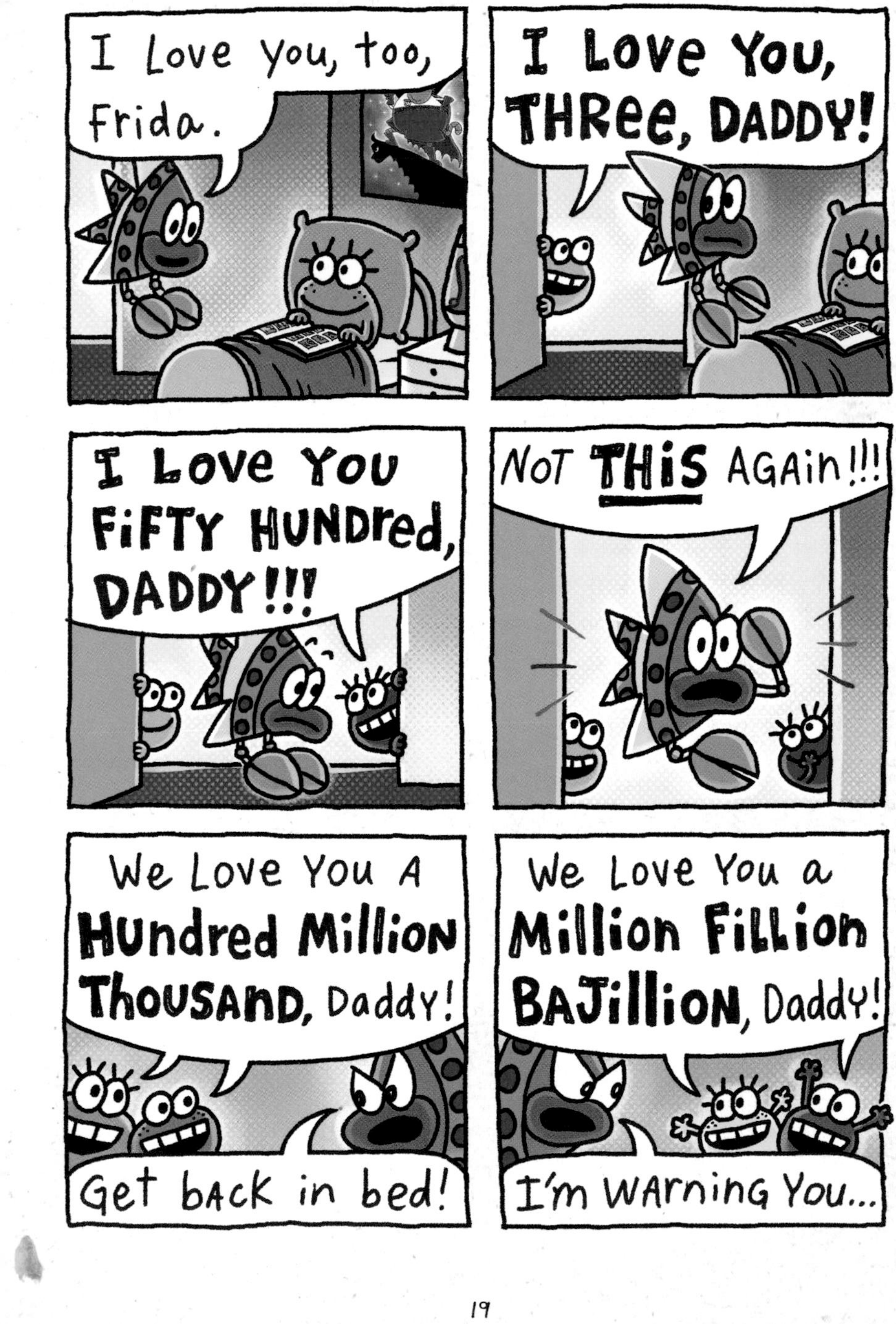
I Love you, too, Frida.
I Love You, THRee, DADDY!
I Love You FiFTY HUNDred, DADDY!!!
NOT THIS AGAin!!!
We Love You A Hundred Million THOUSAND, Daddy!
Get back in bed!
We Love You a Million Fillion BAJillion, Daddy!
I'm WARning You...

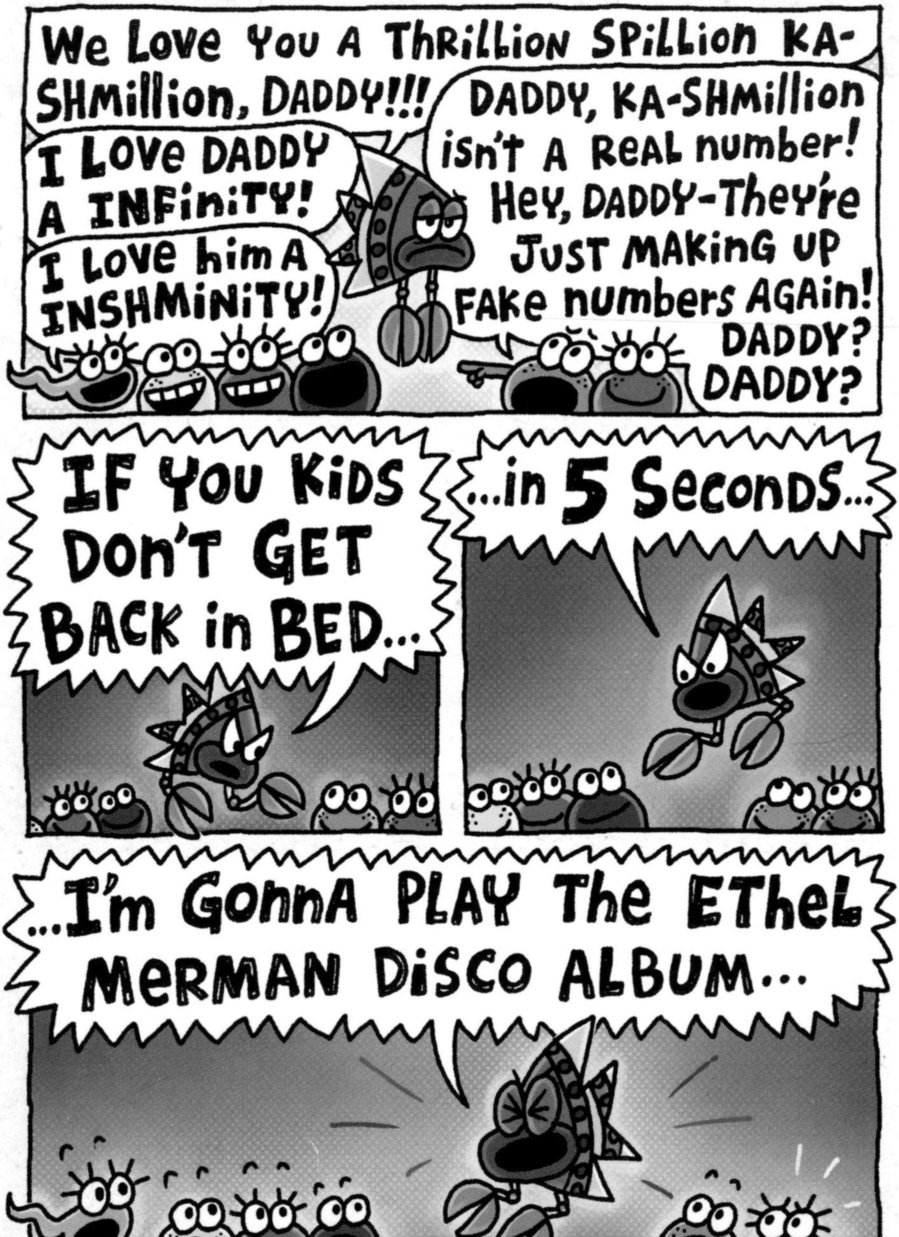
We Love You A Thrillion Spillion KA-SHMillion, DADDY!!!
I Love DADDY A INFINITY!
I Love him A INSHMINITY!
DADDY, KA-SHMillion isn't A REAL number! Hey, DADDY-They're JUST MAKING UP Fake numbers AGAIN! DADDY? DADDY?
IF YOU KIDS DON'T GET BACK in BED...
...in 5 Seconds...
...I'm GonnA PLAY The EThel MerMAN Disco ALBUM...

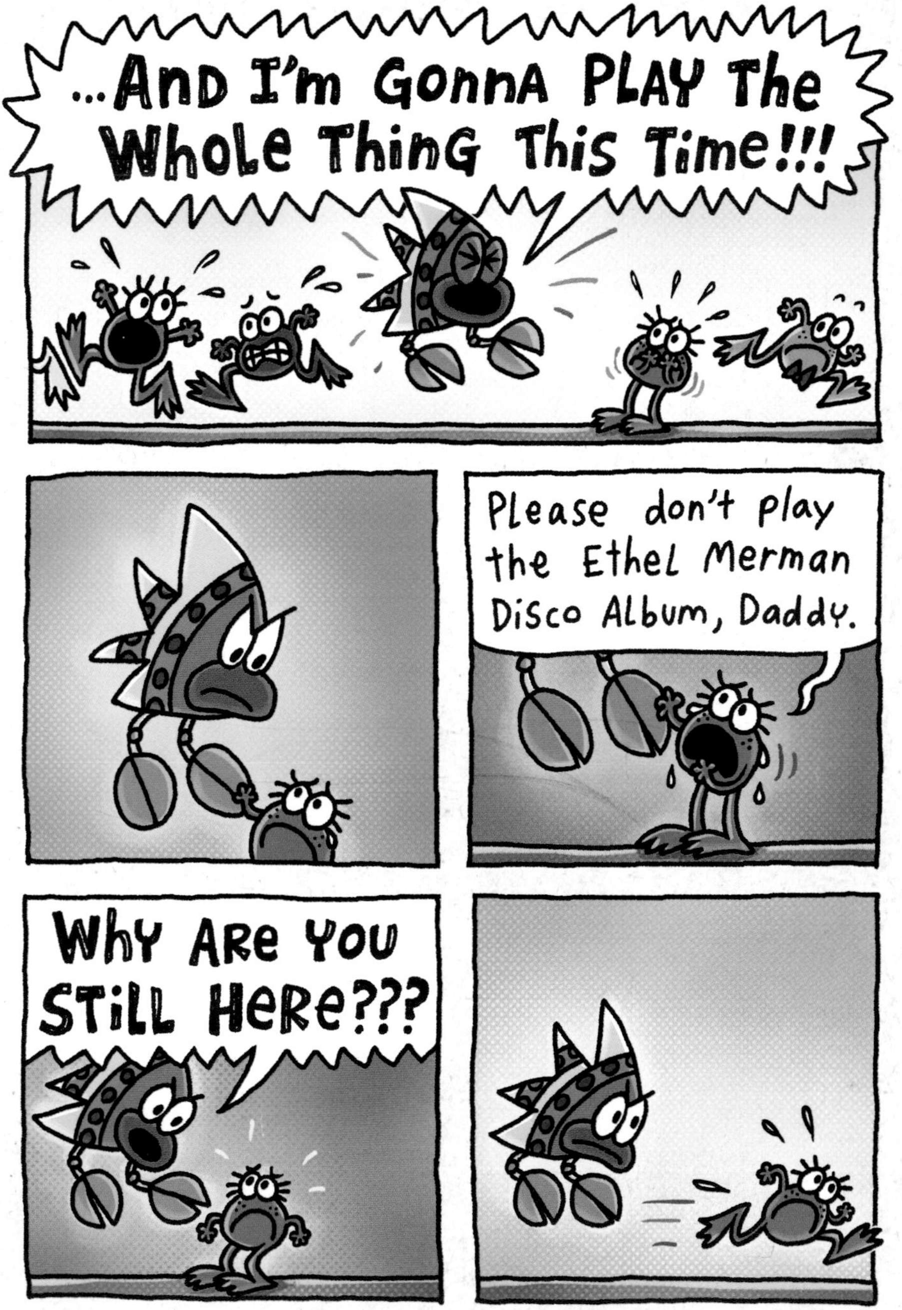
...AND I'M GONNA PLAY THE WHOLE THING THIS TIME!!!
Please don't play the Ethel Merman Disco Album, Daddy.
WHY ARE YOU STILL HERE???

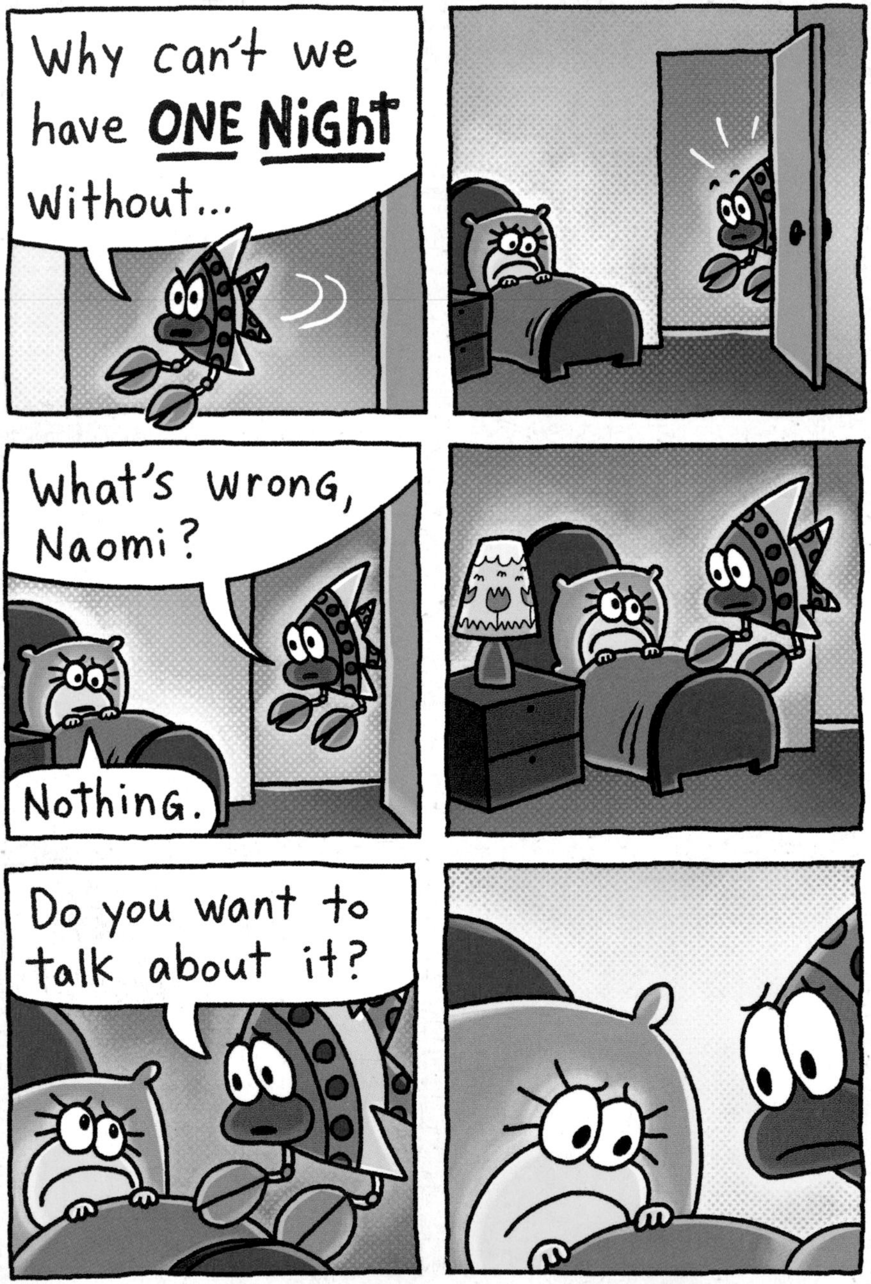
Why can't we have ONE NIGHT without...
What's wrong, Naomi?
Nothing.
Do you want to talk about it?

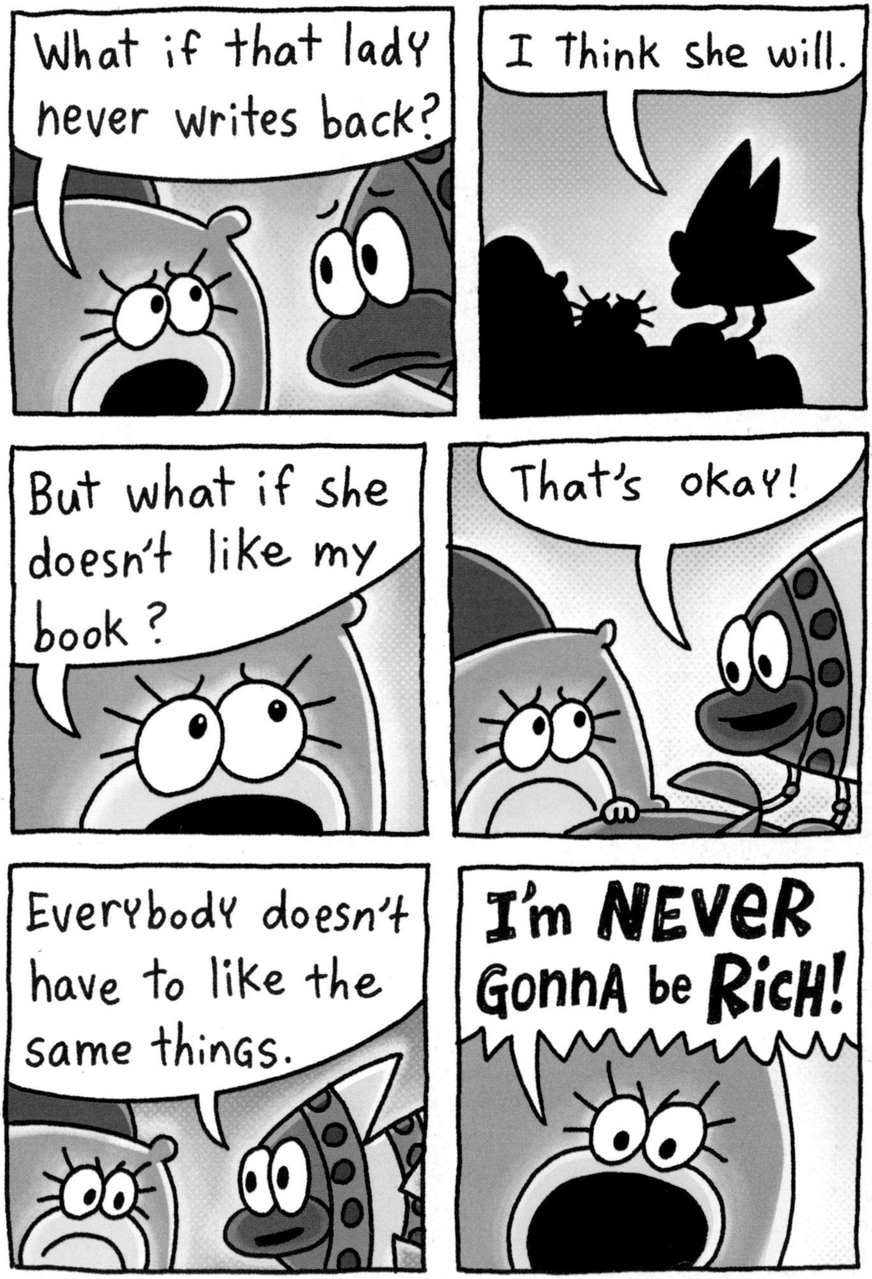
What if that lady never writes back?
I think she will.
But what if she doesn't like my book?
That's okay!
Everybody doesn't have to like the same things.
I'm NEVER GONNA be RICH!

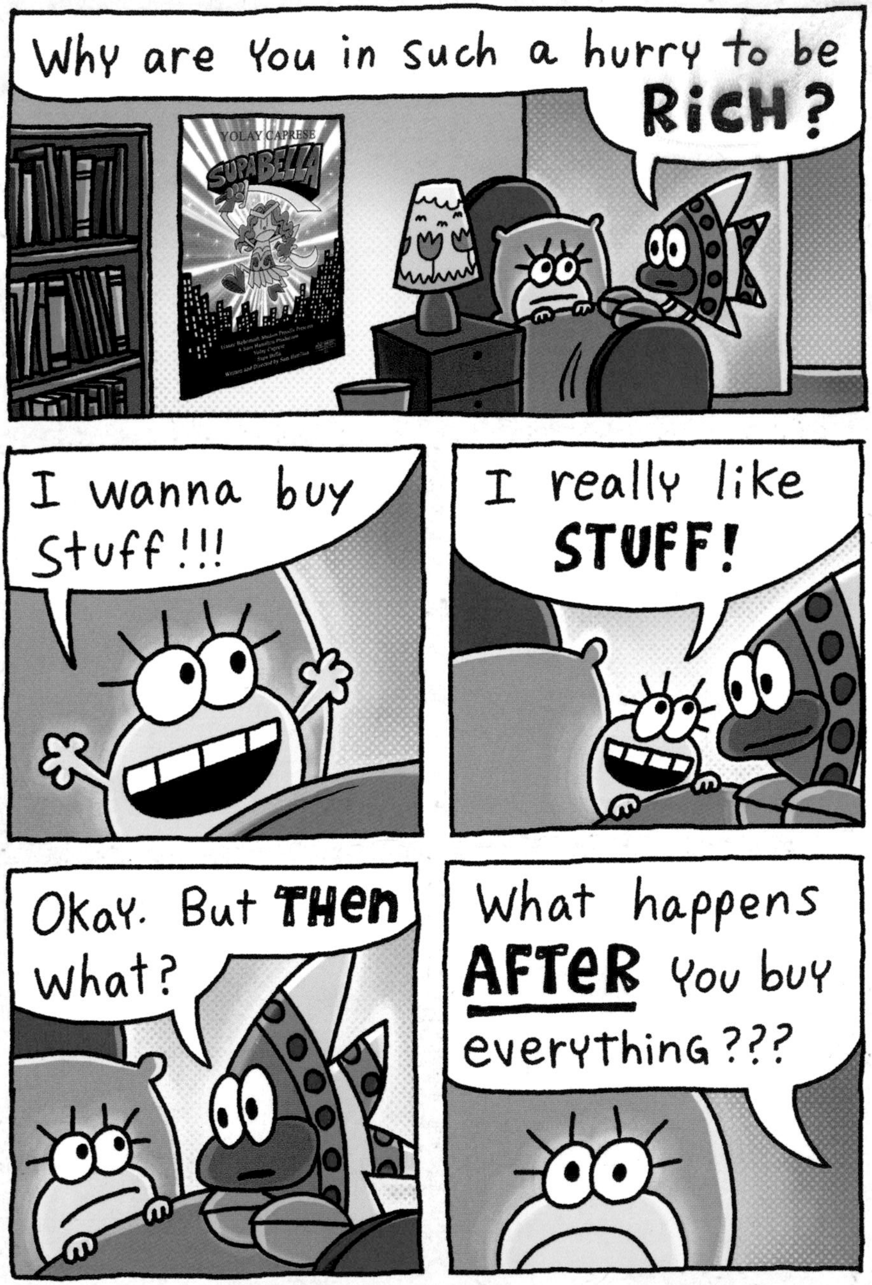
Why are You in such a hurry to be RICH?
I wanna buy Stuff!!!
I really like STUFF!
Okay. But THEN what?
What happens AFTER you buy everything???

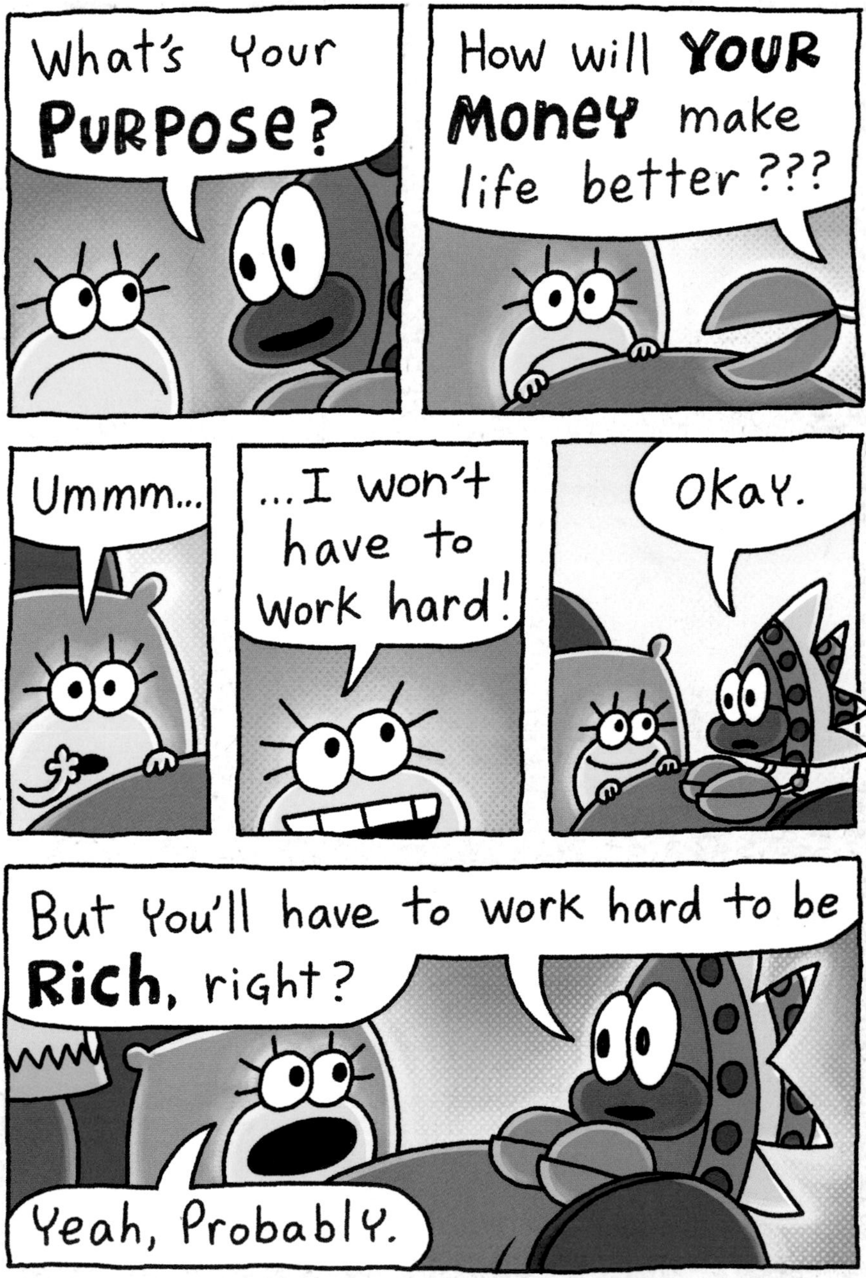
What's your PURPOSE?
How will YOUR MONEY make life better???
Ummm...
...I won't have to work hard!
OKAY.
But you'll have to work hard to be RICH, right?
Yeah, probably.

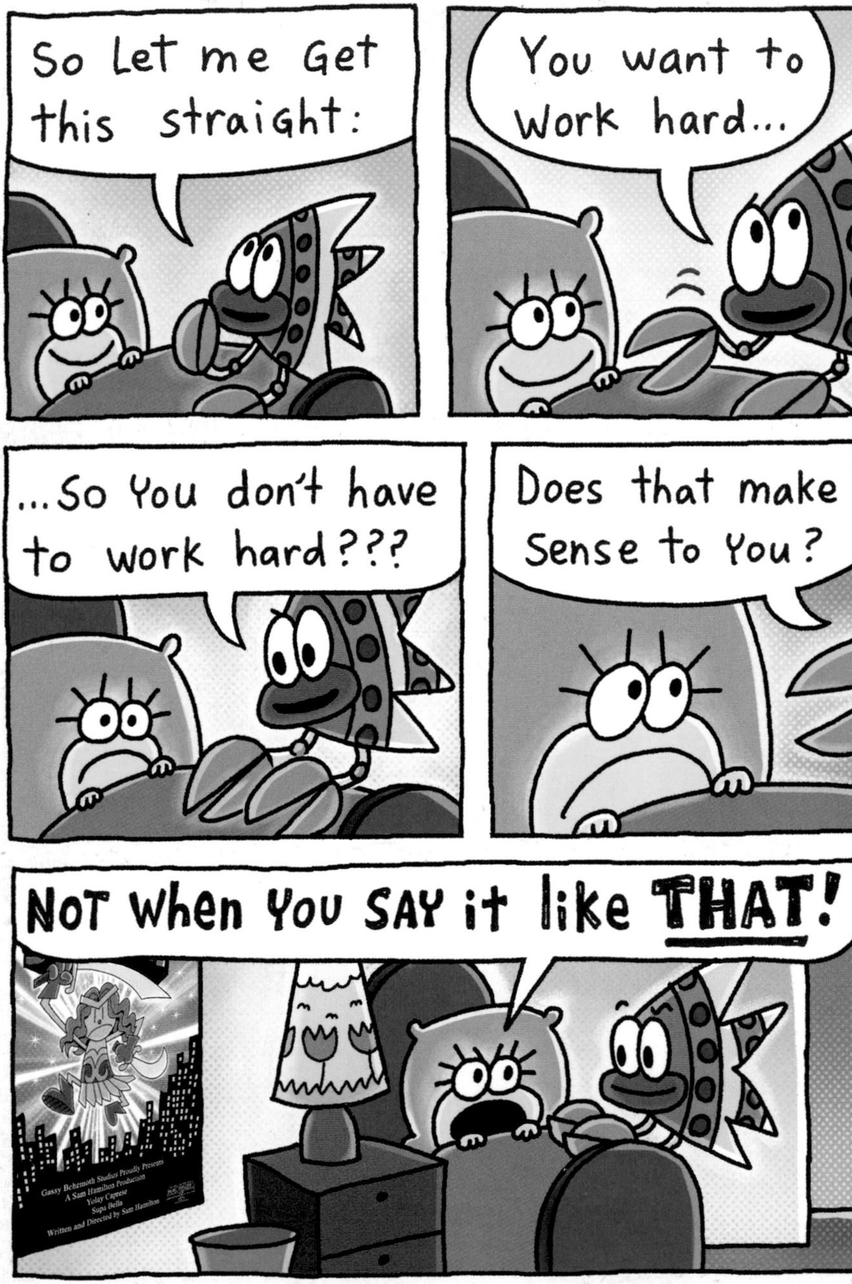
So let me get this straight:
You want to work hard...
...So you don't have to work hard???
Does that make sense to you?
NOT when YOU SAY it like THAT!
Gassy Behemoth Studios Proudly Presents
A Sam Hamilton Production
Yolay Caprese
Supa Bella
Written and Directed by Sam Hamilton

CHAPTER 3

The Big Surprise

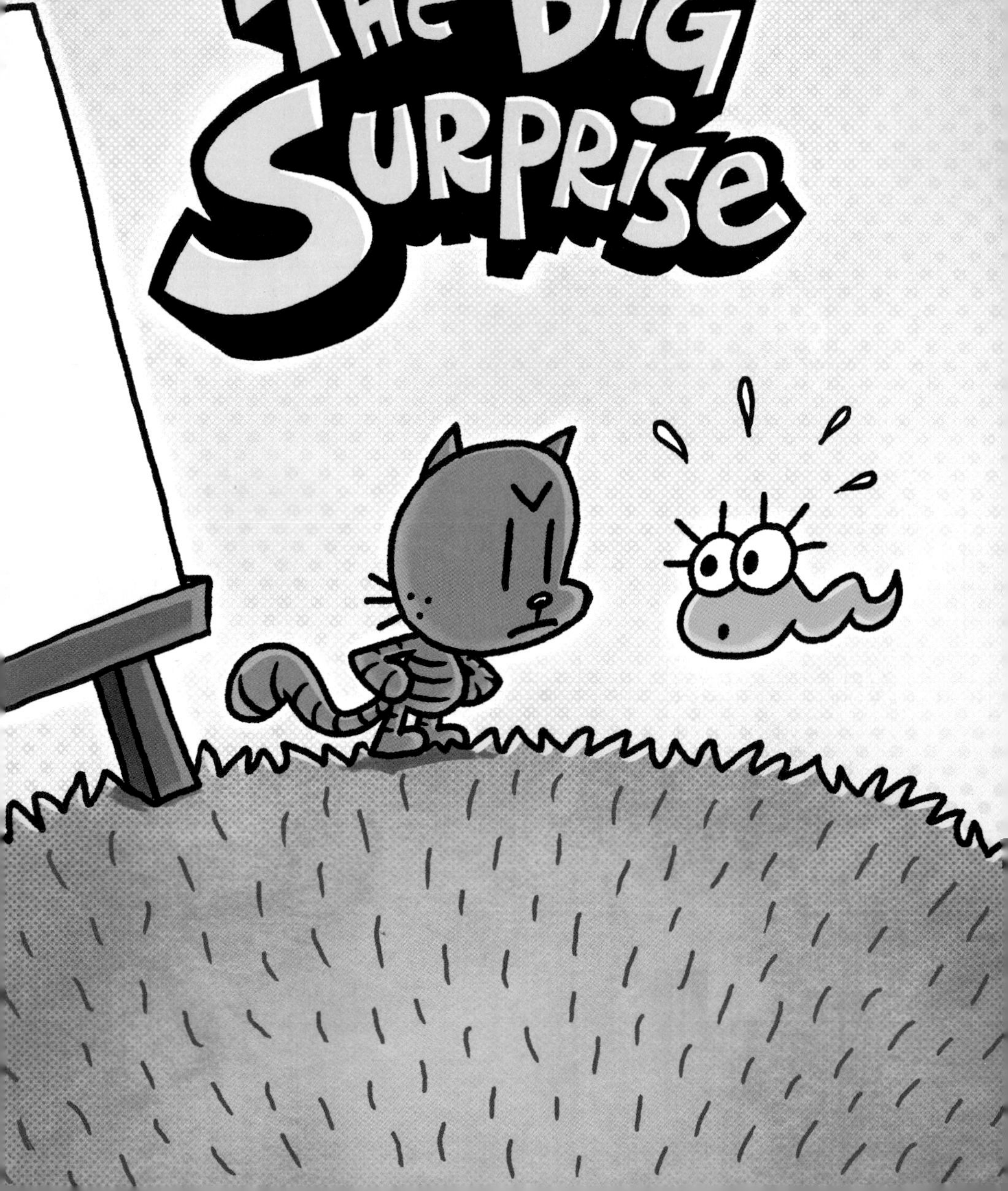

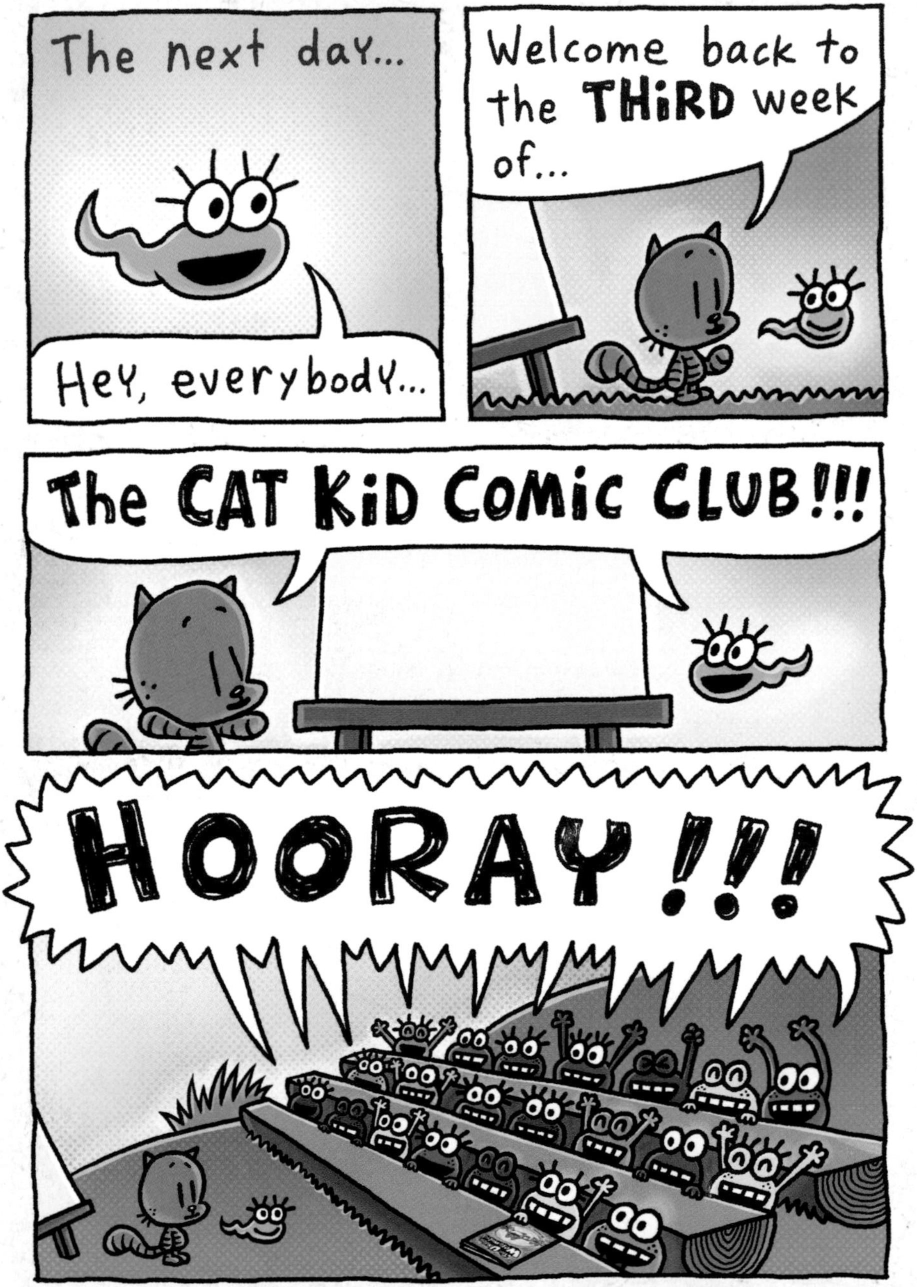

The next day...
Hey, everybody...
Welcome back to the THIRD week of...
The CAT KID COMIC CLUB!!!
HOORAY!!!

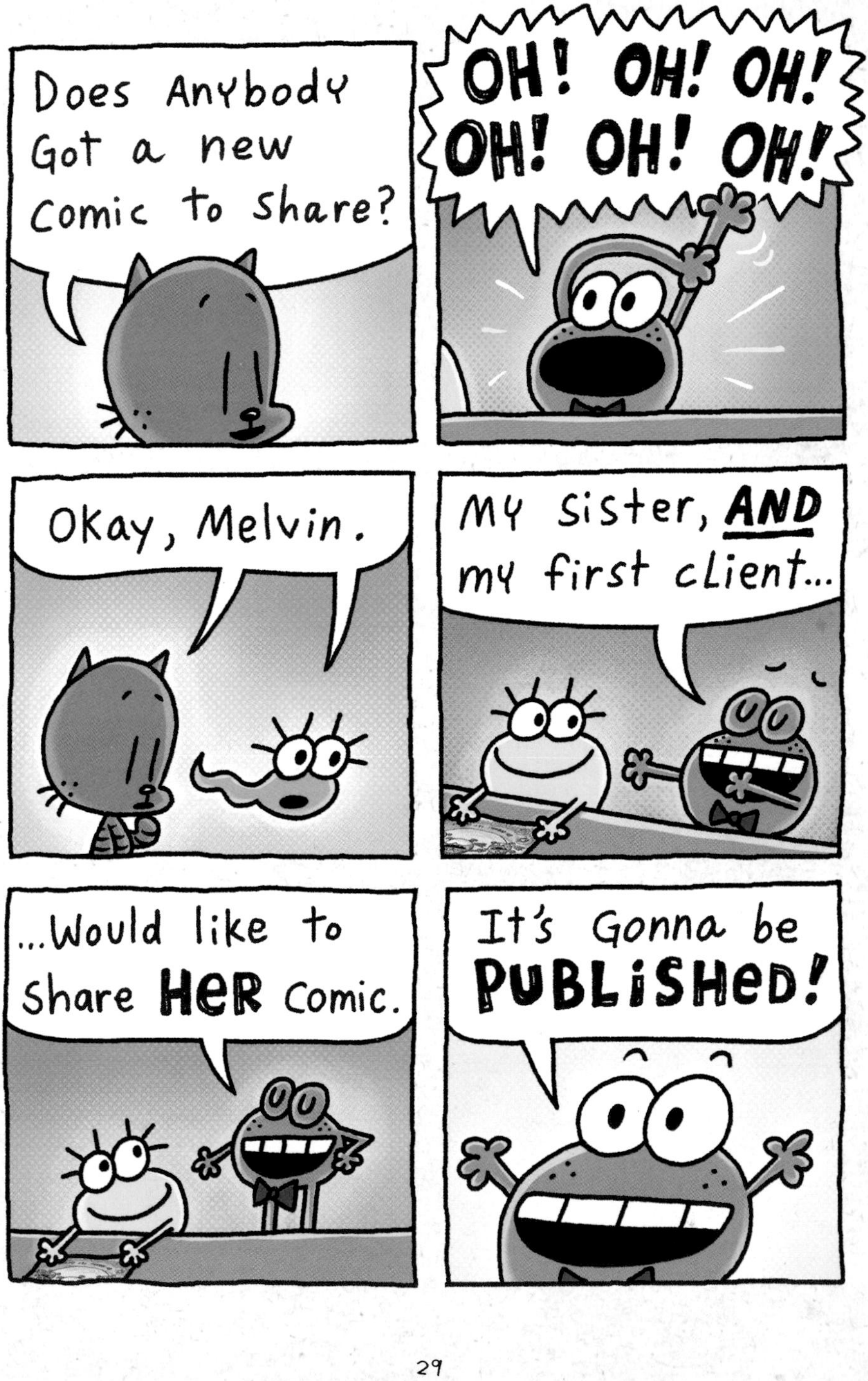
Does Anybody Got a new Comic to Share?
OH! OH! OH! OH! OH! OH!
OKay, Melvin.
My Sister, AND my first cLient...
...Would like to Share HER Comic.
It's Gonna be PUBLiSHED!

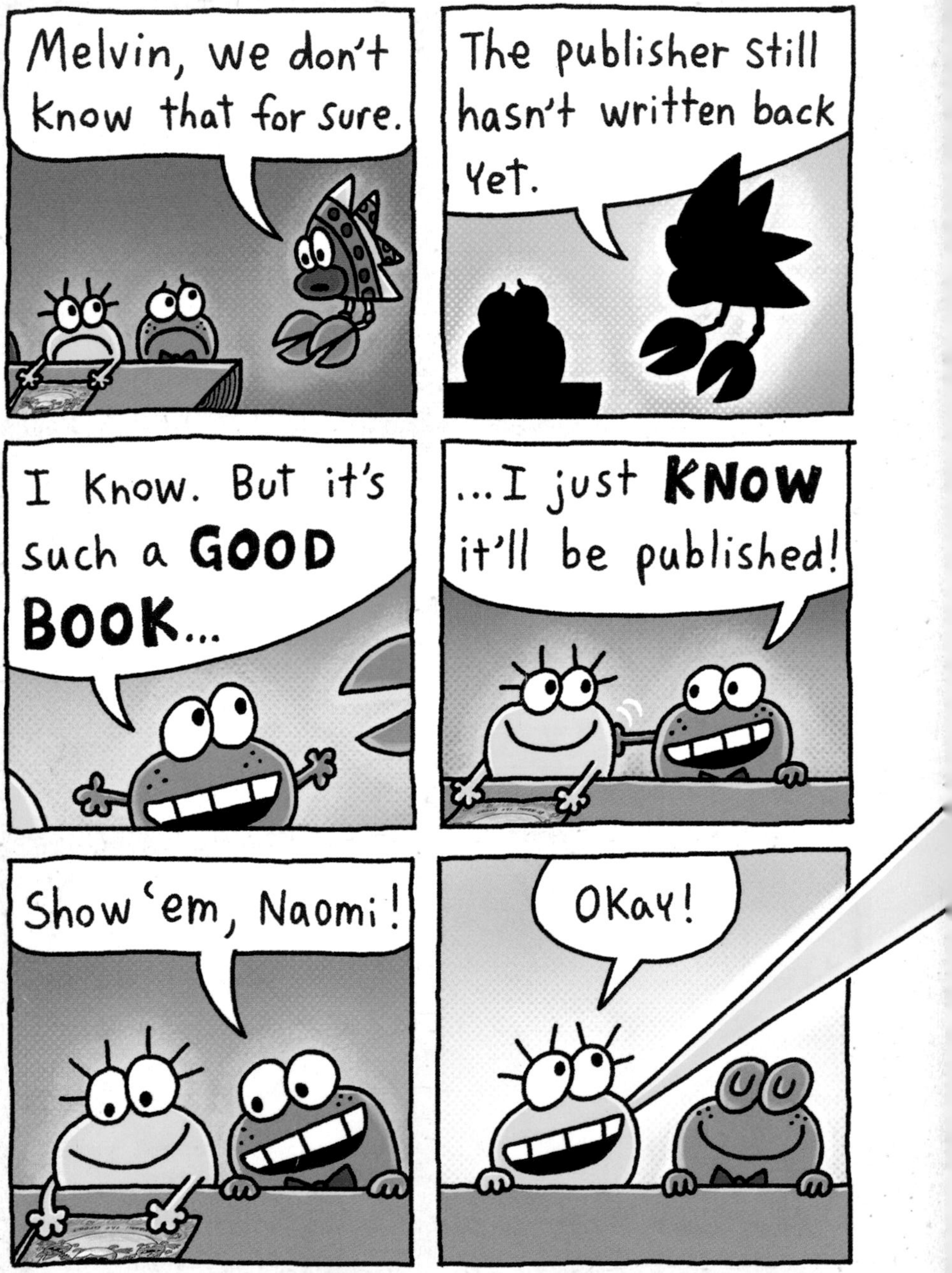
Melvin, we don't know that for sure.
The publisher still hasn't written back yet.
I know. But it's such a **GOOD BOOK**...
...I just **KNOW** it'll be published!
Show 'em, Naomi!
OKay!

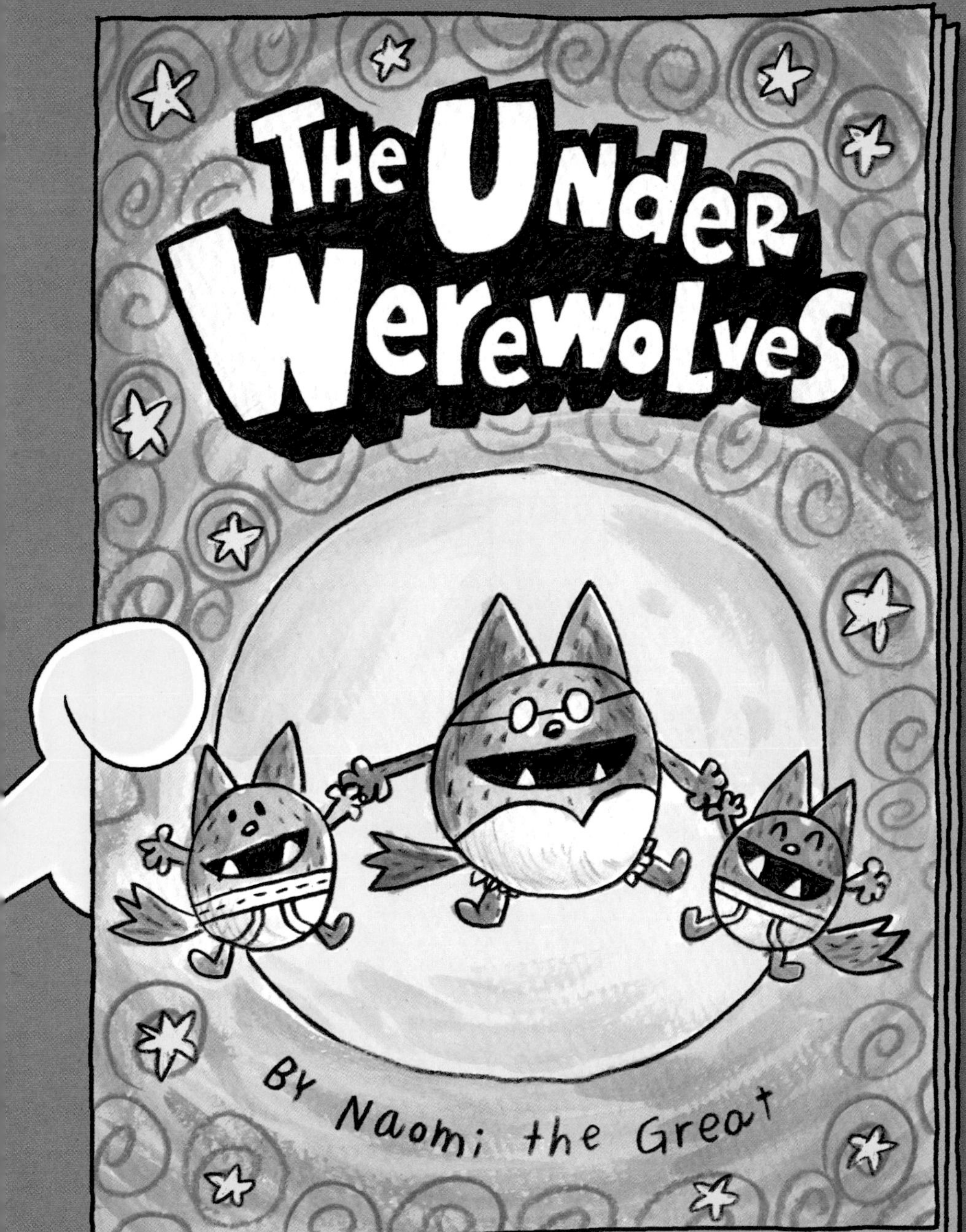
The Under Werewolves
By Naomi the Great

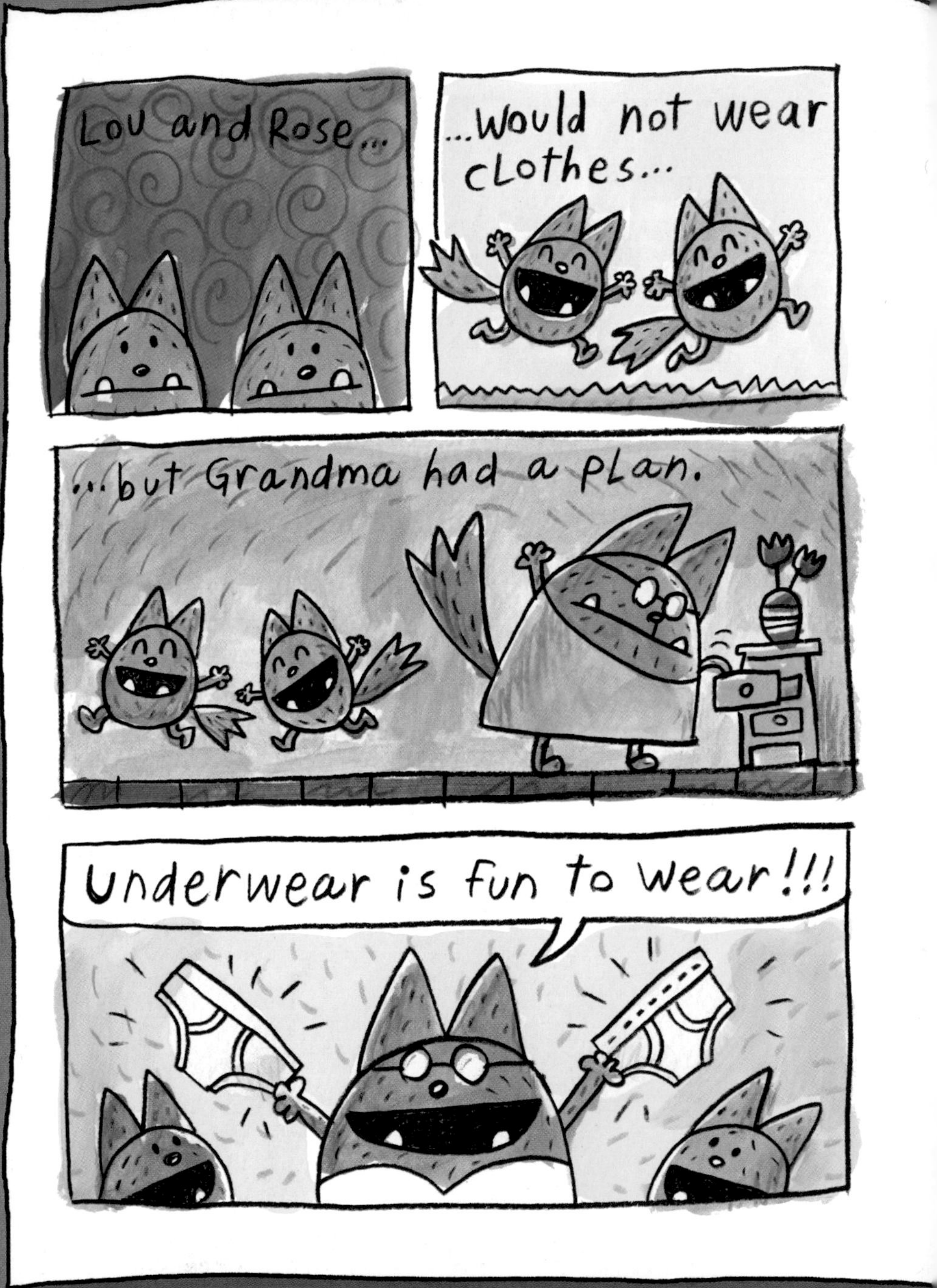
Lou and Rose...
...Would not wear clothes...
...but Grandma had a plan.
Underwear is fun to wear!!!

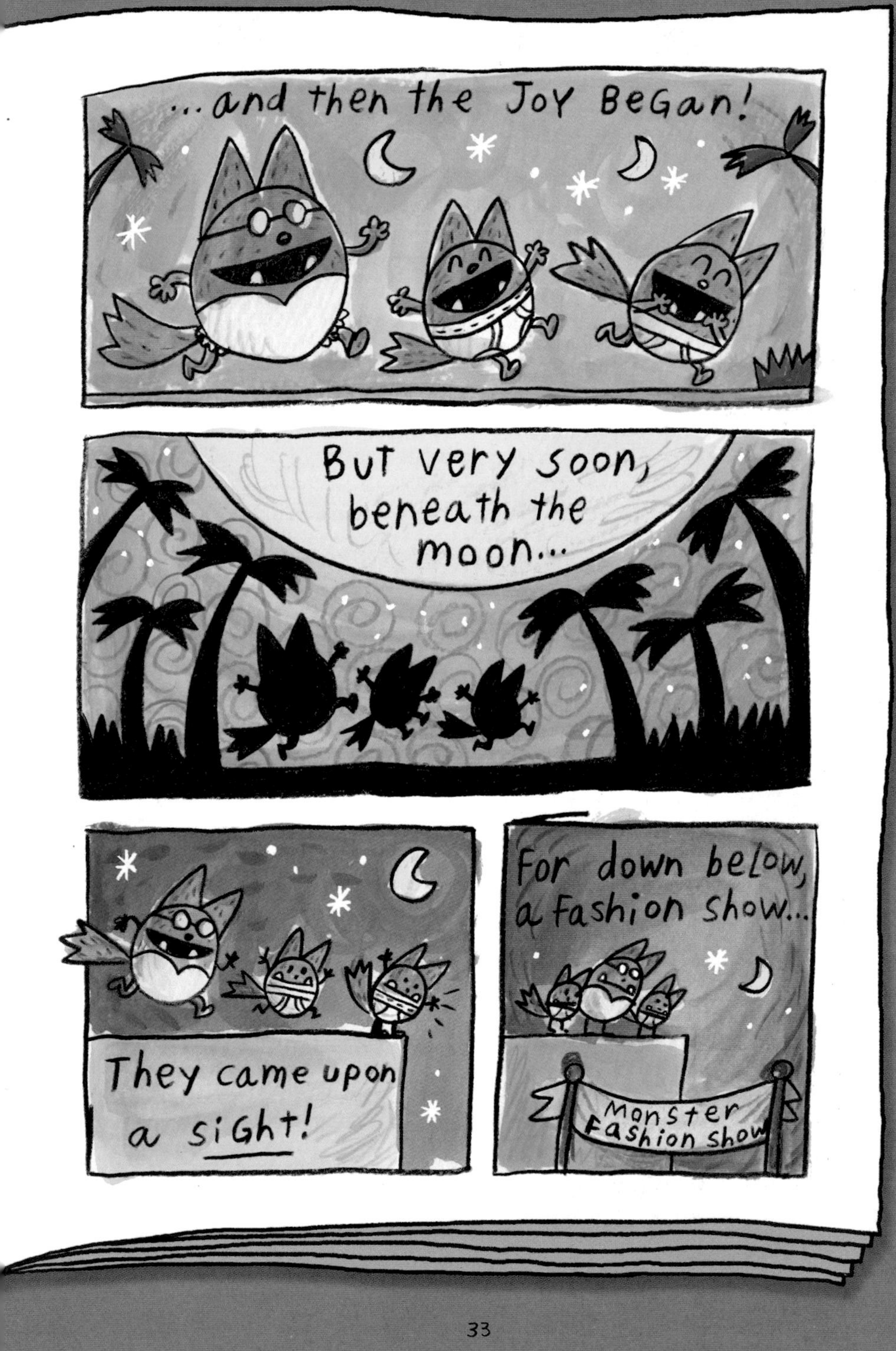
...and then the JOY BeGan!
But very soon, beneath the moon...
They came upon a siGht!
For down below, a fashion show...
Monster Fashion Show

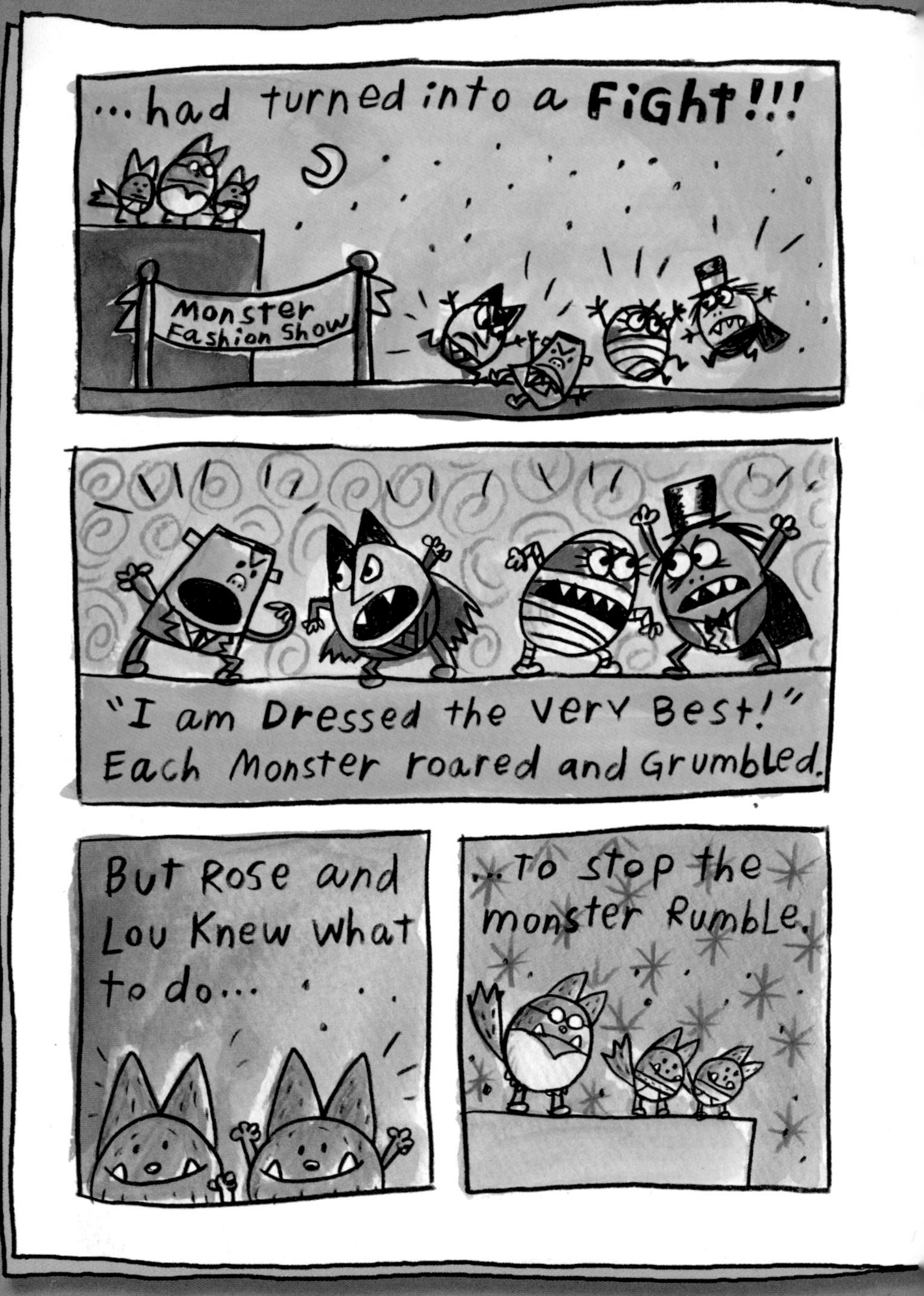
...had turned into a FIGHT!!!
Monster Fashion Show
"I am Dressed the Very Best!" Each Monster roared and Grumbled.
But Rose and Lou Knew what to do...
...To stop the monster Rumble.

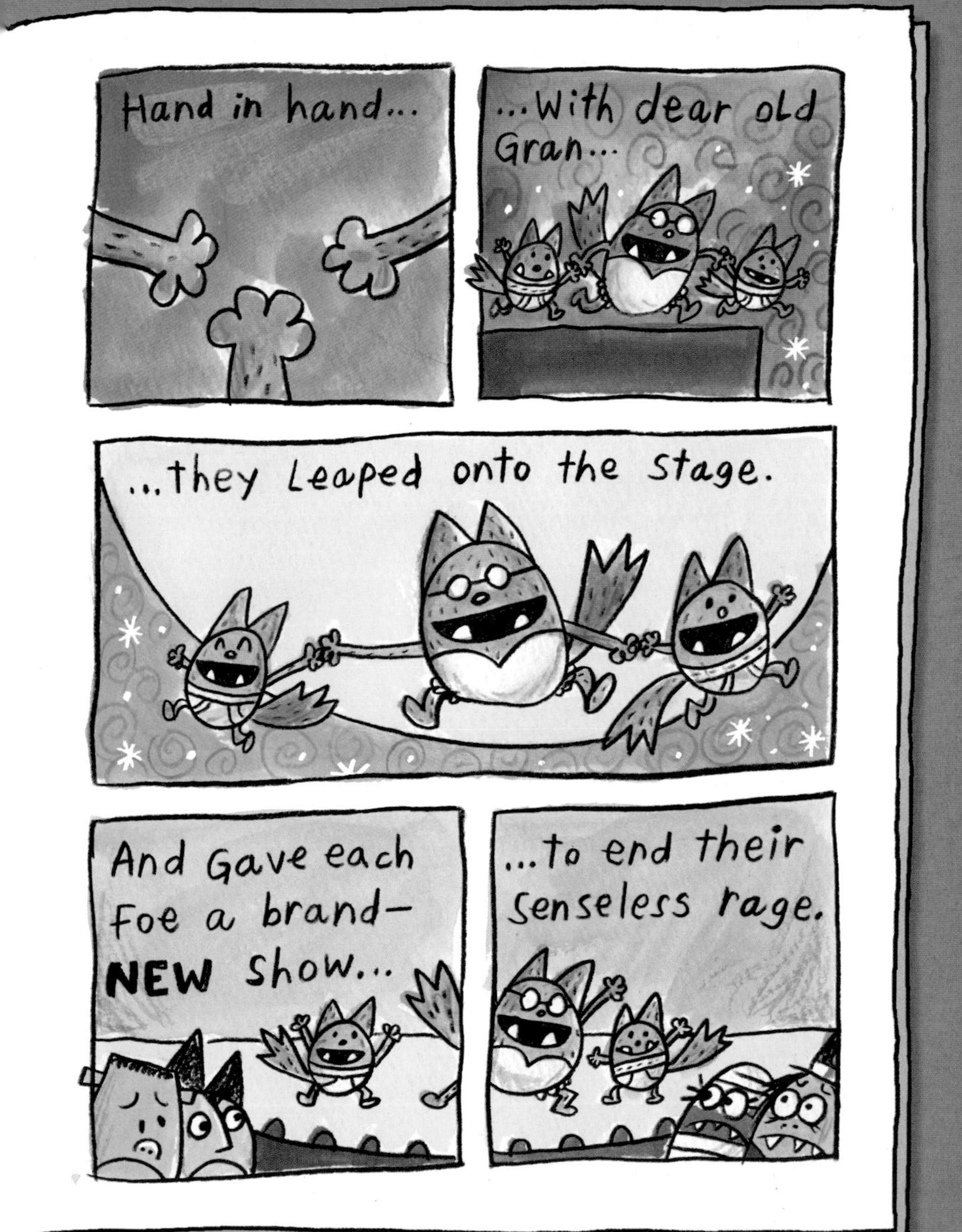
Hand in hand...
...With dear old Gran...
...they Leaped onto the stage.
And Gave each Foe a brand-NEW show...
...to end their senseless rage.

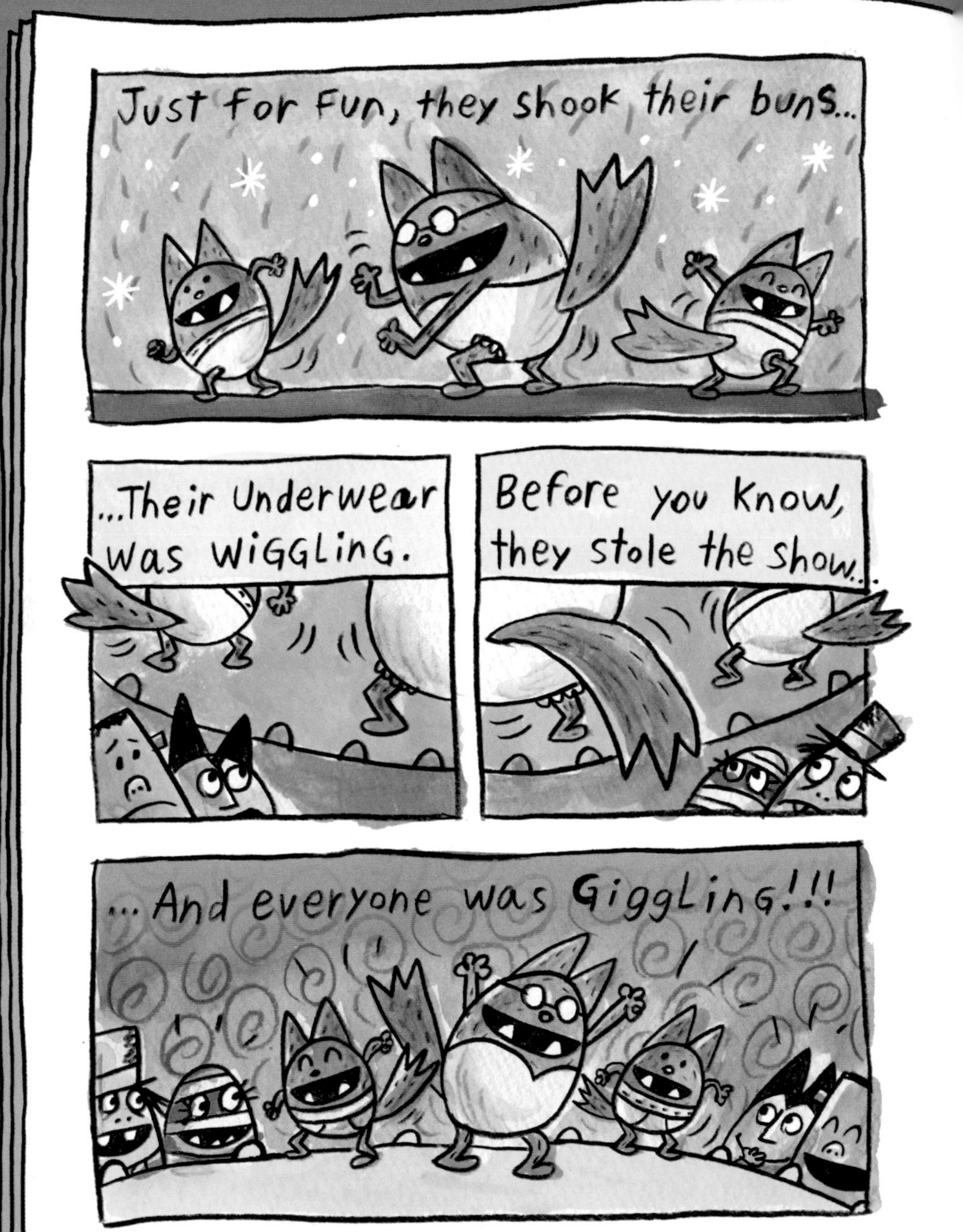
Just for Fun, they shook their buns...
...Their Underwear was WIGGLING.
Before you know, they stole the show...
...And everyone was Giggling!!!

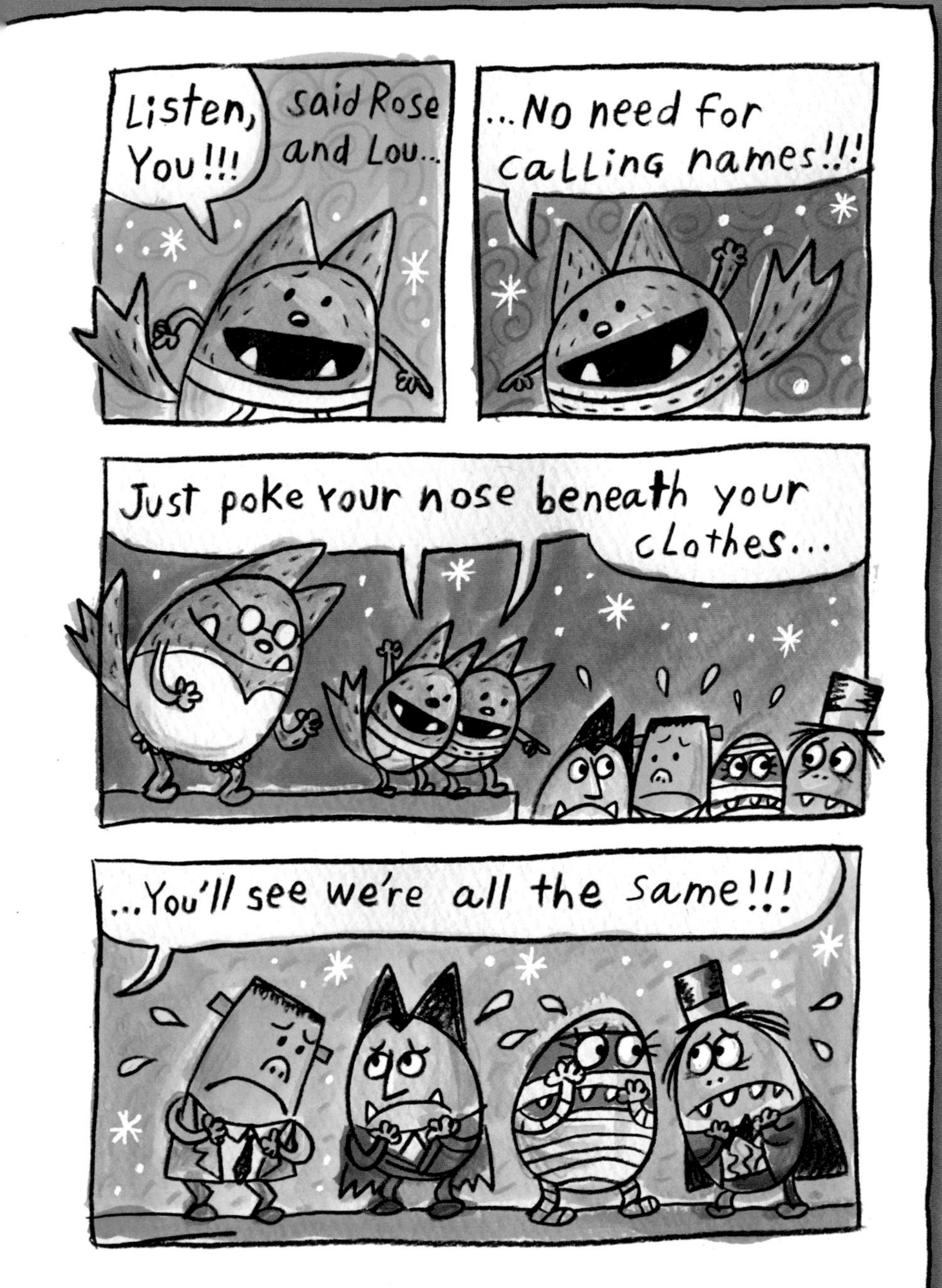
Listen, You!!!
said Rose and Lou...
...No need for calling names!!!
Just poke your nose beneath your clothes...
...You'll see we're all the same!!!

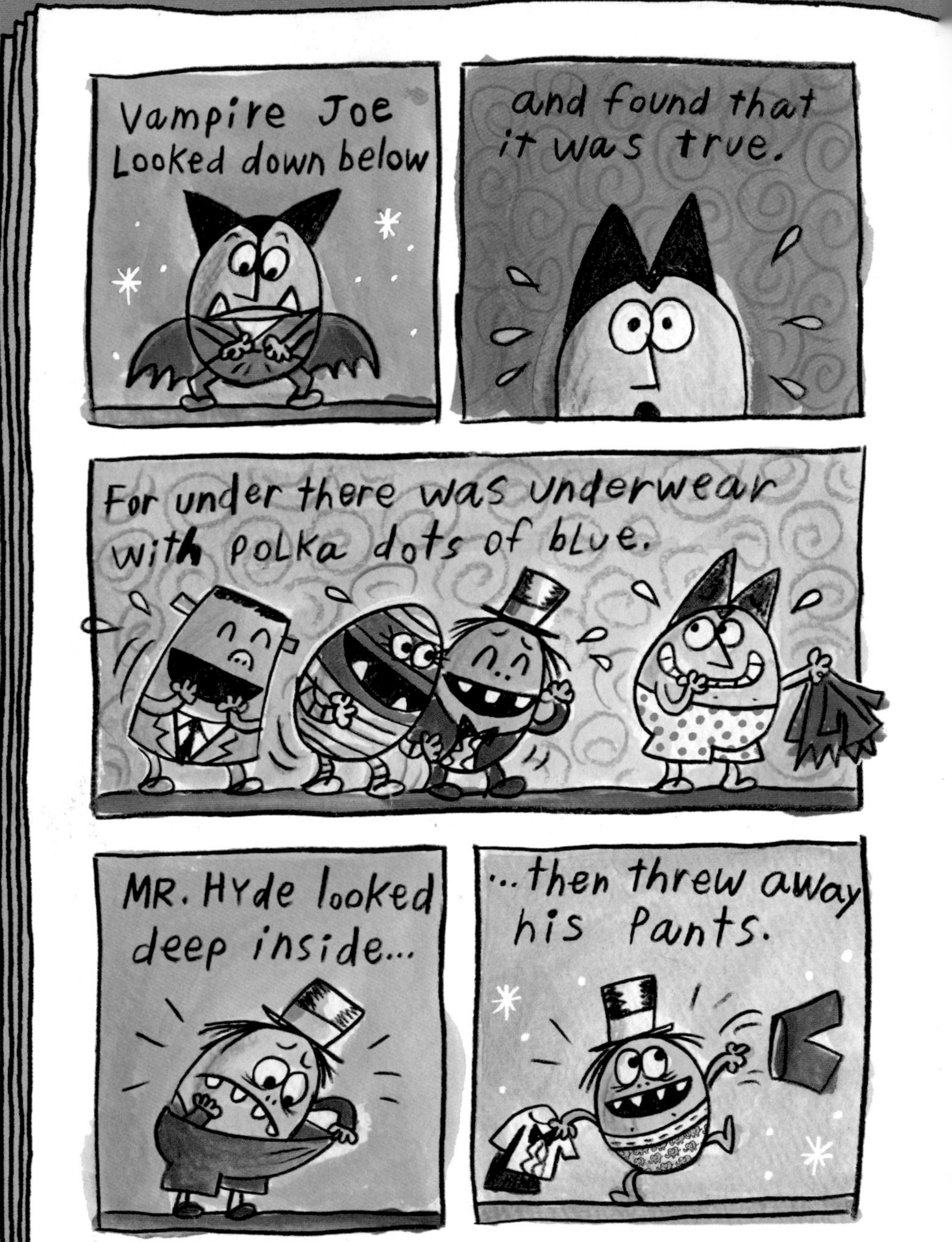
Vampire Joe
Looked down below
and found that
it was true.
For under there was underwear
with polka dots of blue.
MR. HYde looked
deep inside...
...then threw away
his Pants.

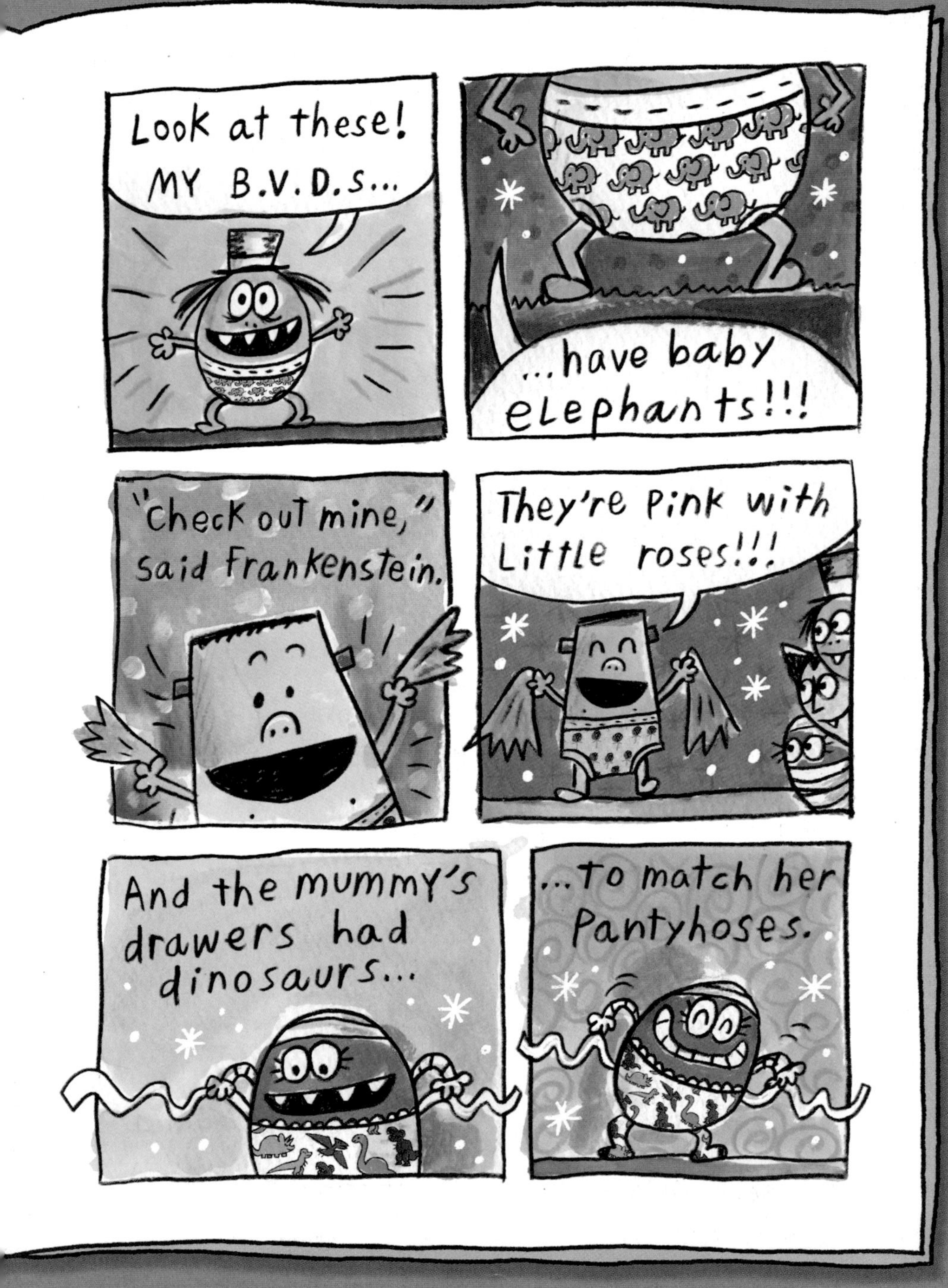
Look at these! MY B.V.D.s...
...have baby elephants!!!
"Check out mine," said Frankenstein.
They're Pink with Little roses!!!
And the mummy's drawers had dinosaurs...
...to match her Pantyhoses.

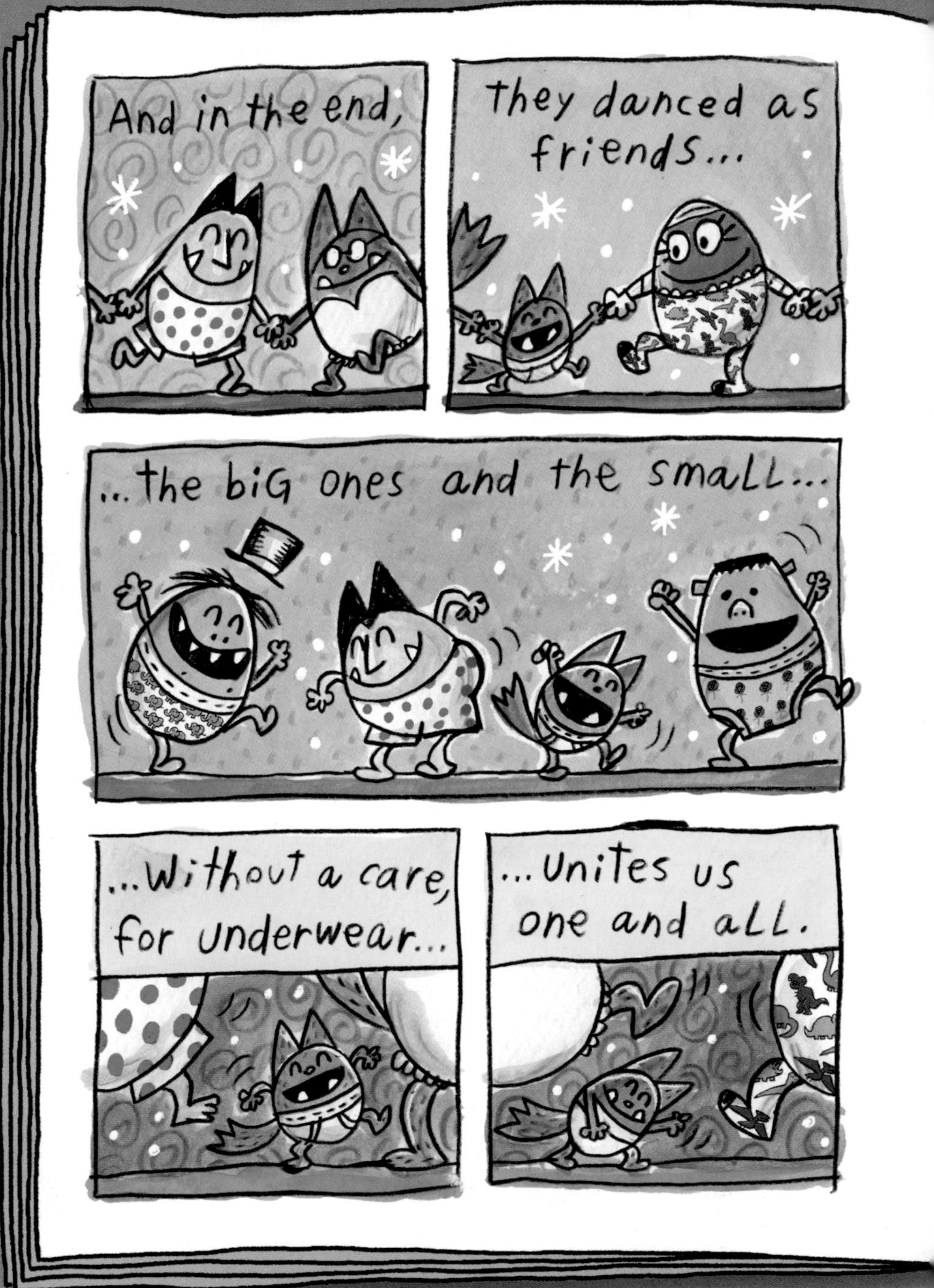
And in the end,
they danced as friends...
...the biG ones and the smaLL...
...Without a care, for underwear...
...Unites us one and aLL.

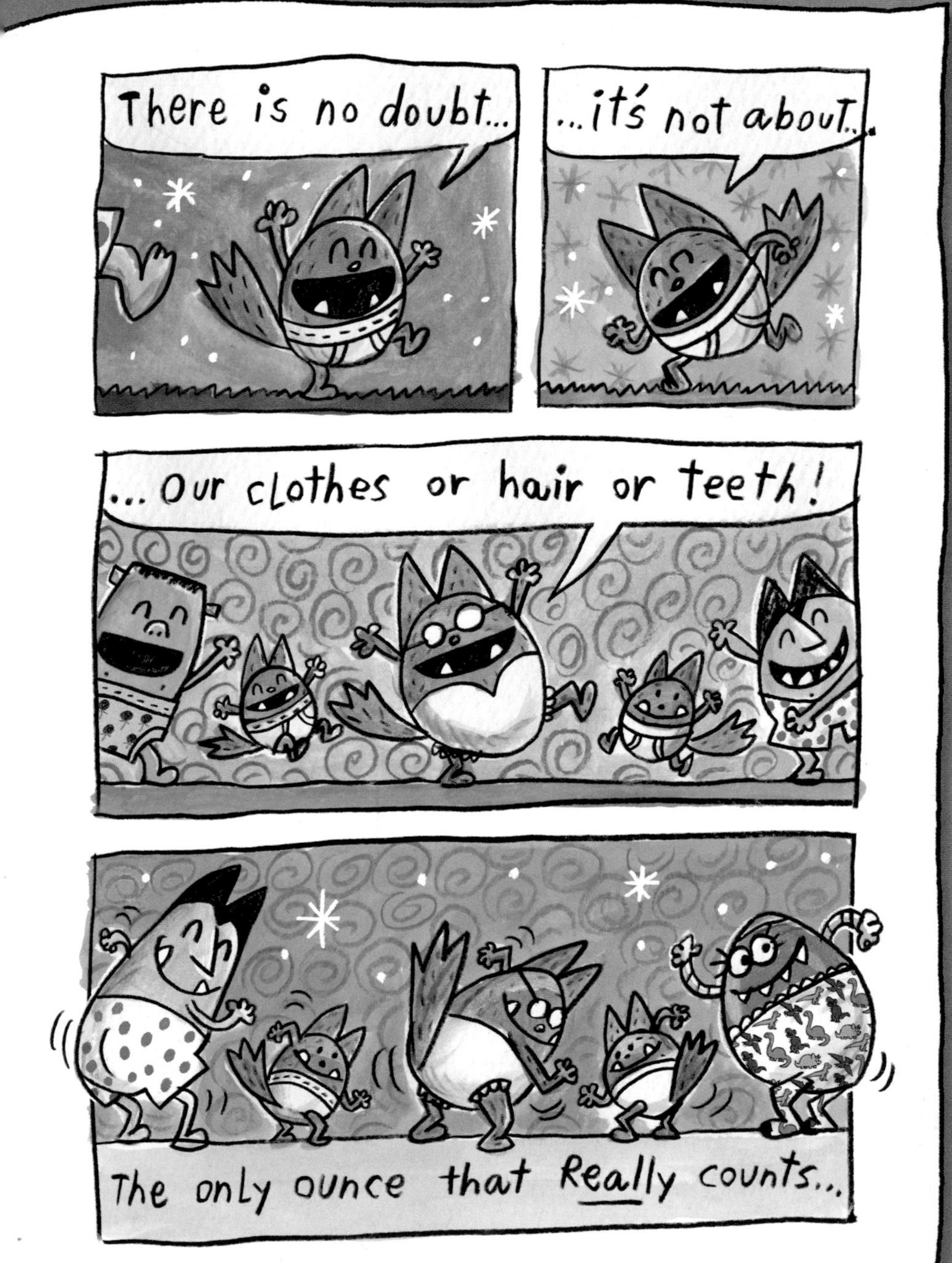
There is no doubt...
...it's not about...
...Our clothes or hair or teeth!
The only ounce that Really counts...

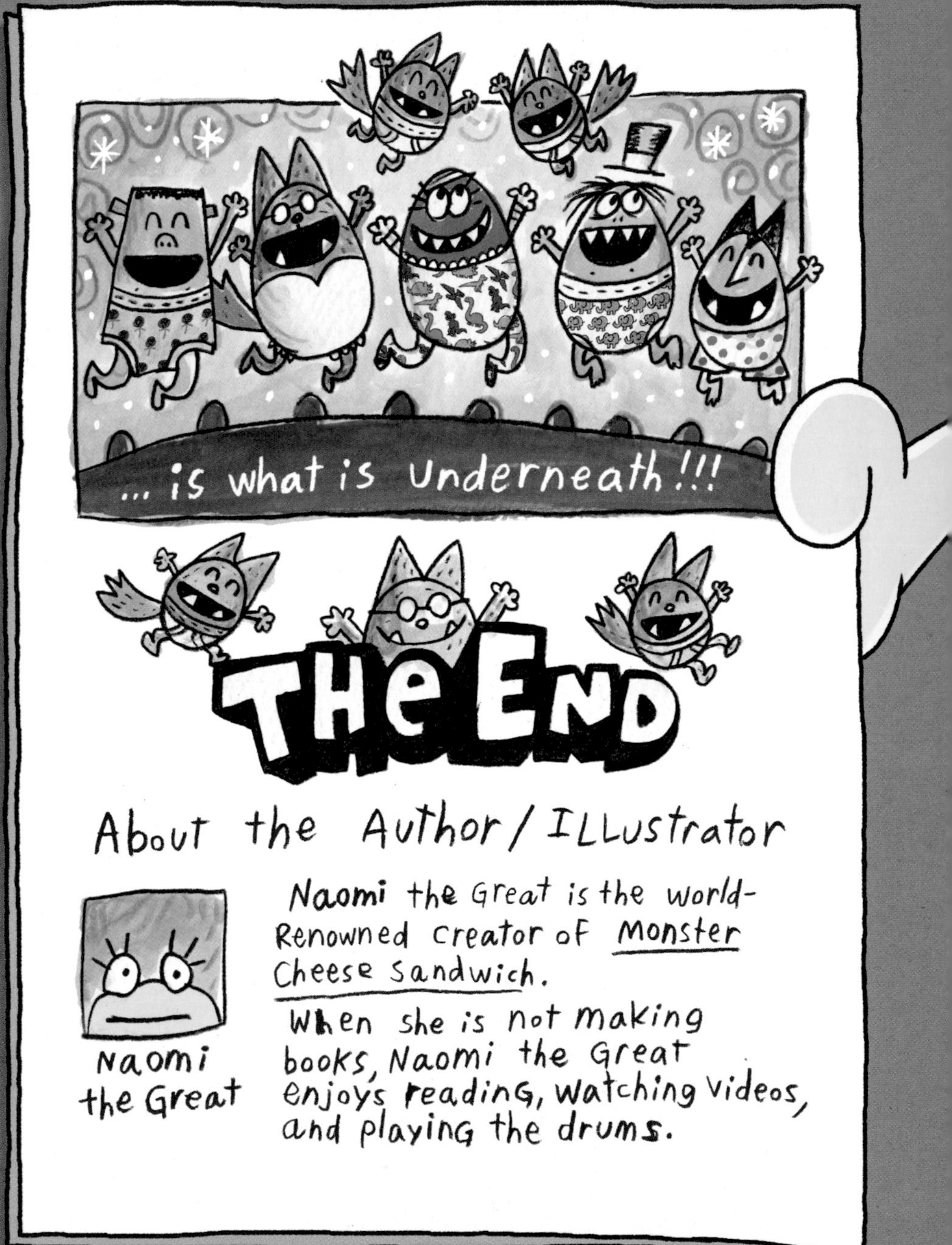
... is what is underneath!!!
THE END
About the Author/ILLustrator
Naomi the Great is the world-Renowned creator of Monster Cheese Sandwich.
When she is not making books, Naomi the Great enjoys reading, watching videos, and playing the drums.
Naomi the Great

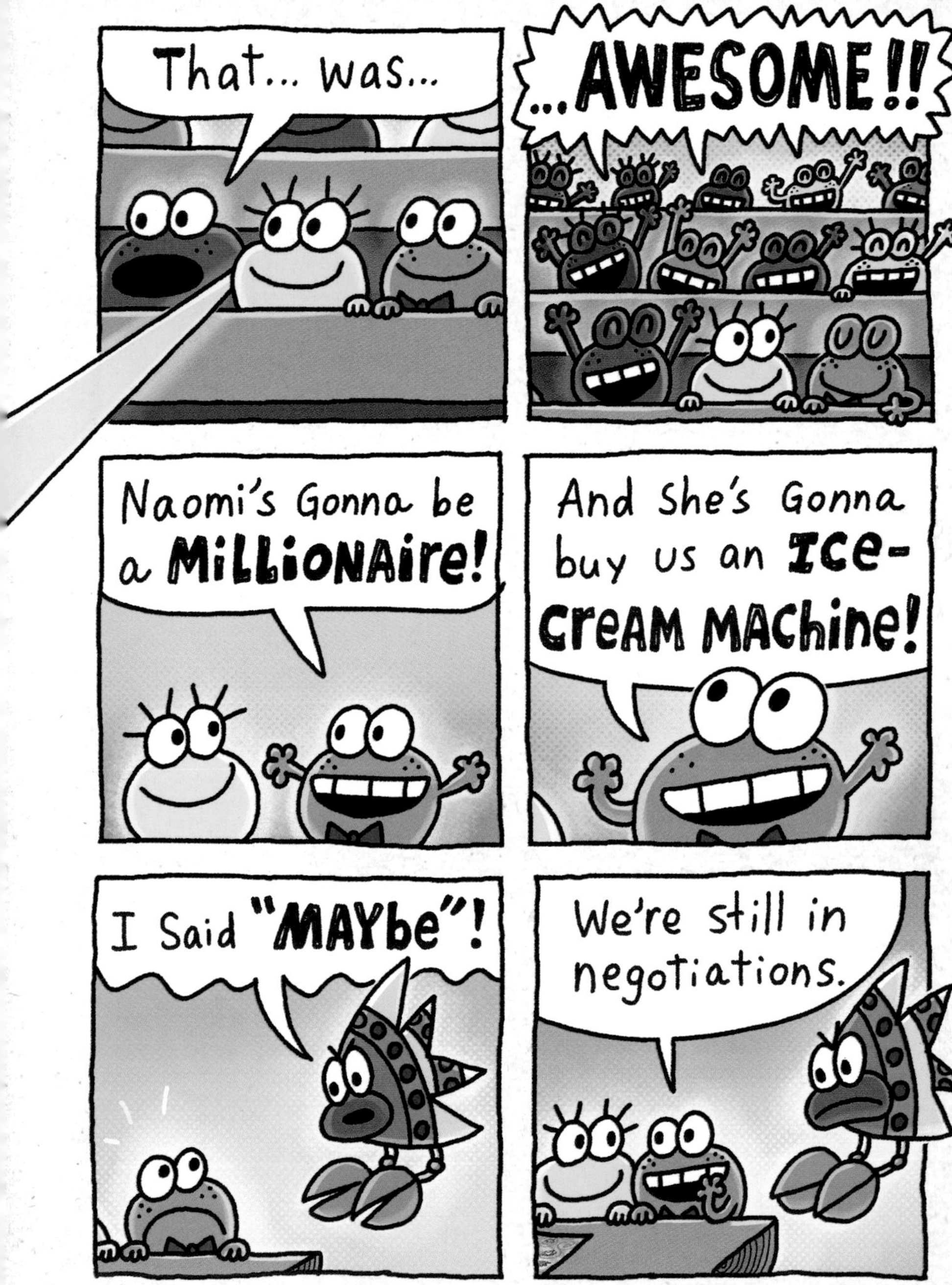
That... was...
...AWESOME!!
Naomi's Gonna be a MILLIONAIRE!
And She's Gonna buy us an ICE-CREAM MACHINE!
I Said "MAYbe"!
We're still in negotiations.

I LOVE ICE CREAM!
Me too!!!
MY favorite flAvor is SWIRL!
"SWirL" isn't A FLAVOR!
Sweeet!
Mine too!
Is Too!!!
So when will it be published?
Beats me!
And how do You even Know a publisher?
We don't.
They Do!!

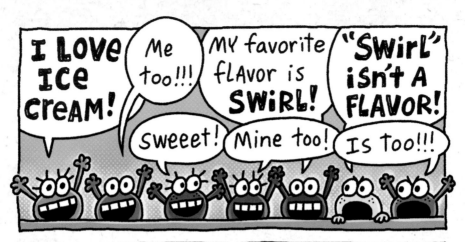

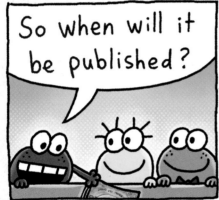

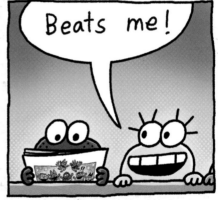

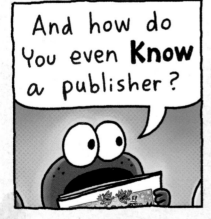

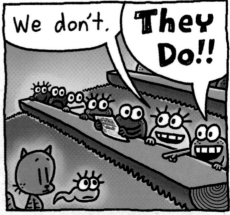

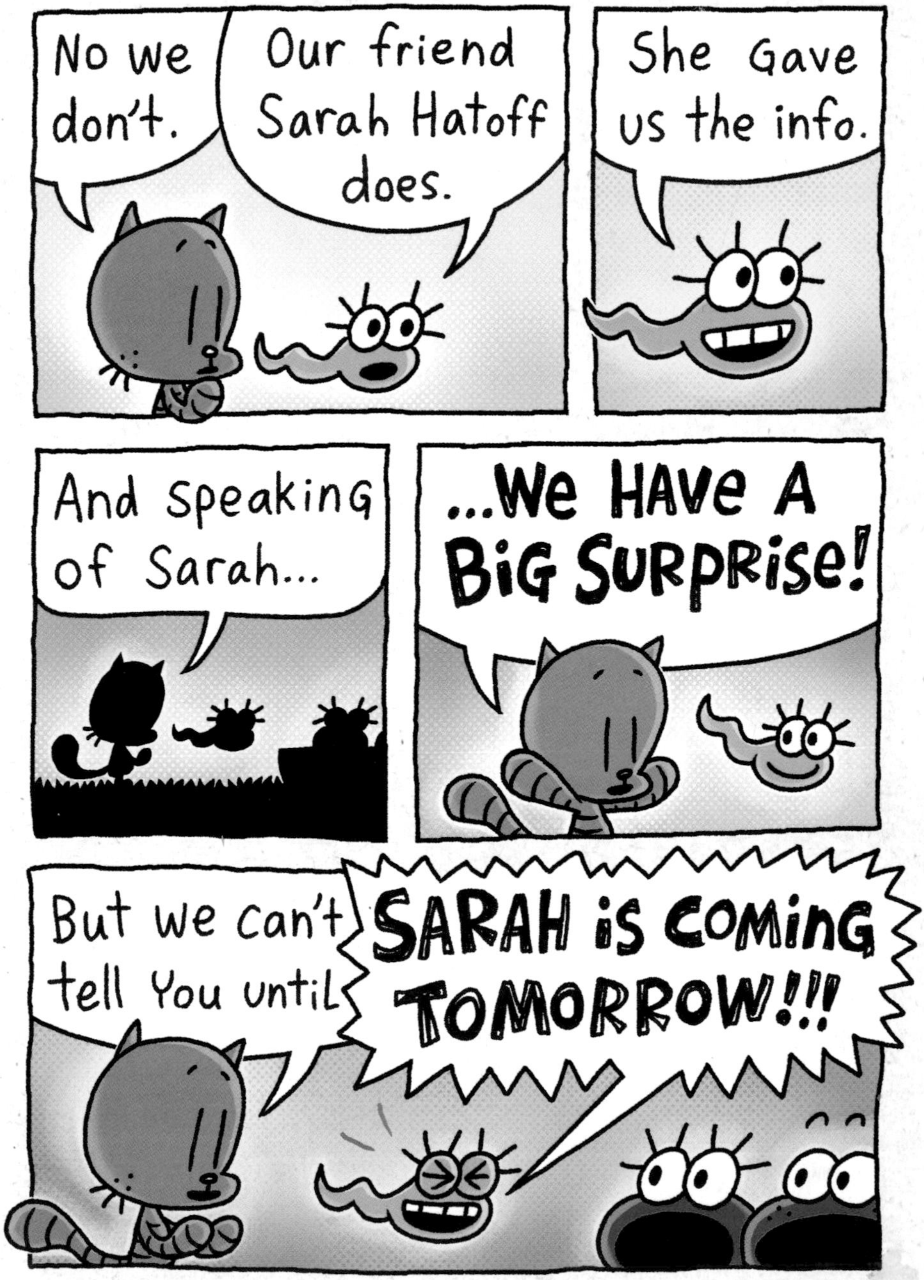
No we don't.
Our friend Sarah Hatoff does.
She Gave us the info.
And speaking of Sarah...
...WE HAVE A BIG SURPRISE!
But we can't tell You until
SARAH IS COMING TOMORROW!!!

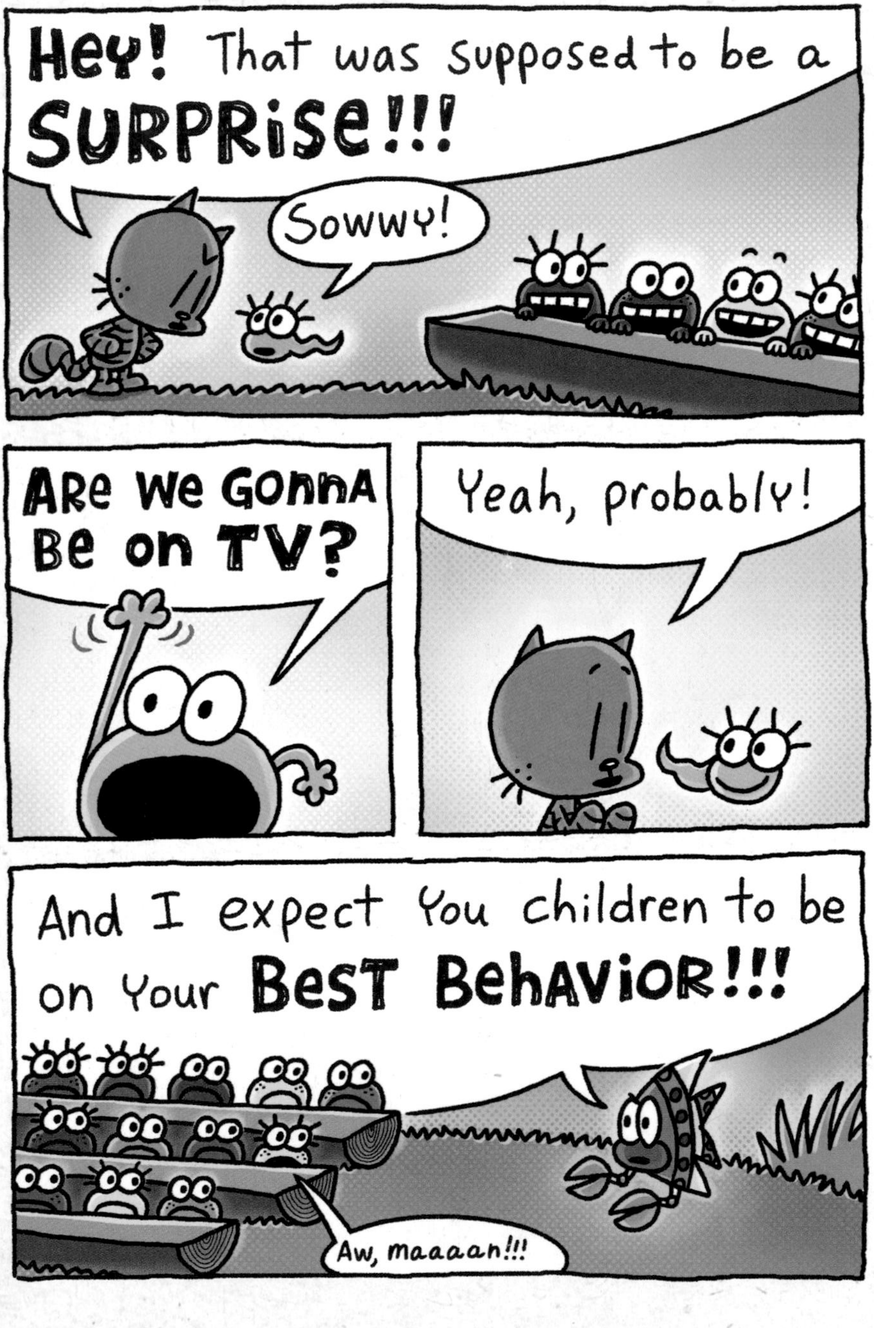
HEY! That was supposed to be a SURPRISE!!!
Sowwy!
ARE WE GONNA BE on TV?
Yeah, probably!
And I expect You children to be on Your BEST BEHAVIOR!!!
Aw, maaaan!!!

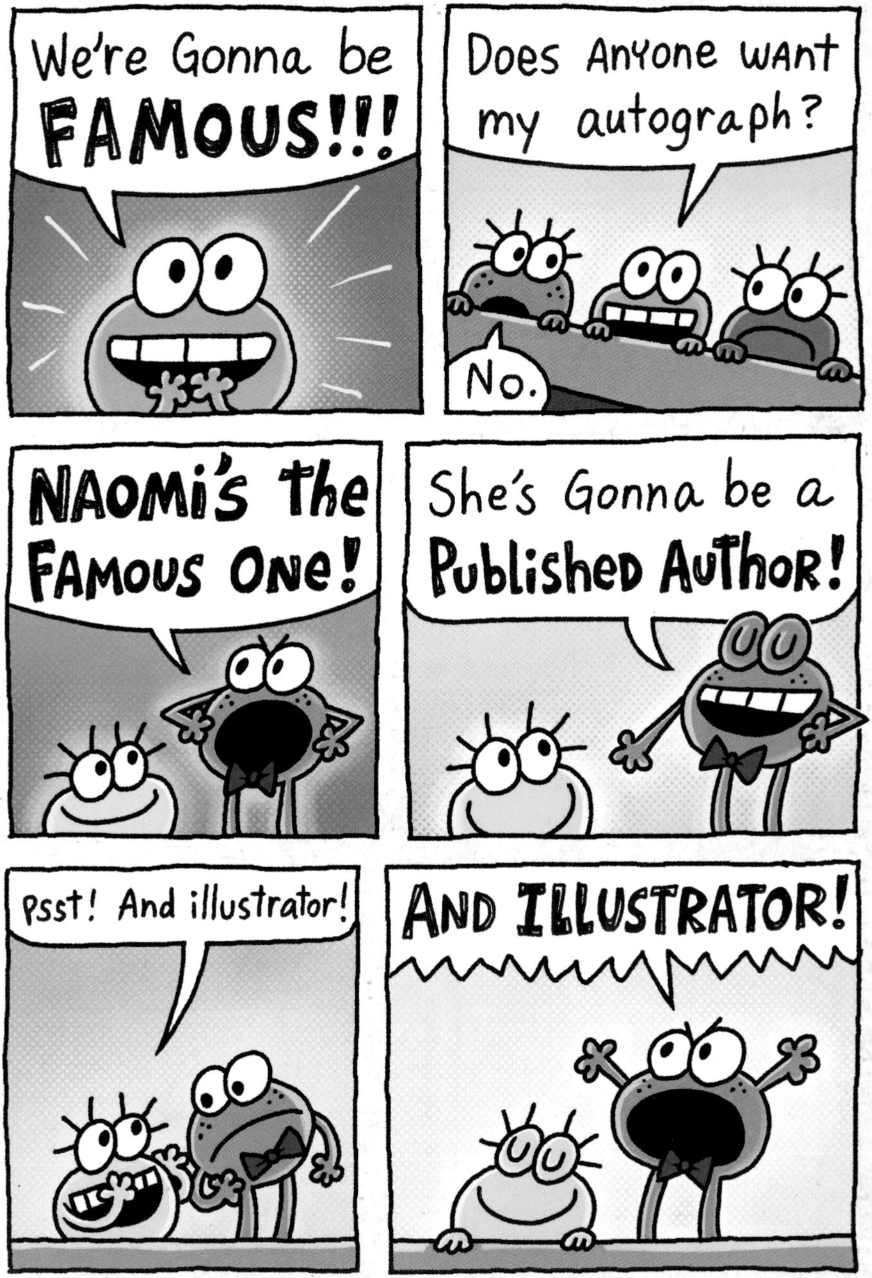
We're Gonna be FAMOUS!!!
Does Anyone WANT my autograph?
No.
NAOMI'S the FAMOUS ONE!
She's Gonna be a Published Author!
Psst! And illustrator!
AND ILLUSTRATOR!

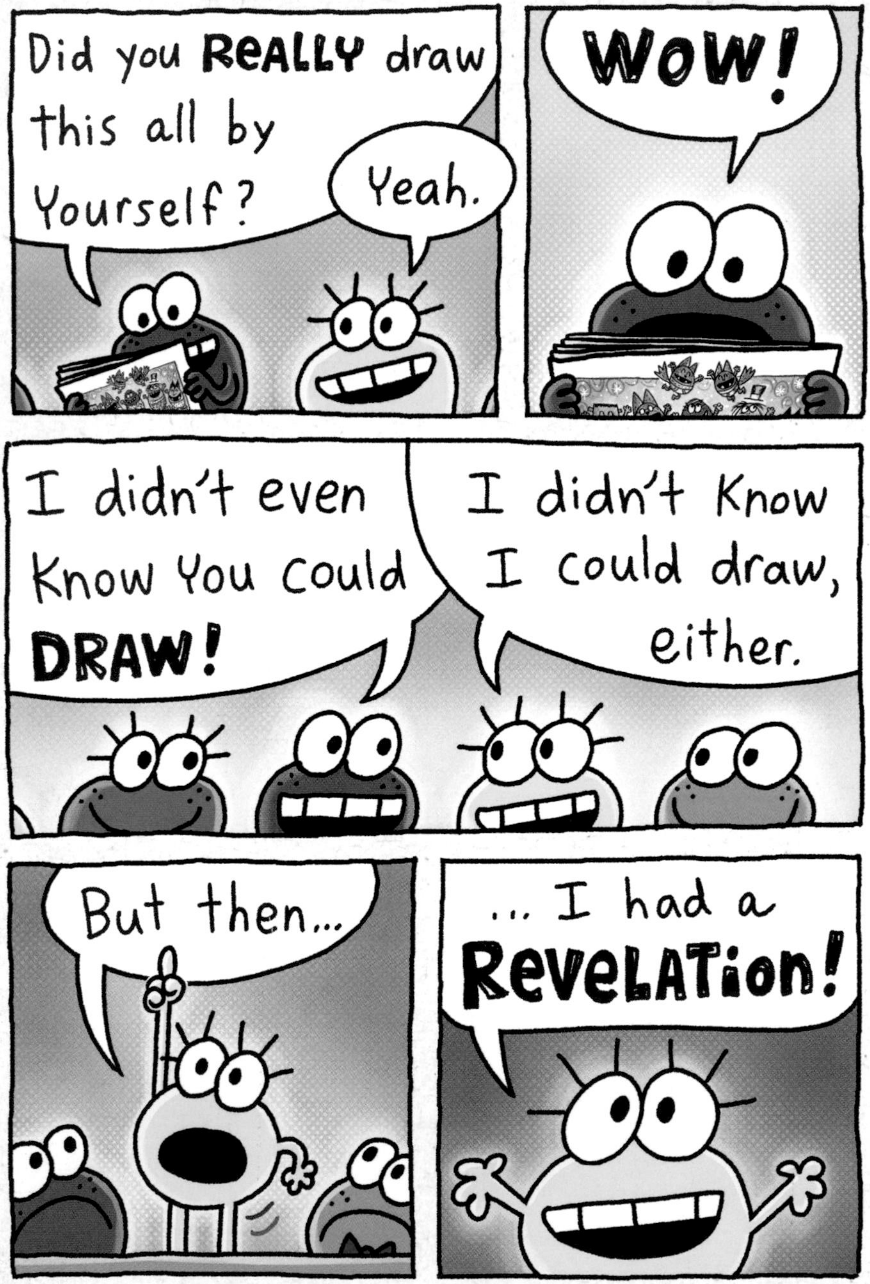
Did you REALLY draw this all by Yourself?
Yeah.
WOW!
I didn't even Know You could DRAW!
I didn't Know I could draw, either.
But then...
... I had a REVELATION!

CHAPTER 4
NAOMI'S REVELATION

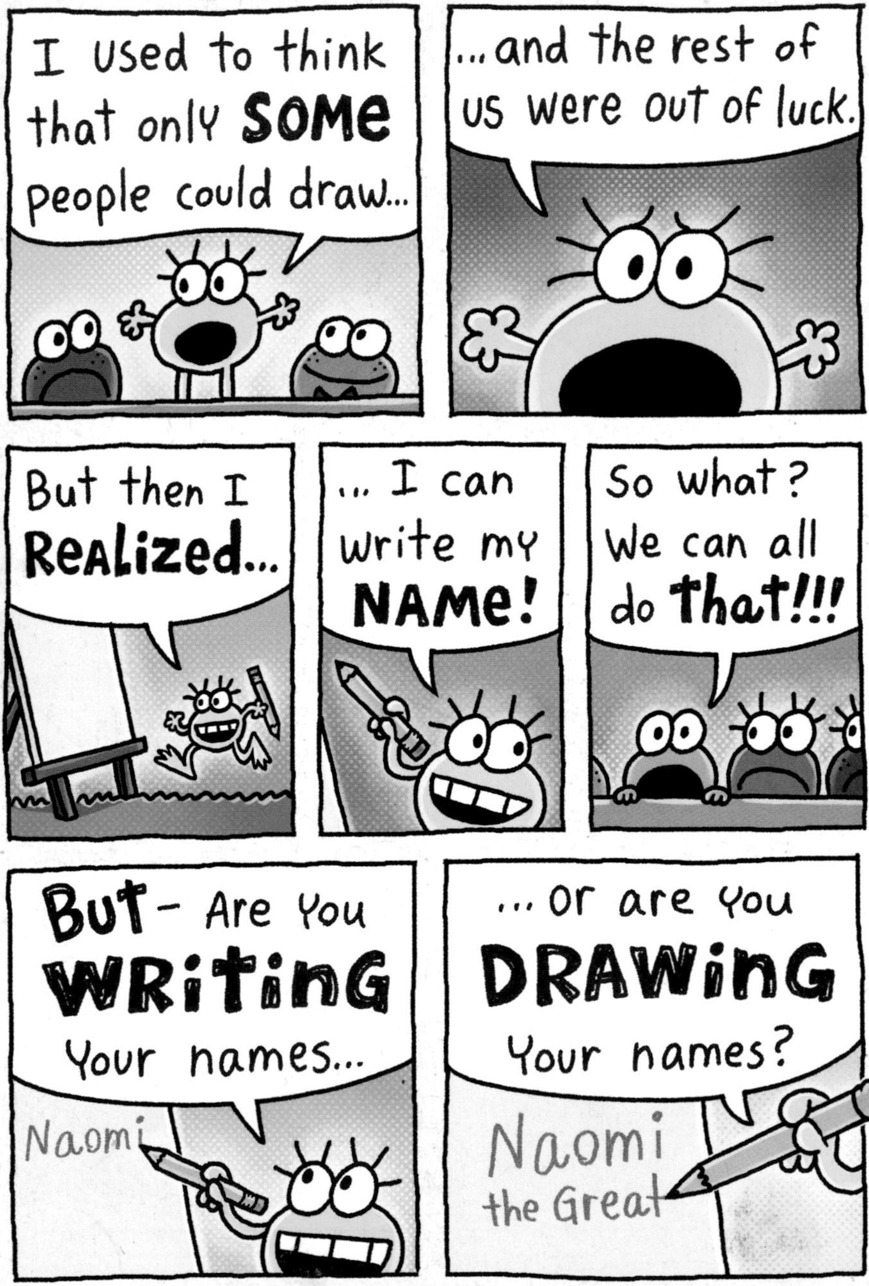
I used to think that only SOME people could draw...
...and the rest of us were out of luck.
But then I REALIZED...
... I can write my NAME!
So what? We can all do THAT!!!
BUT- Are you WRITING your names...
Naomi
... or are you DRAWING your names?
Naomi the Great

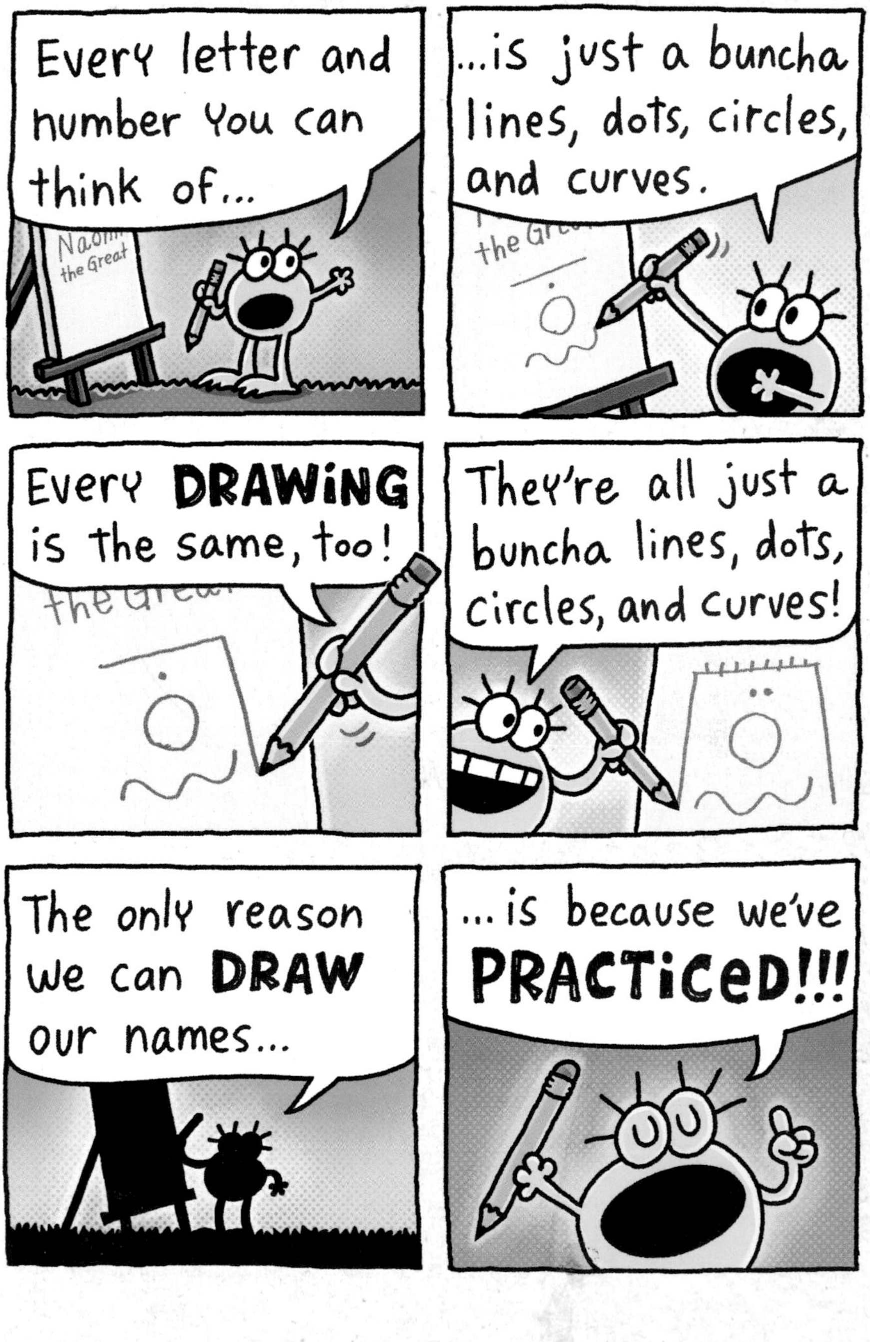
Every letter and number you can think of...
...is just a buncha lines, dots, circles, and curves.
Every **DRAWiNG** is the same, too!
They're all just a buncha lines, dots, circles, and curves!
The only reason we can **DRAW** our names...
... is because we've **PRACTiCeD!!!**

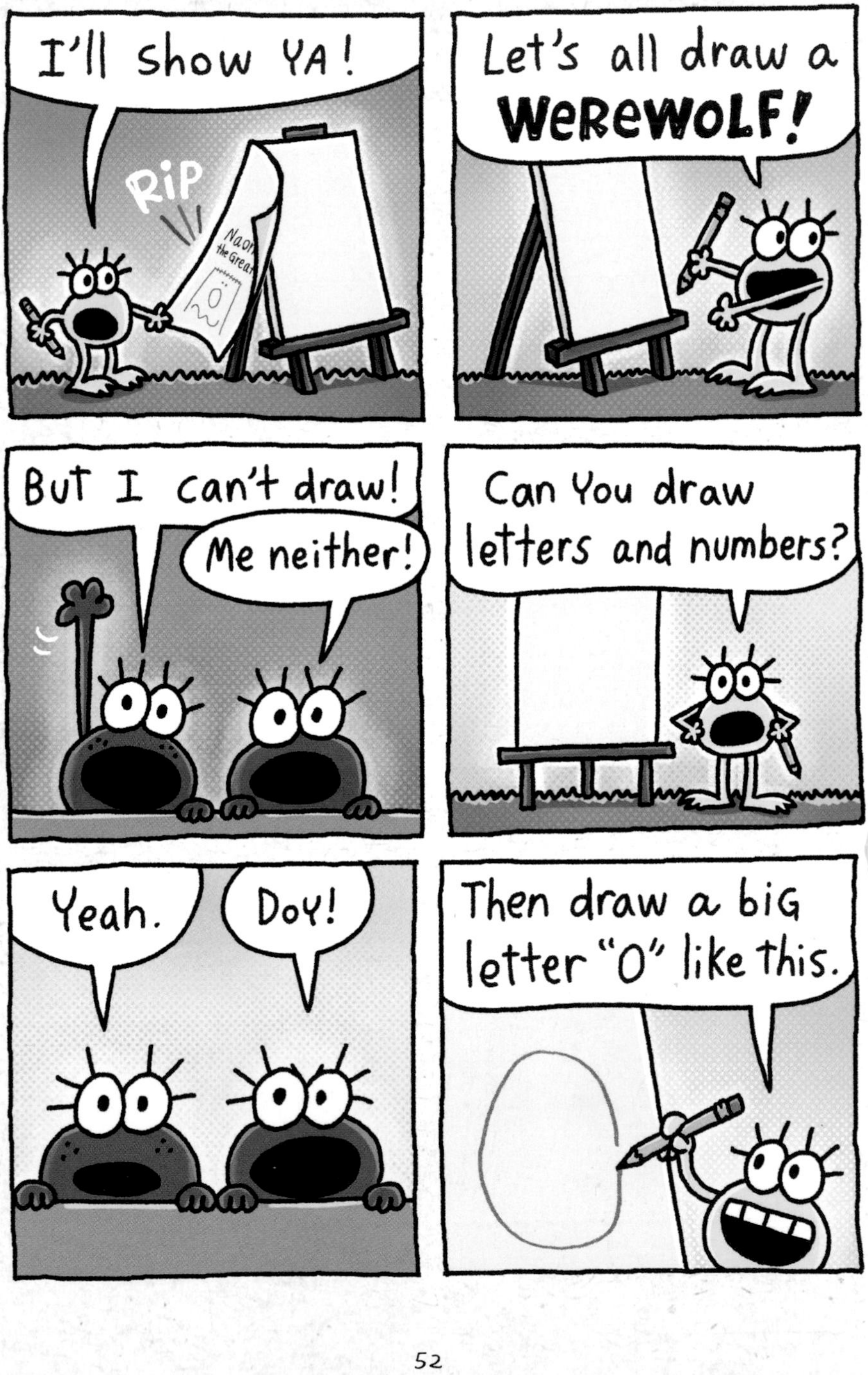
I'll show YA!
RIP
Let's all draw a WEREWOLF!
But I can't draw!
Me neither!
Can You draw letters and numbers?
Yeah.
DOY!
Then draw a big letter "O" like this.

Now, draw a biG letter "M" on top.

Add two periods...

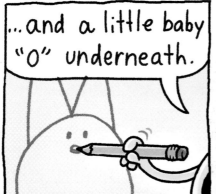

...and a little baby "O" underneath.

Now, make a **BiG** capital "D"...

...but make it **SiDEWAYS**...

...and put two little upside-down "U"s riGht here.

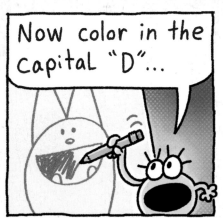

Now color in the capital "D"...

... except for the "U" parts.

WOW! HEY! We're DRAWING! WE RULE!

The arms and legs are easy!

You just draw a sideways "C"...

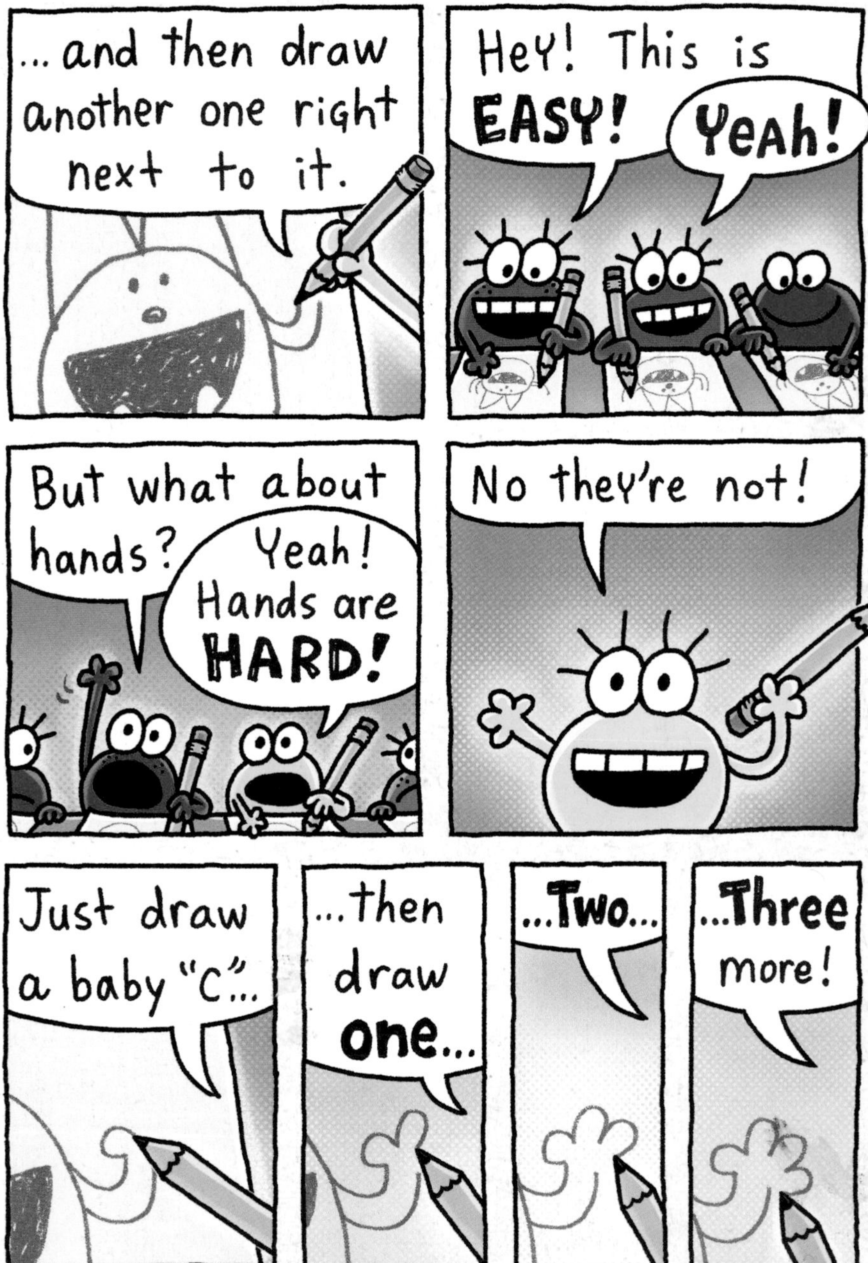
...and then draw another one right next to it.
Hey! This is EASY!
Yeah!
But what about hands?
Yeah! Hands are HARD!
No they're not!
Just draw a baby "C"...
...then draw one...
...Two...
...Three more!

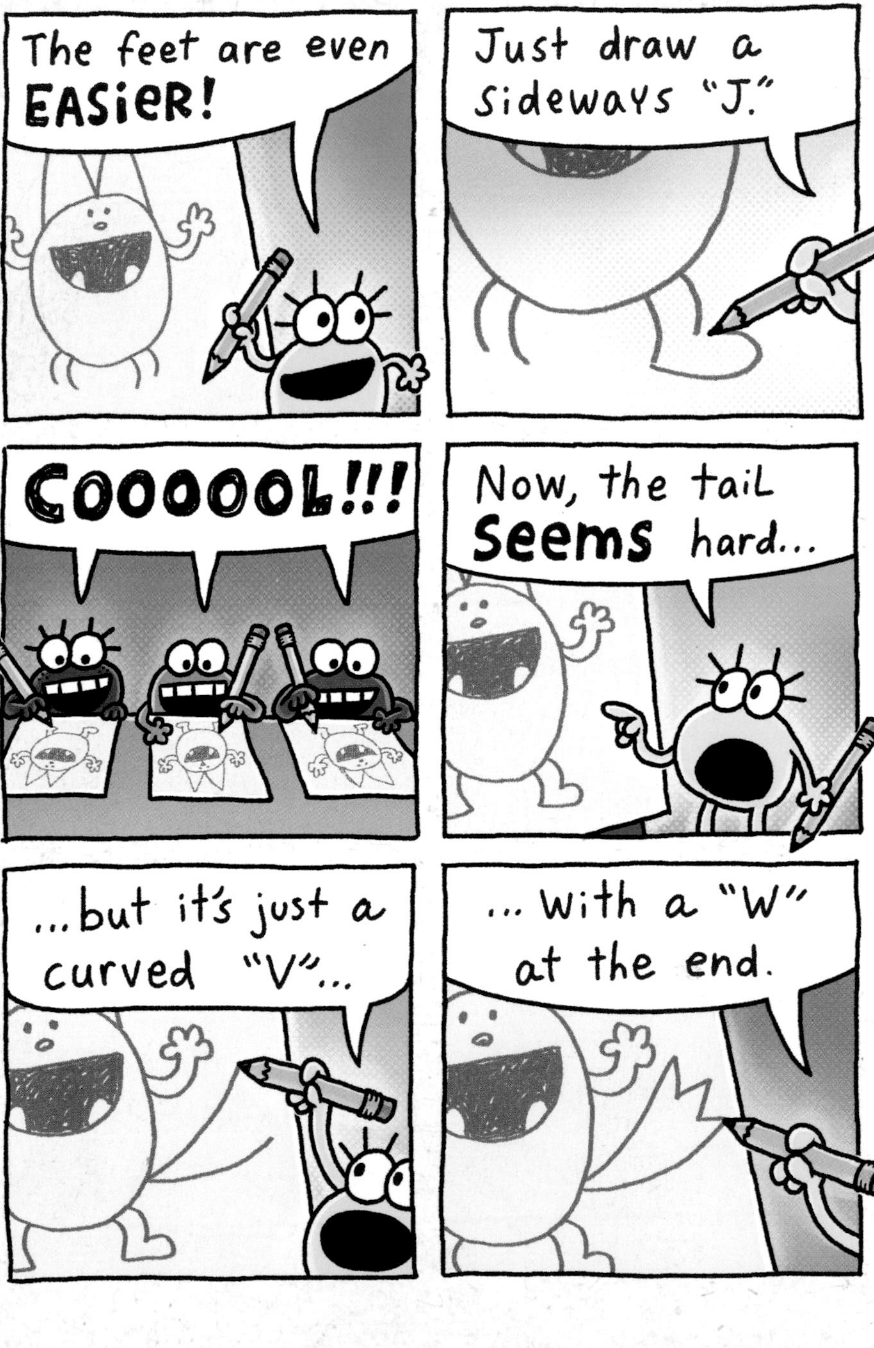

The feet are even EASIER!
Just draw a sideways "J."
COOOOOL!!!
Now, the tail Seems hard...
...but it's just a curved "V"...
... with a "W" at the end.

And for fur, just draw a buncha little baby lines.

Hey! MY werewolf is **NAKED!!!**

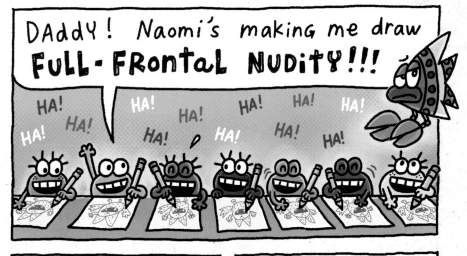

DAddY! Naomi's making me draw **FULL-FRONTAL NUDitY!!!**

HA! HA! HA! HA! HA! HA! HA! HA! HA! HA! HA! HA!

Alright, alright...

HA! HA! HA! HA! HA! HA! HA!

...Who can tell me the lesson you just learned?

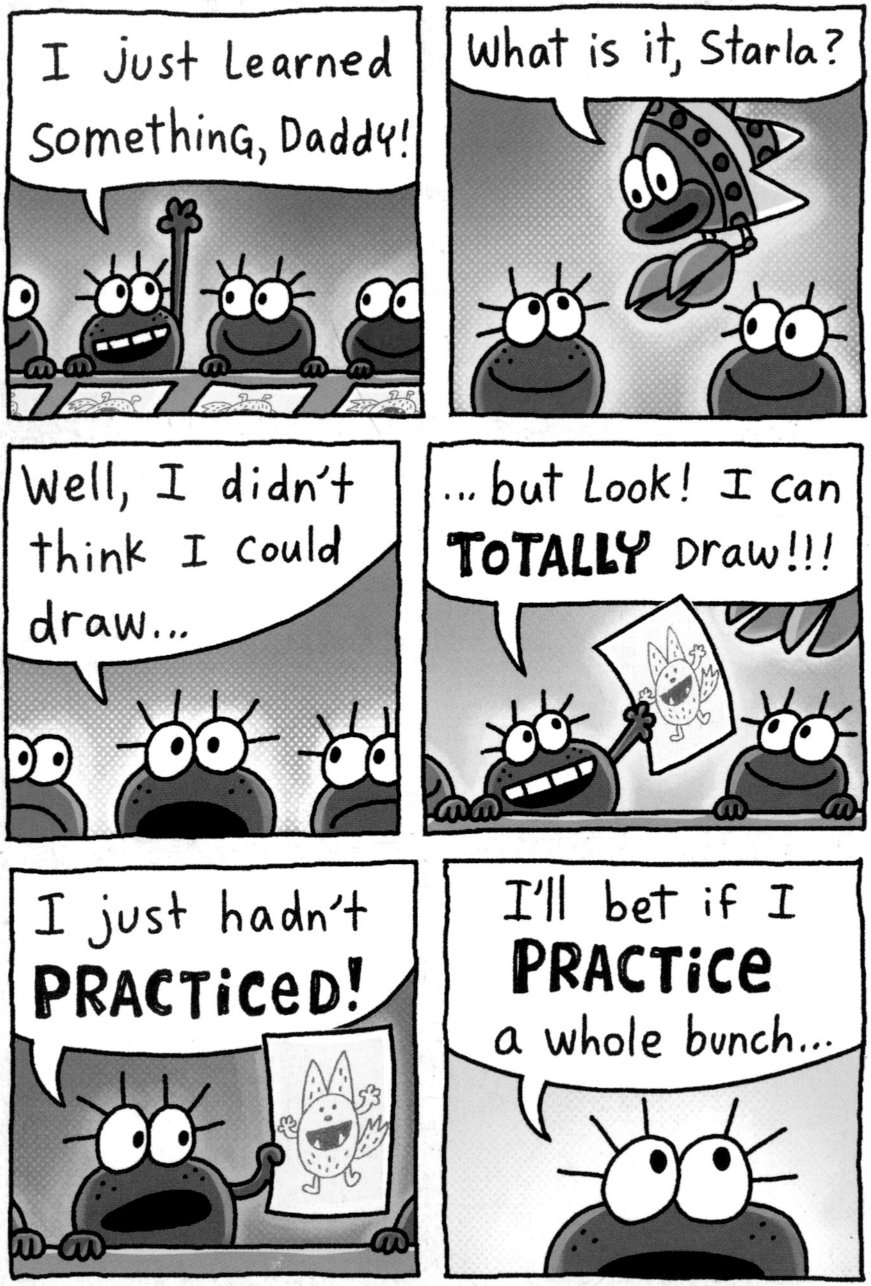
I just learned something, Daddy!
What is it, Starla?
Well, I didn't think I could draw...
... but look! I can TOTALLY draw!!!
I just hadn't PRACTICED!
I'll bet if I PRACTICE a whole bunch...

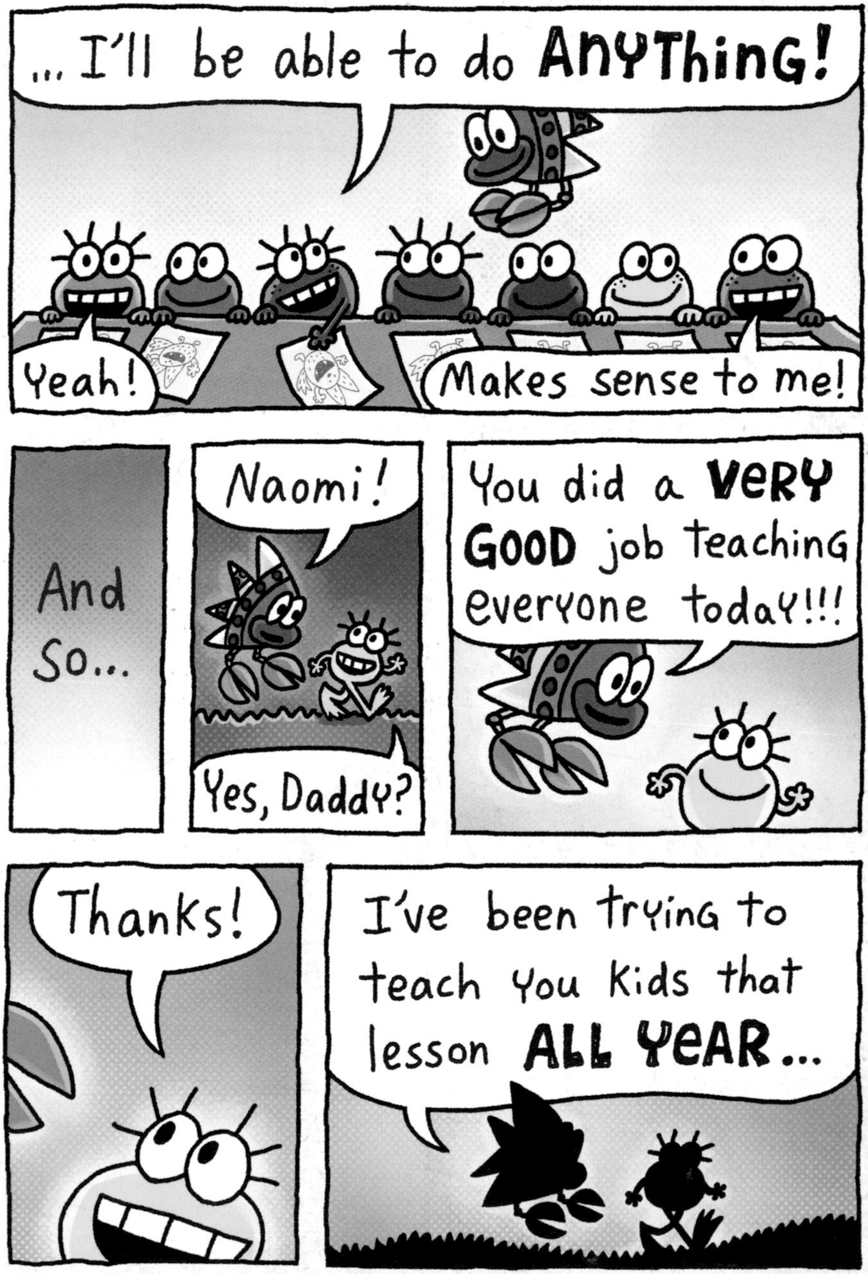
...I'll be able to do ANYTHING!
Yeah!
Makes sense to me!
And so...
Naomi!
Yes, Daddy?
You did a VERY GOOD job teaching everyone today!!!
Thanks!
I've been trying to teach you kids that lesson ALL YEAR...

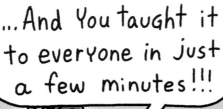

...And You taught it to everyone in just a few minutes!!!

Maybe You've found Your PURPOSE!

Maybe You're Going to be a TEACHER!

Do teachers make a lot of money?

Well, not usually. But they—

PASS!

CHAPTER 5

SHE WRITES BACK

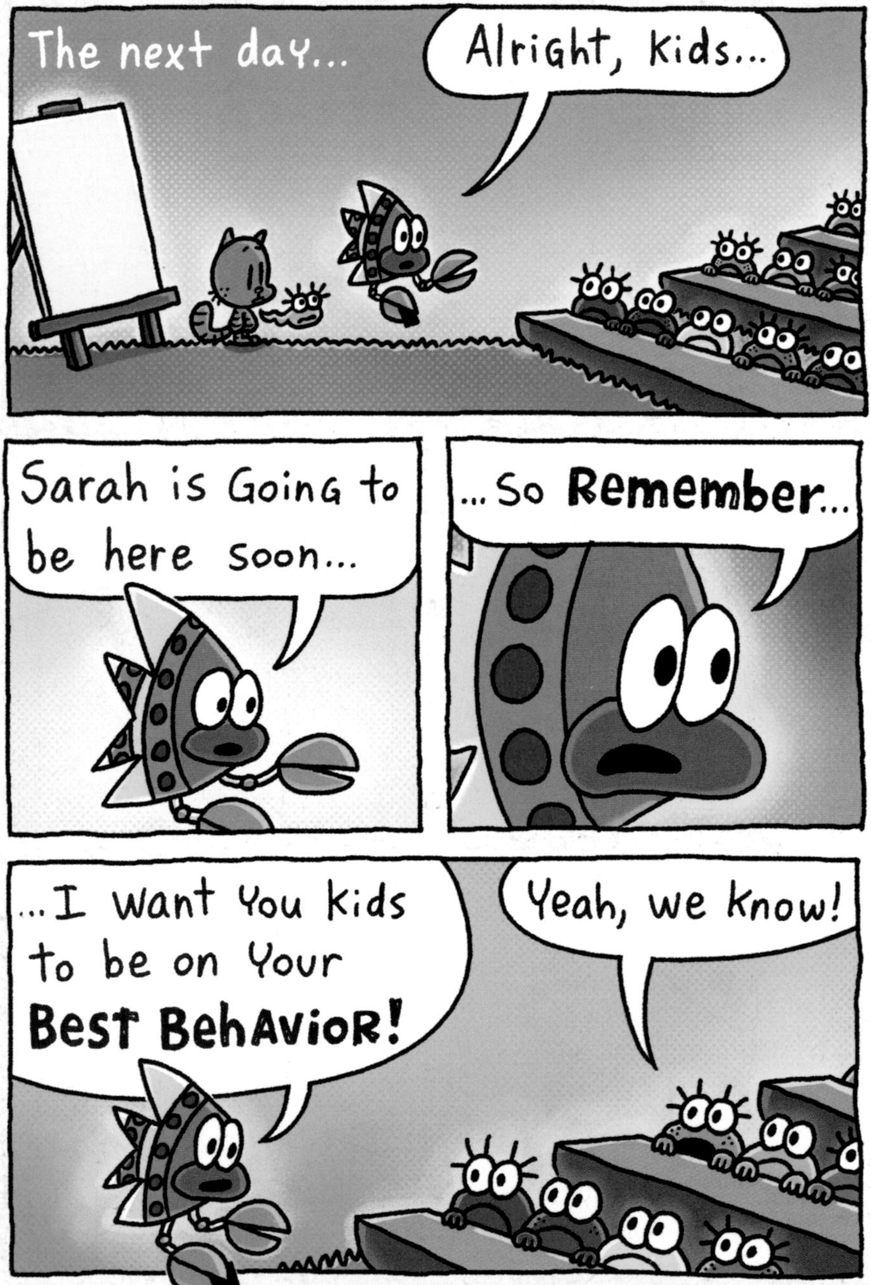
The next day...
Alright, kids...
Sarah is Going to be here soon...
...So Remember...
...I want You kids to be on Your Best Behavior!
Yeah, we know!

And I don't want you calling her **"SARAH."**

Why not?

It's **DISRESPECTFUL!**

You're **KIDS!** She's an **ADULT!**

You should call her **"MS. HATOFF."**

Ms. Hatoff
Ms. Hatoff
Ms. Hatoff
Ms. Hatoff
Ms. Hatoff
Ms. Hatoff
Ms. Hatoff
Ms. Hatoff
Ms. Hatoff
Ms. Hatoff

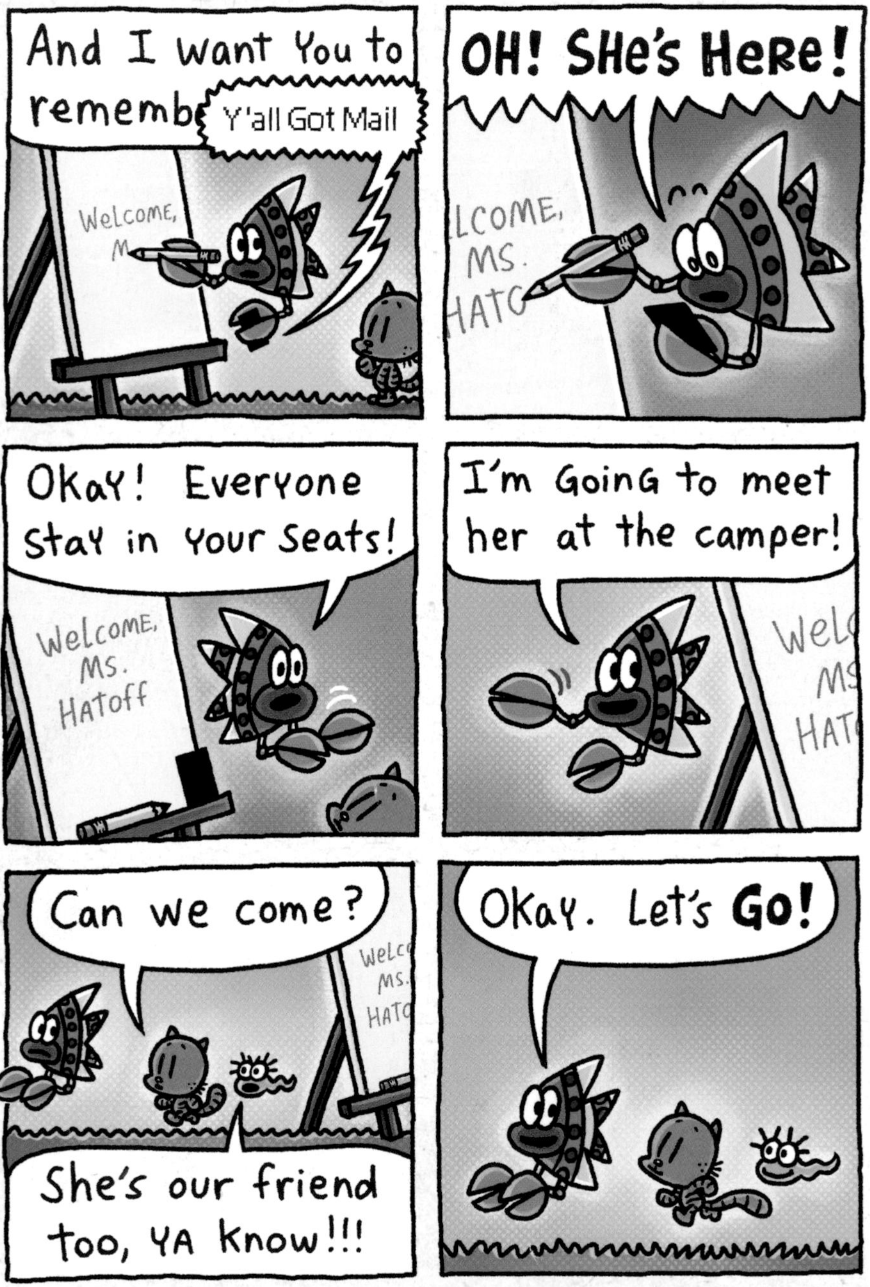
And I want you to rememb
Y'all Got Mail
WELCOME, M
OH! SHE's HERE!
LCOME, MS. HATO
OKAY! Everyone stay in your seats!
WELCOME, MS. HATOFF
I'm Going to meet her at the camper!
WELC MS HATO
Can we come?
WELC MS. HATO
She's our friend too, YA know!!!
OKAY. Let's GO!

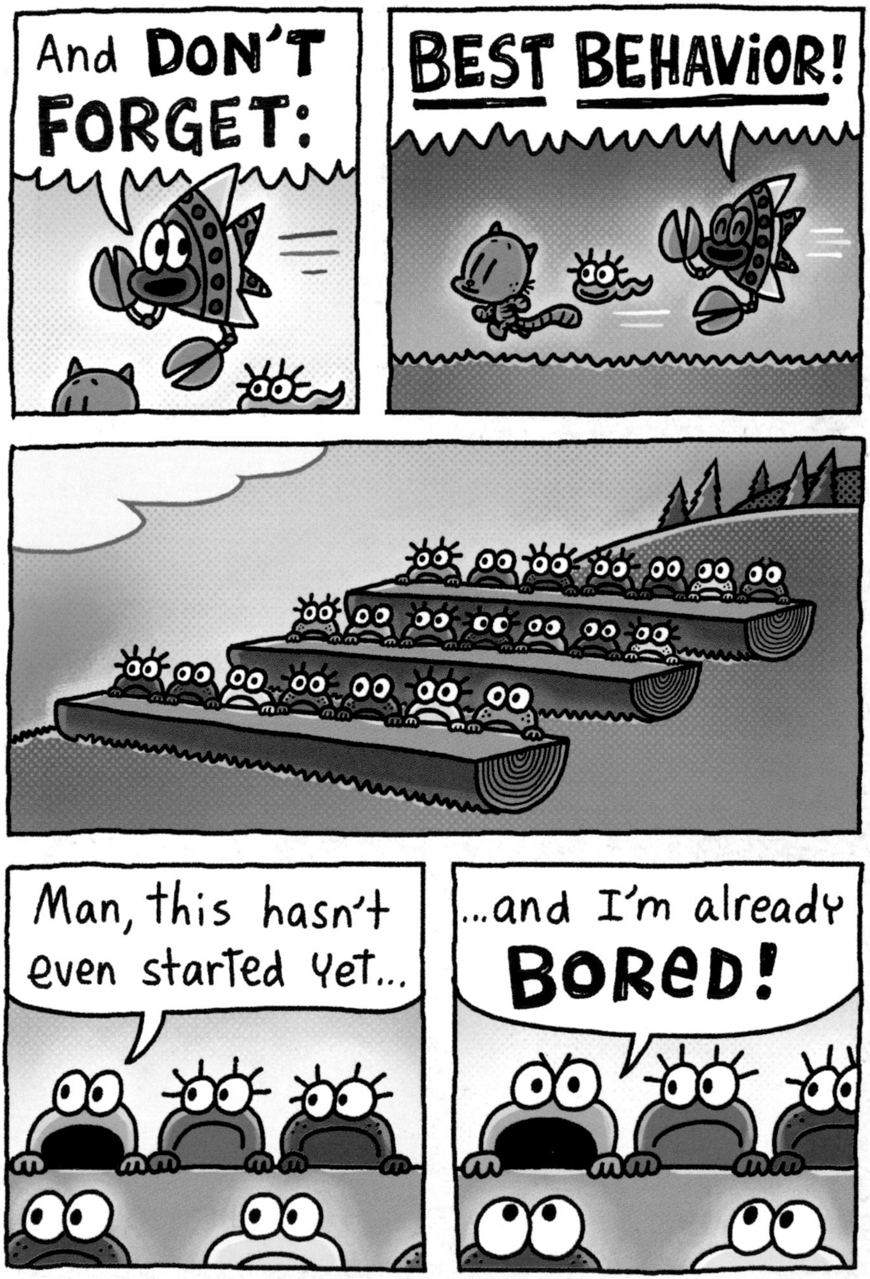
And DON'T FORGET:
BEST BEHAVIOR!
Man, this hasn't even started yet...
...and I'm already BORED!

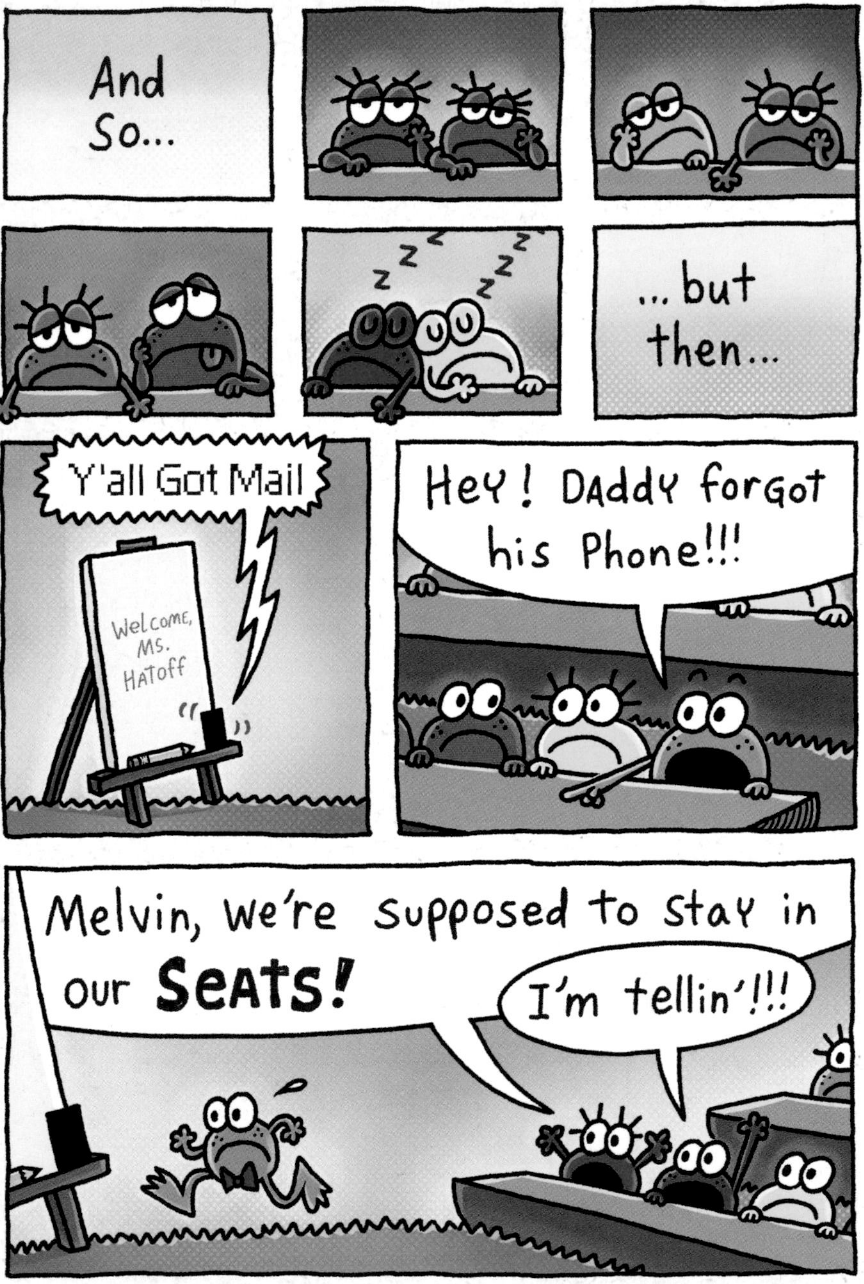
And So...
... but then...
Y'all Got Mail
Welcome, Ms. HATOFF
Hey! DADDY forGot his Phone!!!
Melvin, we're supposed to stay in our SEATS!
I'm tellin'!!!

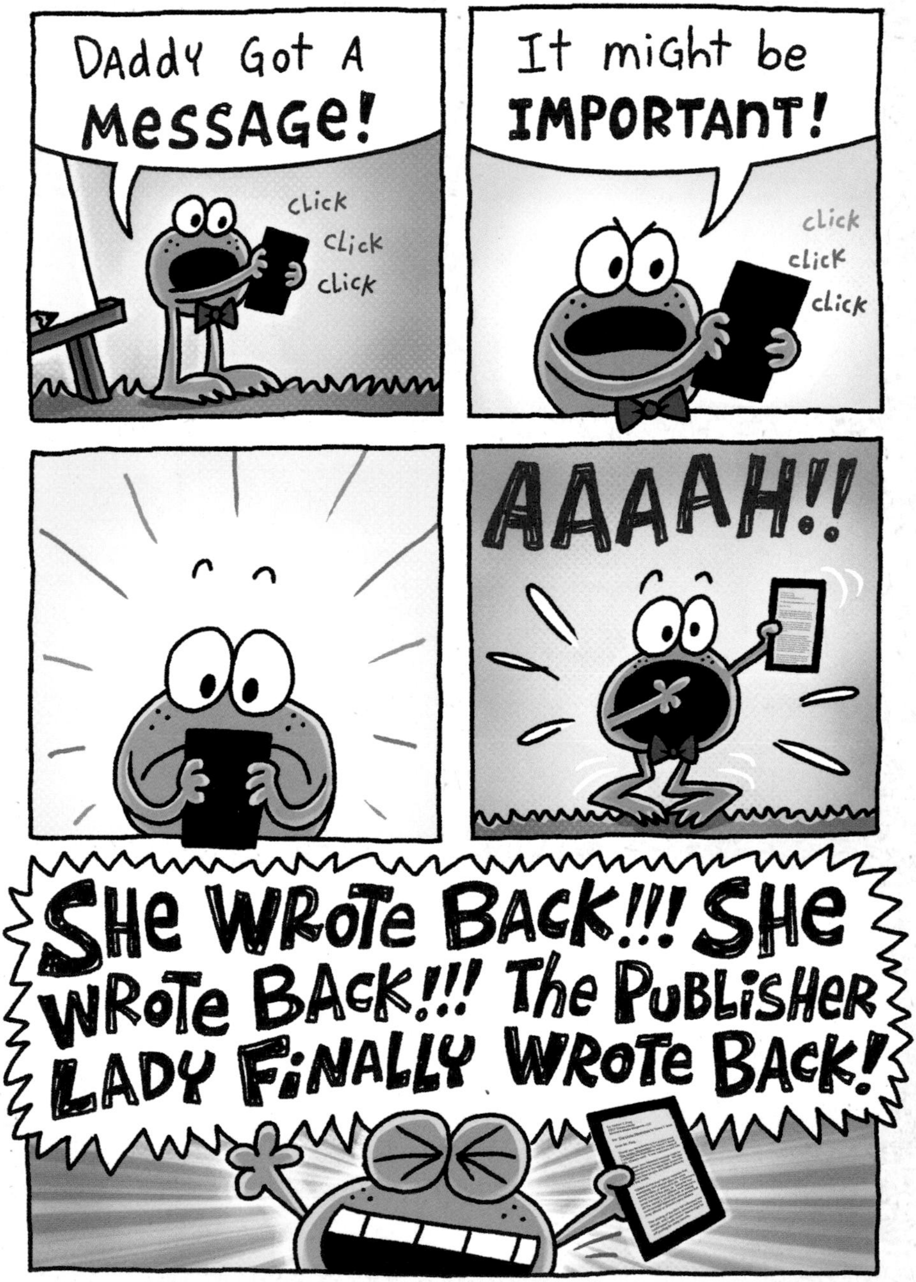

DAddy Got A MeSSAGe!
cLick
cLick
cLick
It might be IMPORTANT!
cLick
cLick
cLick
AAAAH!!
SHe WRoTe BACK!!! SHe WRoTe BACK!!! The PuBLiSHeR LADY FiNALLY WRoTe BACK!

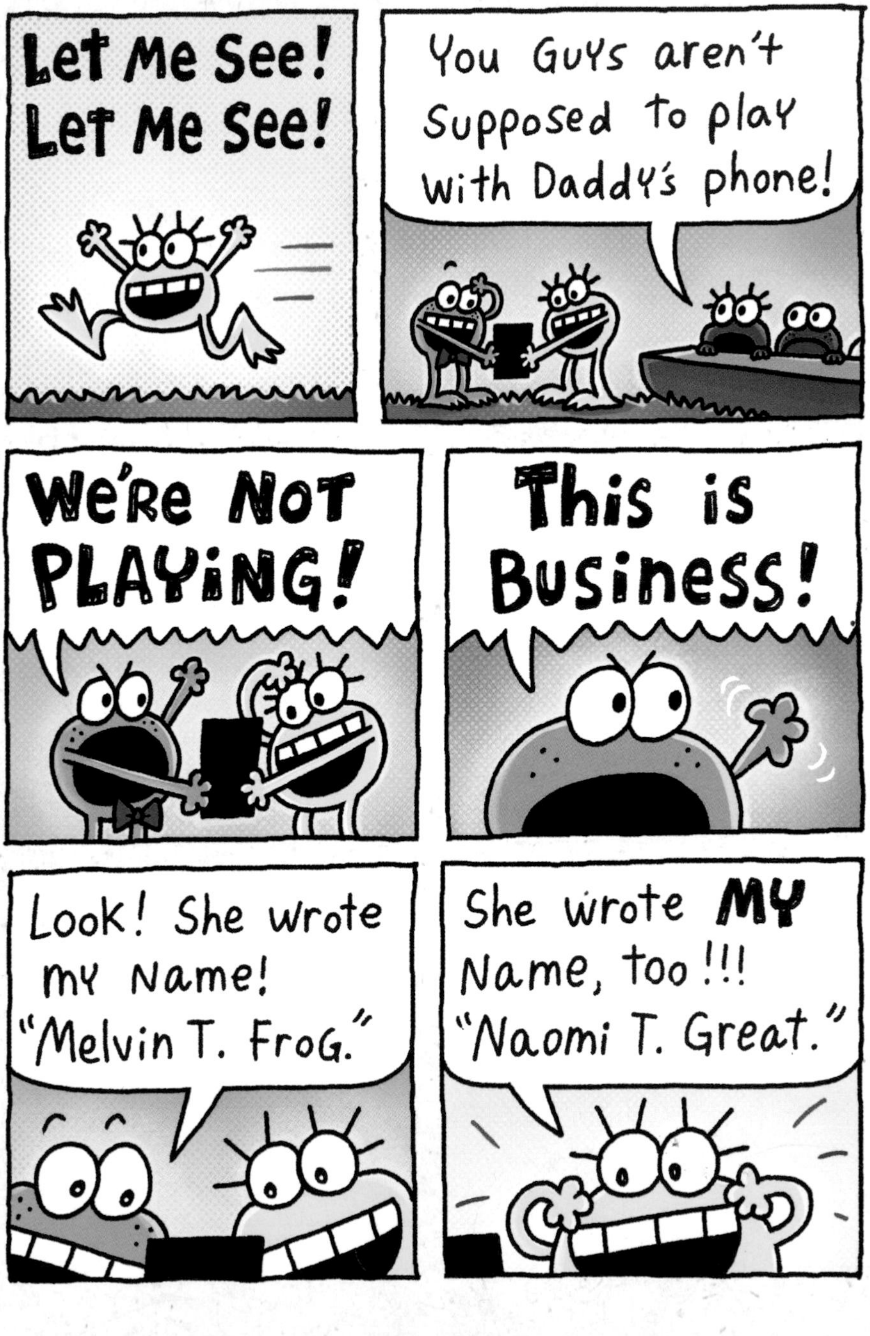
Let Me See! Let Me See!
You GUYS aren't Supposed to play with Daddy's phone!
We're NOT PLAYING!
This is Business!
Look! She wrote my Name! "Melvin T. FroG."
She wrote MY Name, too!!! "Naomi T. Great."

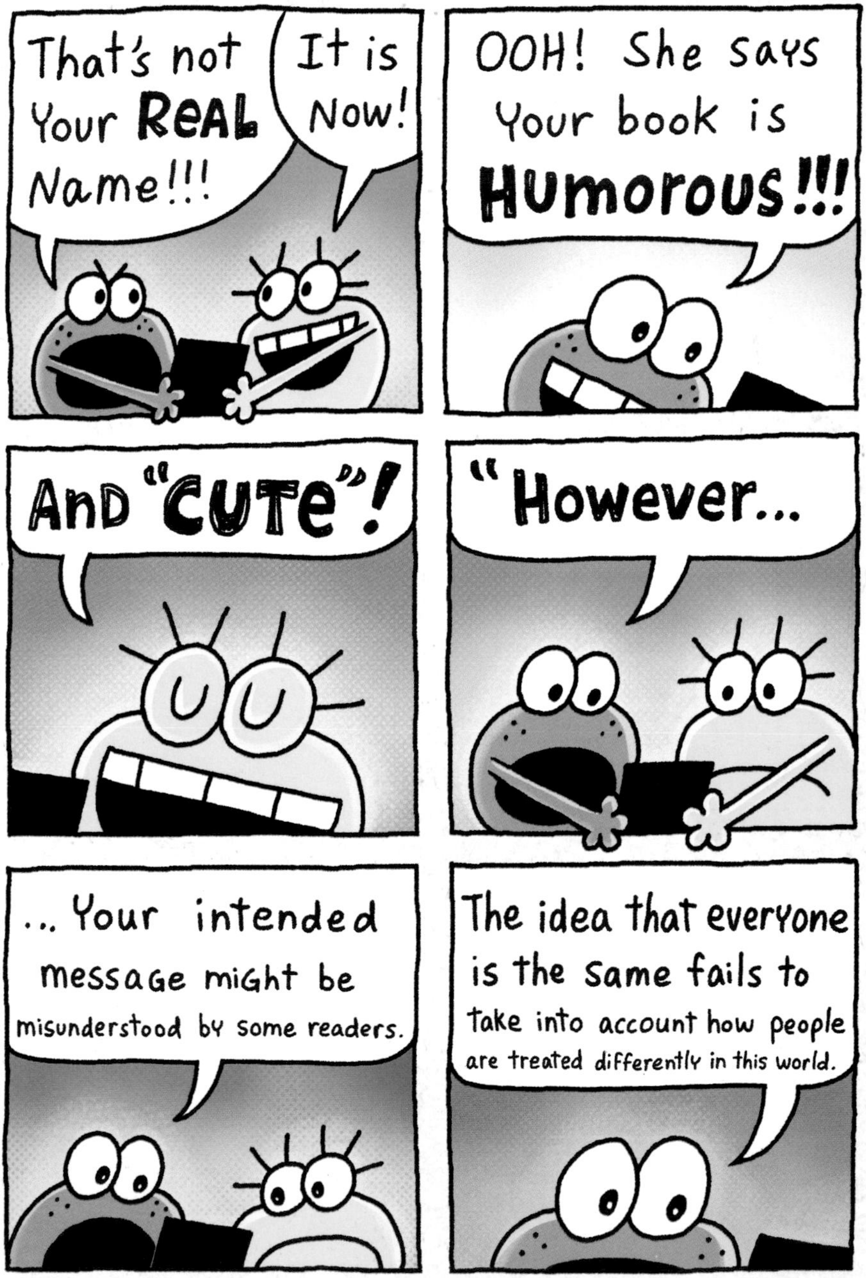
That's not Your REAL Name!!!
It is Now!
OOH! She says Your book is HUMOROUS!!!
AND "CUTE"!
"However...
... Your intended message might be misunderstood by some readers.
The idea that everyone is the same fails to take into account how people are treated differently in this world.

'Global sameness' fails to recognize that everybody isn't always given the same opportunities or chances in life. Furthermore, some lines in the story (i.e. 'just poke your nose beneath your clothes, you'll see we're all the same'), could be seen as making controversial statements about gender that may offend or diminish many readers."

Just skip to the end!

NO! I'm READING!

You Read too slow!

Give it to me! NO!!!

Let Go! Give it !!!

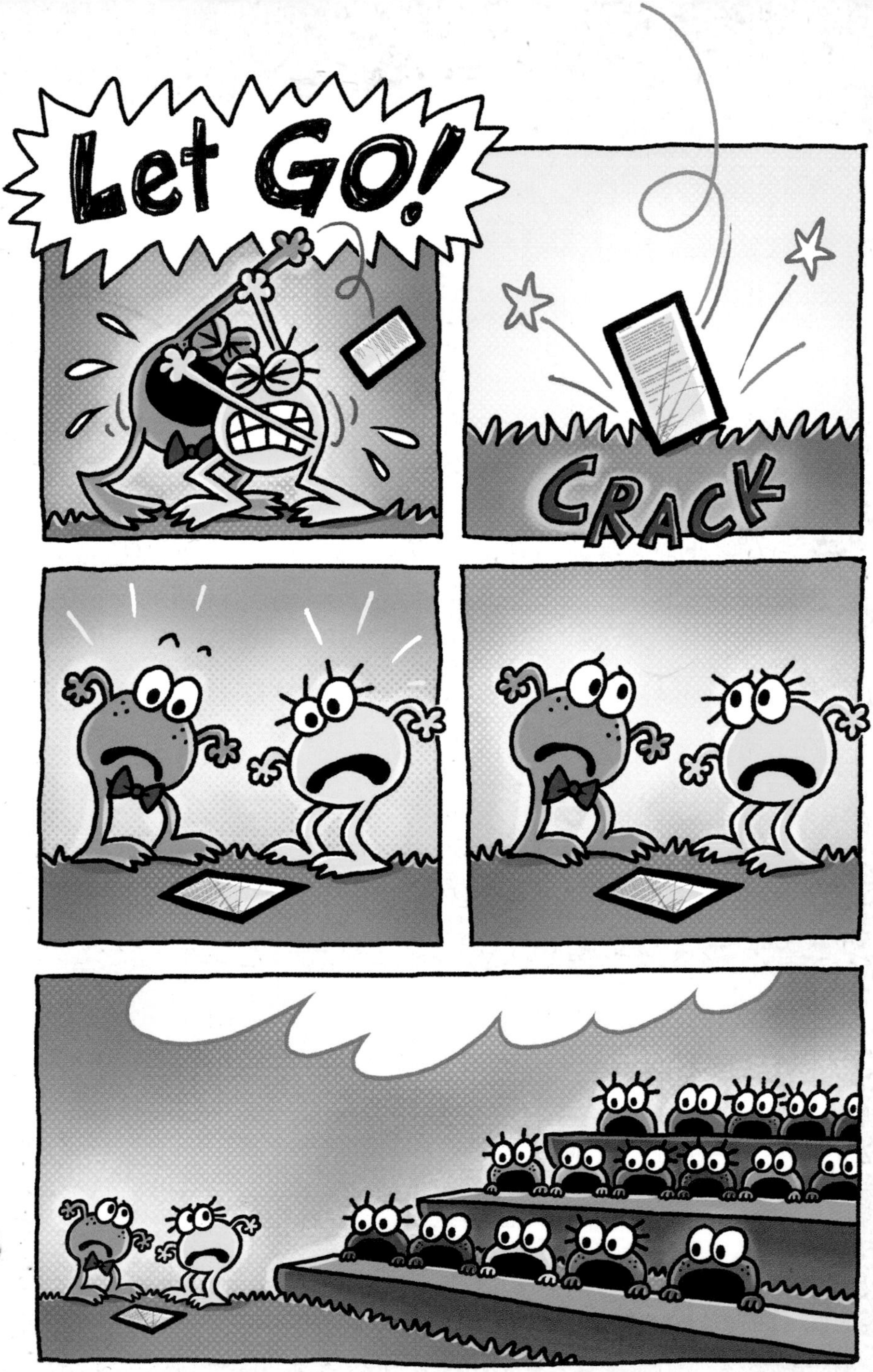
Let GO!
CRACK

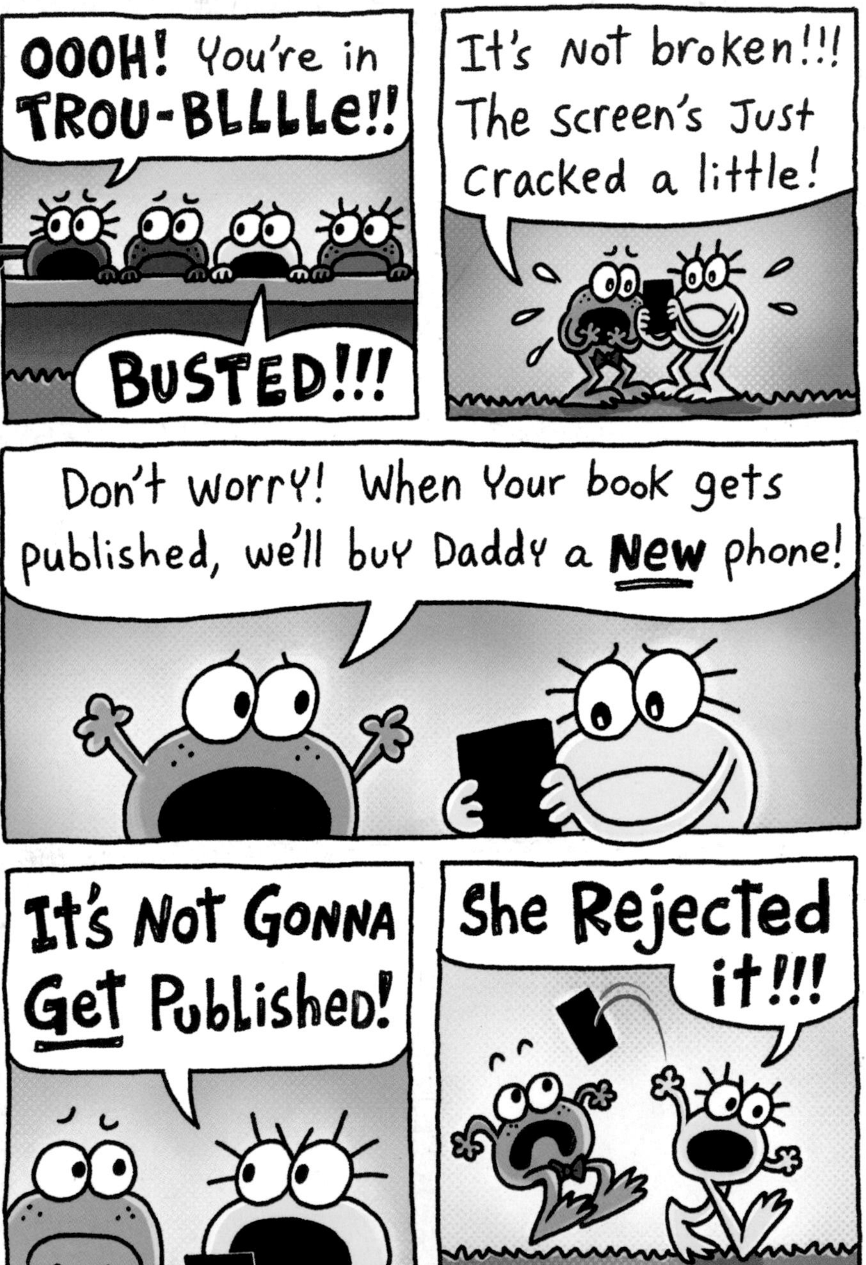
OOOH! You're in TROU-BLLLLe!!
BUSTED!!!
It's Not broken!!! The screen's Just cracked a little!
Don't worry! When your book gets published, we'll buy Daddy a NEW phone!
It's Not GONNA Get Published!
She Rejected it!!!

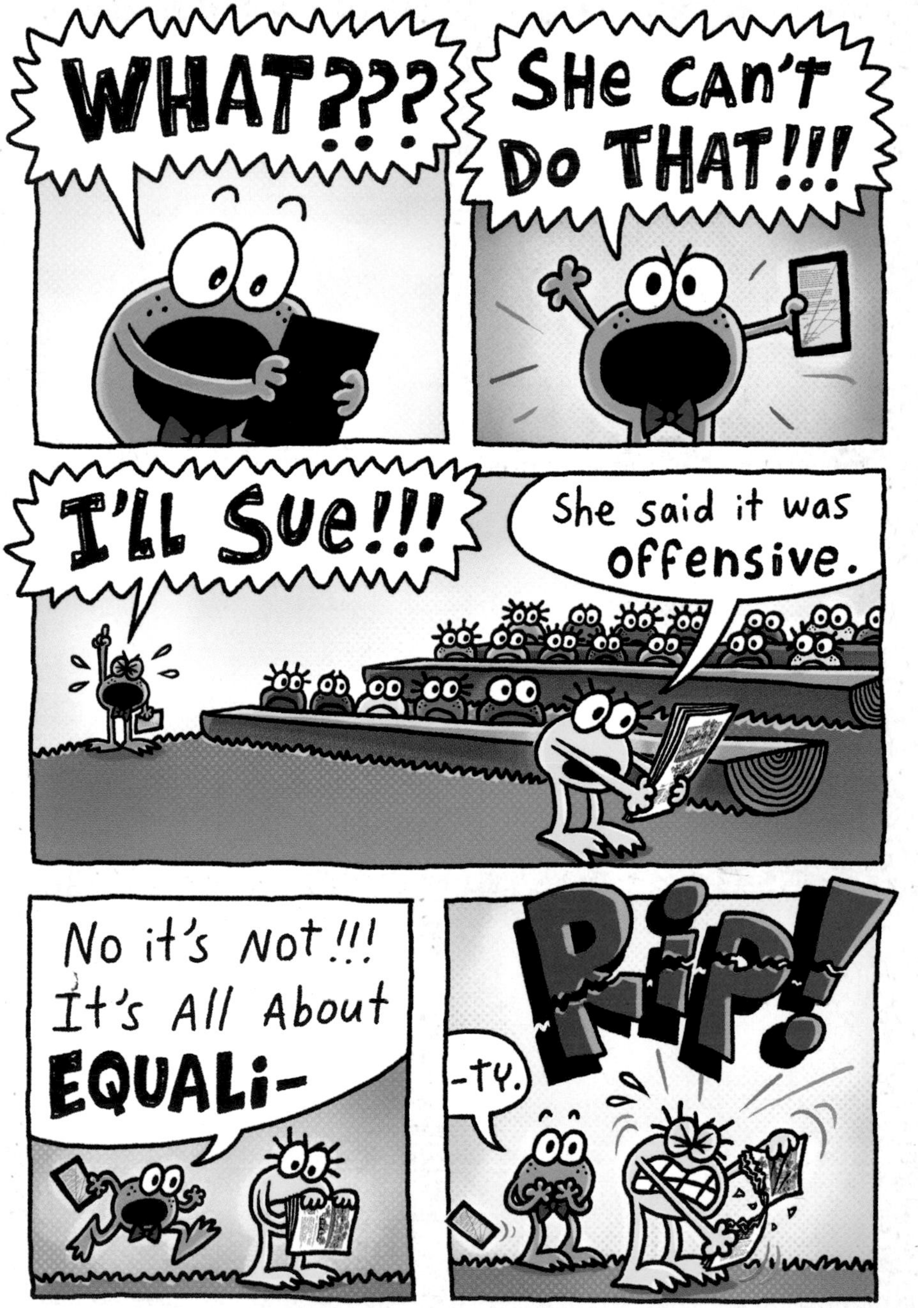
WHAT???
She can't DO THAT!!!
I'LL Sue!!!
She said it was offensive.
No it's Not!!! It's All About EQUALi-
RiP!
-TY.

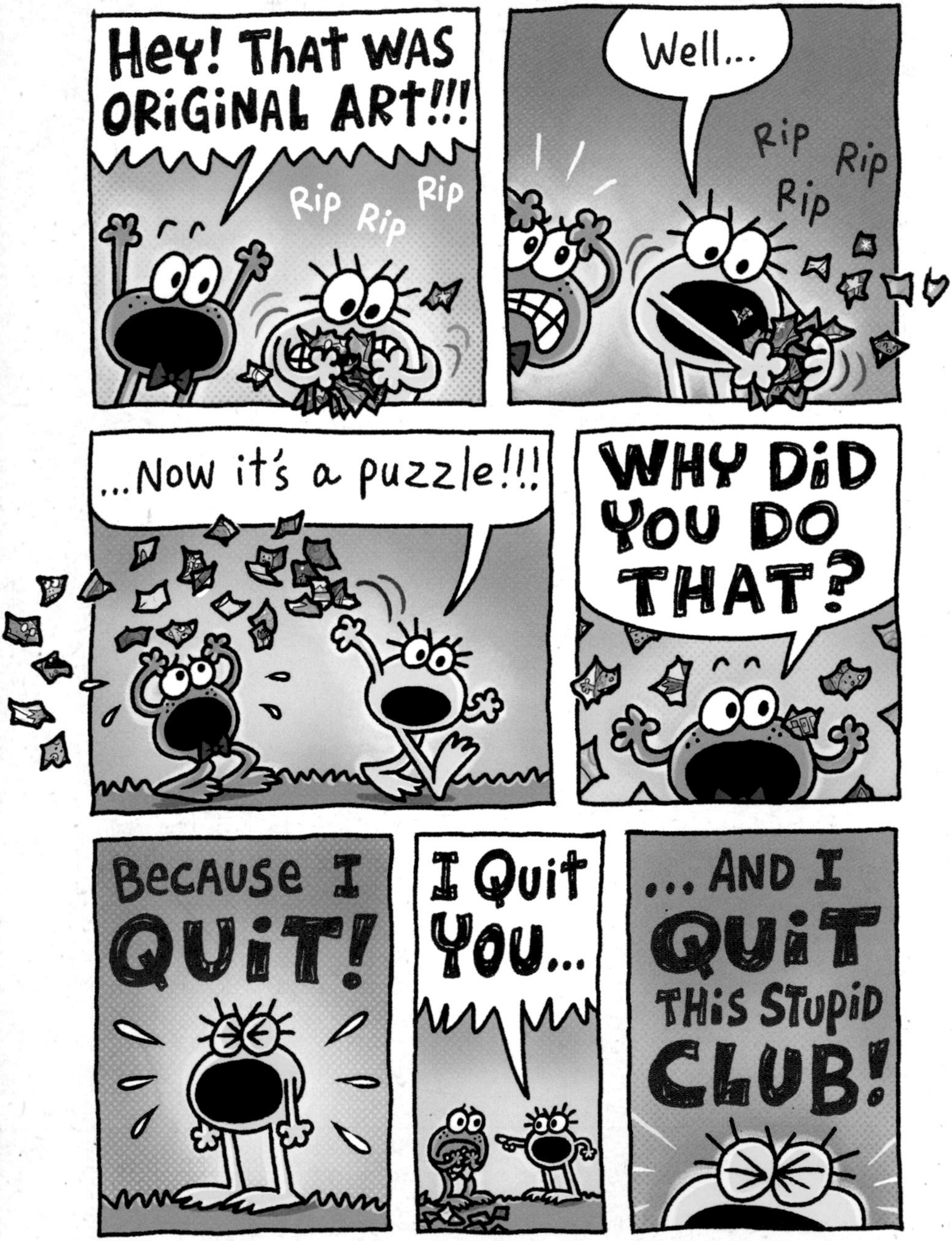
Hey! That WAS ORIGINAL ART!!!
Rip Rip Rip
Well...
Rip Rip Rip
...Now it's a puzzle!!!
WHY DID YOU DO THAT?
Because I QUIT!
I Quit YOU...
... AND I QUIT THIS STUPID CLUB!

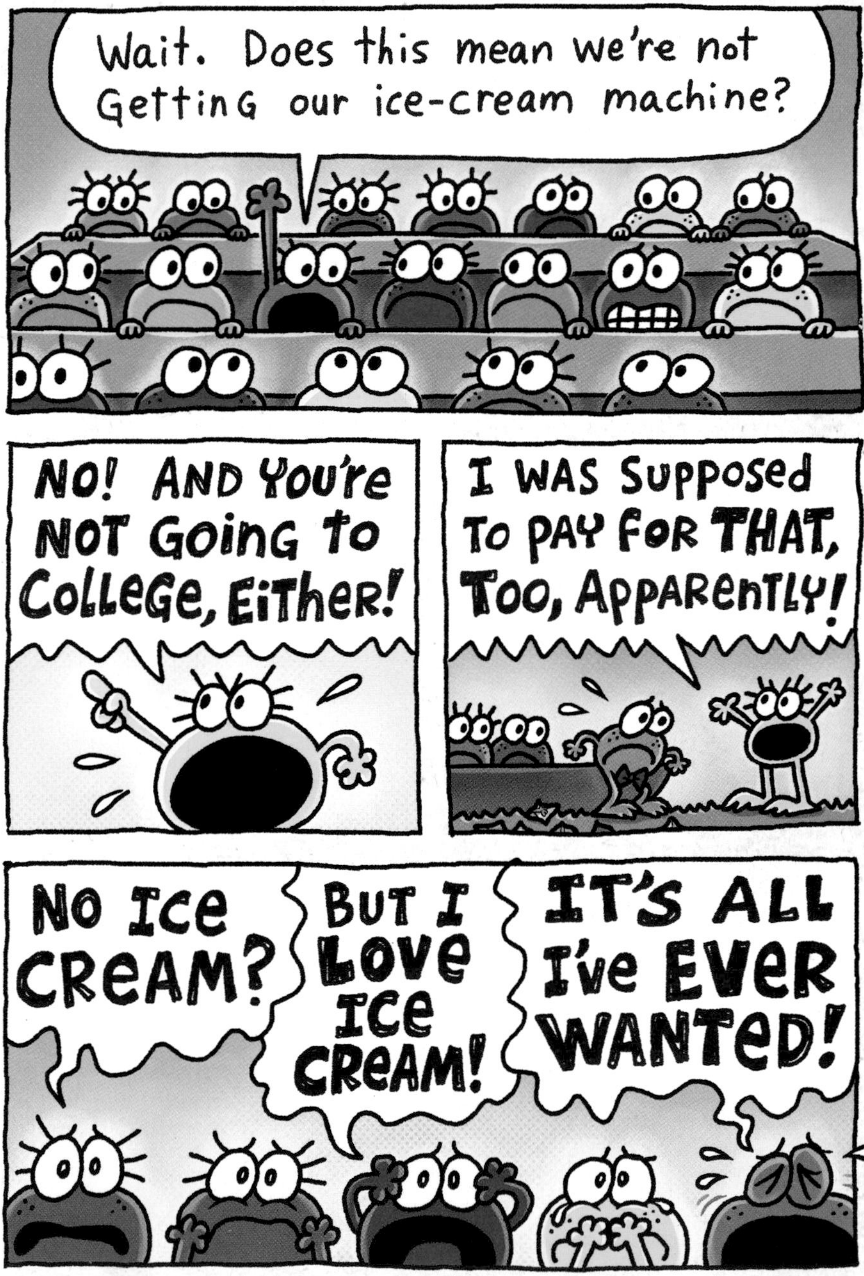
Wait. Does this mean we're not Getting our ice-cream machine?
NO! AND YOU'RE NOT GOING TO COLLEGE, EITHER!
I WAS SUPPOSED TO PAY FOR THAT, TOO, APPARENTLY!
NO ICE CREAM?
BUT I LOVE ICE CREAM!
IT'S ALL I'VE EVER WANTED!

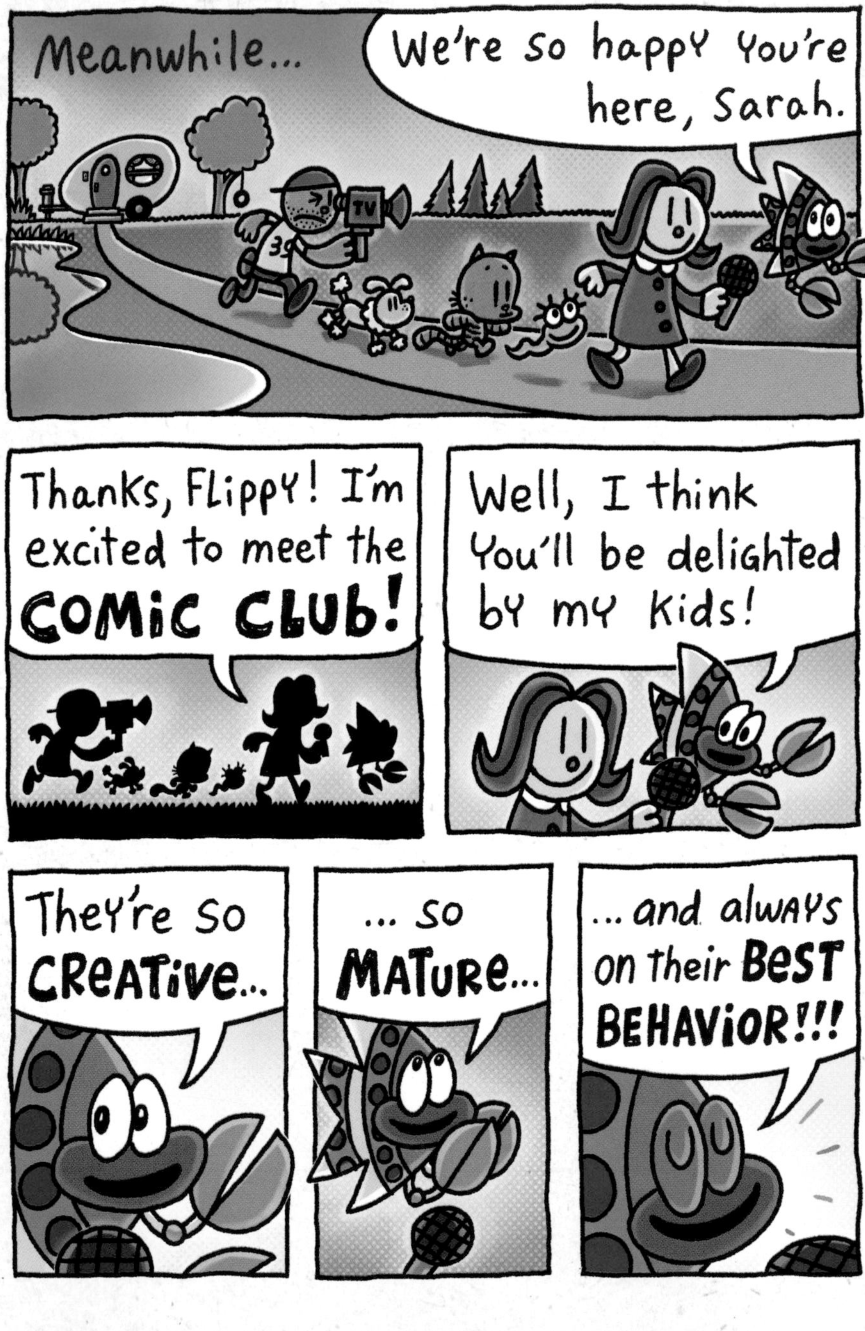
Meanwhile...
We're so happy you're here, Sarah.
TV
Thanks, Flippy! I'm excited to meet the COMIC CLUB!
Well, I think you'll be delighted by my kids!
They're so CREATIVE...
... so MATURE...
... and always on their BEST BEHAVIOR!!!

CHAPTER 6

Our Worst Behavior

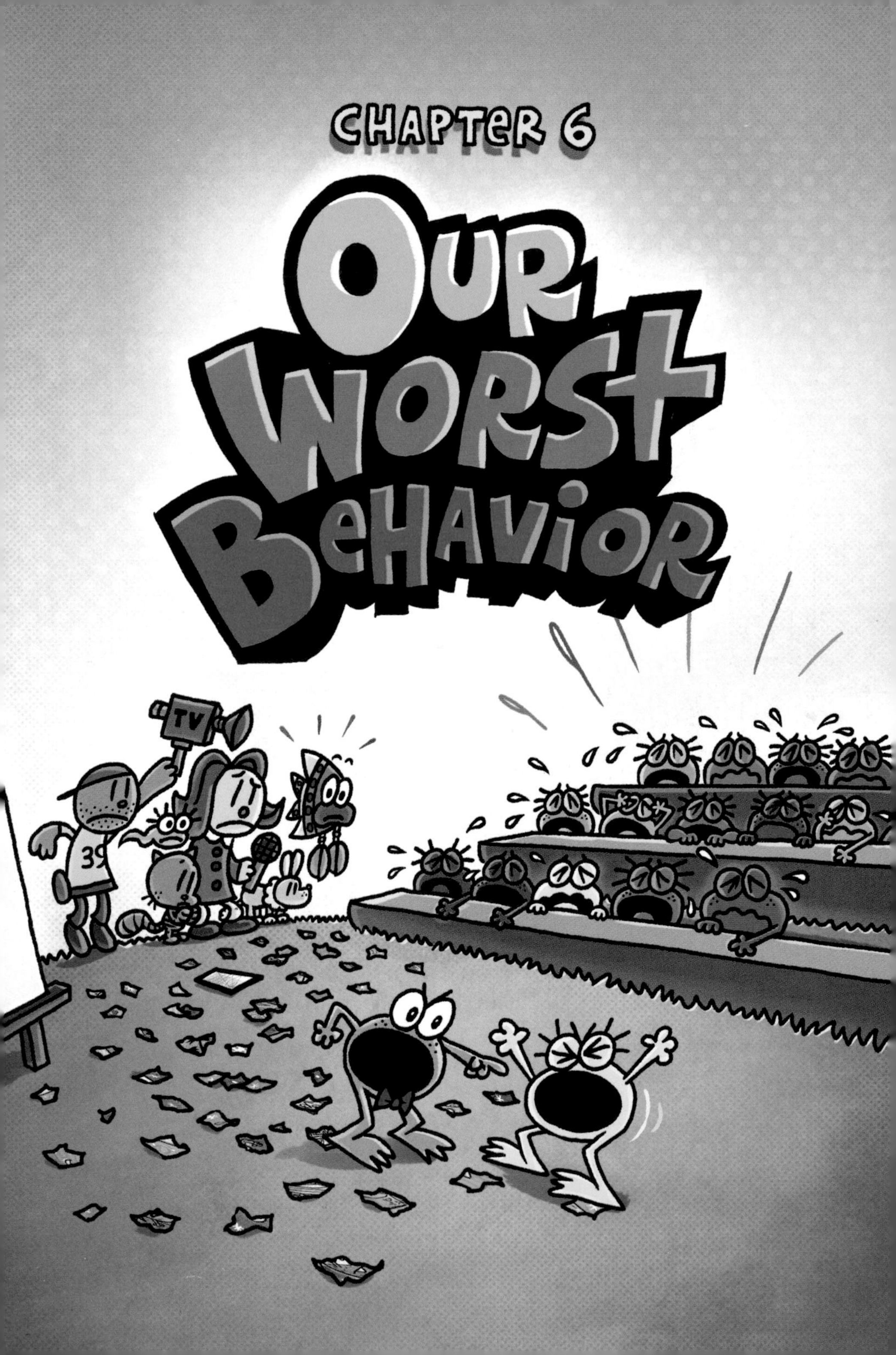
TV

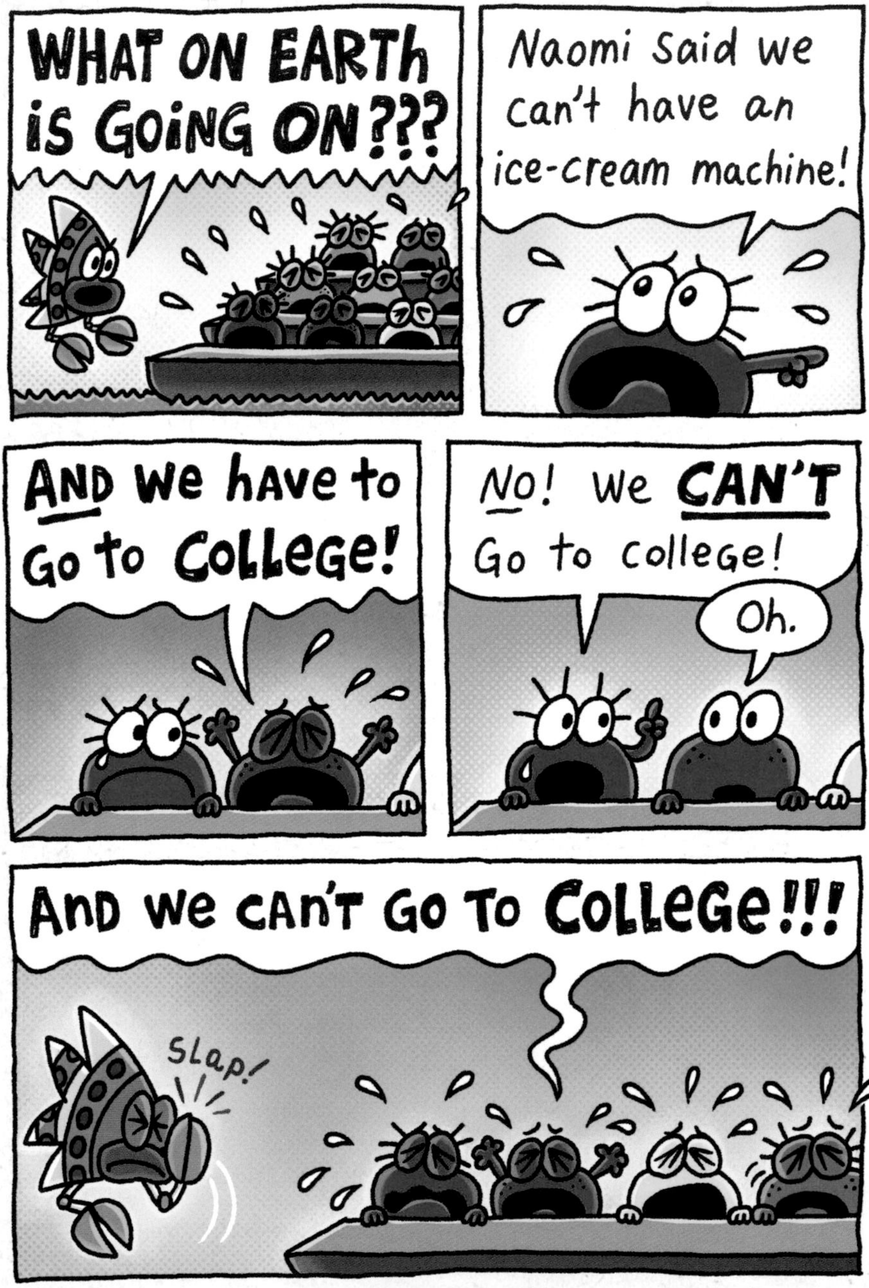
WHAT ON EARTH is GOING ON???
Naomi said we can't have an ice-cream machine!
AND we have to Go to COLLEGE!
NO! We CAN'T Go to college!
Oh.
AND WE CAN'T GO TO COLLEGE!!!
Slap!

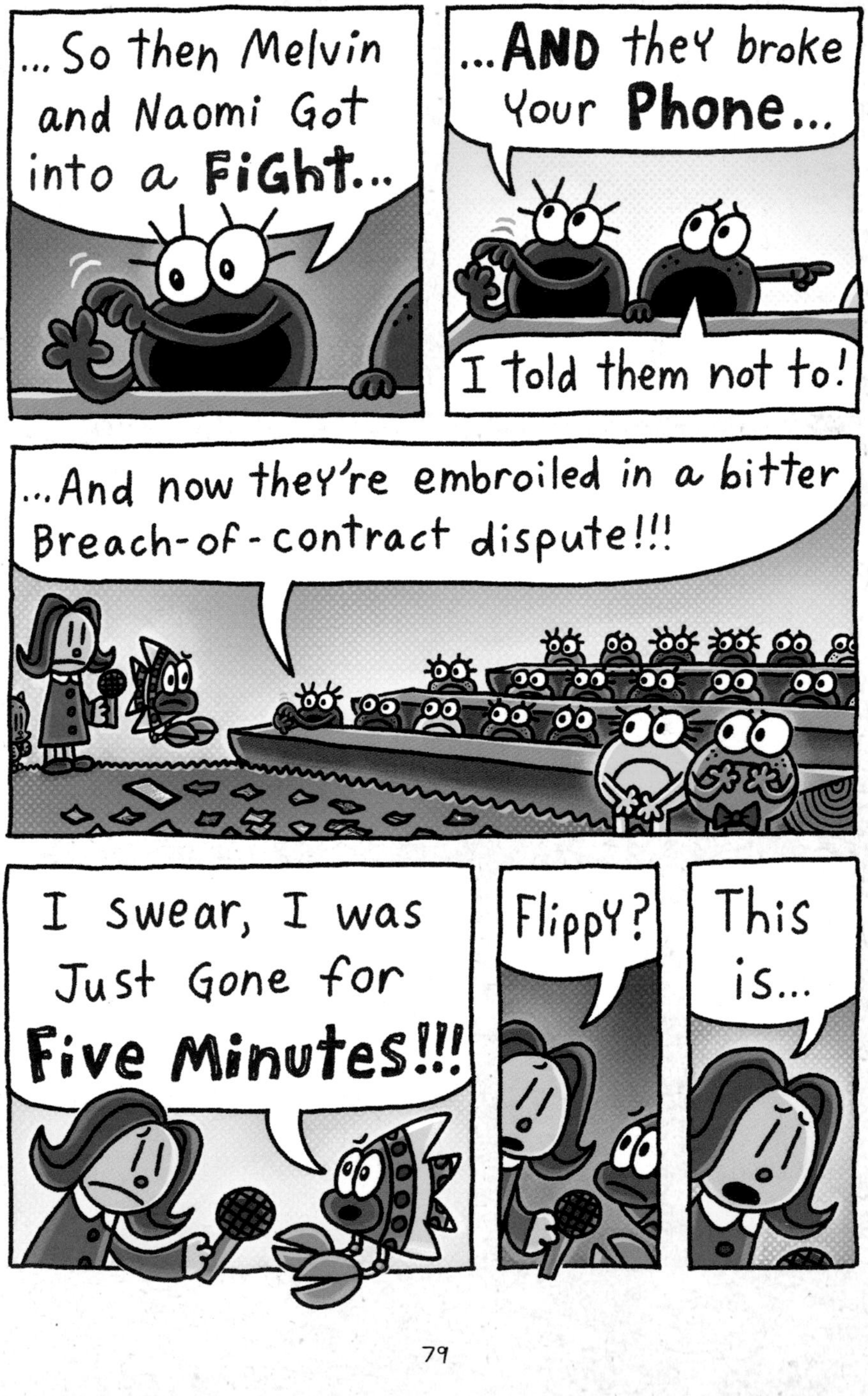
...So then Melvin and Naomi Got into a FiGht...
...AND they broke Your Phone...
I told them not to!
...And now they're embroiled in a bitter Breach-of-contract dispute!!!
I swear, I was Just Gone for Five Minutes!!!
Flippy?
This is...

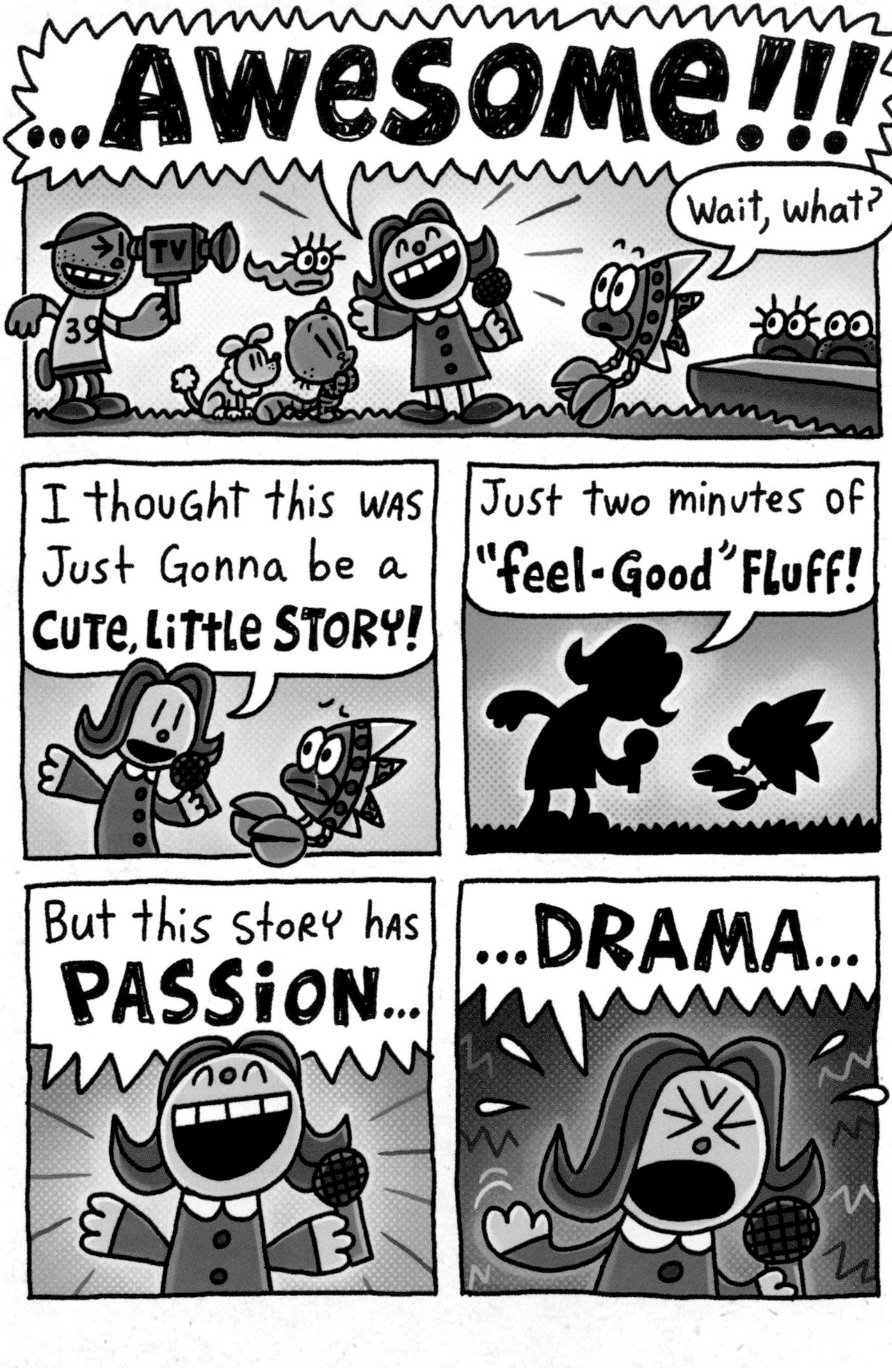

...AWESOME!!!
Wait, what?
I thought this WAS Just Gonna be a CUTE, LITTLE STORY!
Just two minutes of "feel-Good" FLUFF!
But this story has PASSION...
...DRAMA...

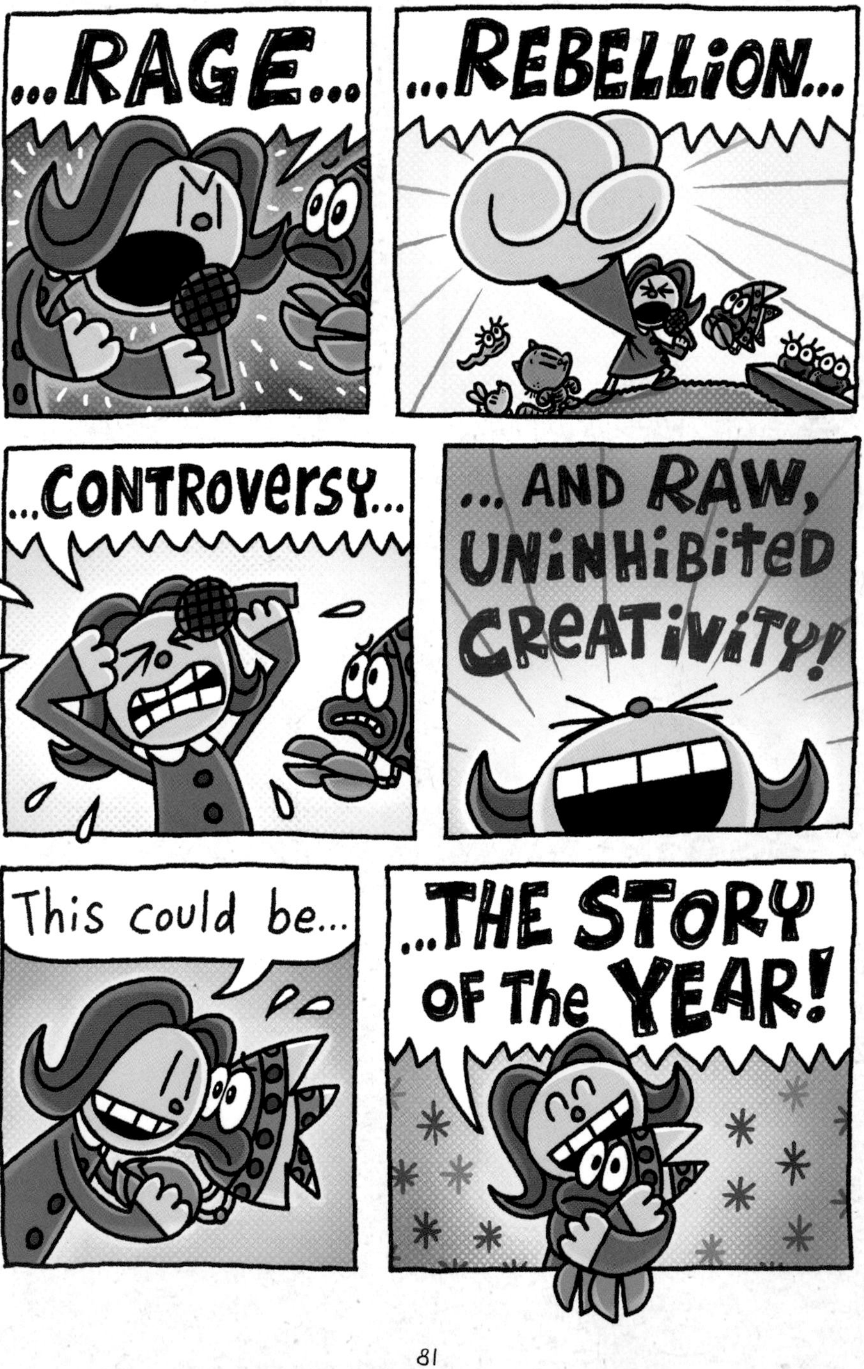
...RAGE...
...REBELLION...
...CONTROVERSY...
... AND RAW, UNINHIBITED CREATIVITY!
This could be...
...THE STORY OF THE YEAR!

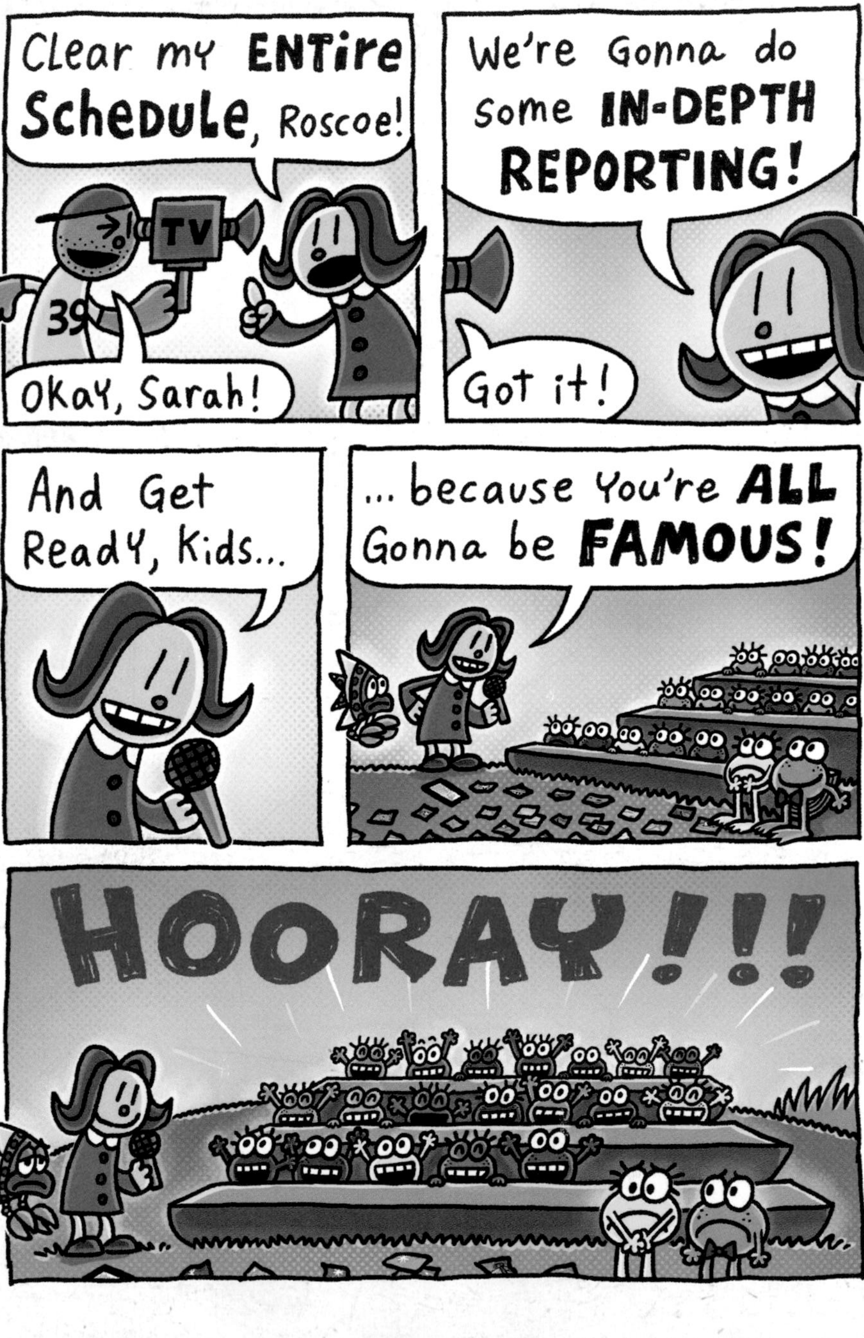
Clear my ENTire Schedule, Roscoe!
OKay, Sarah!
TV
39
We're Gonna do some IN-DEPTH REPORTING!
Got it!
And Get Ready, Kids...
...because You're ALL Gonna be FAMOUS!
HOORAY!!!

CHAPTER 7

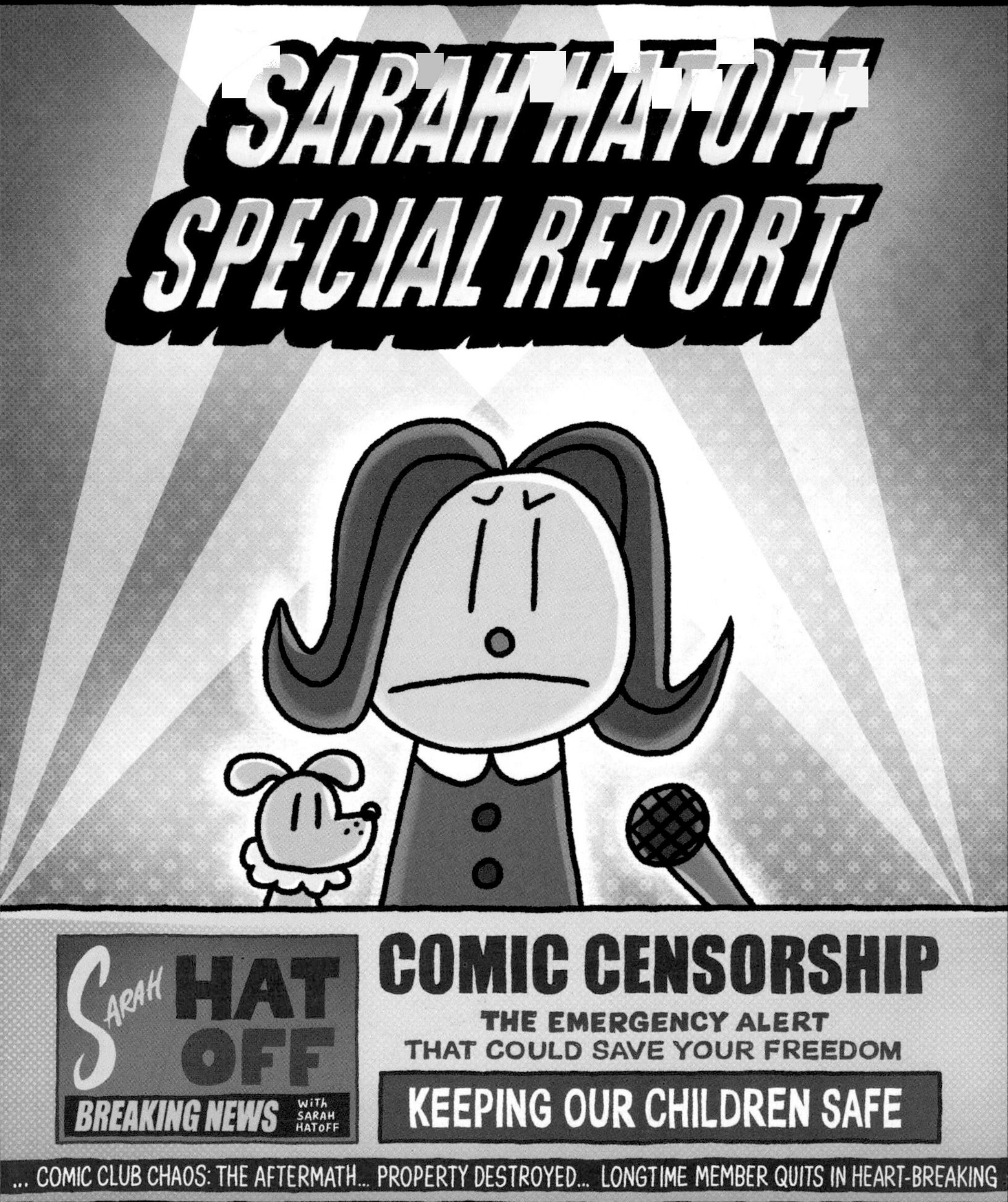
SARAH HATOFF SPECIAL REPORT
SARAH HAT OFF
BREAKING NEWS
WITH SARAH HATOFF
COMIC CENSORSHIP
THE EMERGENCY ALERT
THAT COULD SAVE YOUR FREEDOM
KEEPING OUR CHILDREN SAFE
... COMIC CLUB CHAOS: THE AFTERMATH... PROPERTY DESTROYED... LONGTIME MEMBER QUITS IN HEART-BREAKING

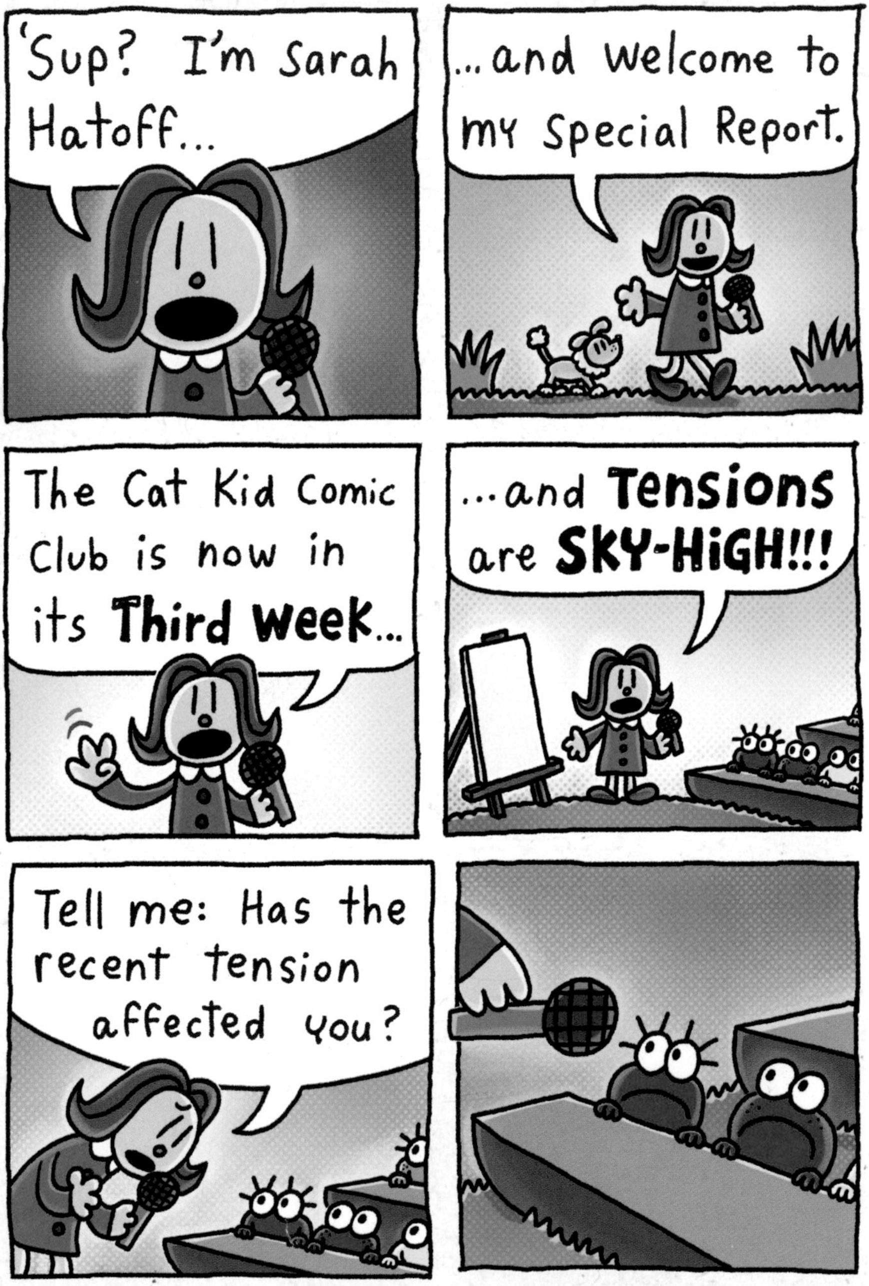
'Sup? I'm Sarah Hatoff...
...and welcome to my Special Report.
The Cat Kid Comic Club is now in its **Third Week**...
...and **Tensions** are **SKY-HiGH!!!**
Tell me: Has the recent tension affected you?

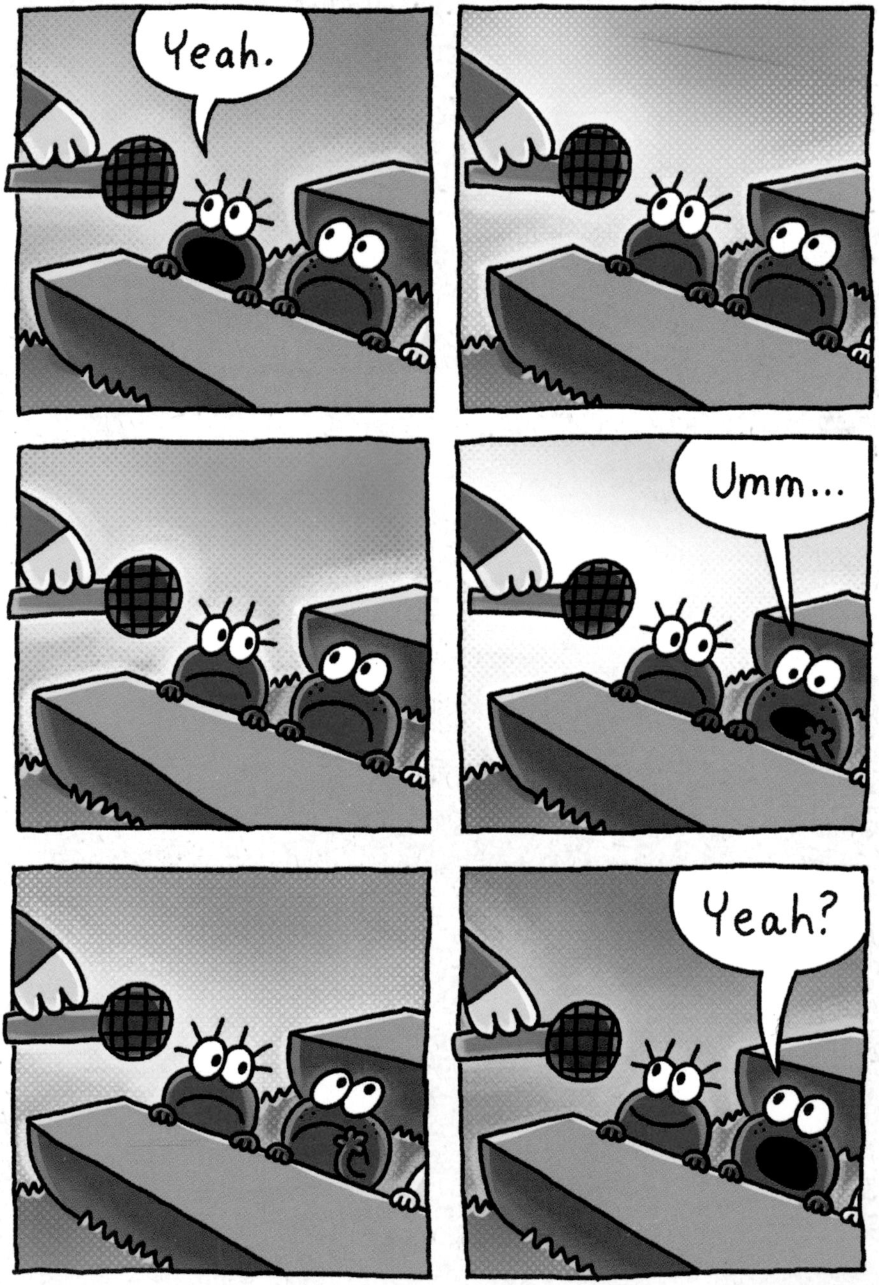
Yeah.
Umm...
Yeah?

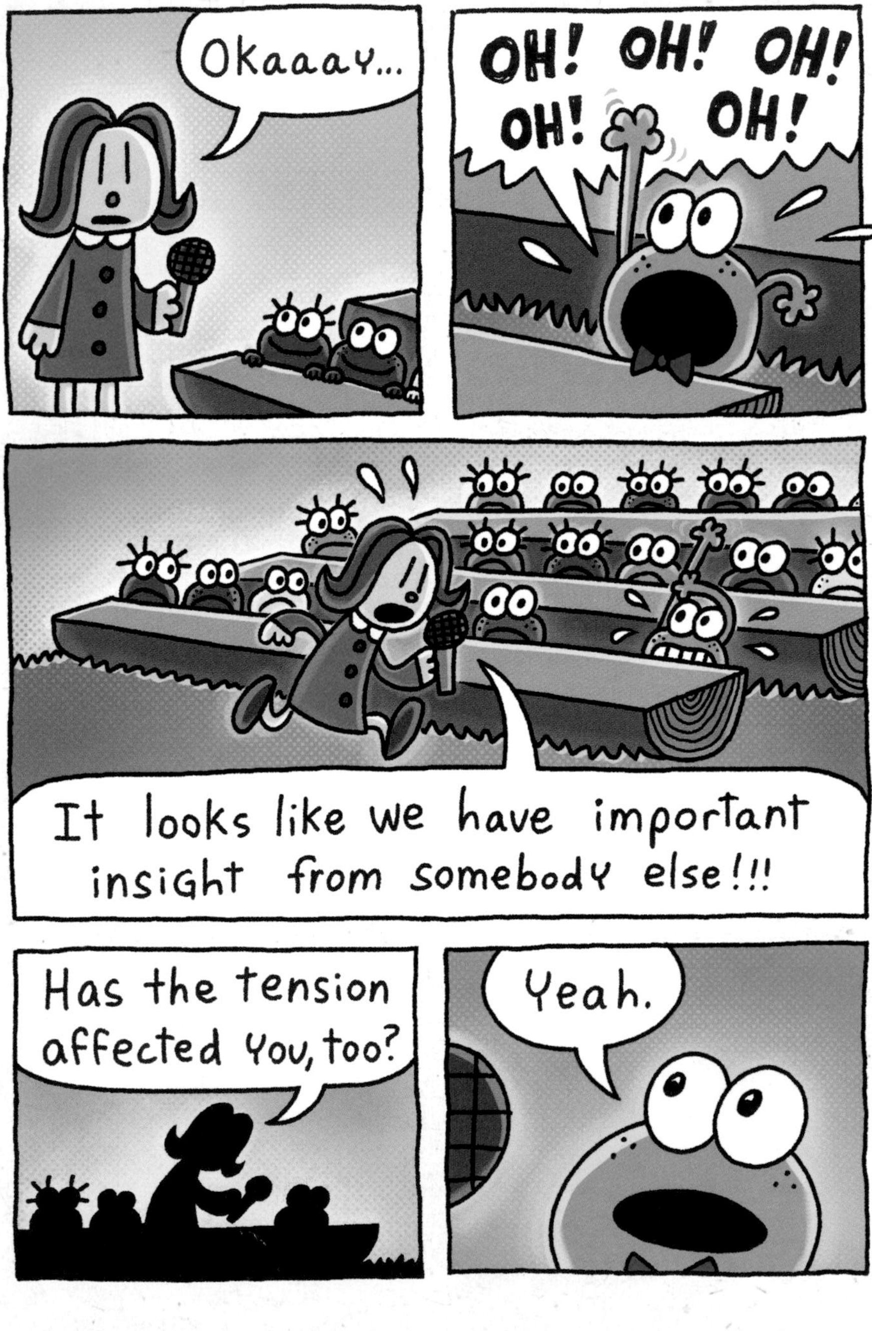
Okaaay...
OH! OH! OH! OH! OH!
It looks like we have important insight from somebody else!!!
Has the tension affected you, too?
Yeah.

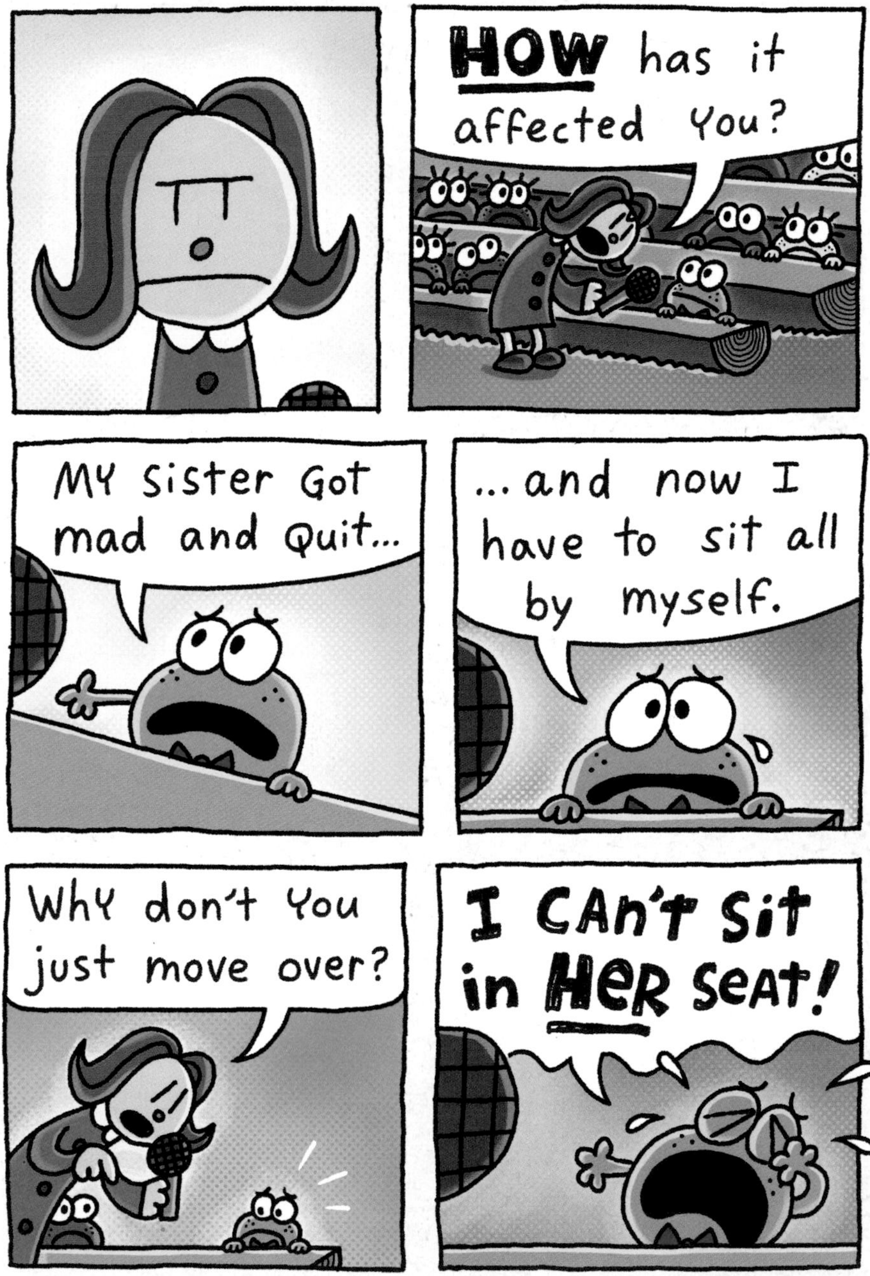
HOW has it affected You?
MY Sister Got mad and Quit...
...and now I have to sit all by myself.
WhY don't You just move over?
I CAN'T Sit in HER SEAT!

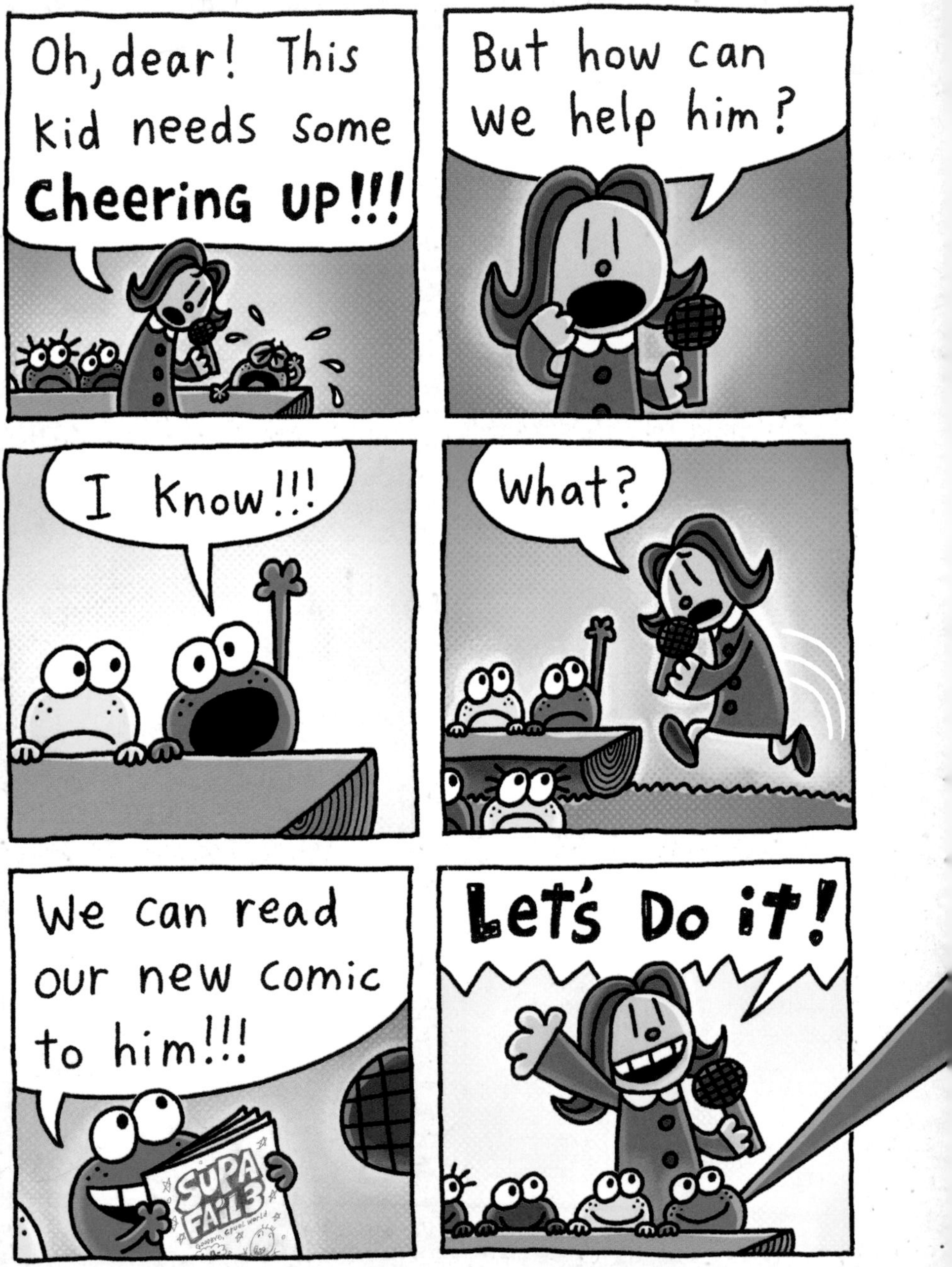
Oh, dear! This kid needs some CHEERING UP!!!
But how can we help him?
I Know!!!
What?
We can read our new comic to him!!!
SUPA FAIL 3
Let's Do it!

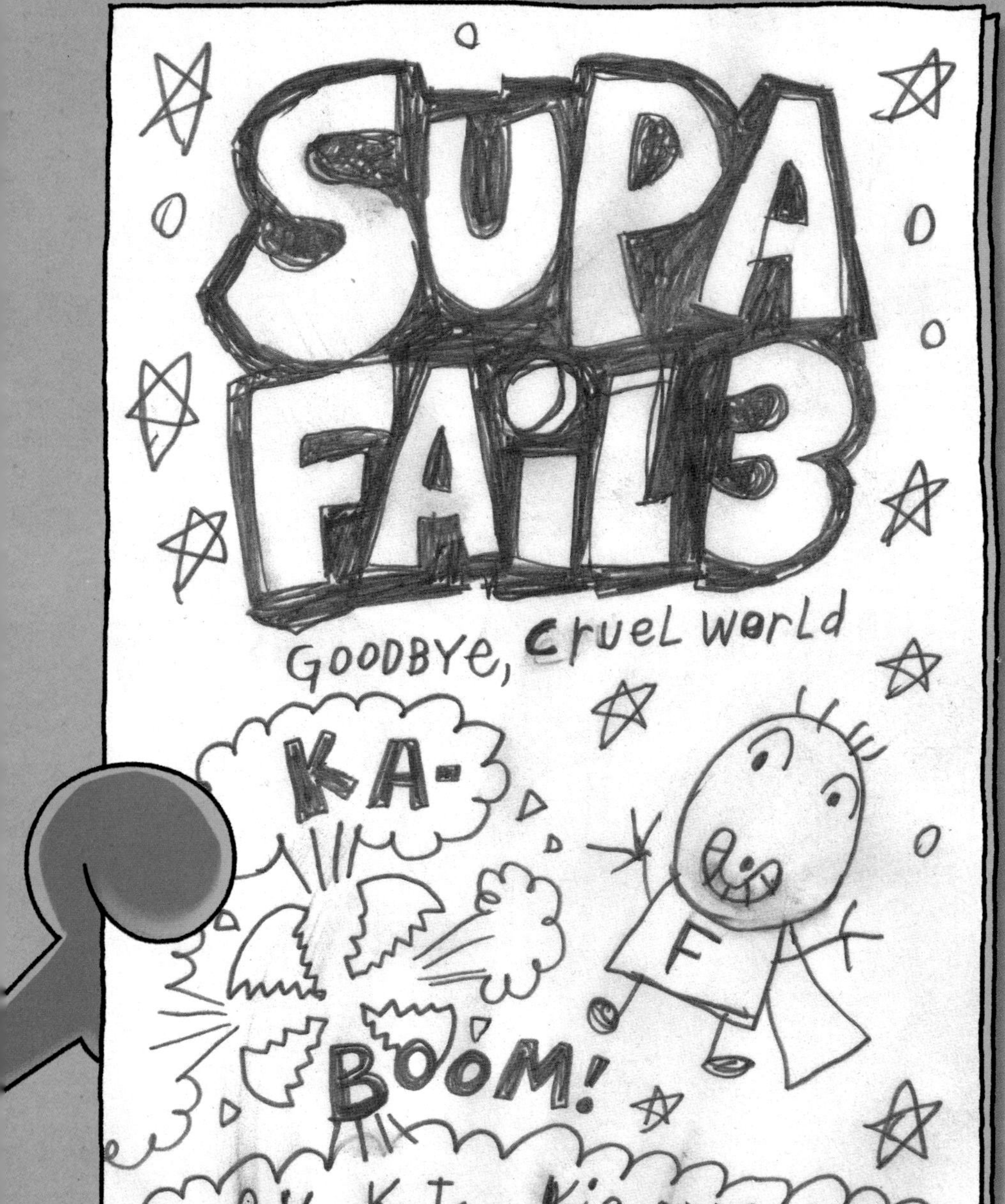
SUPA FAIL 3
GOODBYE, CRUEL WORLD
KA-
BOOM!
F
BY K.T., Kip, and Curly

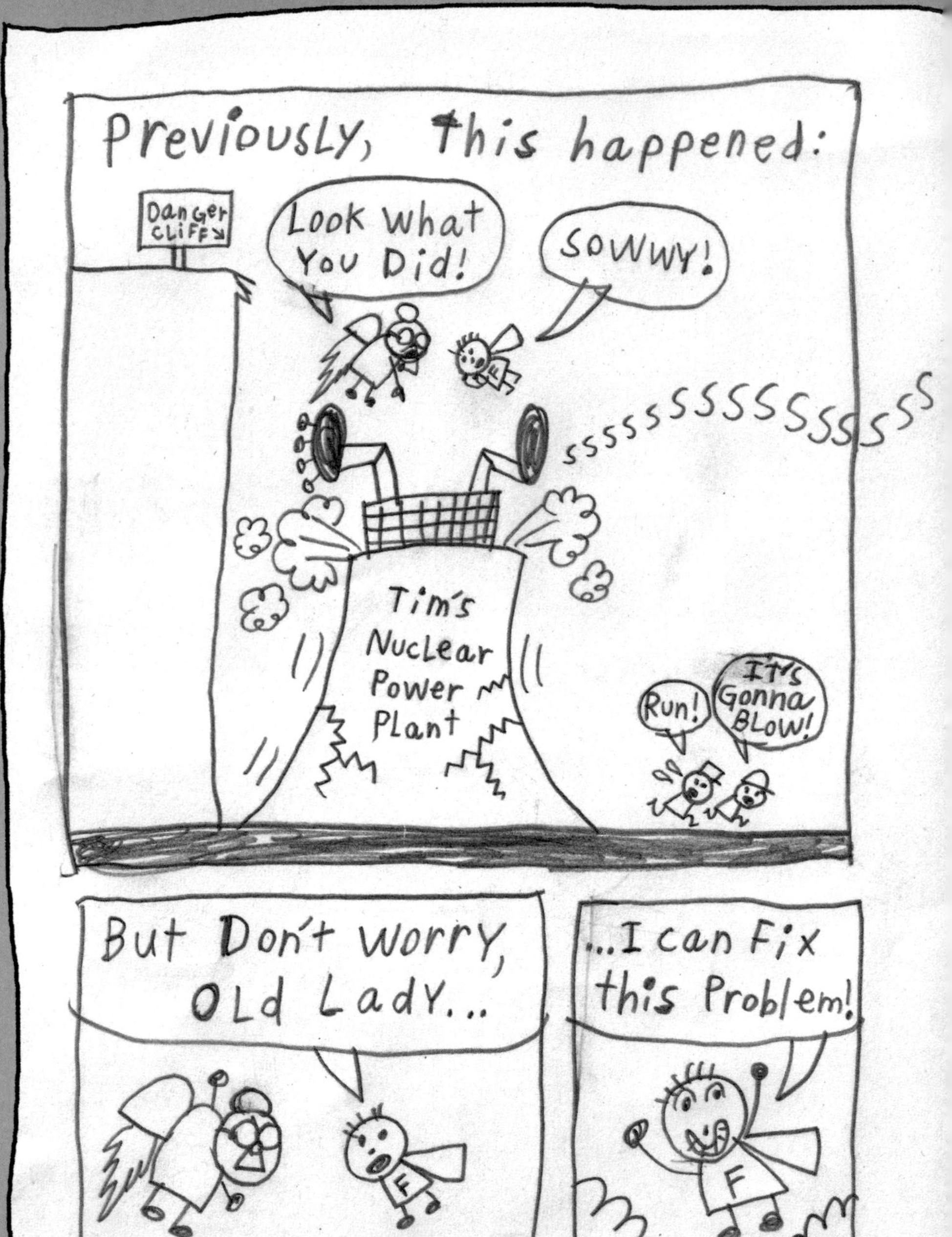
Previously, this happened:
Danger CLIFF
Look What You Did!
SOWWY!
SSSSSSSSSSSSSSSSS
Tim's Nuclear Power Plant
Run!
It's Gonna BLOW!
But Don't worry, OLd Lady...
...I can Fix this Problem!

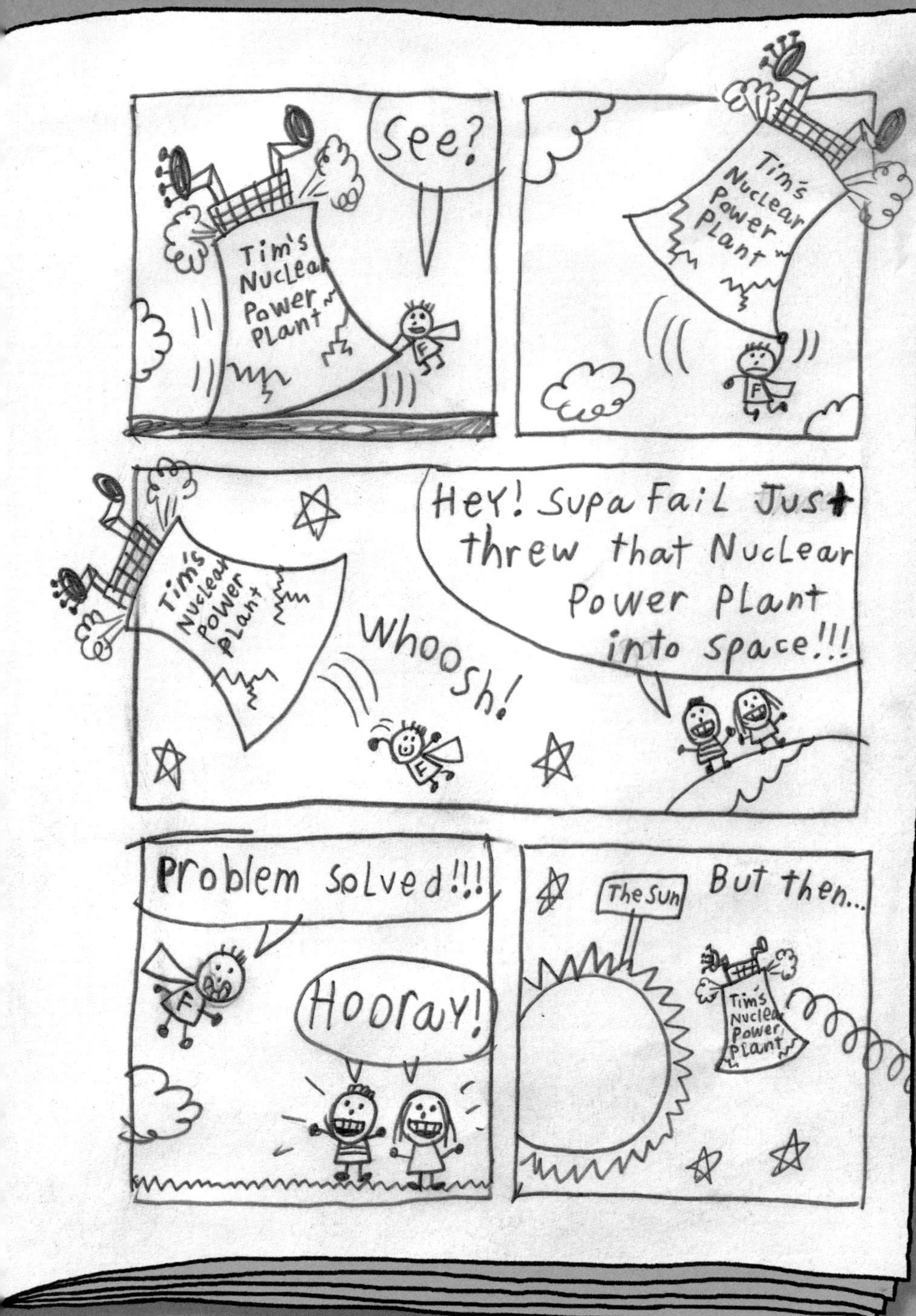

See?
Tim's Nuclear Power Plant
Tim's Nuclear Power Plant
Tim's Nuclear Power Plant
Hey! Supa Fail Just threw that Nuclear Power Plant into space!!!
Whoosh!
Problem solved!!!
Hooray!
The Sun
But then...
Tim's Nuclear Power Plant

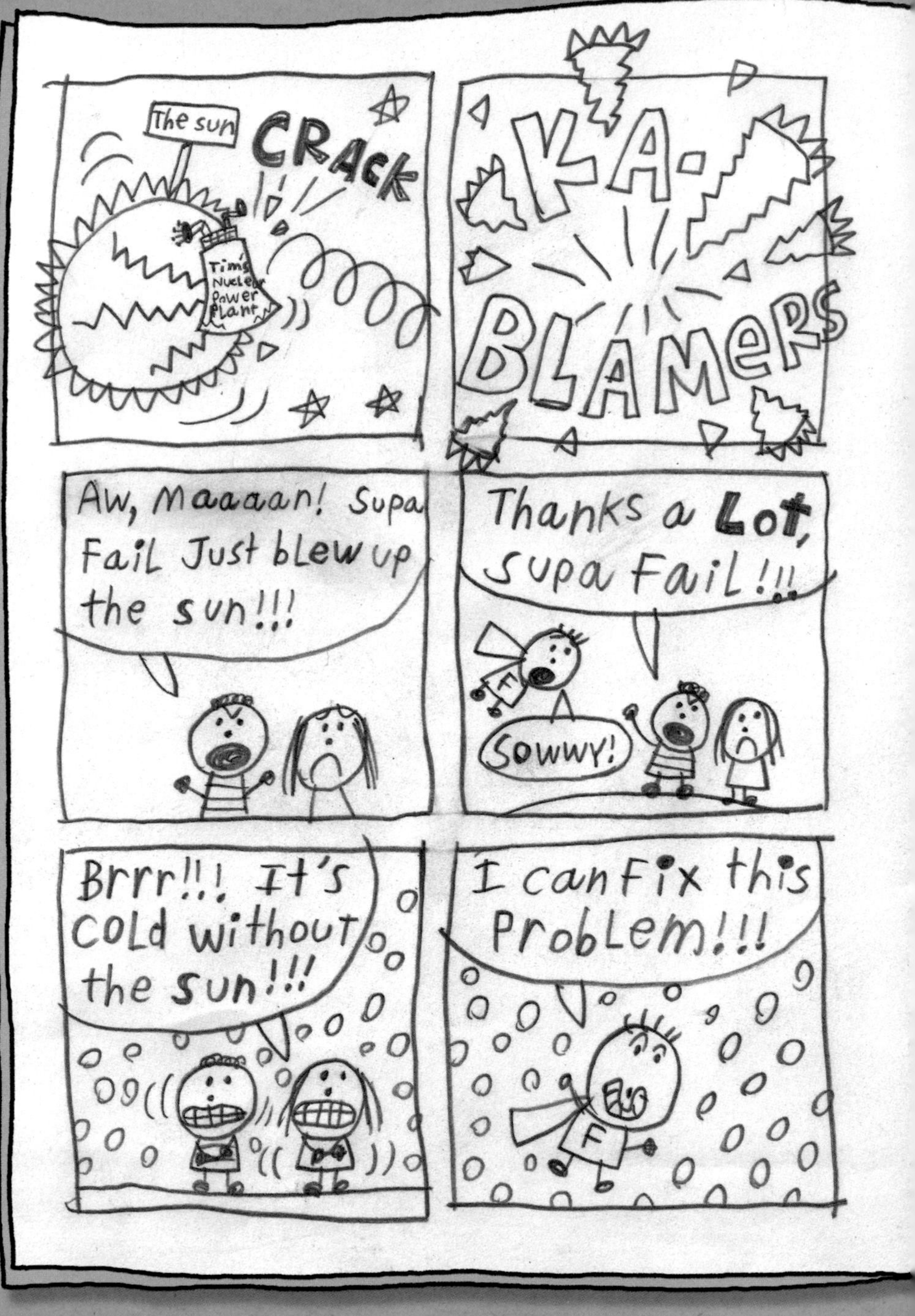
The sun
CRACK
Tim's Nuclear Power Plant
KA-BLAMERS
Aw, Maaaan! Supa Fail Just blew up the sun!!!
Thanks a Lot, Supa Fail!!!
SOWWY!
Brrr!!! It's cold without the sun!!!
I can Fix this Problem!!!

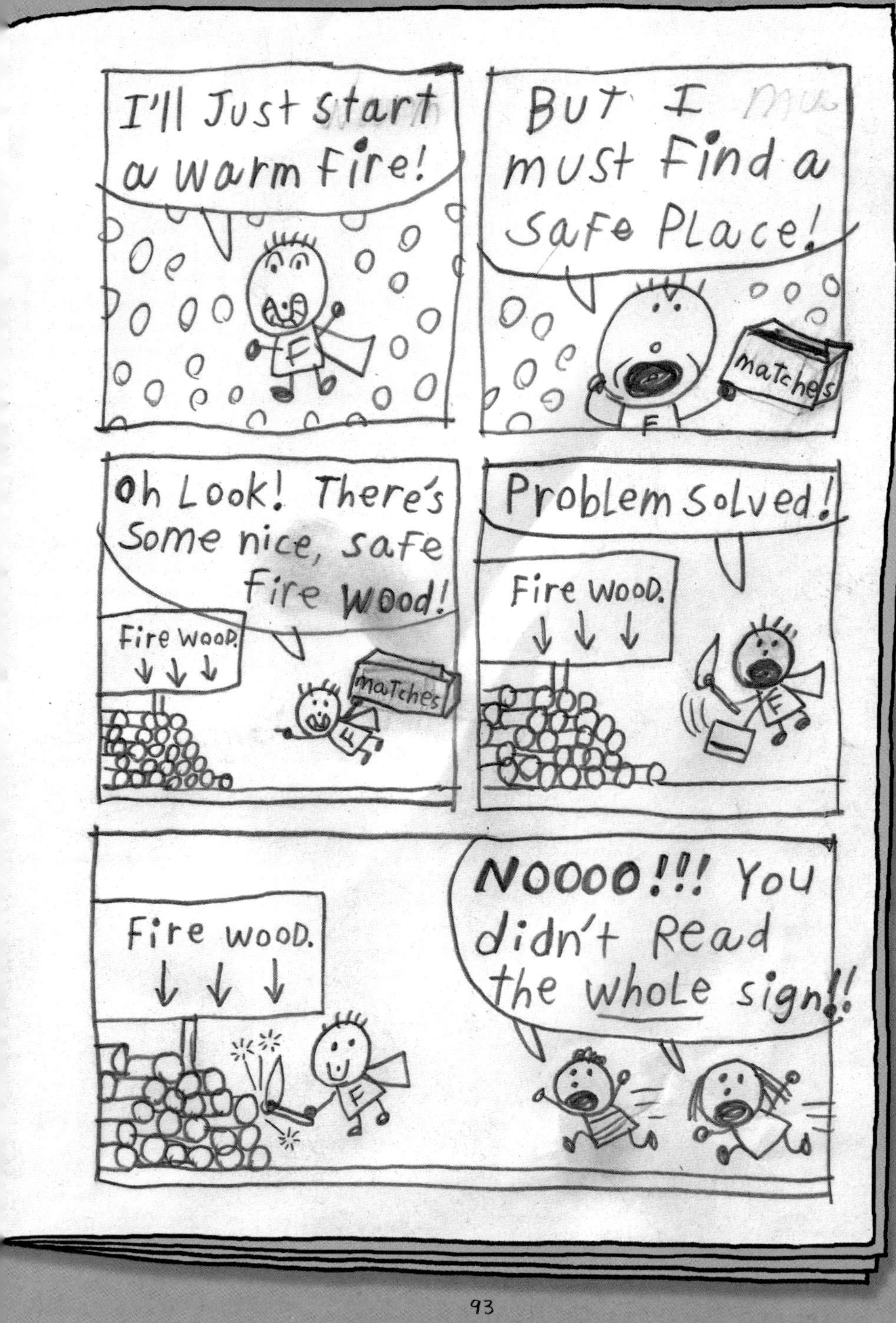
I'll Just start a warm Fire!
But I must Find a safe Place!
matches
Oh Look! There's some nice, safe fire wood!
Fire WOOD.
matches
Problem Solved!
Fire WOOD.
Fire WOOD.
NOOOO!!! You didn't Read the whole sign!!

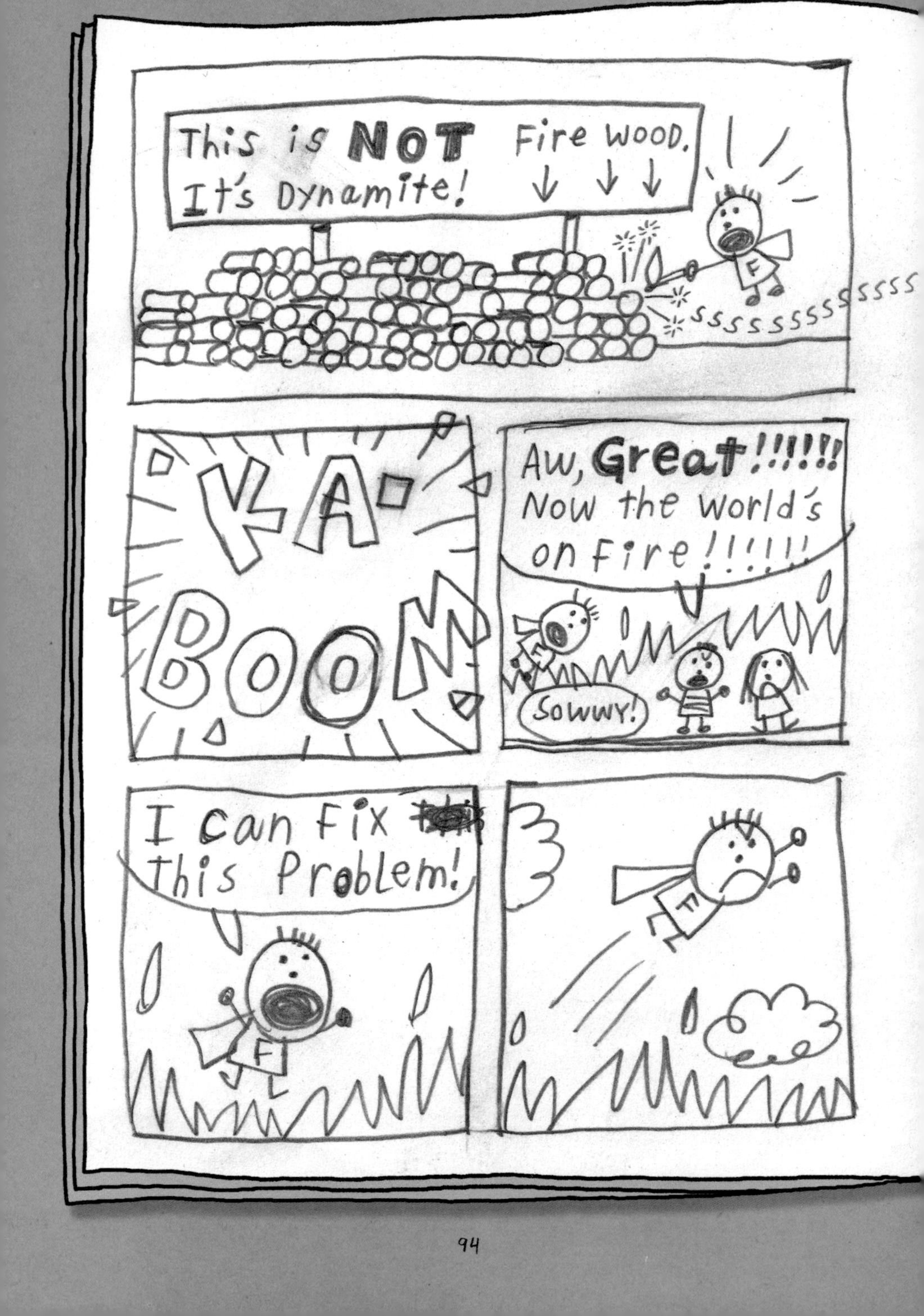
This is NOT Fire WOOD.
It's Dynamite!
SSSSSSSSSSSSSSS
KA-BOOM
Aw, Great!!!!!!
Now the world's on Fire!!!!!!
SOWWY!
I can fix this Problem!

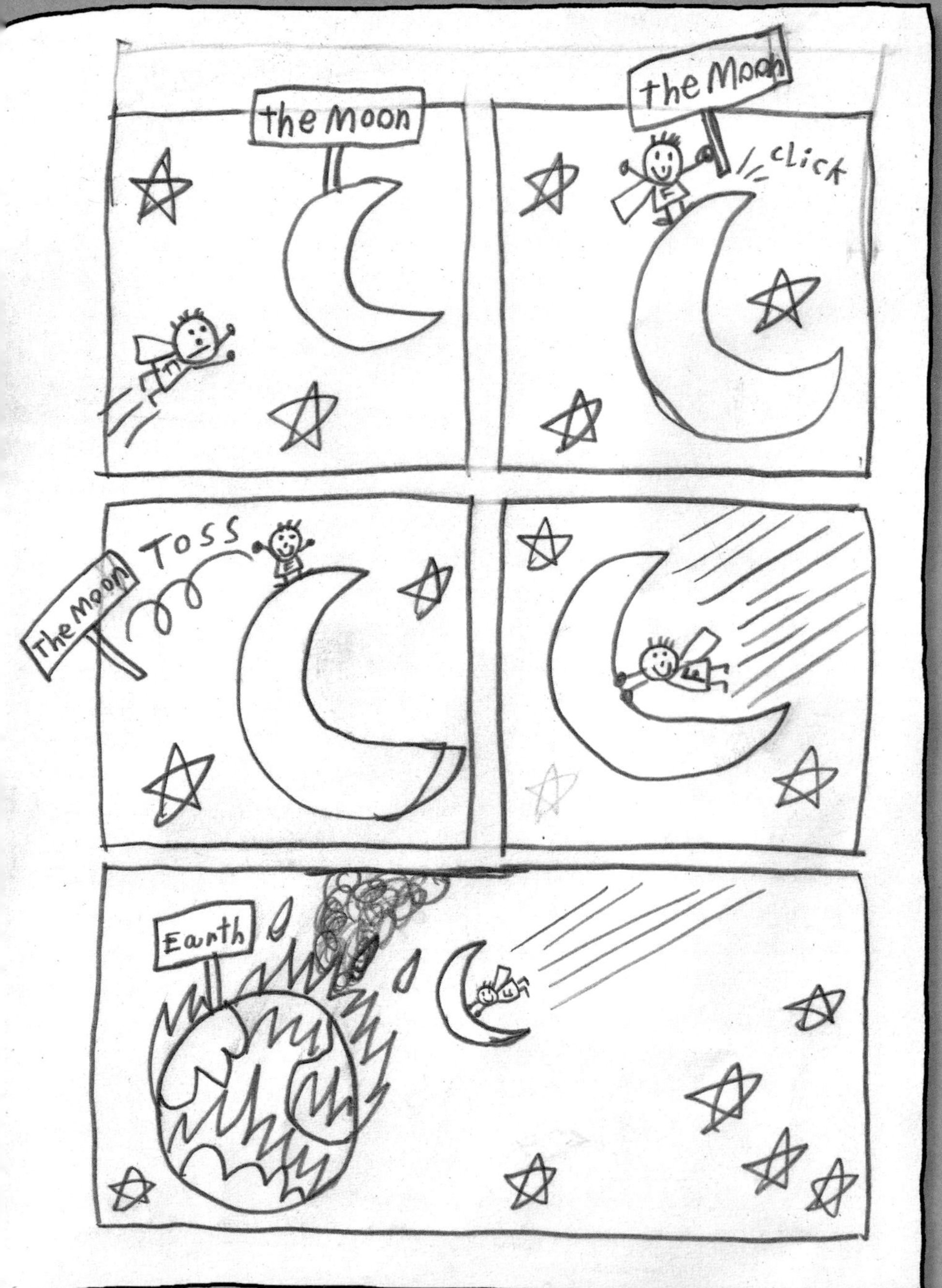
the Moon
the Moon
CLICK
The Moon
TOSS
Earth

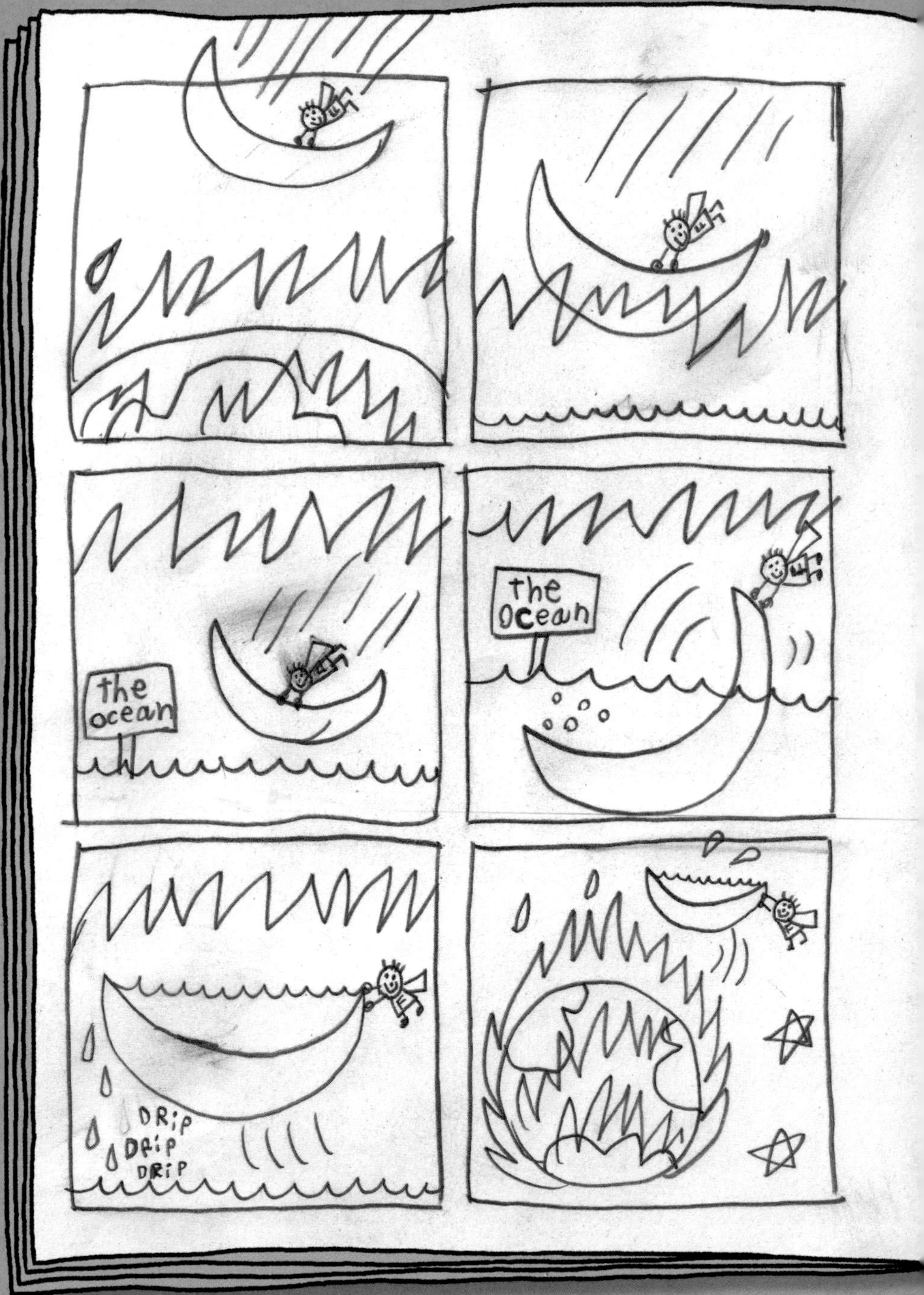
the ocean
the Ocean
DRip
DRip
DRip

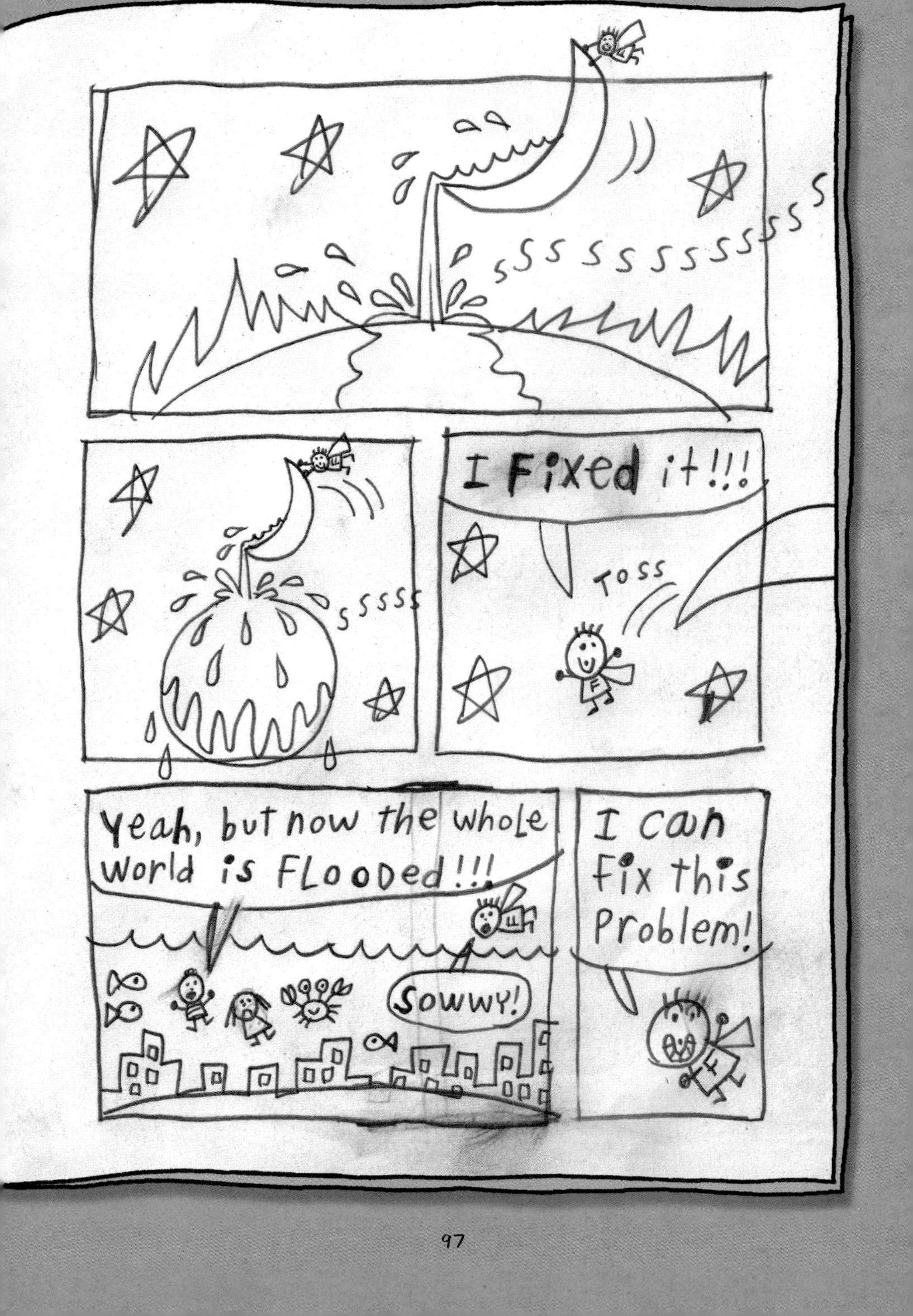
SSSSSSSSSSSSS
SSSSS
I Fixed it!!!
TOSS
Yeah, but now the whole world is FLOODED!!!
SOWWY!
I can fix this Problem!

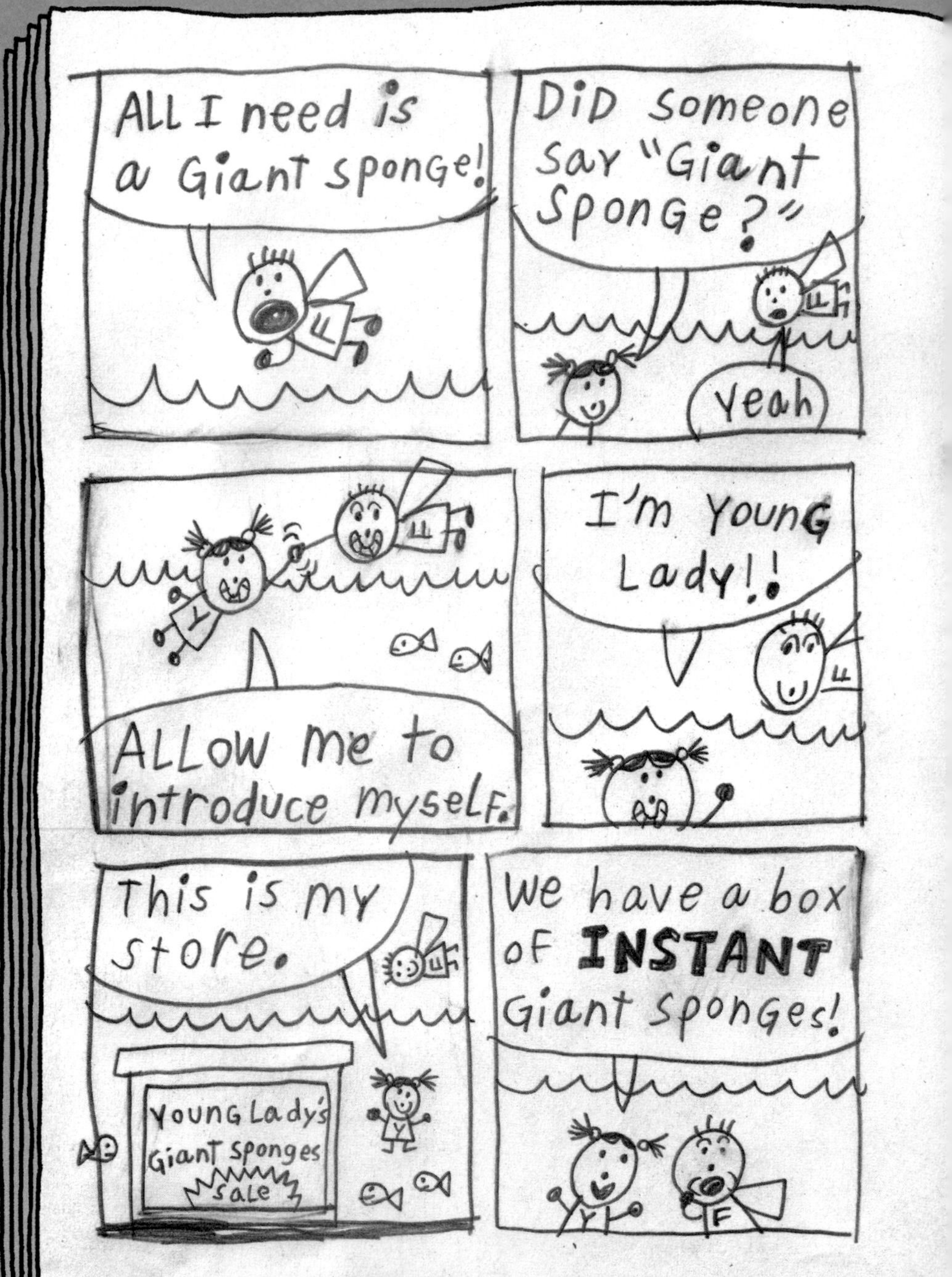
ALL I need is a Giant sponge!
DiD someone say "Giant Sponge?"
Yeah
ALLOW me to introduce myself.
I'm YounG Lady!!
This is my store.
YounG Lady's Giant Sponges
SALE
We have a box of INSTANT Giant sponGes!

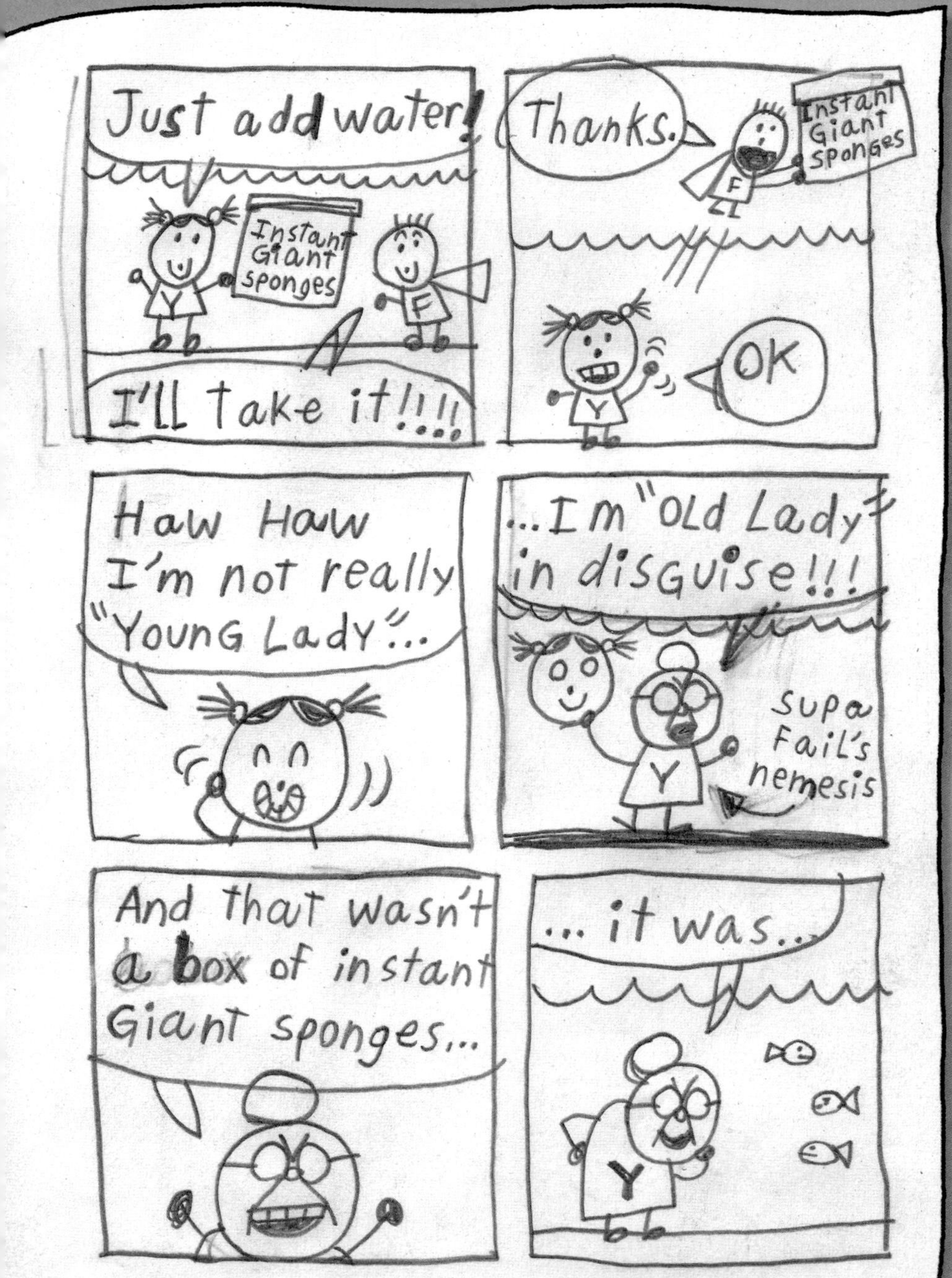
Just add water!
Instant Giant sponges
I'LL take it!!!!
Thanks.
Instant Giant Sponges
OK
Haw Haw I'm not really "YOUNG Lady"...
...I'm "OLD Lady" in disguise!!!
Supa Fail's nemesis
And that wasn't a box of instant Giant sponges...
... it was...

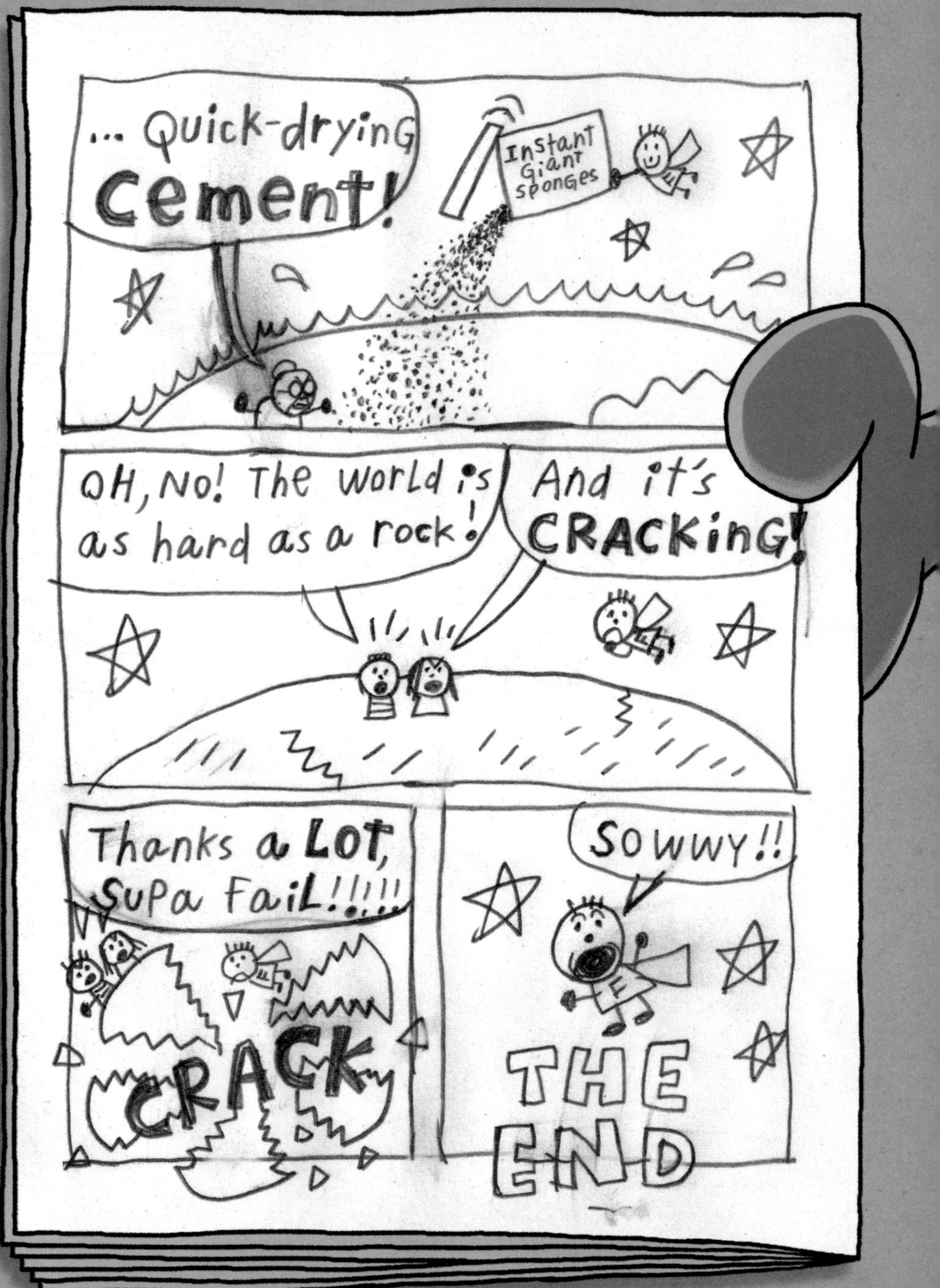
... Quick-drying cement!
Instant Giant sponges
OH, No! The world is as hard as a rock!
And it's CRACKinG!
Thanks a LOT, SuPa FaiL!!!!!
CRACK
SOWWY!!
THE END

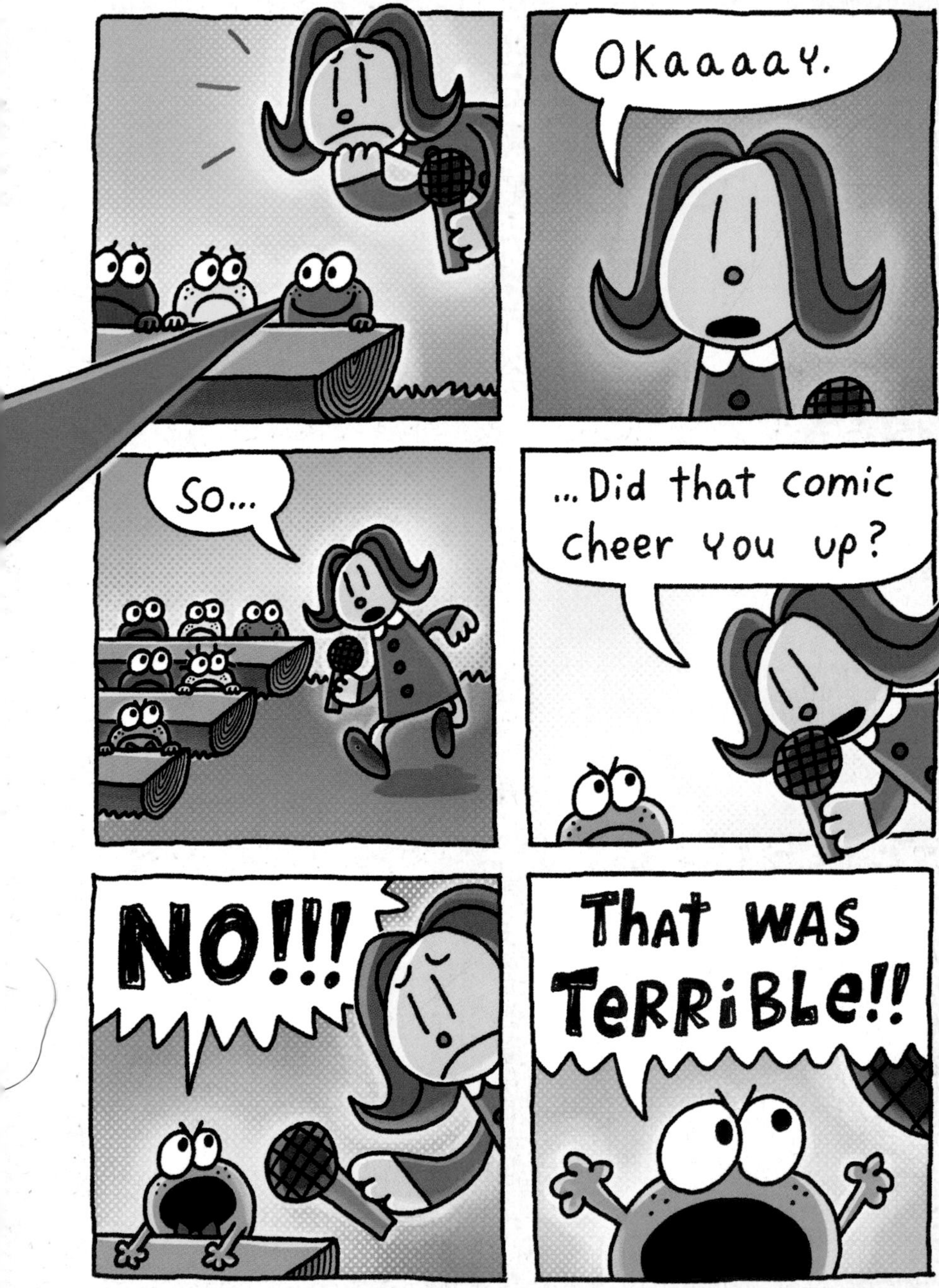
Okaaaay.
So...
...Did that comic cheer you up?
NO!!!
That WAS TeRRiBLe!!

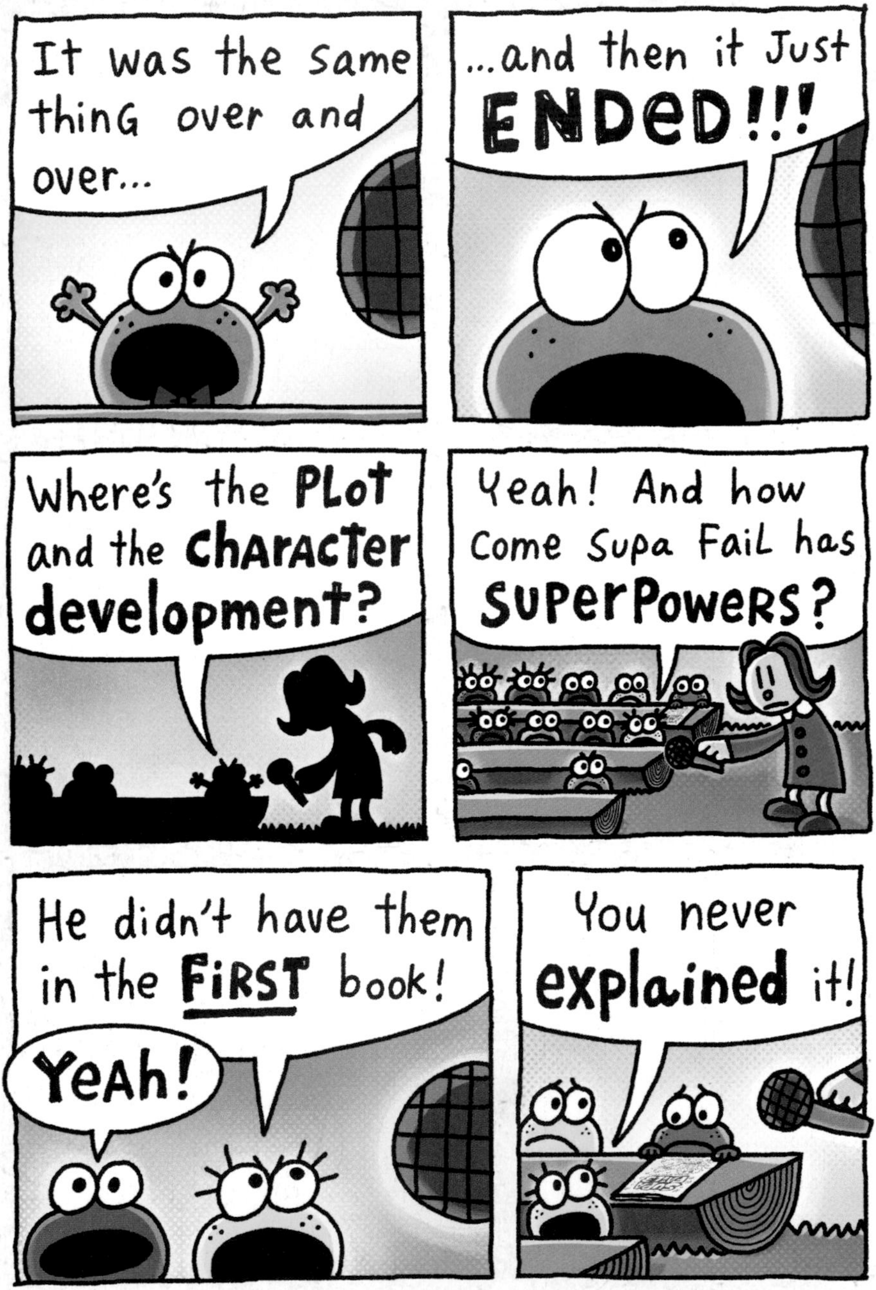
It was the same thing over and over...
...and then it Just ENDED!!!
Where's the PLOT and the CHARACTER development?
Yeah! And how come Supa Fail has SUPERPOWERS?
He didn't have them in the FIRST book!
YeAh!
You never explained it!

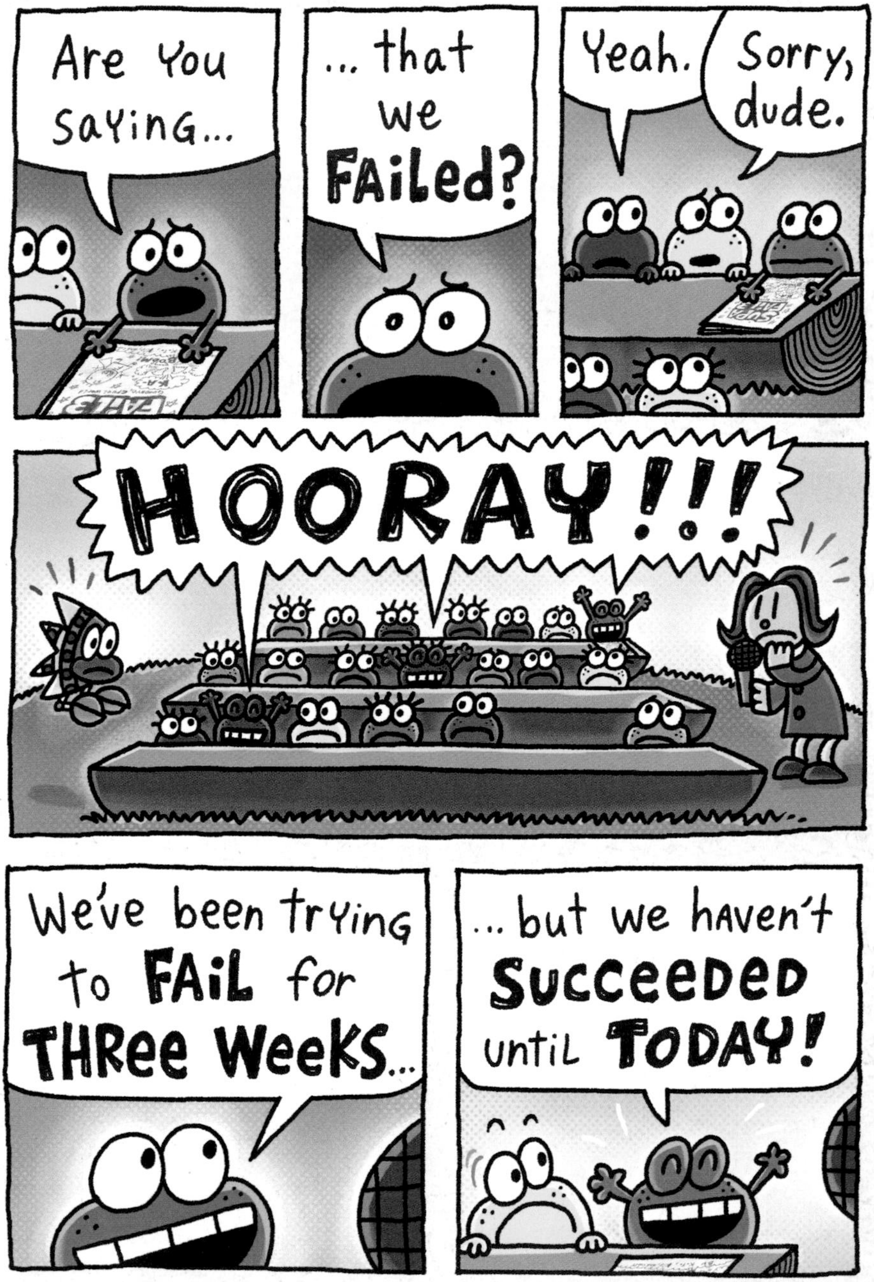
Are you saying...
... that we FAILED?
Yeah.
Sorry, dude.
HOORAY!!!
We've been trying to FAIL for THREE WEEKS...
... but we haven't SUCCEEDED until TODAY!

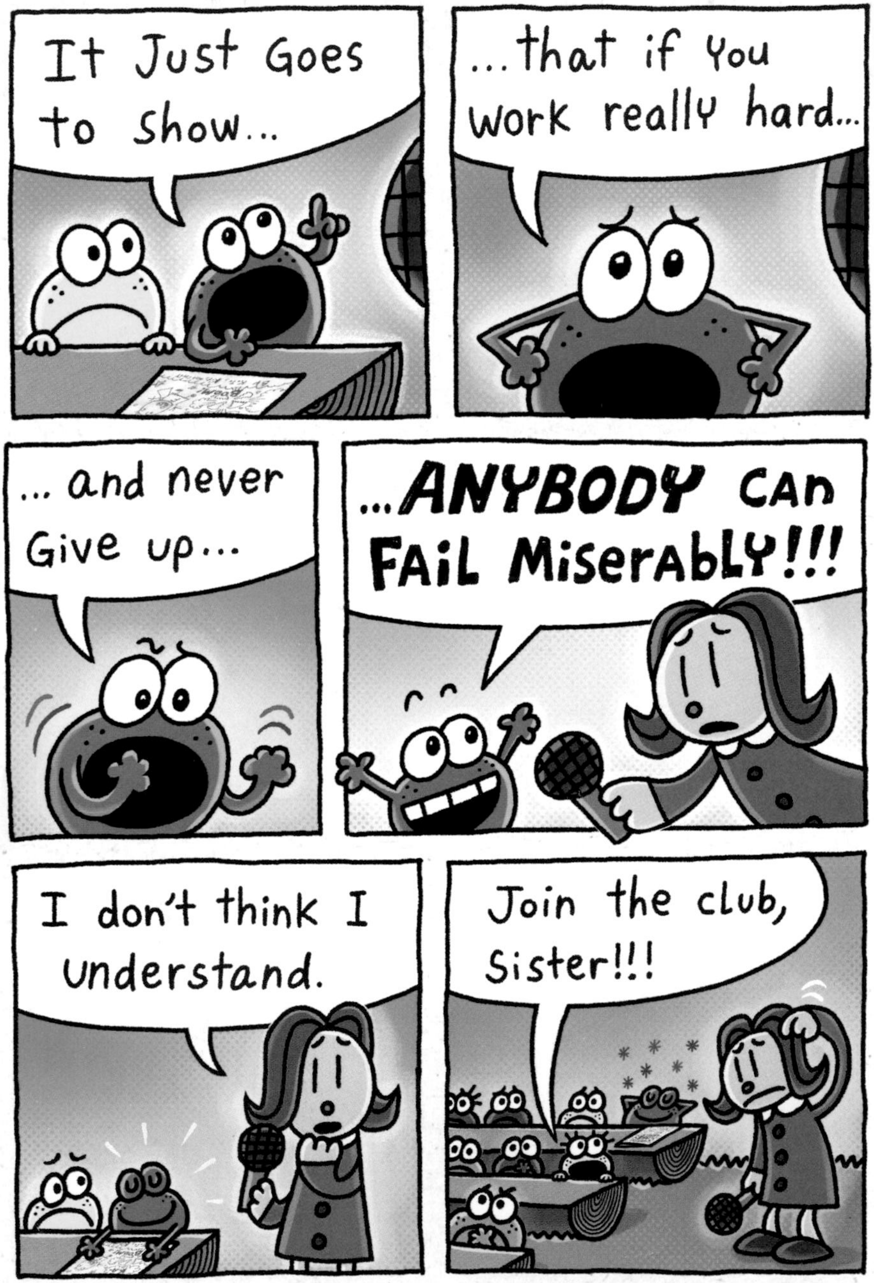
It Just Goes to show...
...that if you work really hard...
... and never Give up...
...ANYBODY CAN FAIL MiSERABLY!!!
I don't think I understand.
Join the club, Sister!!!

CHAPTER 8

The Time Out Rock

Time Out.

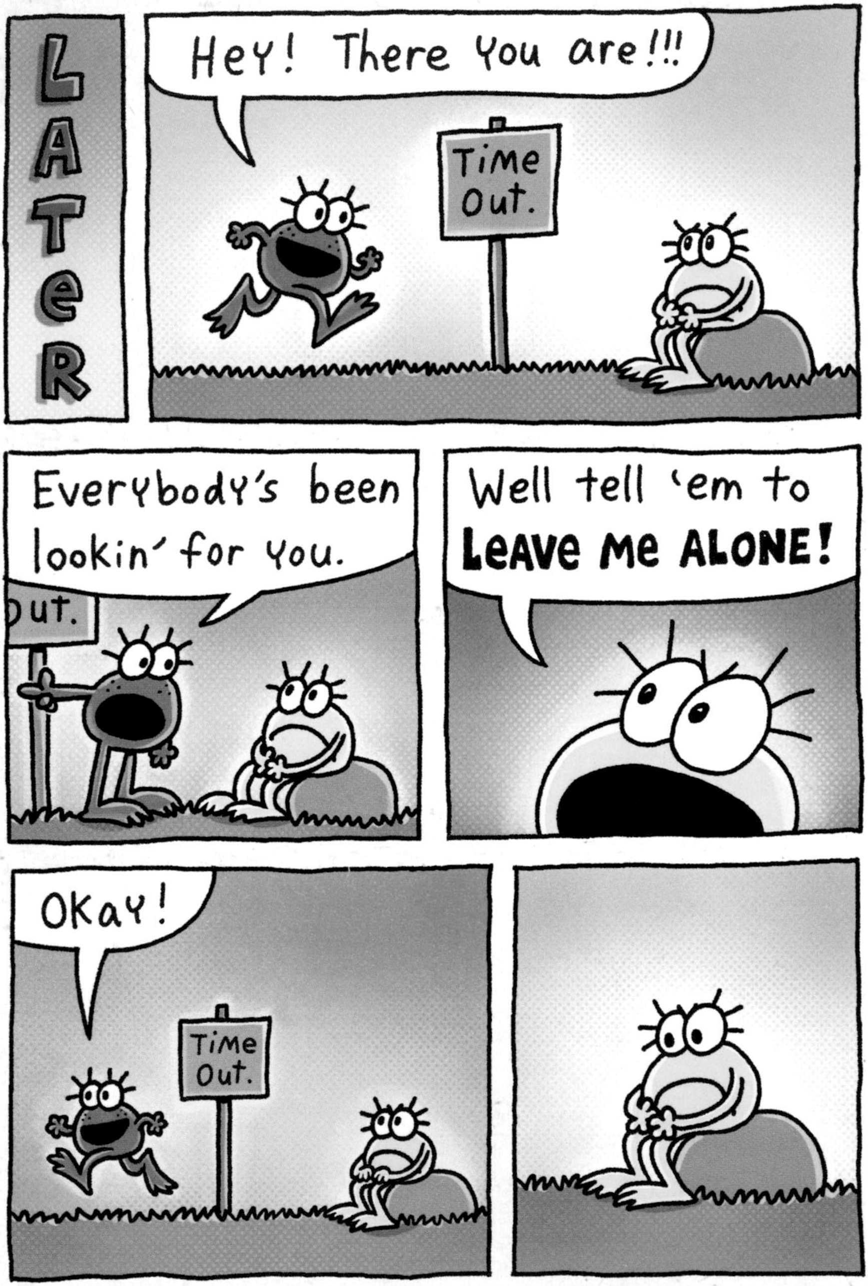
LATER
Hey! There you are!!!
Time Out.
Everybody's been lookin' for you.
ut.
Well tell 'em to LEAVE ME ALONE!
Okay!
Time Out.

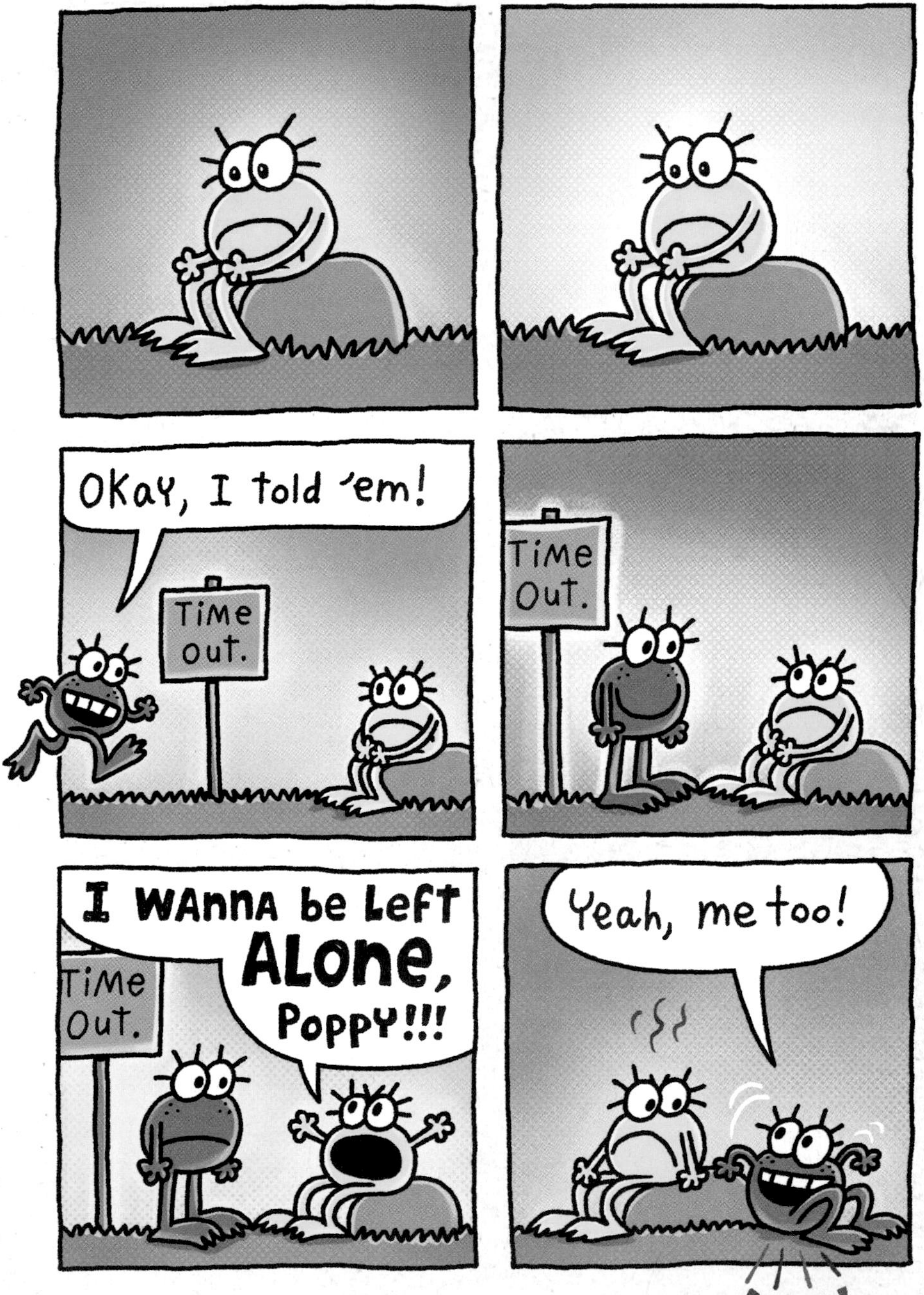
OKay, I told 'em!
Time out.
Time Out.
I WANNA be Left ALONE, POPPY!!!
Time Out.
Yeah, me too!
PLOP!

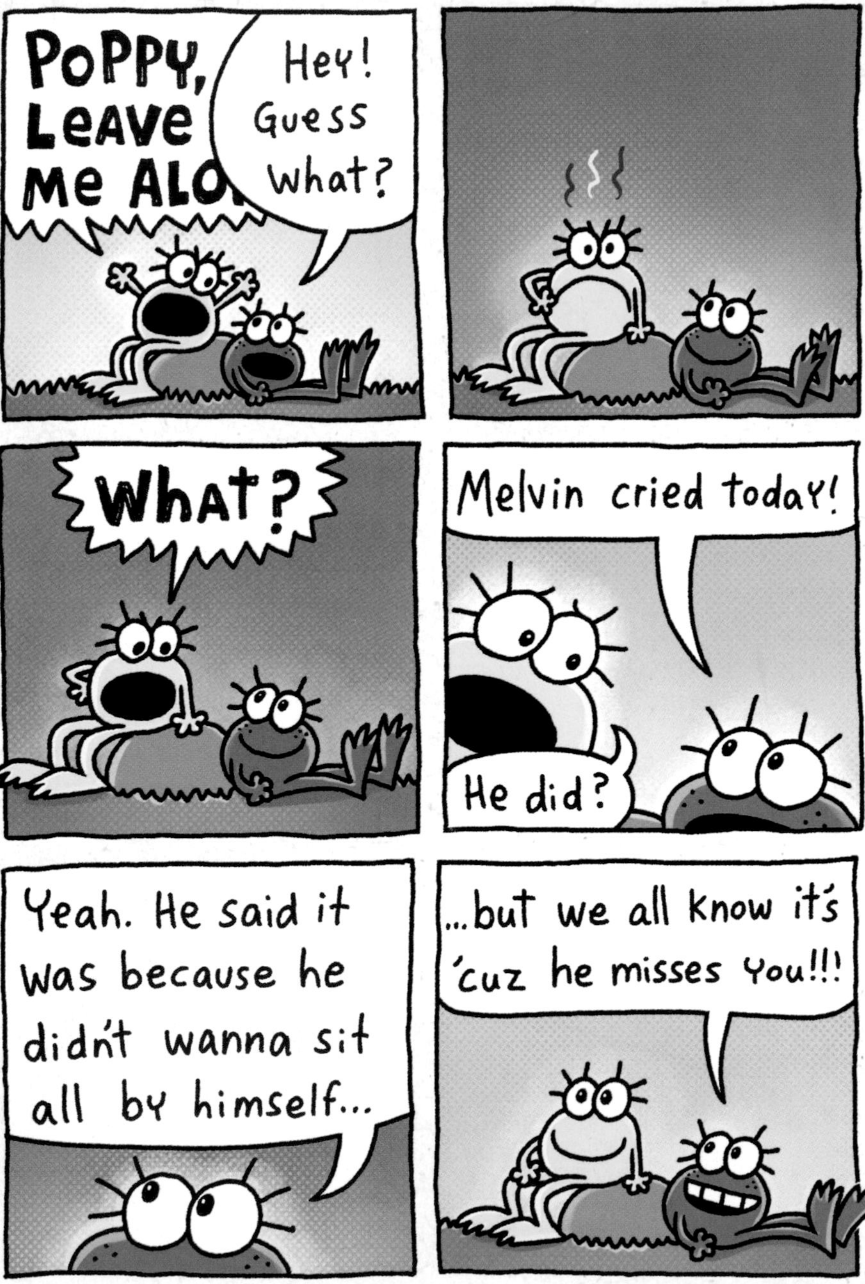
POPPY, LEAVE ME ALO
Hey! Guess what?
WHAT?
Melvin cried today!
He did?
Yeah. He said it was because he didn't wanna sit all by himself...
...but we all know it's 'cuz he misses you!!!

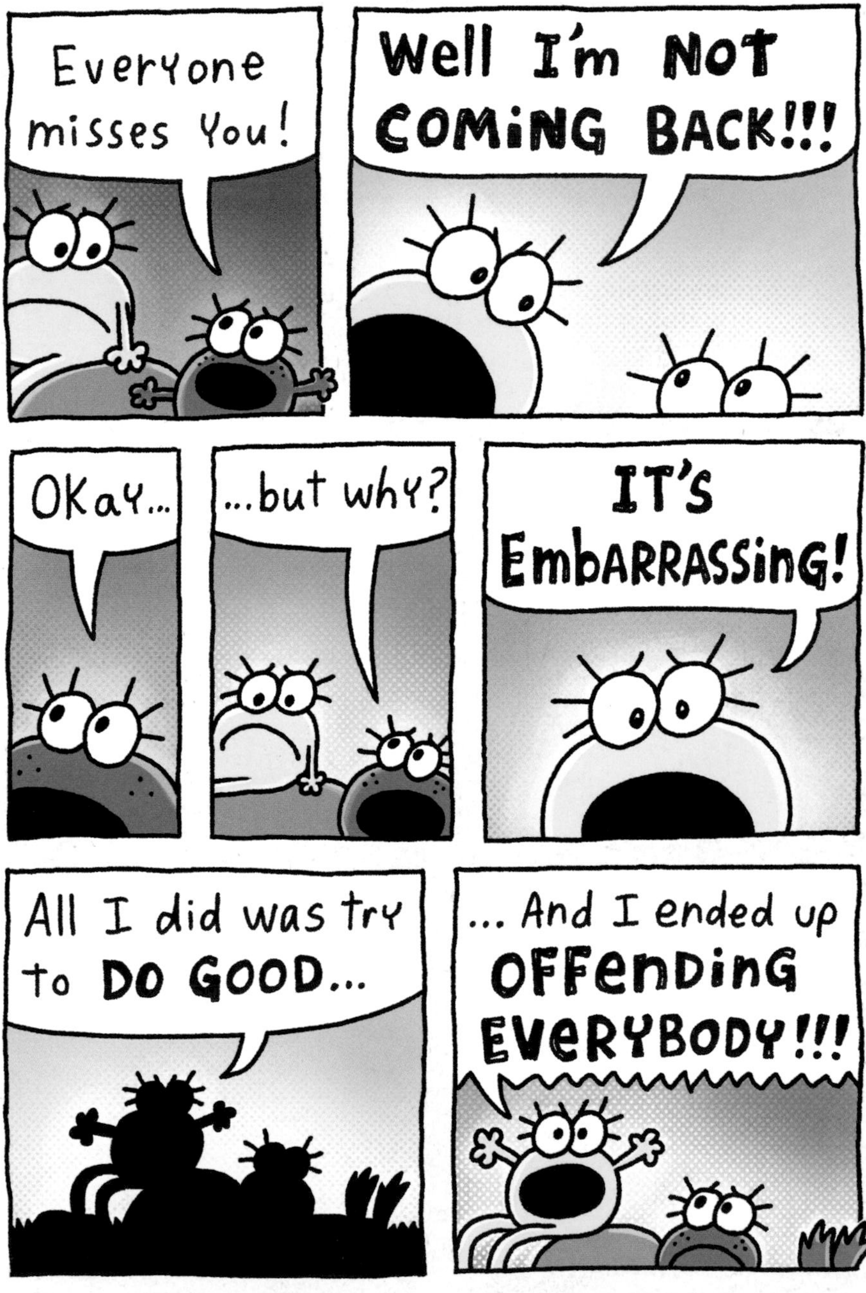
Everyone misses You!
Well I'm NOT COMING BACK!!!
OKay...
...but why?
IT'S Embarrassing!
All I did was try to DO GOOD...
... And I ended up OFFENDING EVERYBODY!!!

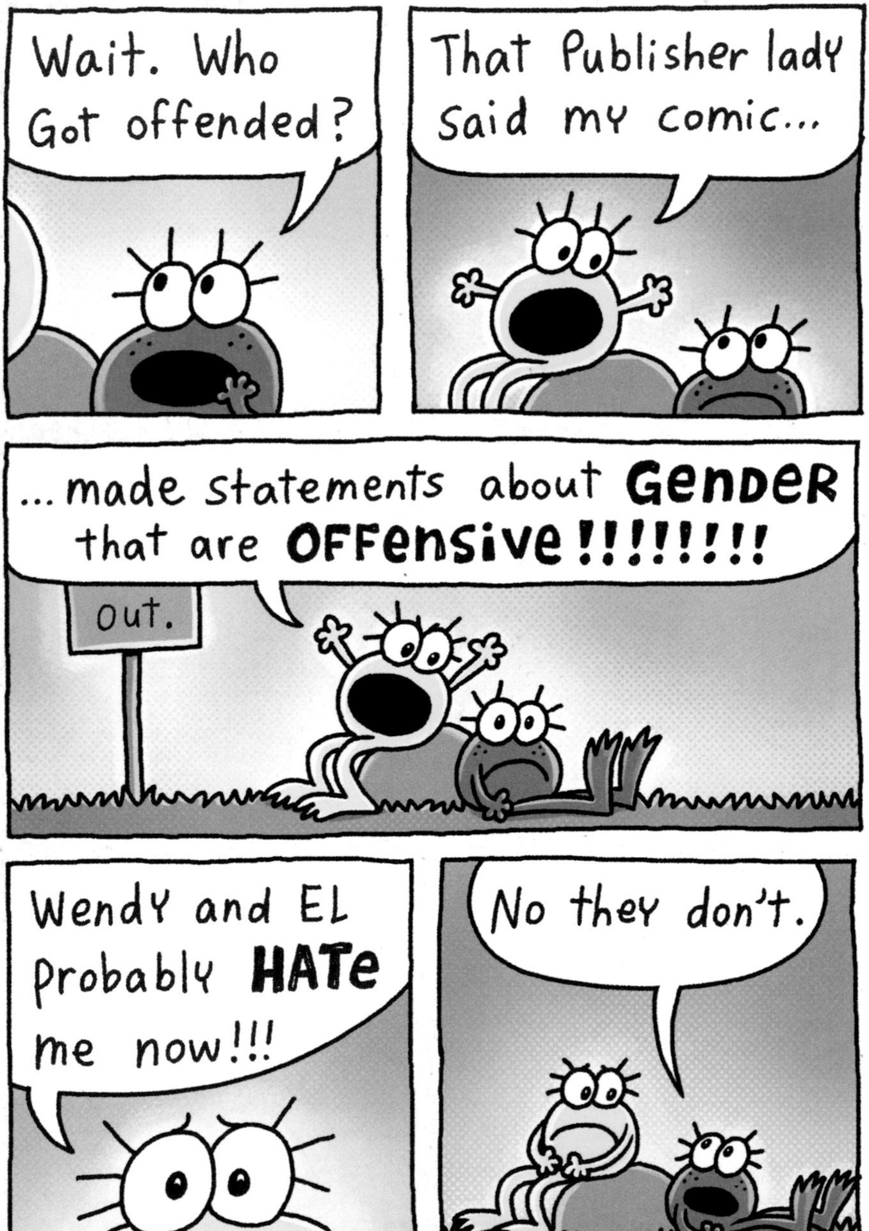
Wait. Who Got offended?
That Publisher lady said my comic...
...made statements about GENDER that are OFFENSIVE!!!!!!!!
out.
Wendy and EL probably HATe me now!!!
No they don't.

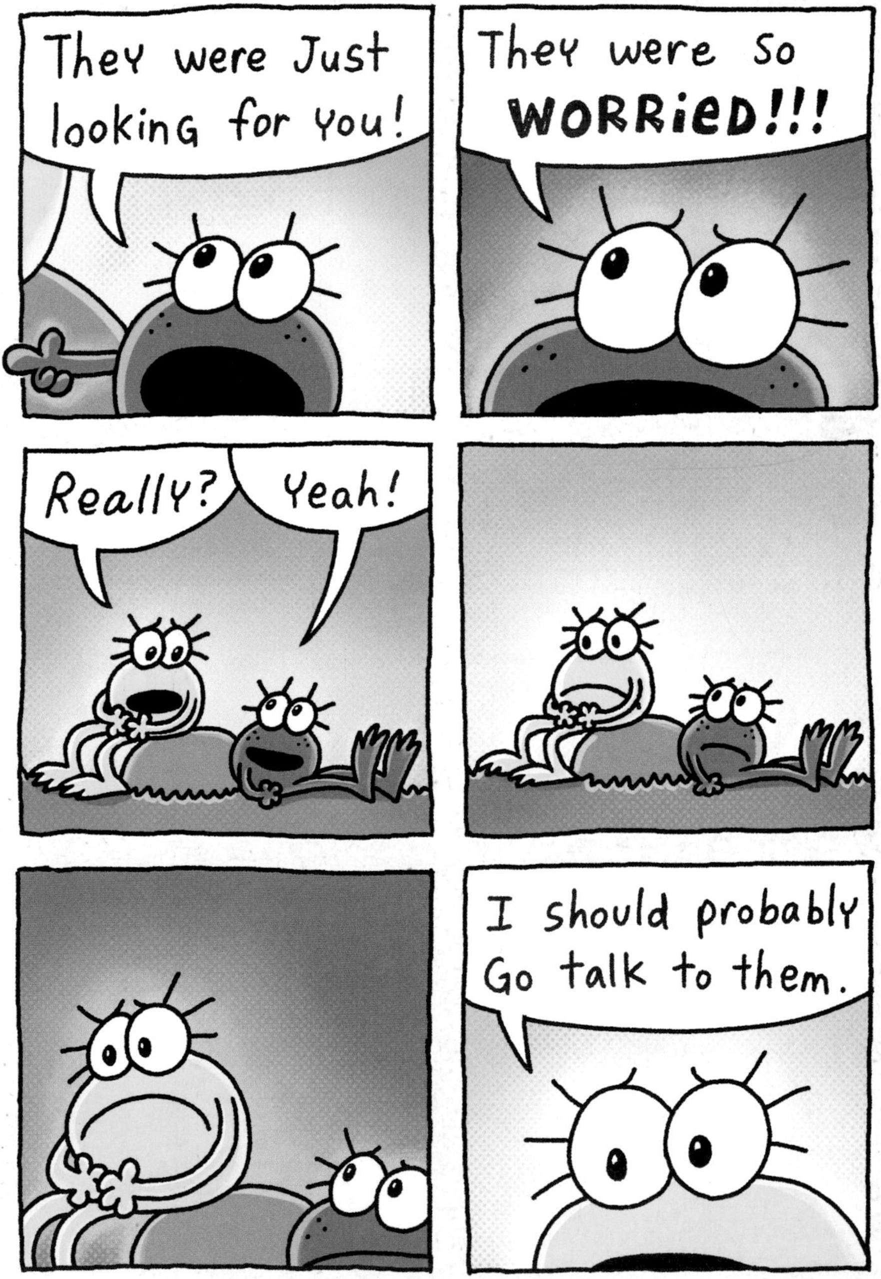
They were Just looking for you!
They were So WORRIED!!!
Really?
Yeah!
I should probably Go talk to them.

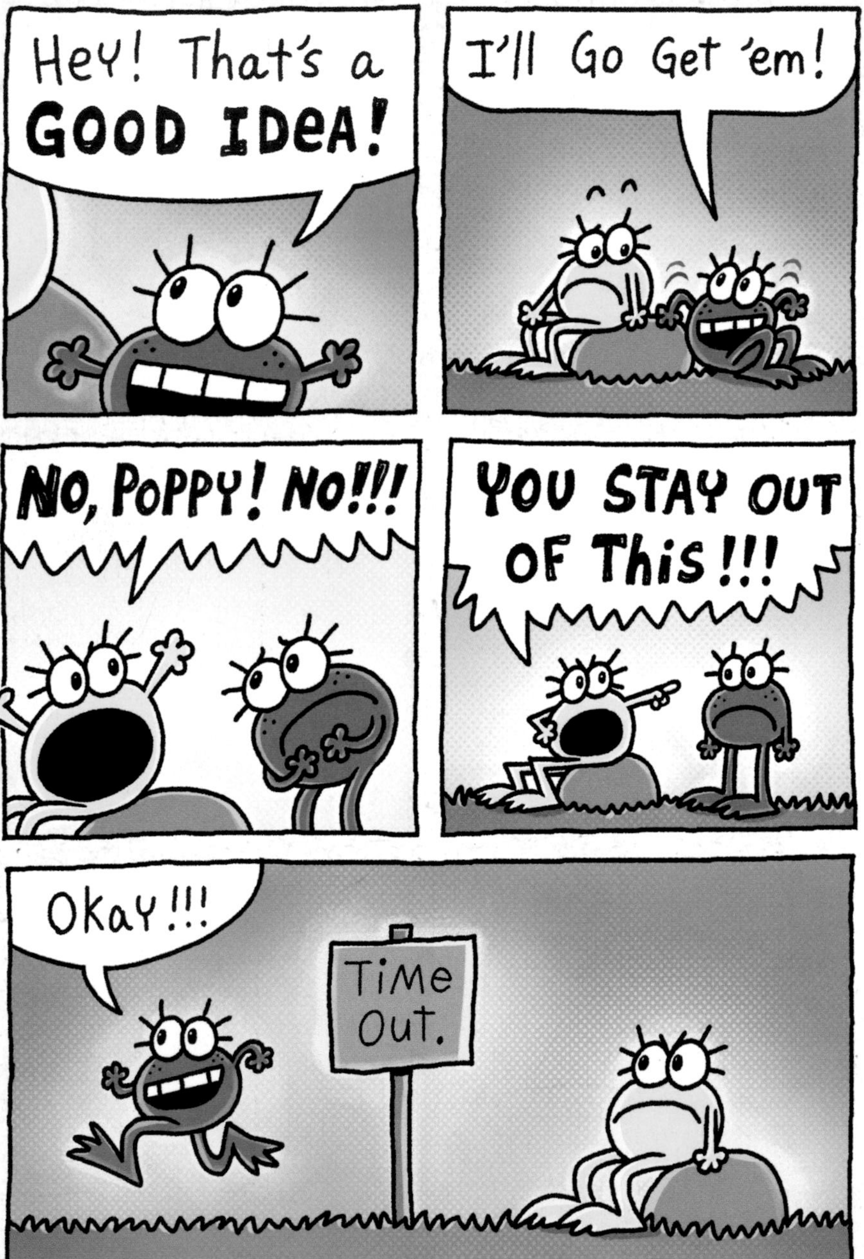
Hey! That's a GOOD IDEA!
I'll Go Get 'em!
NO, POPPY! NO!!!
YOU STAY OUT OF This!!!
Okay!!!
TiMe Out.

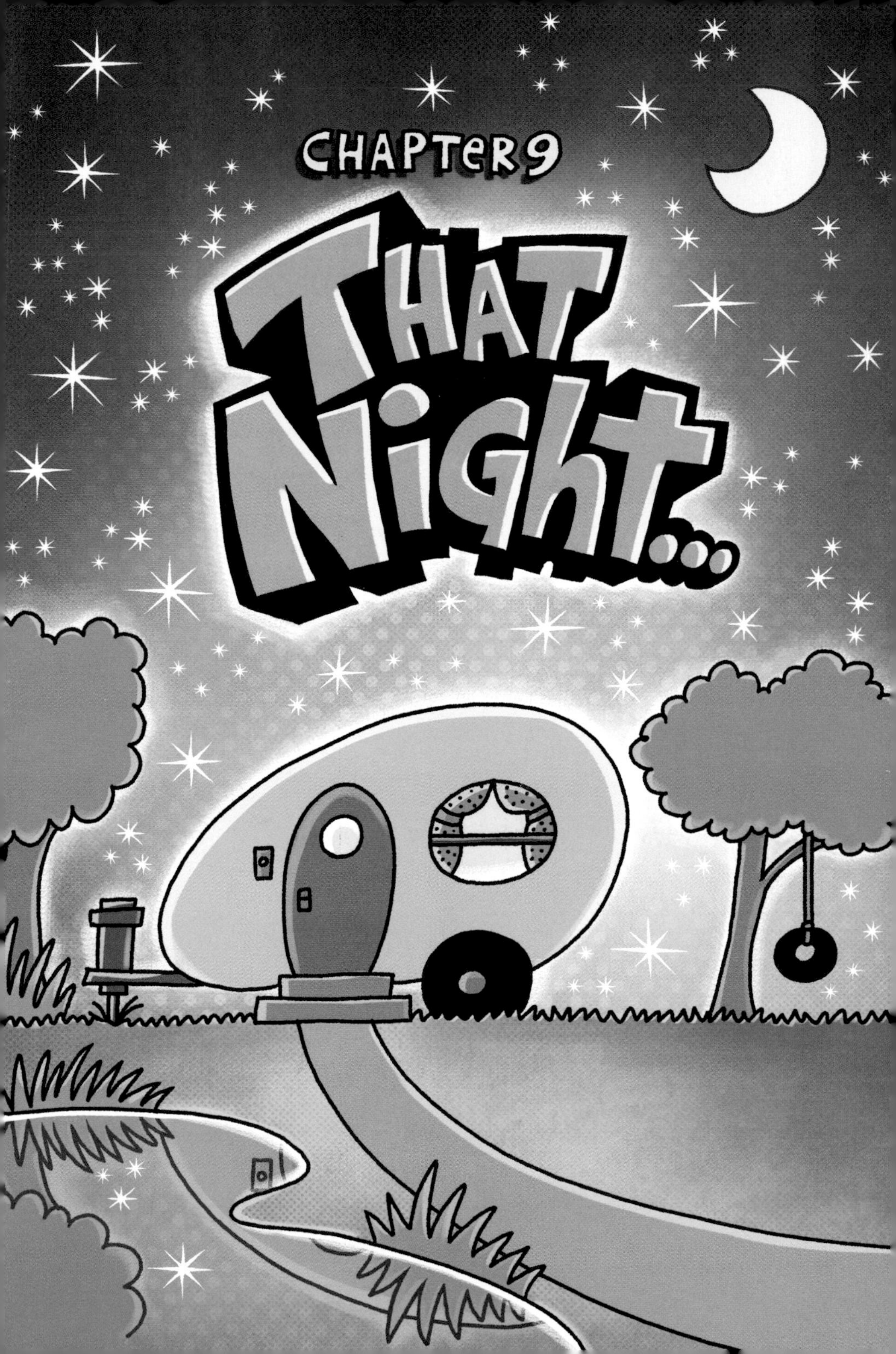
CHAPTER 9
THAT NIGHT...

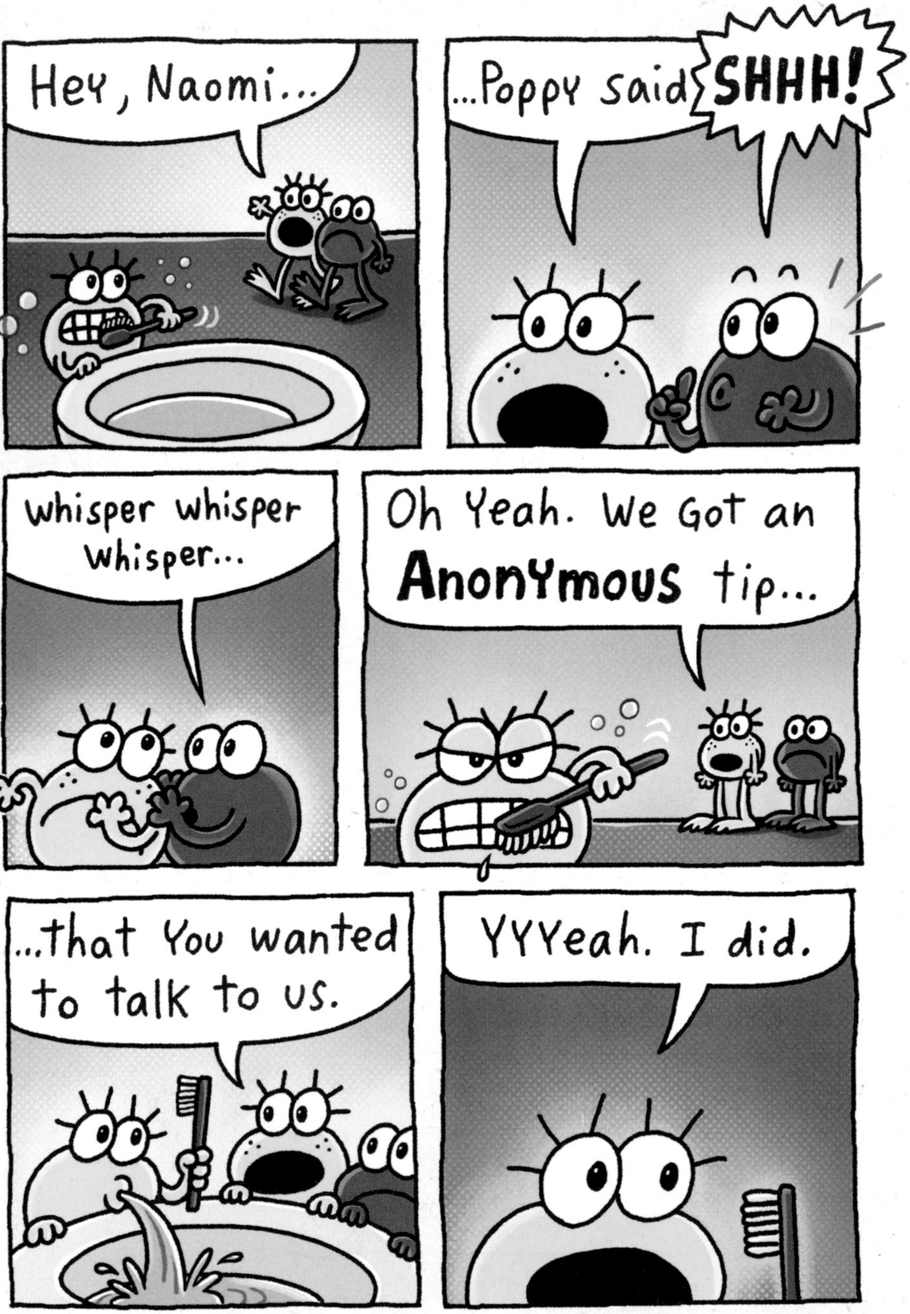
Hey, Naomi...
...Poppy said
SHHH!
whisper whisper whisper...
Oh Yeah. We Got an ANONYMOUS tip...
...that You wanted to talk to us.
YYYeah. I did.

I wanted to Say I'm Sorry.
About the ice-cream machine?
No. About my Comic.
Oh.
How come?
I didn't mean for it to be HURTFUL!
Gilbert
K.T.
Kendrick
Kip
Naomi
What was hurtful about it?

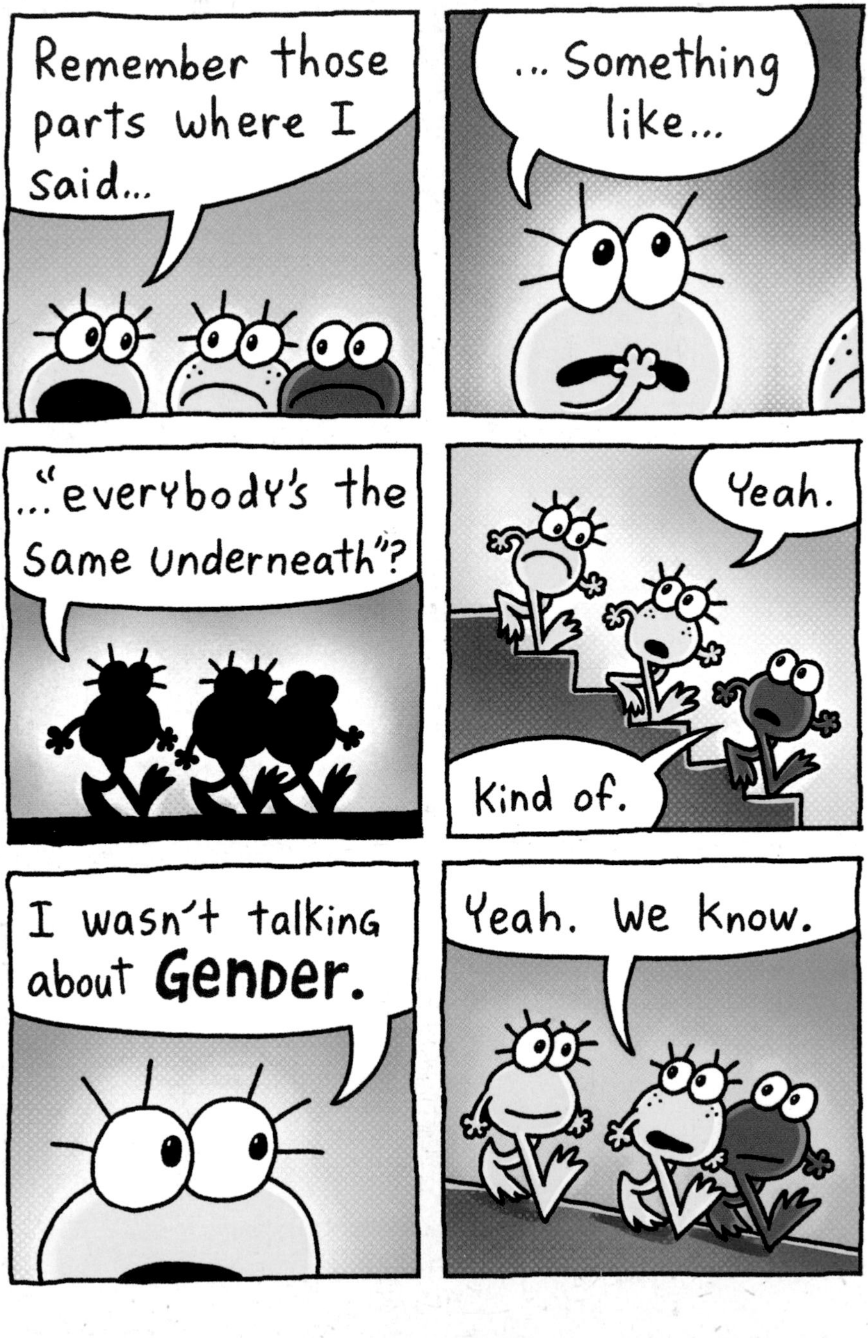
Remember those parts where I said...
... Something like...
..."everybody's the same underneath"?
Yeah.
Kind of.
I wasn't talking about **Gender.**
Yeah. We know.

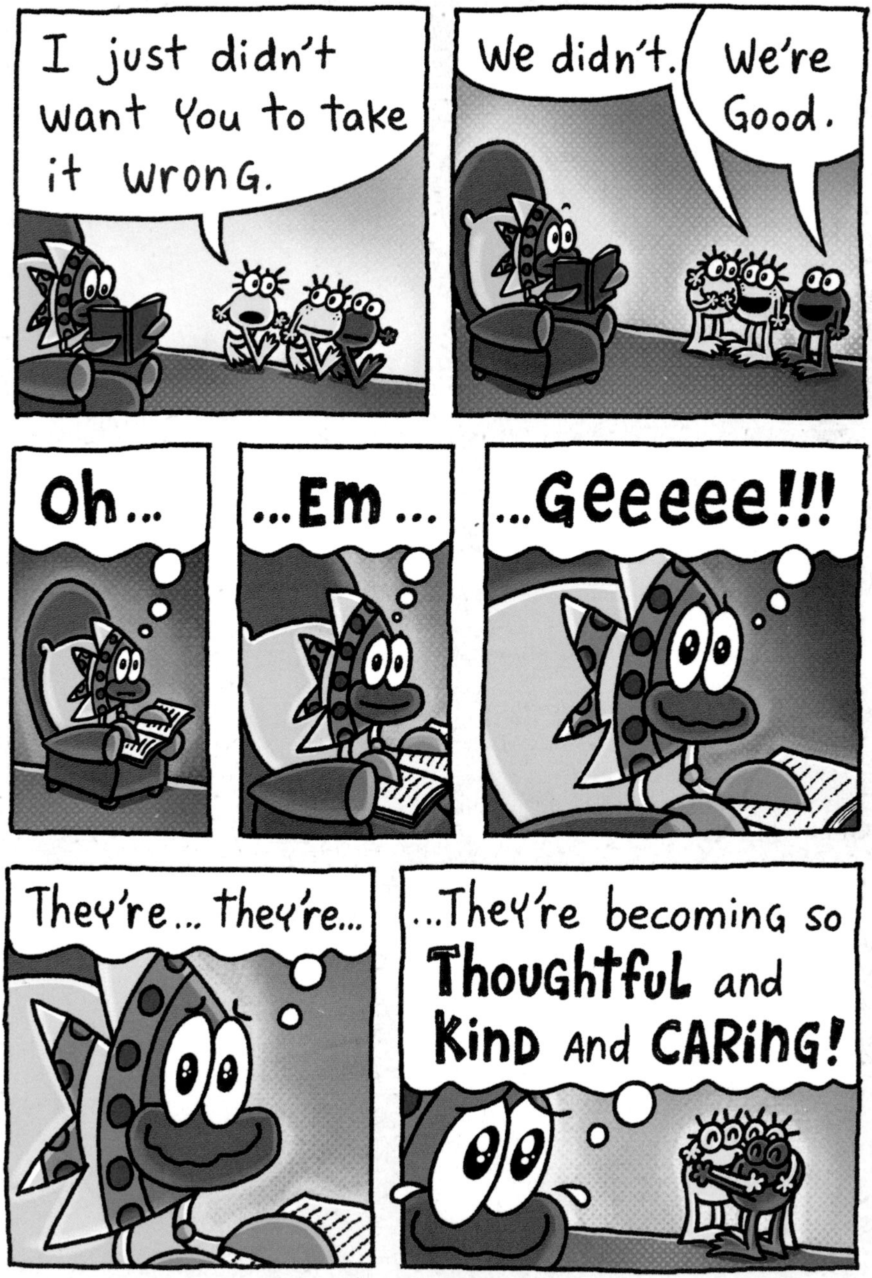
I just didn't want You to take it WRONG.
We didn't.
We're Good.
Oh...
...Em...
...Geeeee!!!
They're... they're...
...They're becoming so THOUGHTFUL and KIND AND CARING!

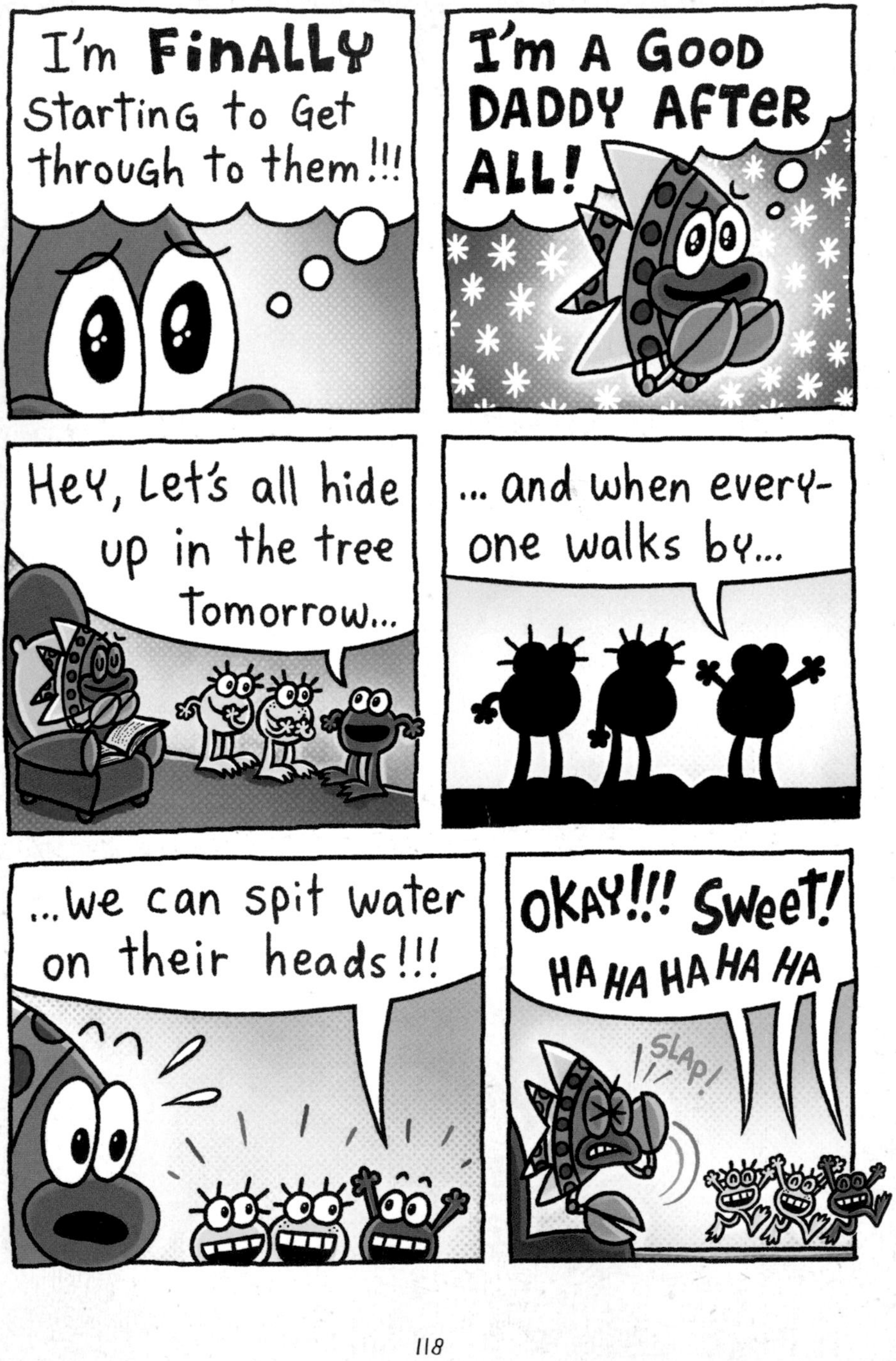
I'm FINALLY Starting to Get through to them!!!
I'm A GOOD DADDY AFTER ALL!
Hey, Let's all hide up in the tree tomorrow...
... and when every-one walks by...
...we can spit water on their heads!!!
OKAY!!! Sweet!
HA HA HA HA HA
SLAP!

CHAPTER 10

New Day, New Comics

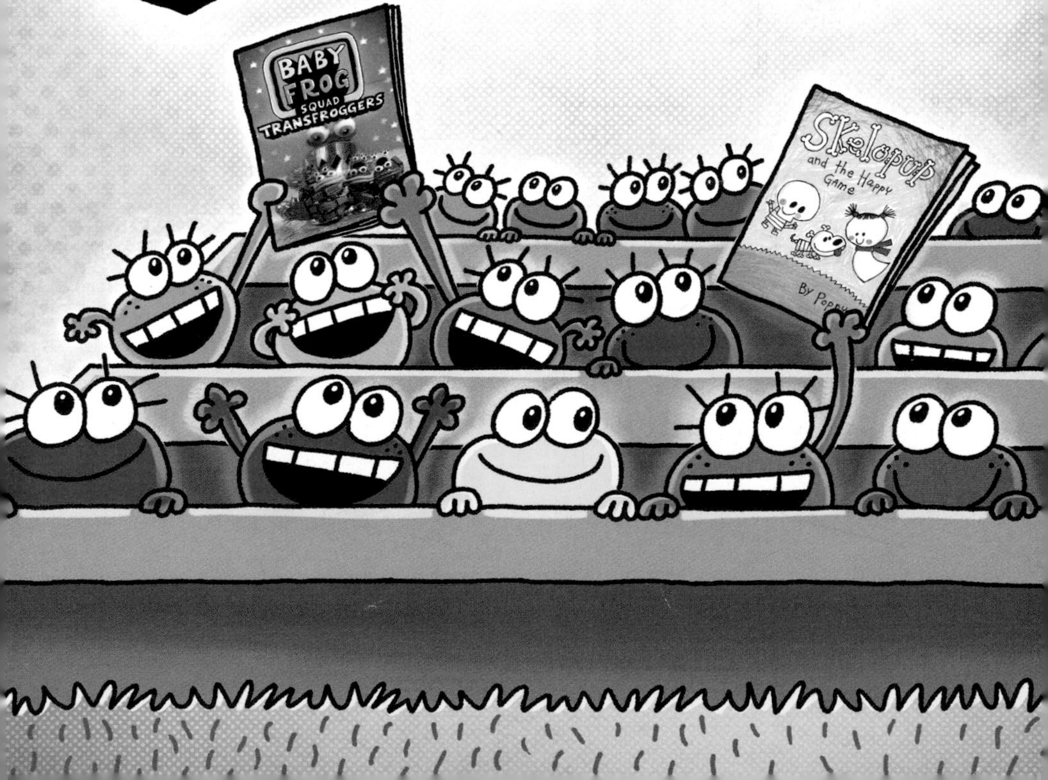
BABY FROG
SQUAD
TRANSFROGGERS
Skelopup
and the Happy Game
By Popp

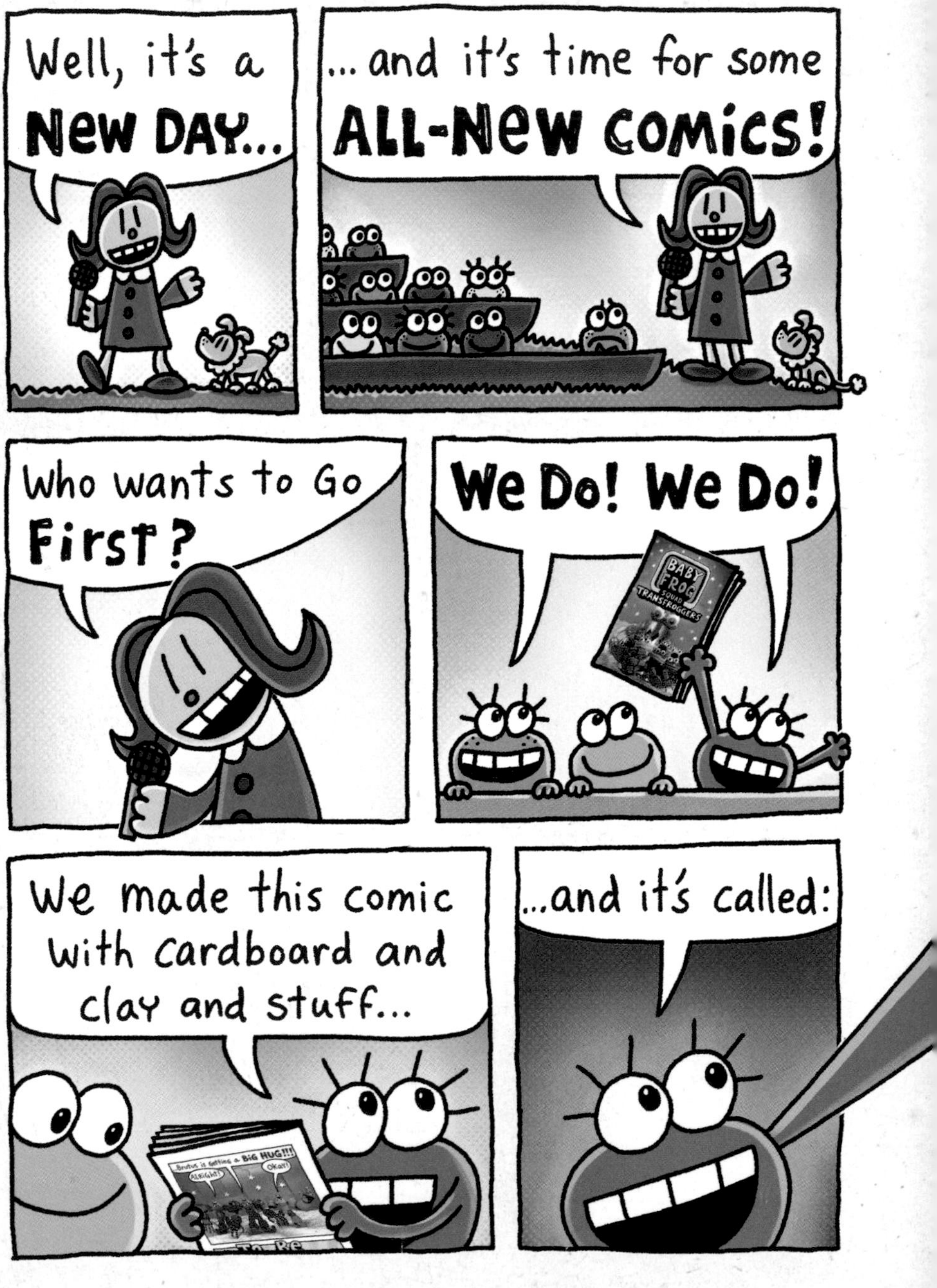
Well, it's a NEW DAY...
...and it's time for some ALL-NEW COMICS!
Who wants to Go FIRST?
We Do! We Do!
BABY FROG SQUAD TRANSFROGGERS
We made this comic with cardboard and clay and stuff...
...and it's called:

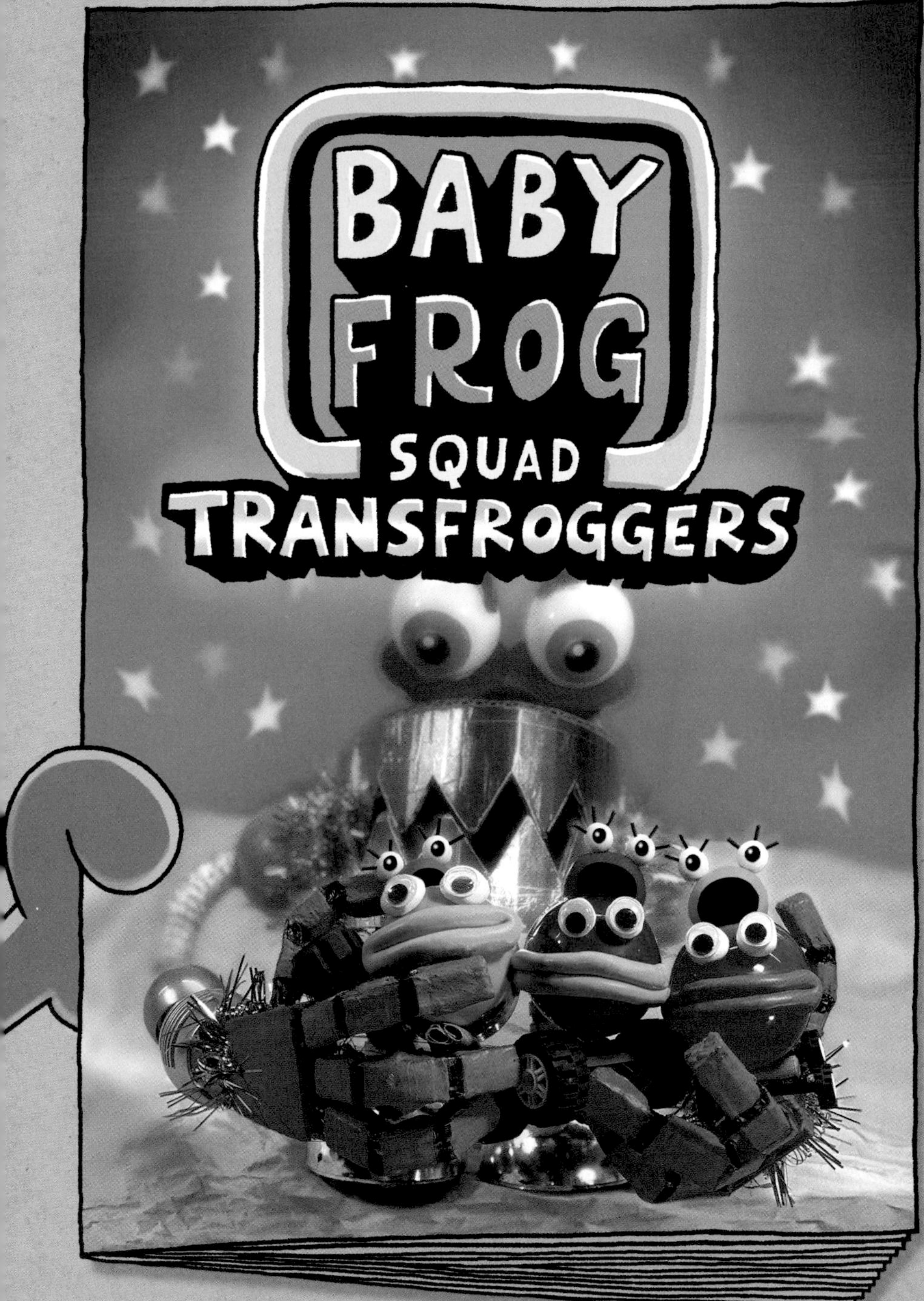
BABY FROG
SQUAD
TRANSFROGGERS

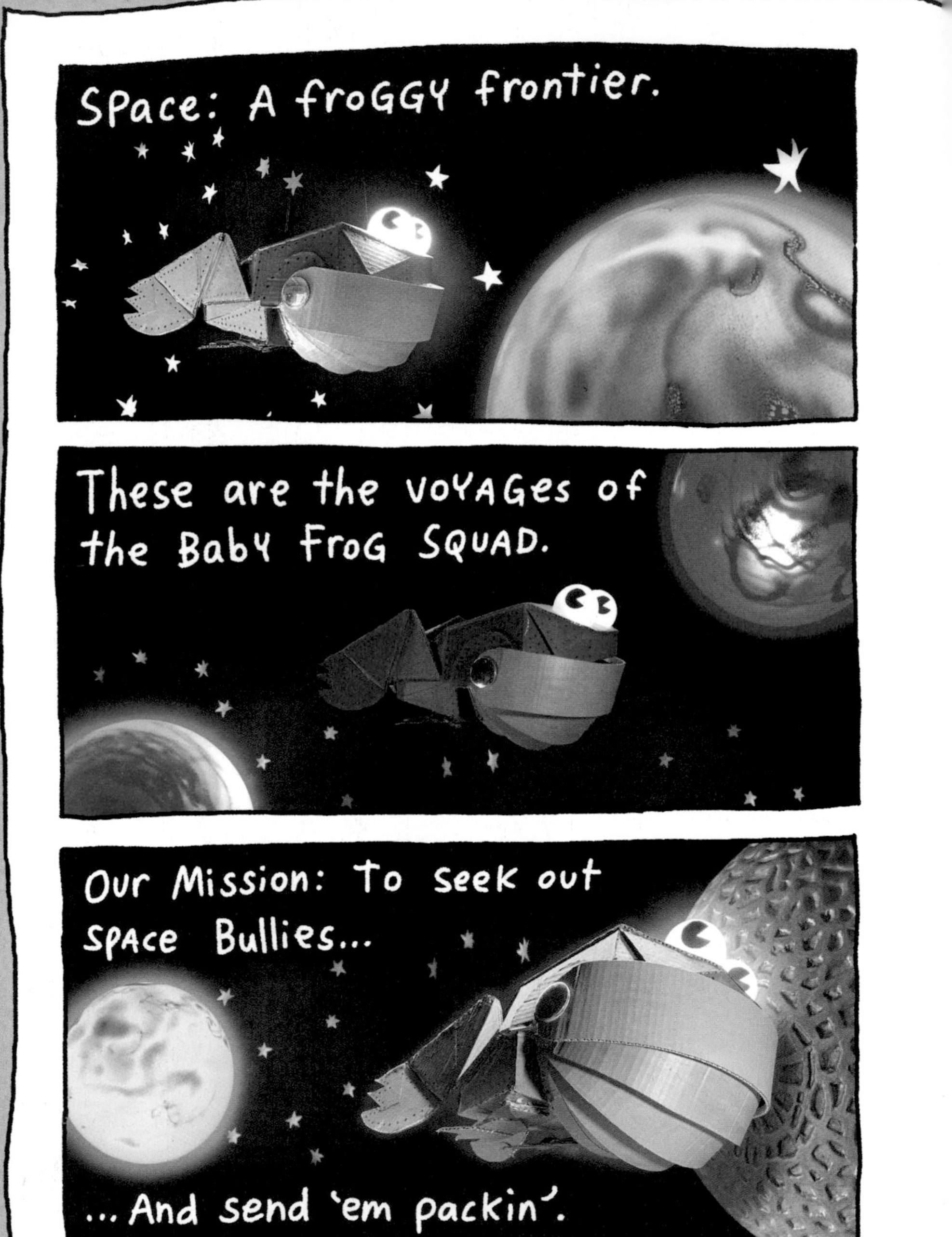
Space: A froGGY frontier.
These are the VOYAGEs of the BabY FroG SQUAD.
Our Mission: To seek out SPAce Bullies...
...And send 'em packin'.

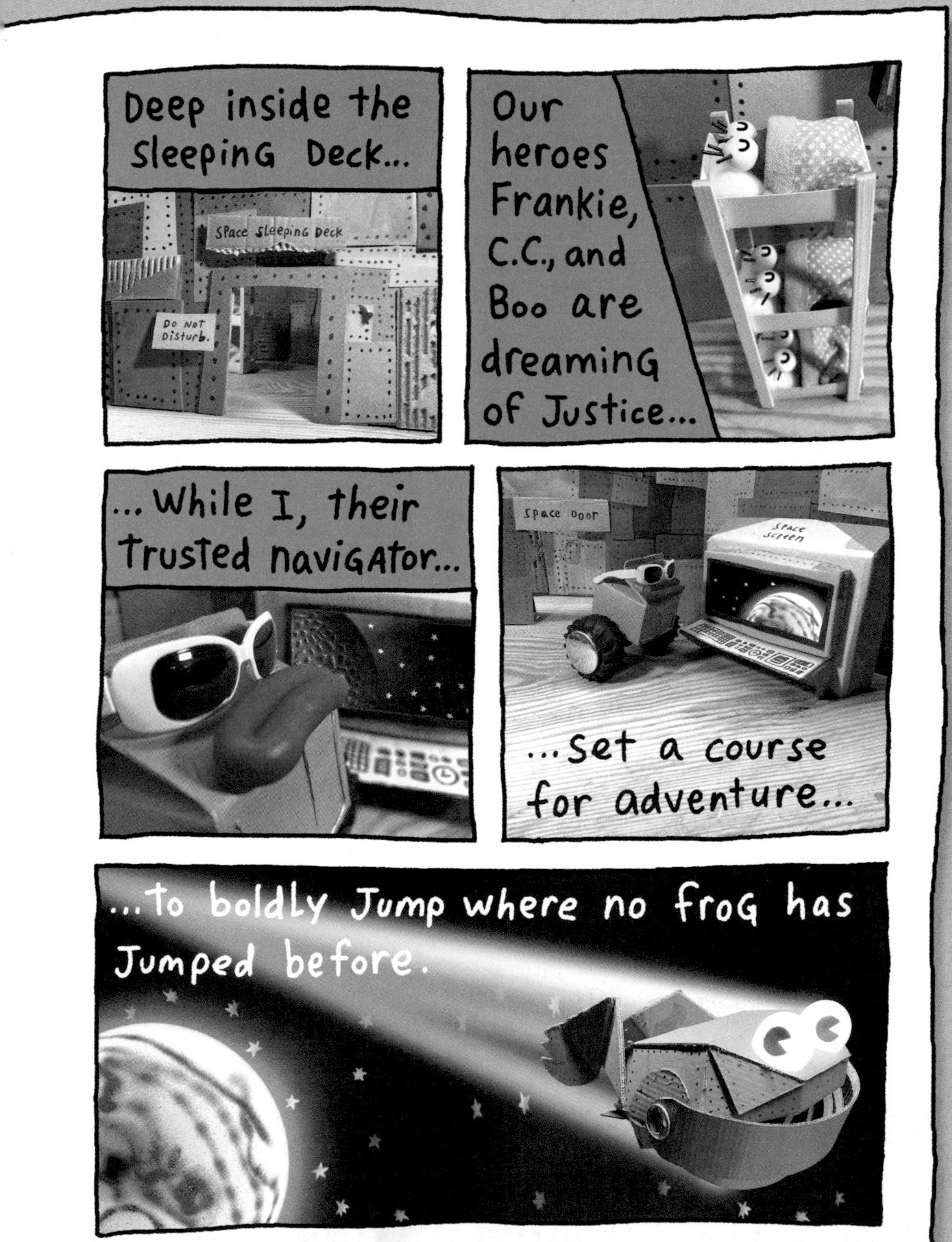
Deep inside the Sleeping Deck...
Space Sleeping Deck
Do Not Disturb.
Our heroes Frankie, C.C., and Boo are dreaming of Justice...
...While I, their trusted navigator...
Space Door
Space Screen
...set a course for adventure...
...to boldly Jump where no frog has Jumped before.

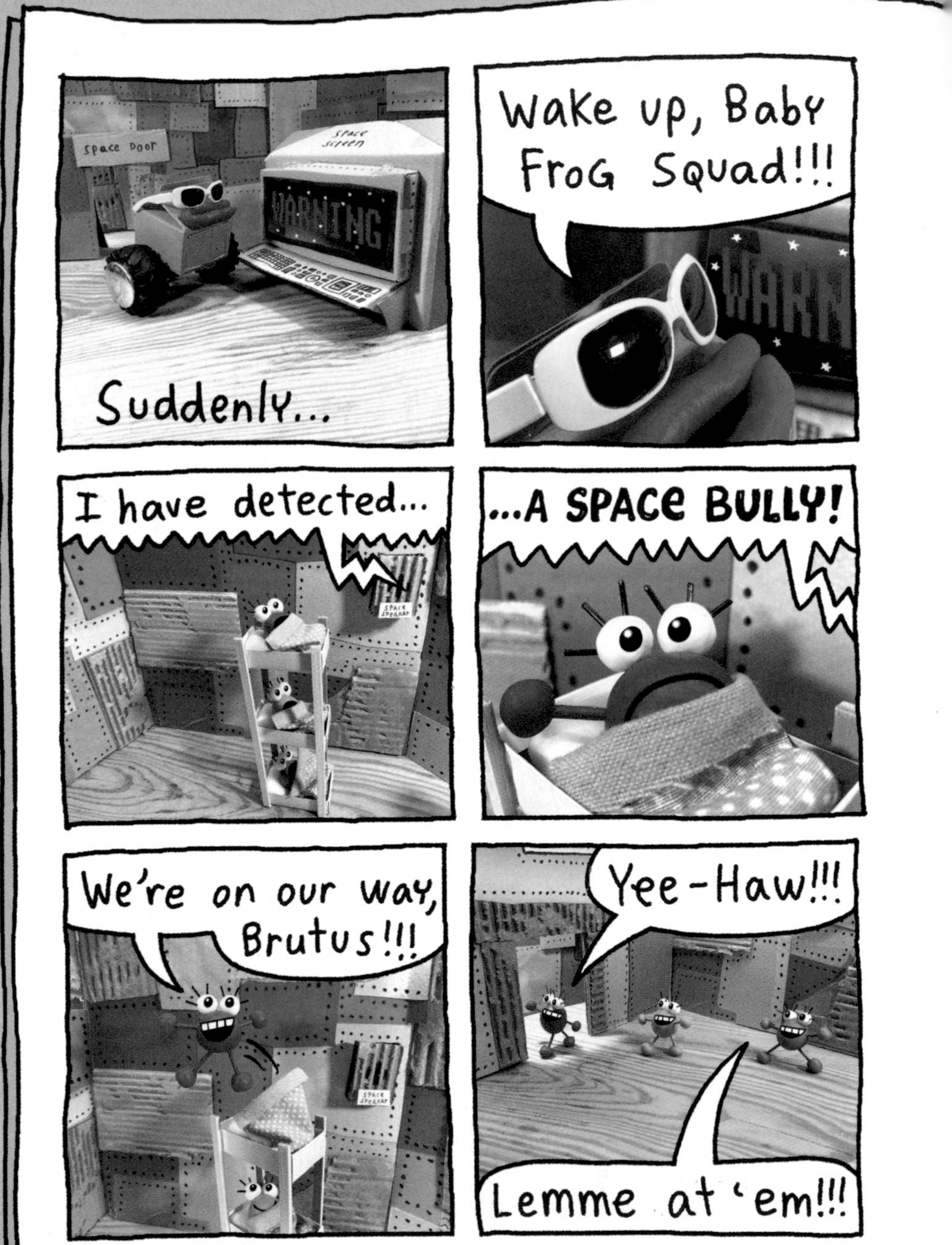
Space Door
Space screen
WARNING
Suddenly...
Wake up, Baby Frog Squad!!!
I have detected...
SPACE SPEAKER
...A SPACE BULLY!
We're on our way, Brutus!!!
SPACE SPEAKER
Yee-Haw!!!
Lemme at 'em!!!

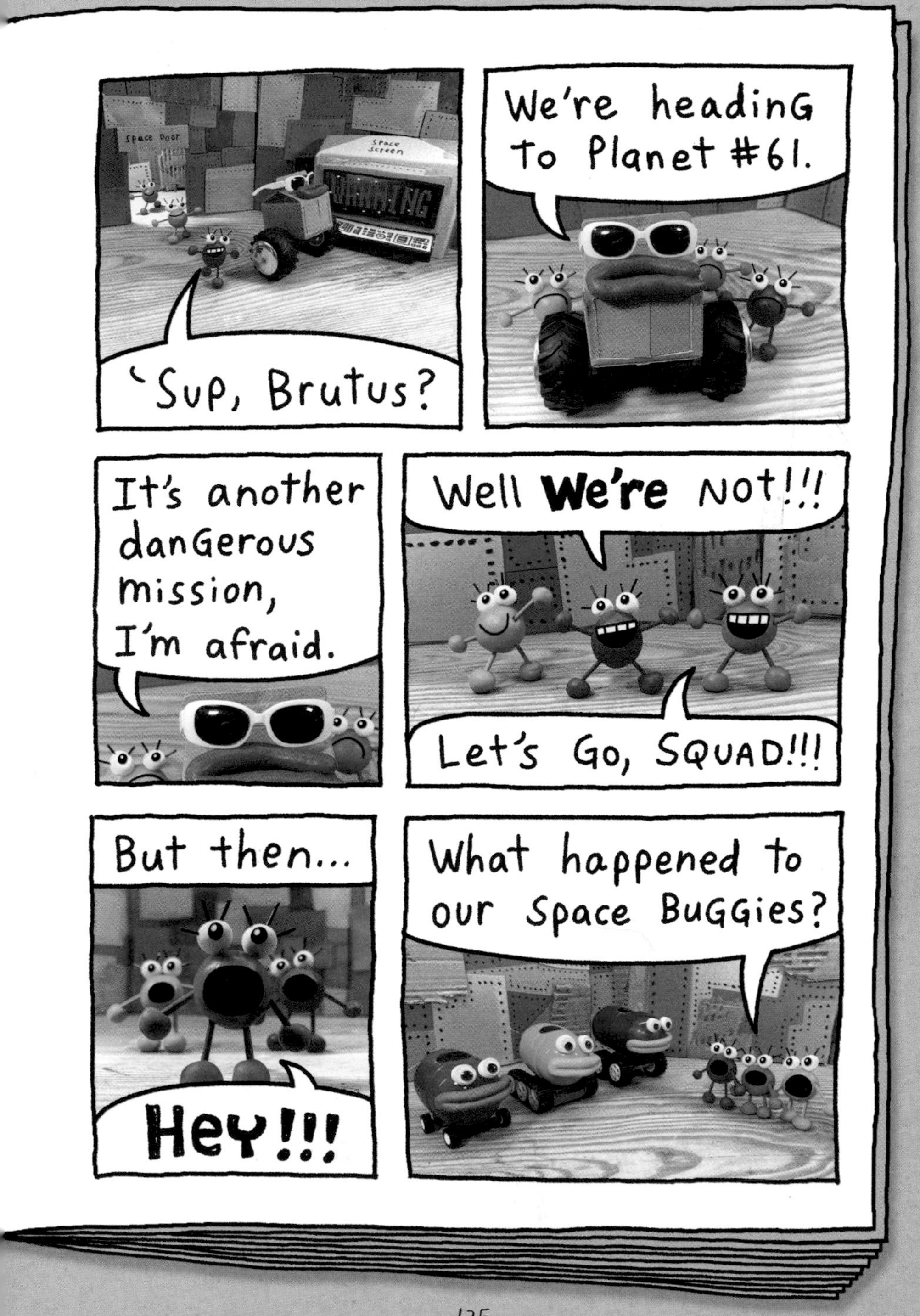
Space Door
Space Screen
WARNING
'Sup, Brutus?
We're heading to Planet #61.
It's another danGerous mission, I'm afraid.
Well **We're** NOT!!!
Let's Go, SQUAD!!!
But then...
HEY!!!
What happened to our Space BuGGies?

I made some improvements while y'all were asleep.

Thanks, Buddy! How can we ever repay you?

How about a hug?

Okay!!!

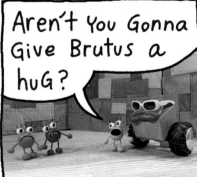

Aren't you gonna give Brutus a hug?

I'm not really a hugger.

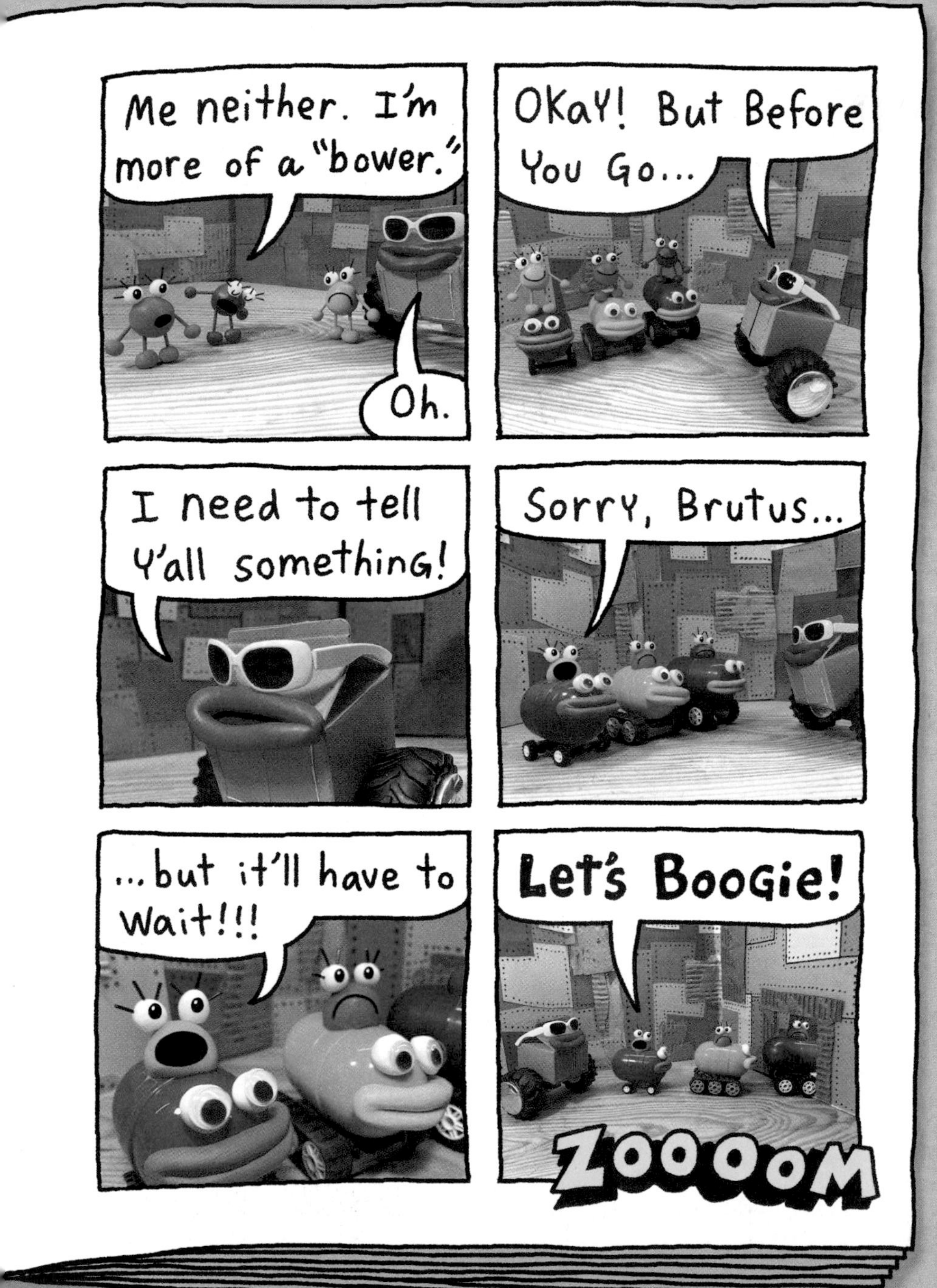
Me neither. I'm more of a "bower."
Oh.
OKAY! But Before You Go...
I need to tell Y'all something!
Sorry, Brutus...
...but it'll have to Wait!!!
Let's Boogie!
ZOOOOM

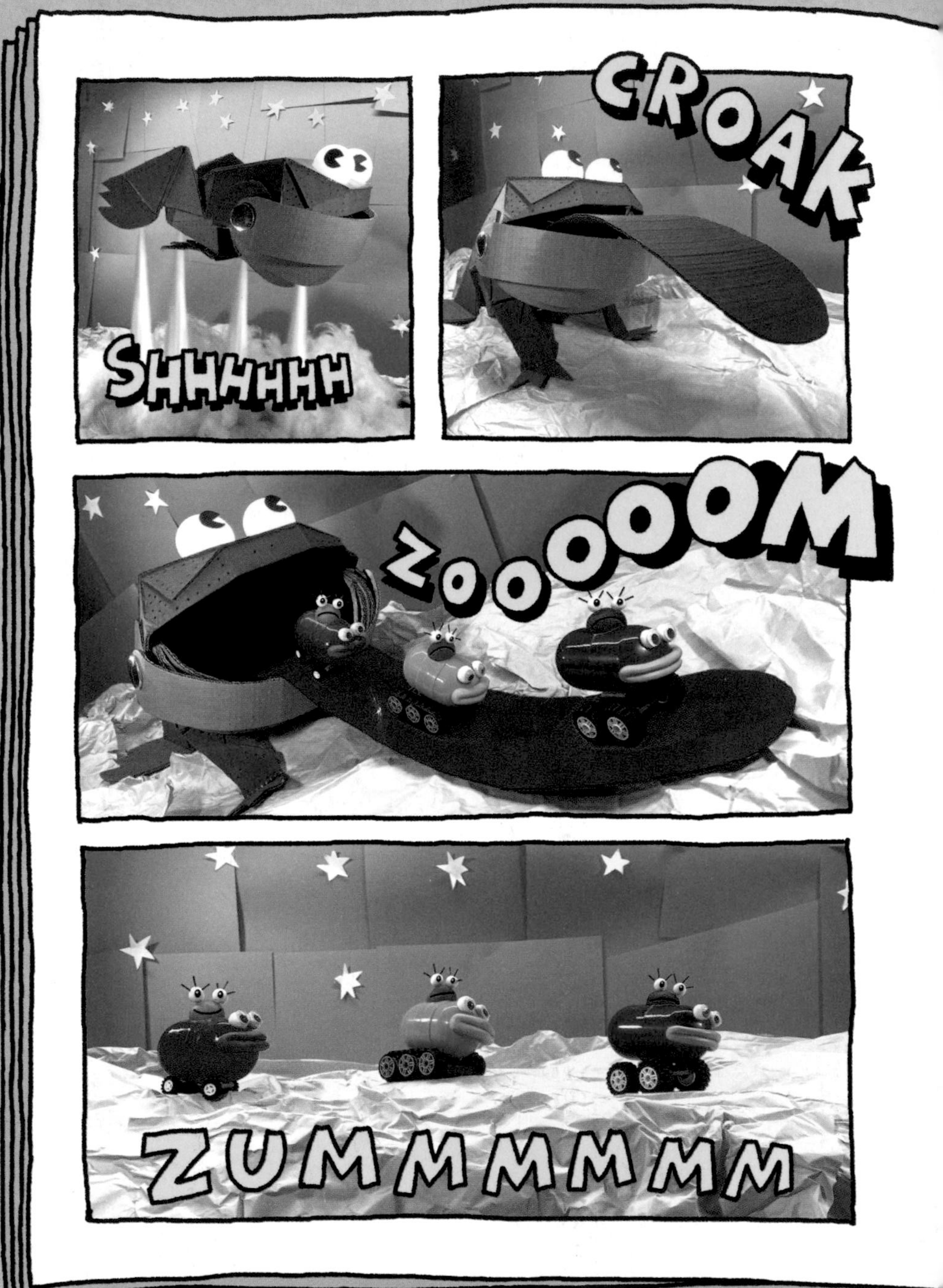
SHHHHHH
CROAK
ZOOOOOOM
ZUMMMMMM

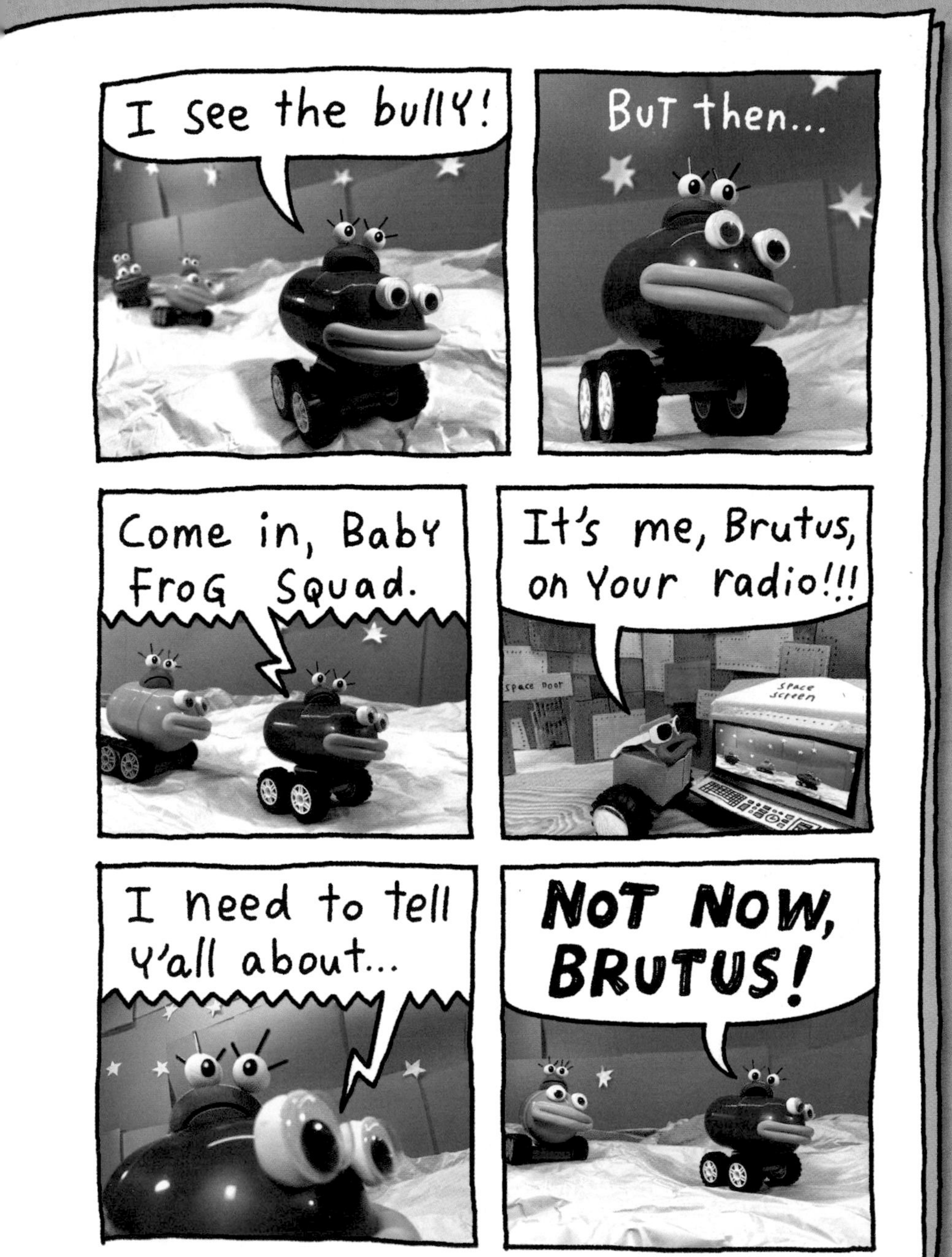
I see the bully!
But then...
Come in, Baby Frog Squad.
It's me, Brutus, on your radio!!!
Space Door
Space Screen
I need to tell y'all about...
NOT NOW, BRUTUS!

We've Got **WORK** to do!

Hey, Bully! CUT it OUT!!!

NO WAY!

Then You leave me no choice!!!

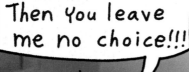

I shall stop this **RUFFIAN**...

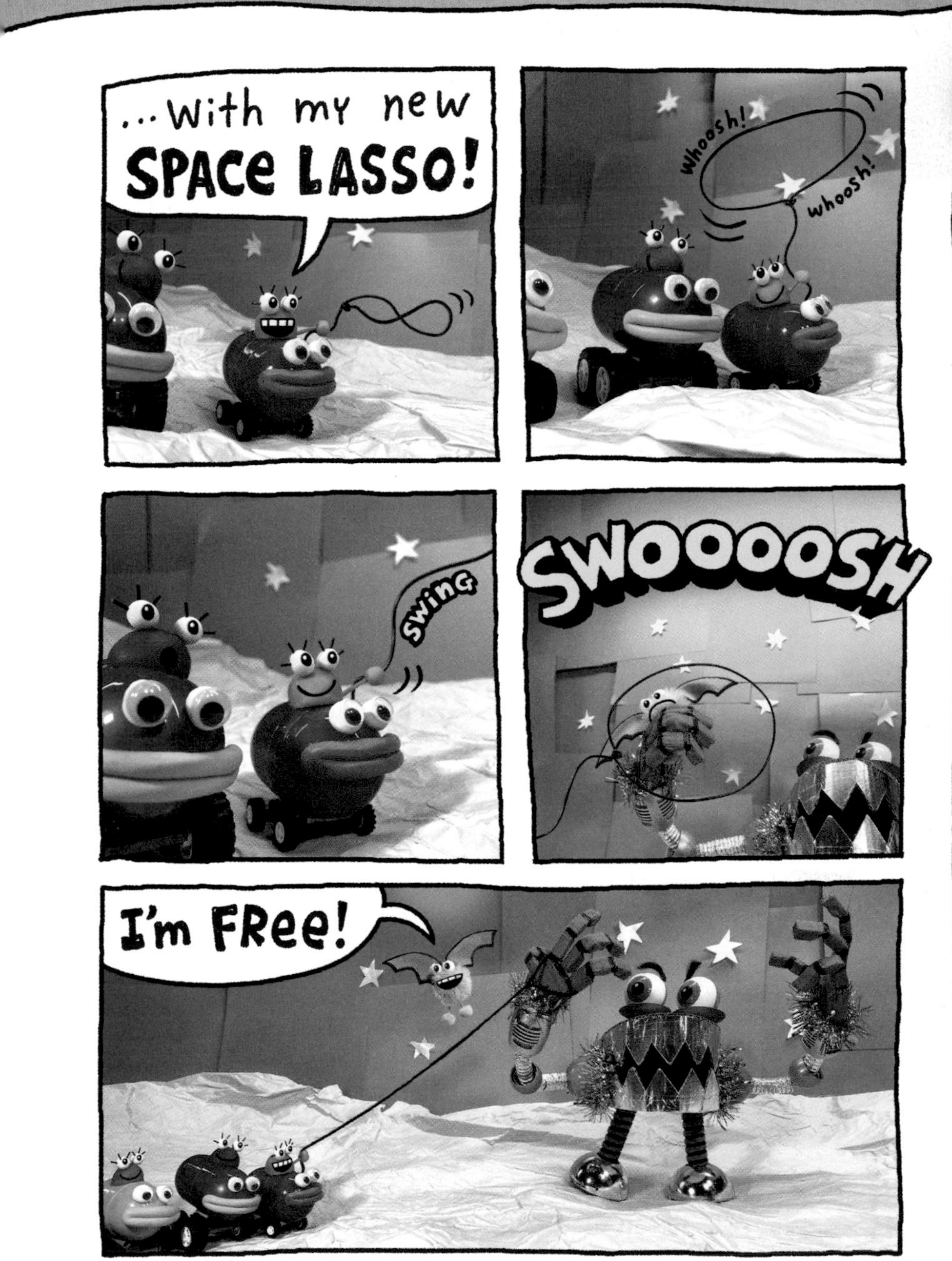
...With my new SPACE LASSO!
Whoosh!
whoosh!
SWING
SWOOOOSH
I'm FRee!

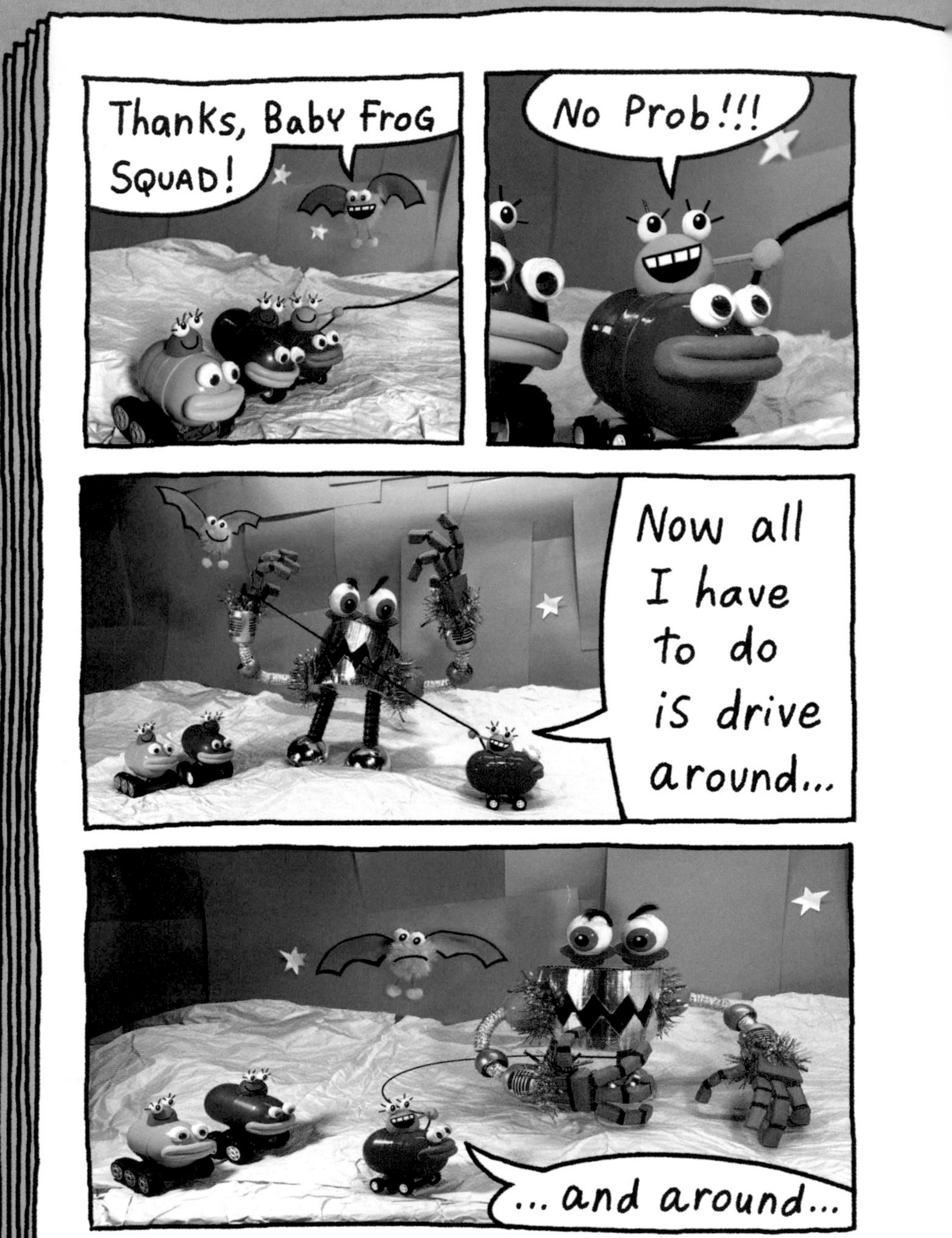
Thanks, Baby Frog Squad!
No Prob!!!
Now all I have to do is drive around...
...and around...

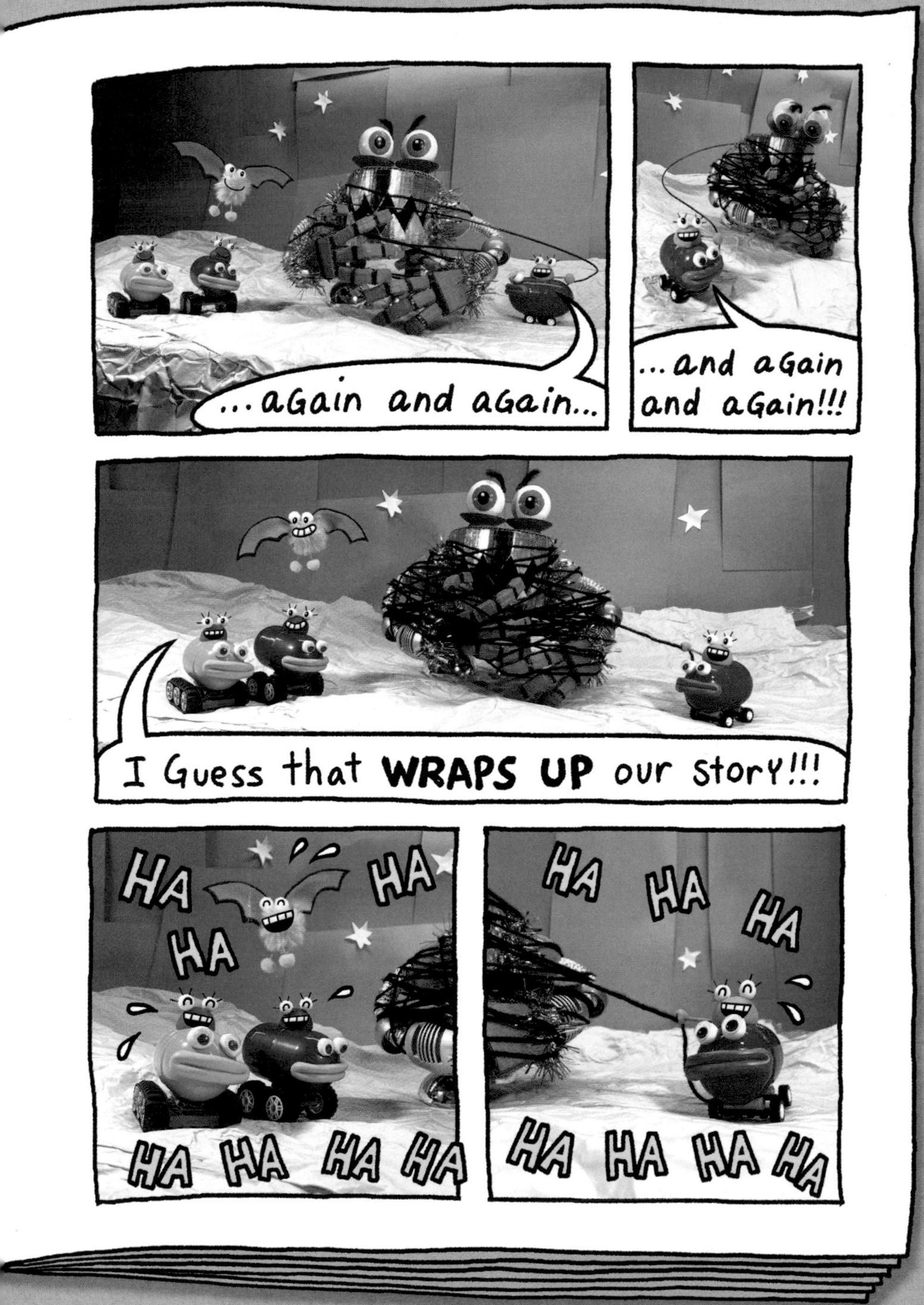
...aGain and aGain...
...and aGain and aGain!!!
I Guess that **WRAPS UP** our story!!!
HA HA HA
HA HA HA HA
HA HA HA
HA HA HA HA

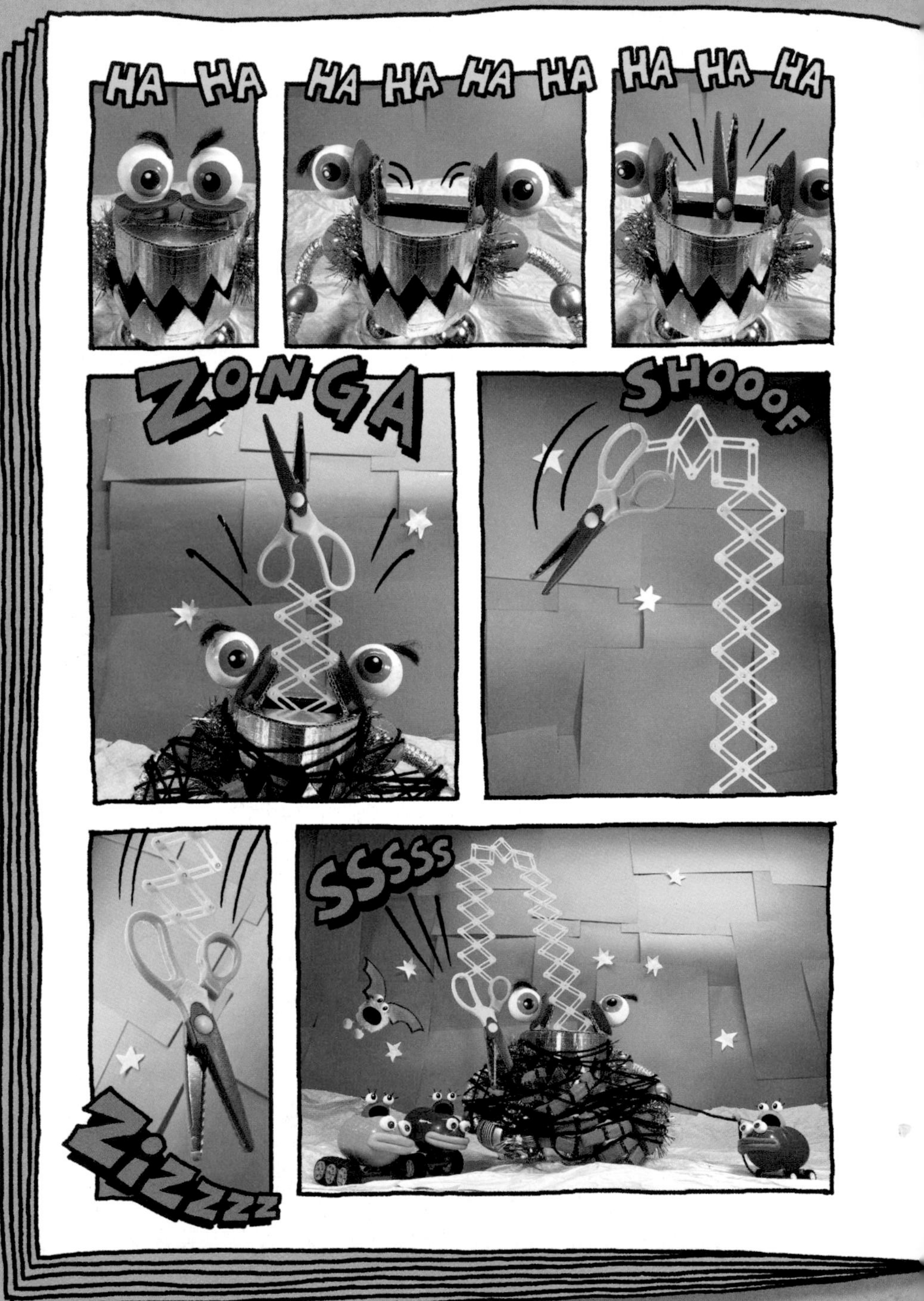
HA HA
HA HA HA HA
HA HA HA
ZONGA
SHOOOF
ZIZZZZ
SSSSS

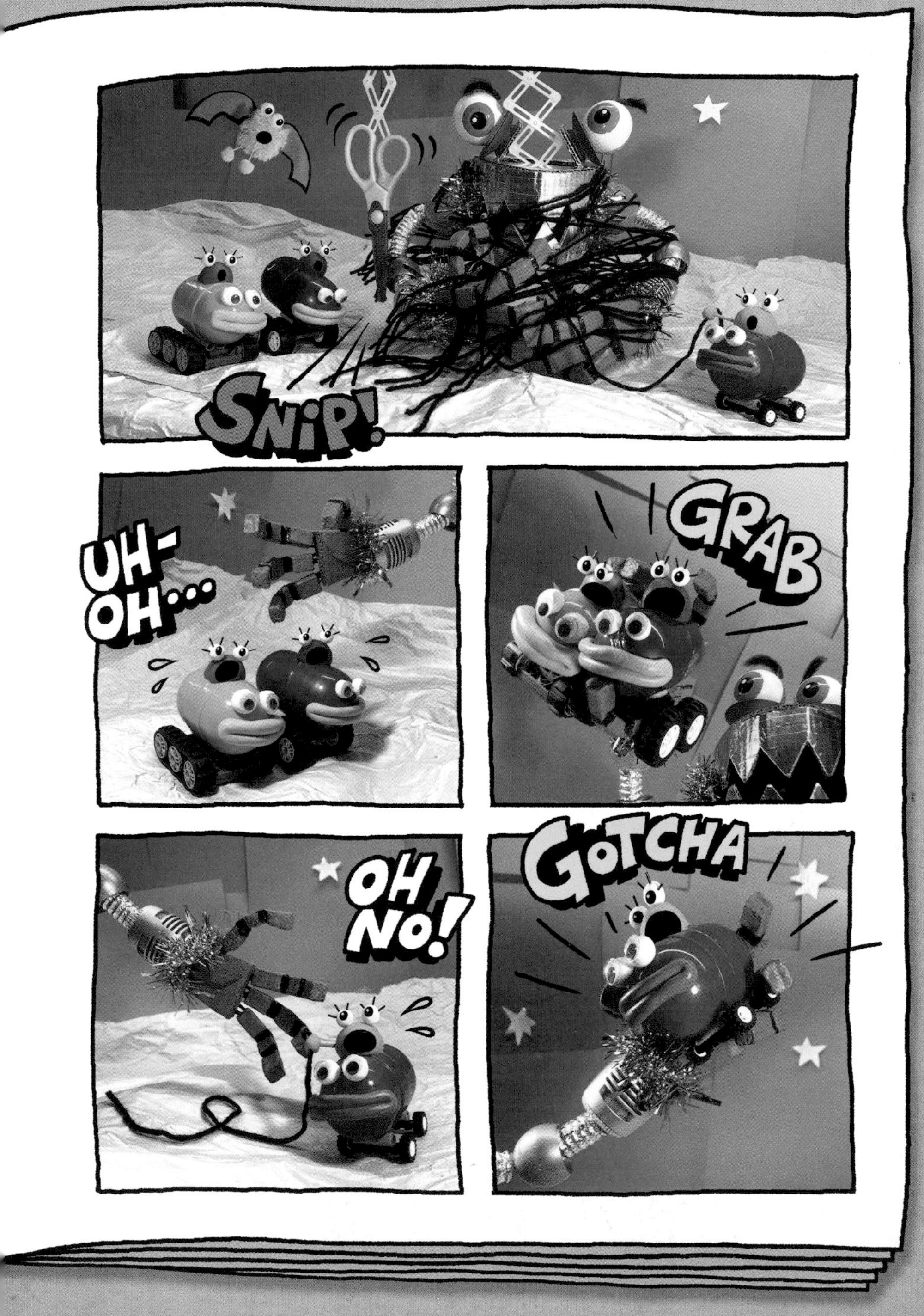
SNIP!
UH-OH...
GRAB
OH NO!
GOTCHA

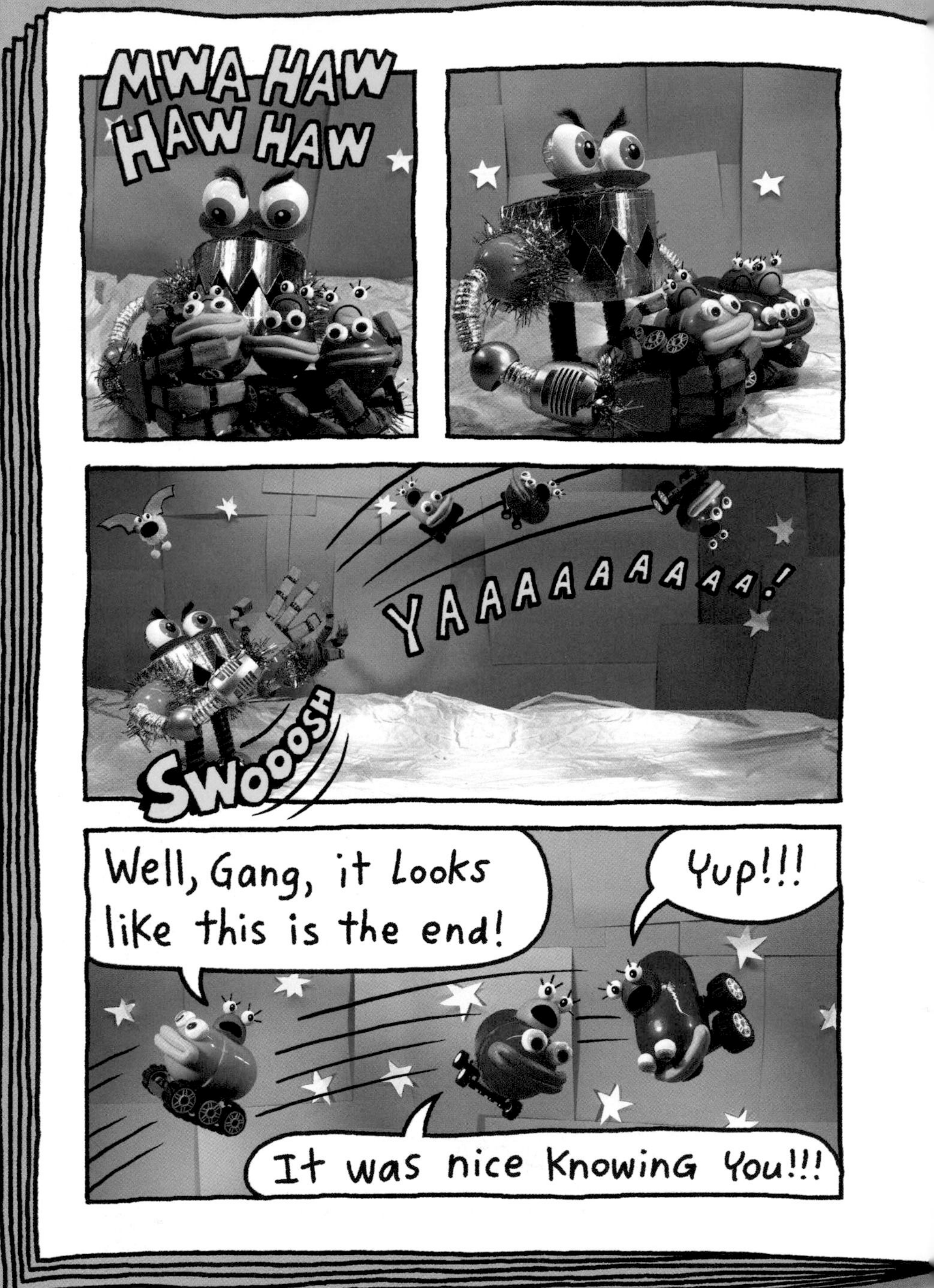
MWA HAW HAW HAW
YAAAAAAAAAA!
SWOOOSH
Well, Gang, it looks like this is the end!
Yup!!!
It was nice knowing you!!!

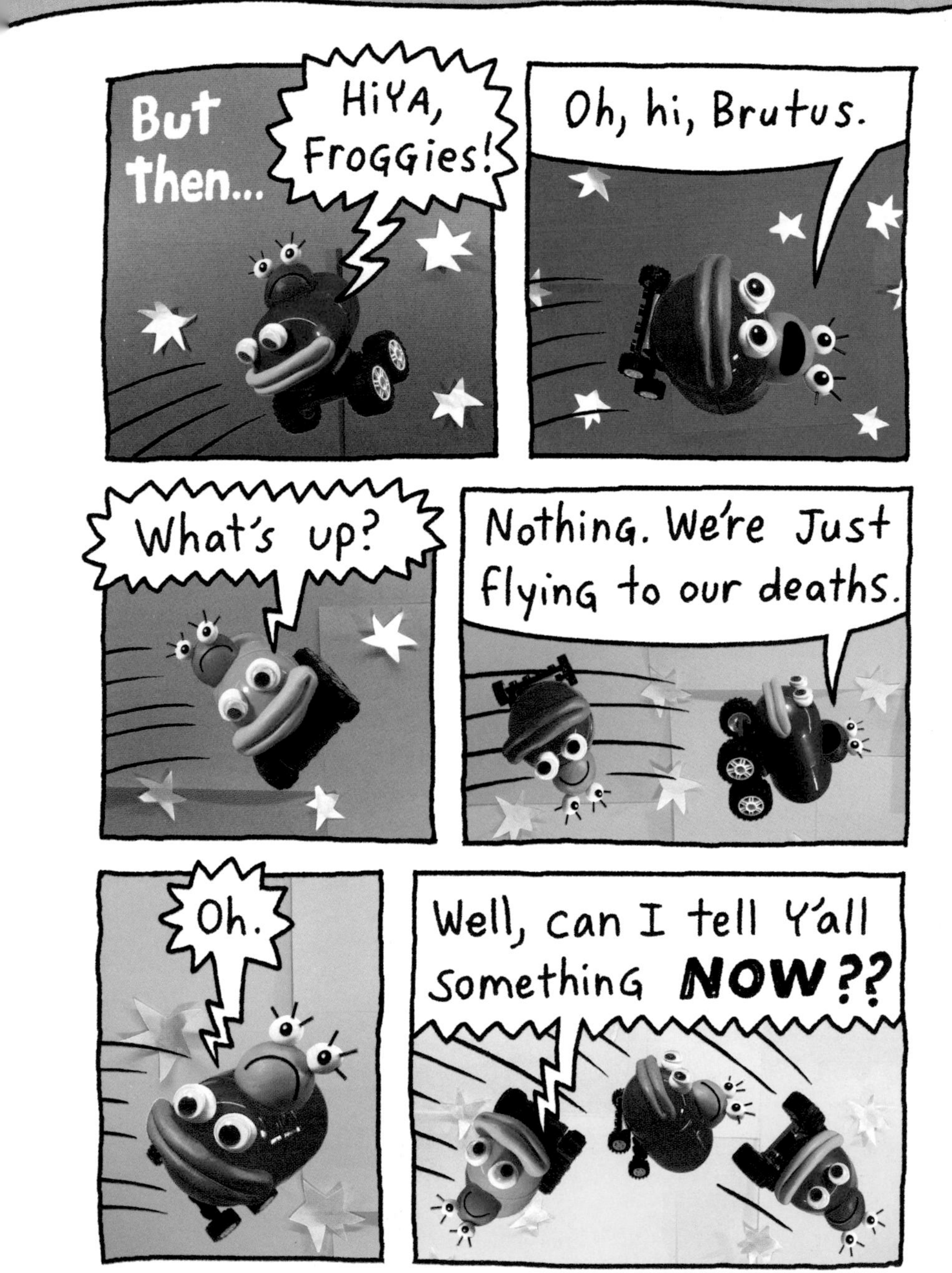
But then...
HiYA, FroGGies!
Oh, hi, Brutus.
What's up?
NothinG. We're Just flyinG to our deaths.
Oh.
Well, can I tell Y'all somethinG **NOW**??

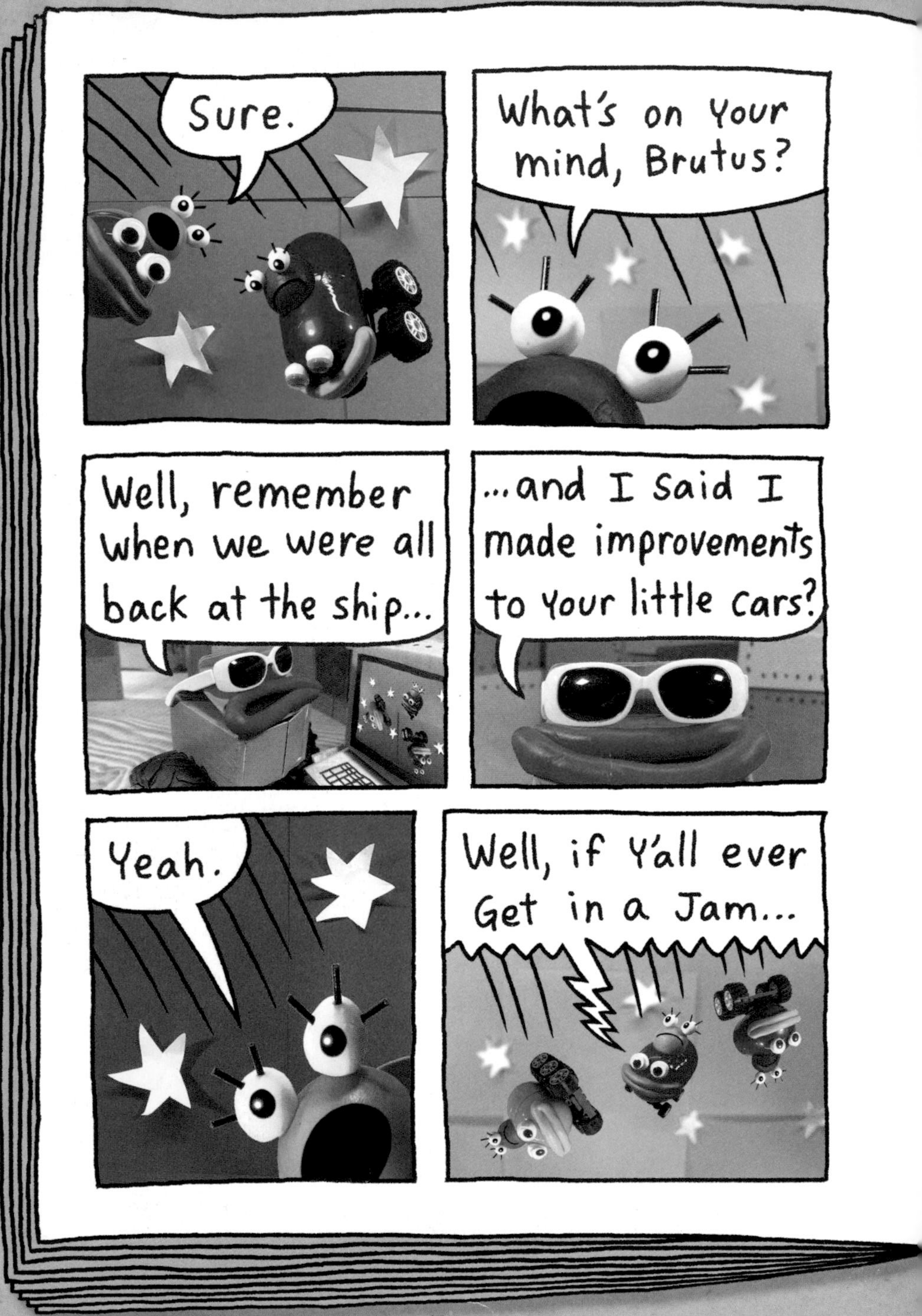
Sure.
What's on your mind, Brutus?
Well, remember when we were all back at the ship...
...and I said I made improvements to your little cars?
Yeah.
Well, if y'all ever get in a jam...

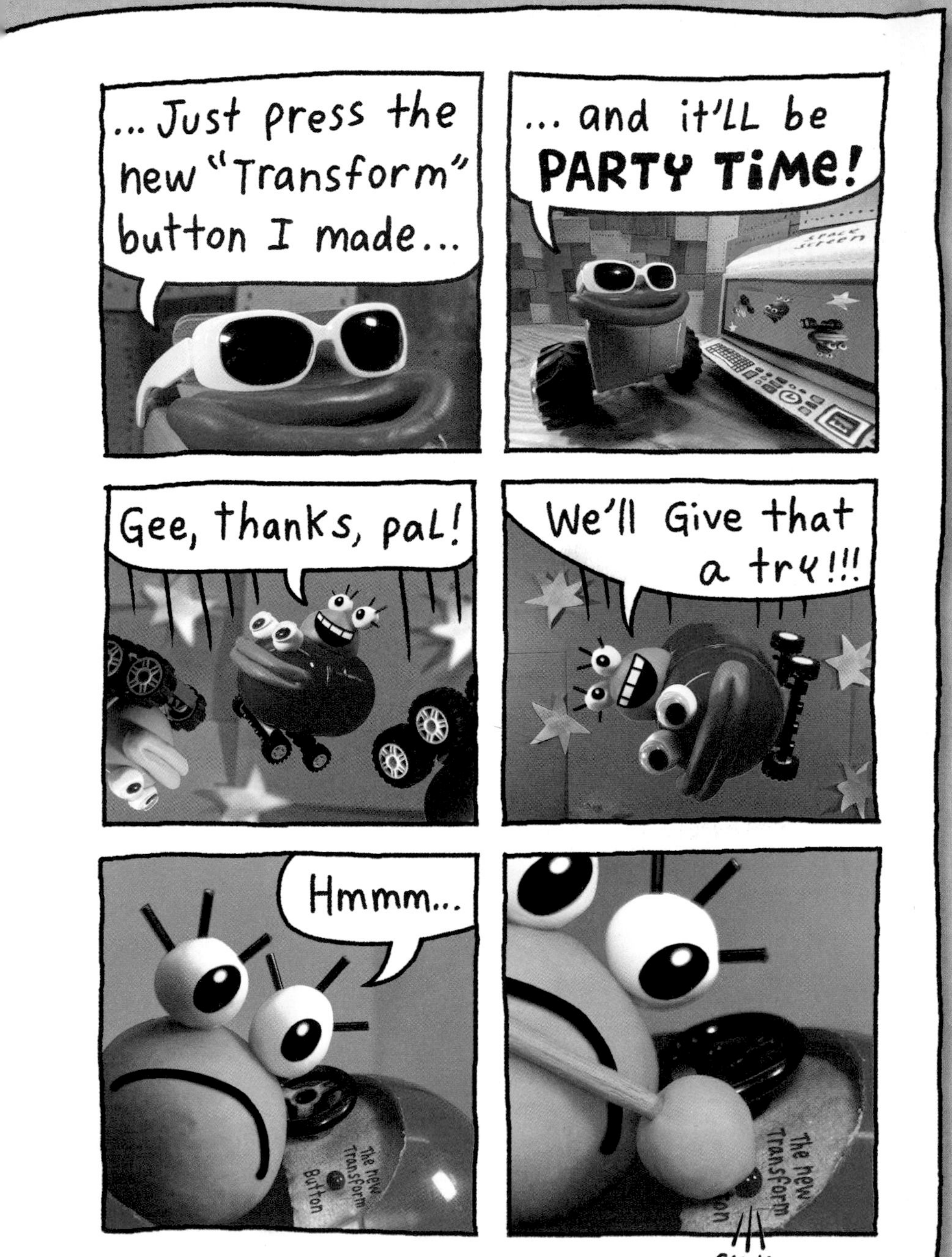
...Just press the new "Transform" button I made...
... and it'LL be **PARTY TiMe!**
Gee, thanks, paL!
We'll Give that a try!!!
Hmmm...
The new Transform Button
The new Transform
CLick

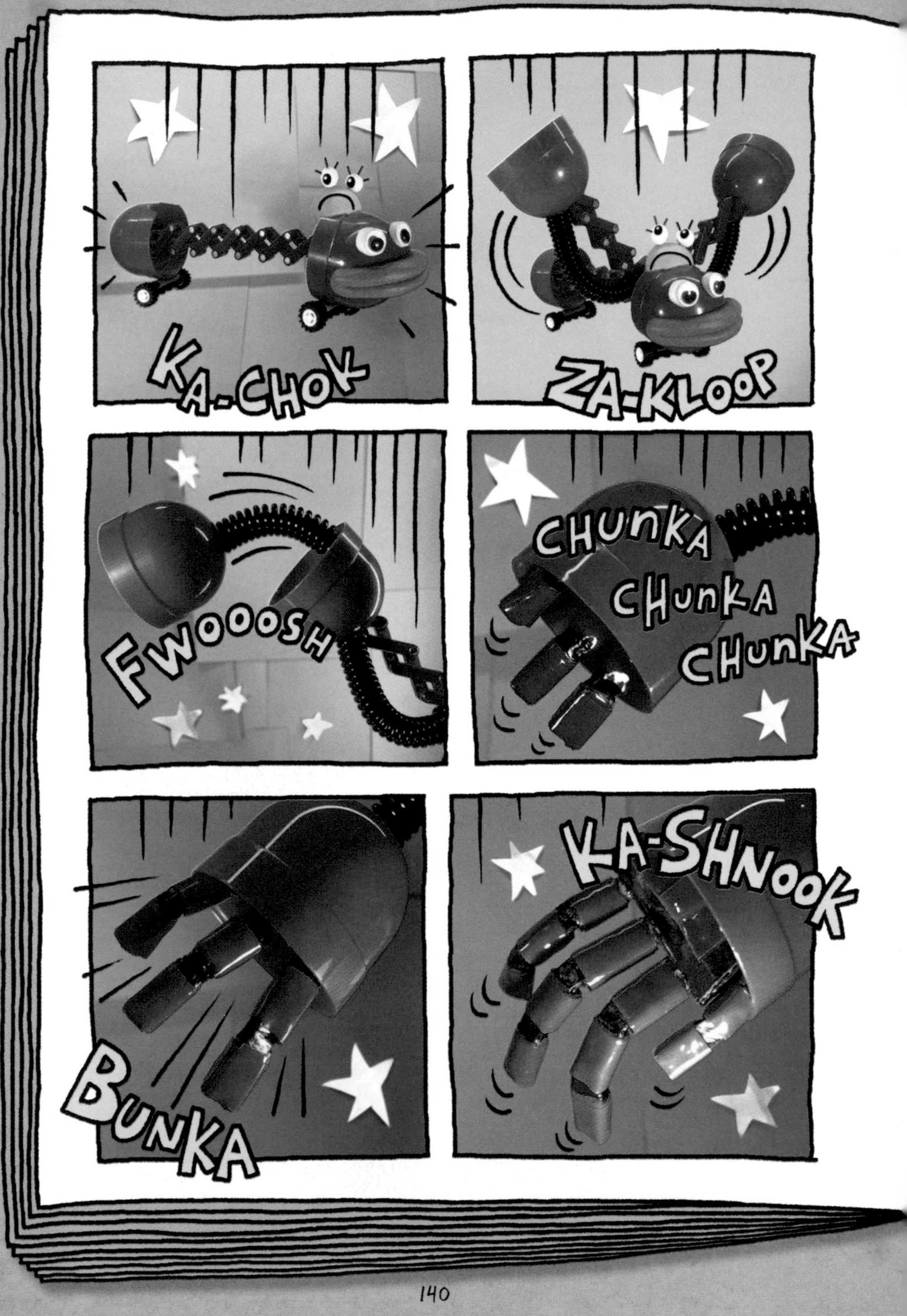
KA-CHOK
ZA-KLOOP
FWOOOSH
CHUNKA
CHUNKA
CHUNKA
BUNKA
KA-SHNOOK

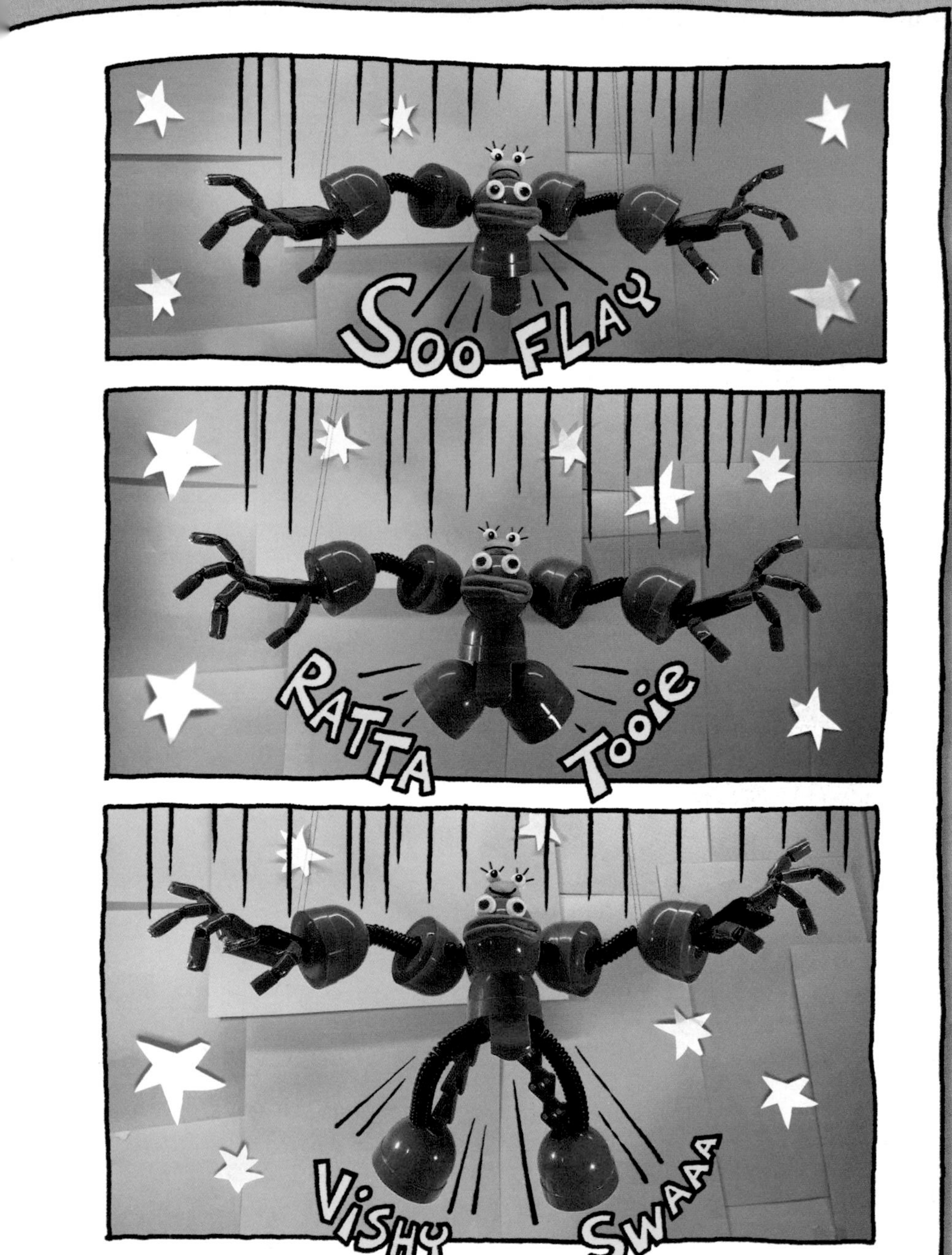
SOO FLAY
RATTA TOOIE
VISHY SWAAA

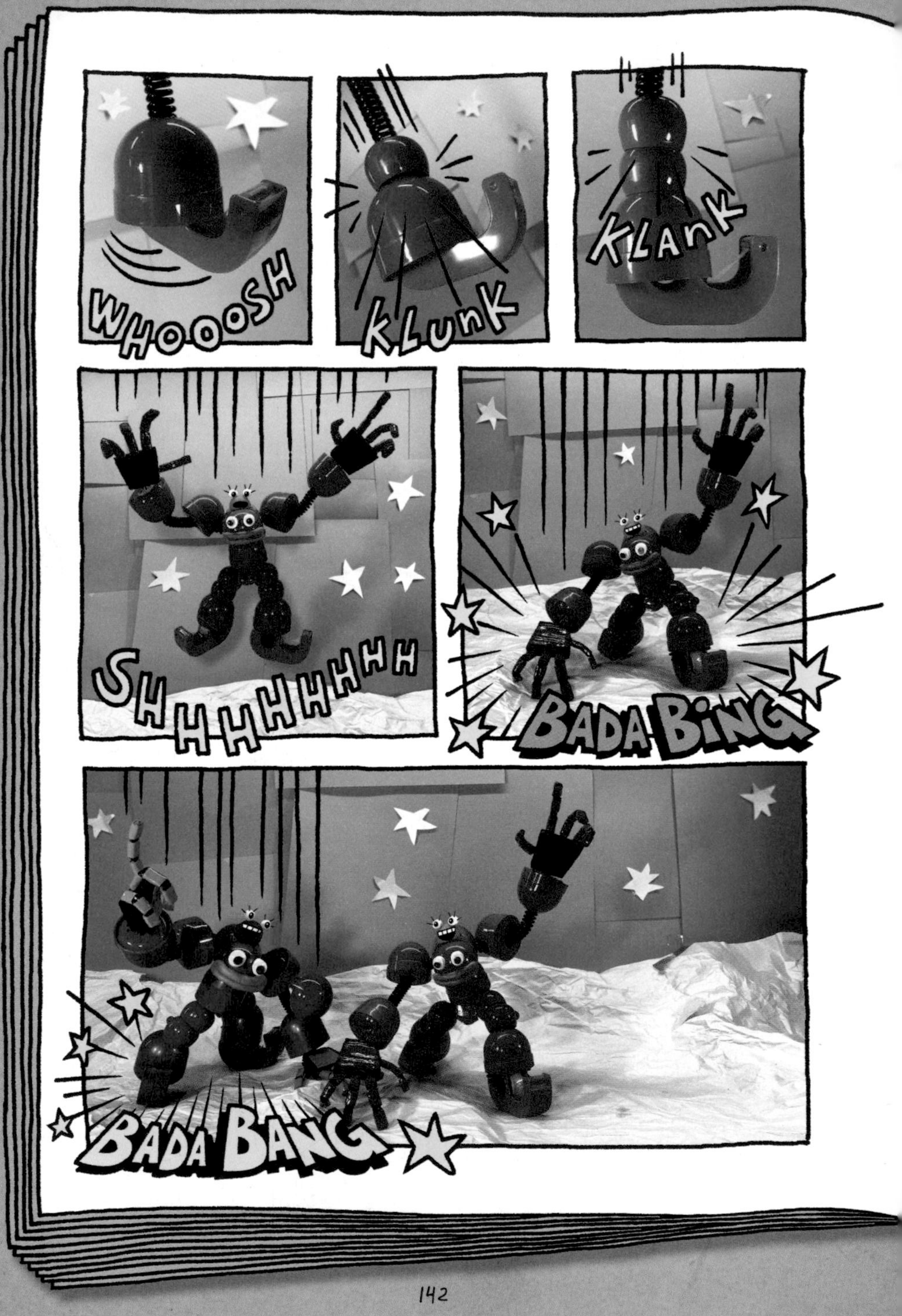
WHOOOSH
KLUNK
KLANK
SHHHHHHHH
BADA BING
BADA BANG

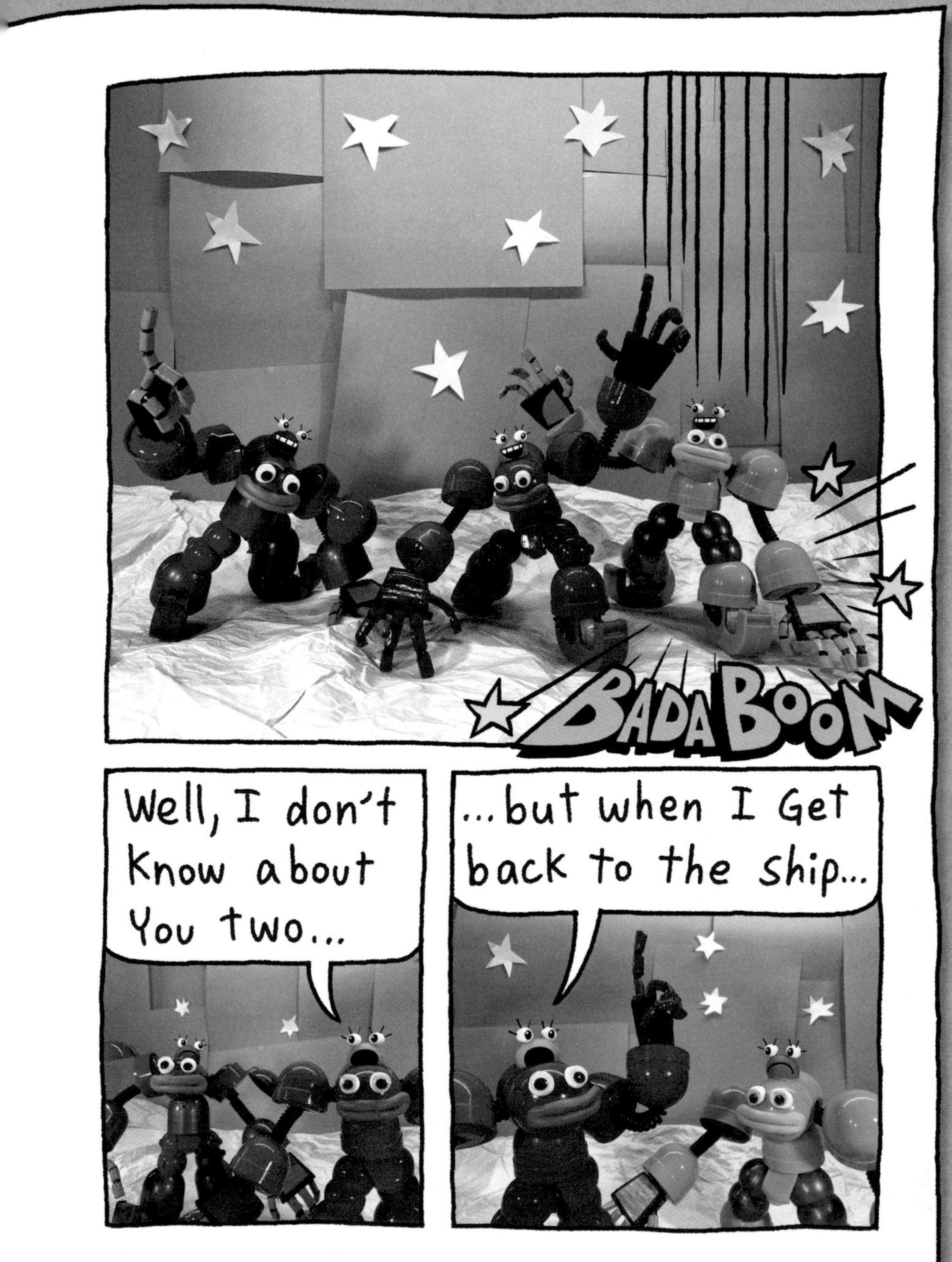
BADA BOOM
Well, I don't Know about You two...
...but when I Get back to the ship...

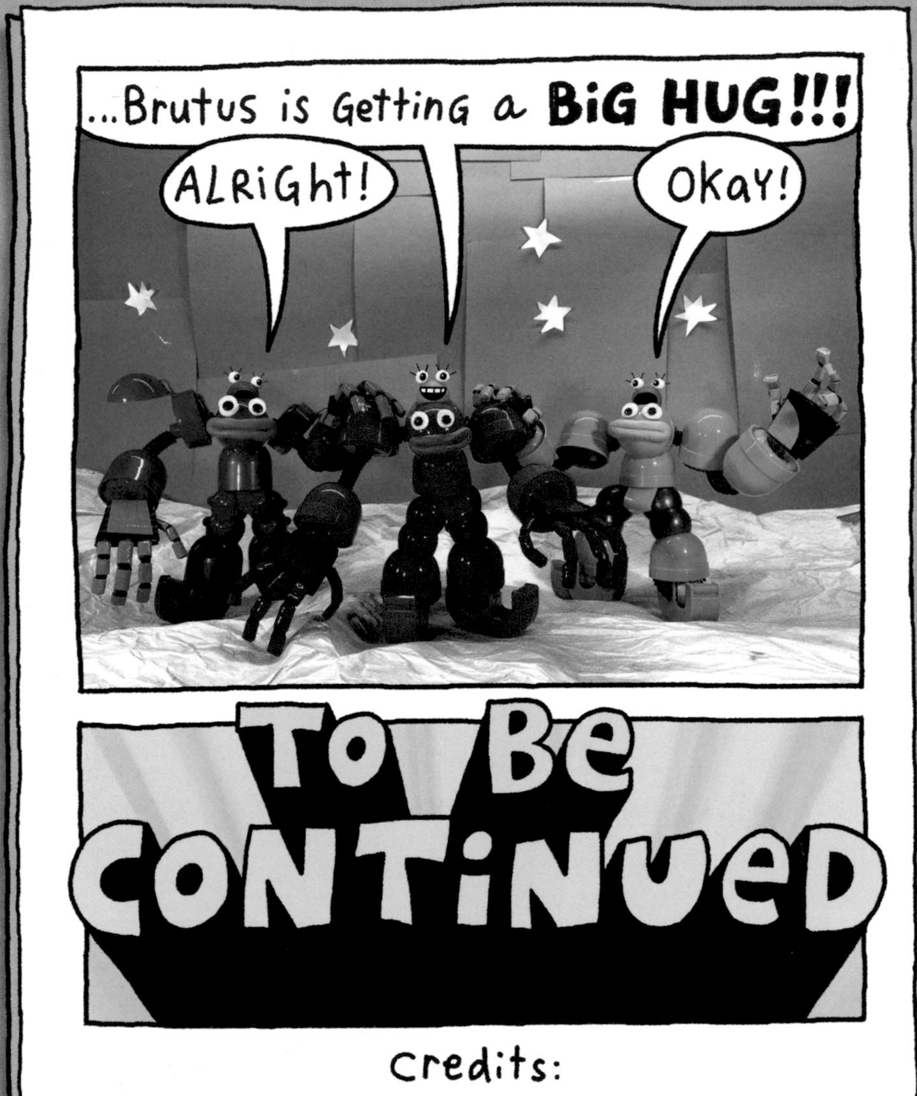
...Brutus is Getting a BiG HUG!!!
ALRiGht!
OKaY!
To Be CONTiNUeD
credits:
story by: BiLLie
art by: Frida and EL and Deb
photography and editing by: Billie and EL

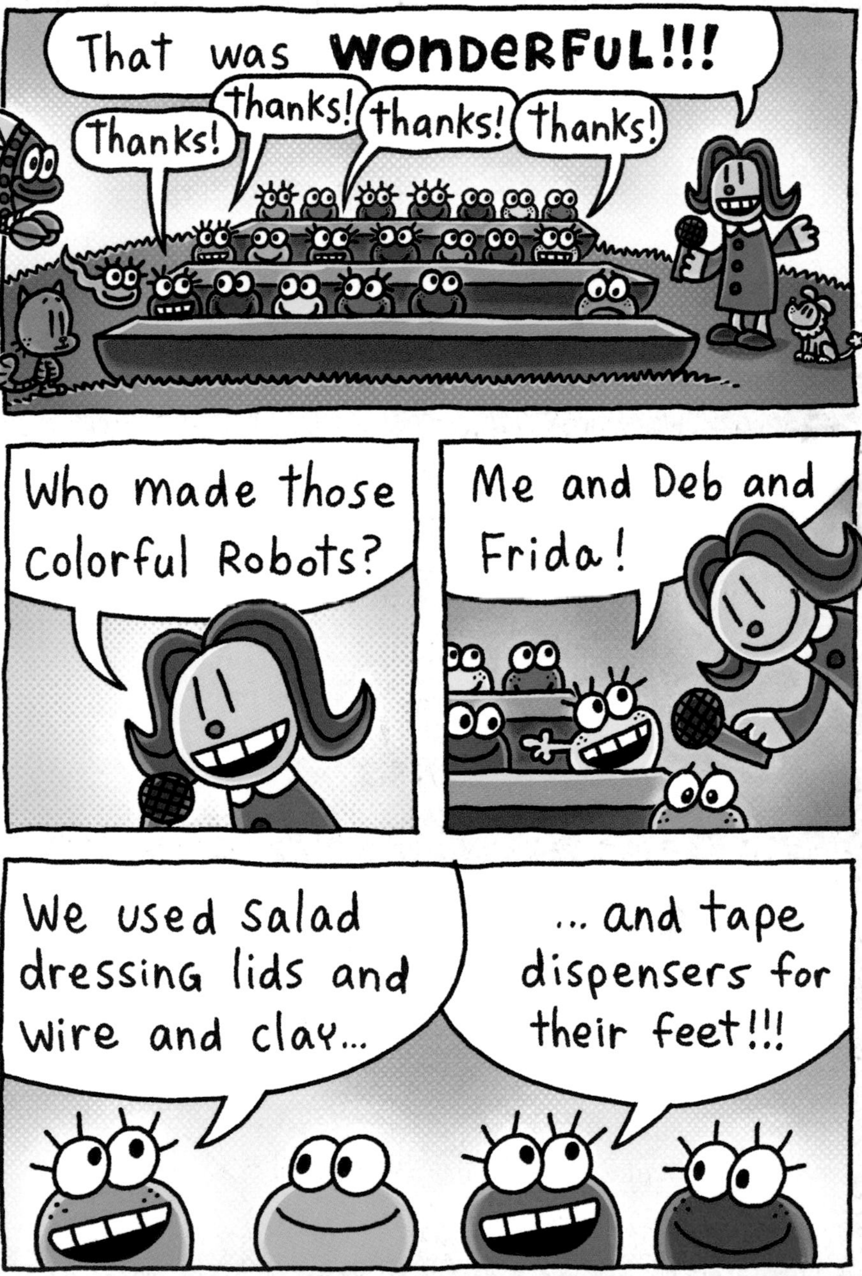
That was WONDERFUL!!!
Thanks!
thanks!
thanks!
thanks!
Who made those Colorful Robots?
Me and Deb and Frida!
We used salad dressing lids and wire and clay...
... and tape dispensers for their feet!!!

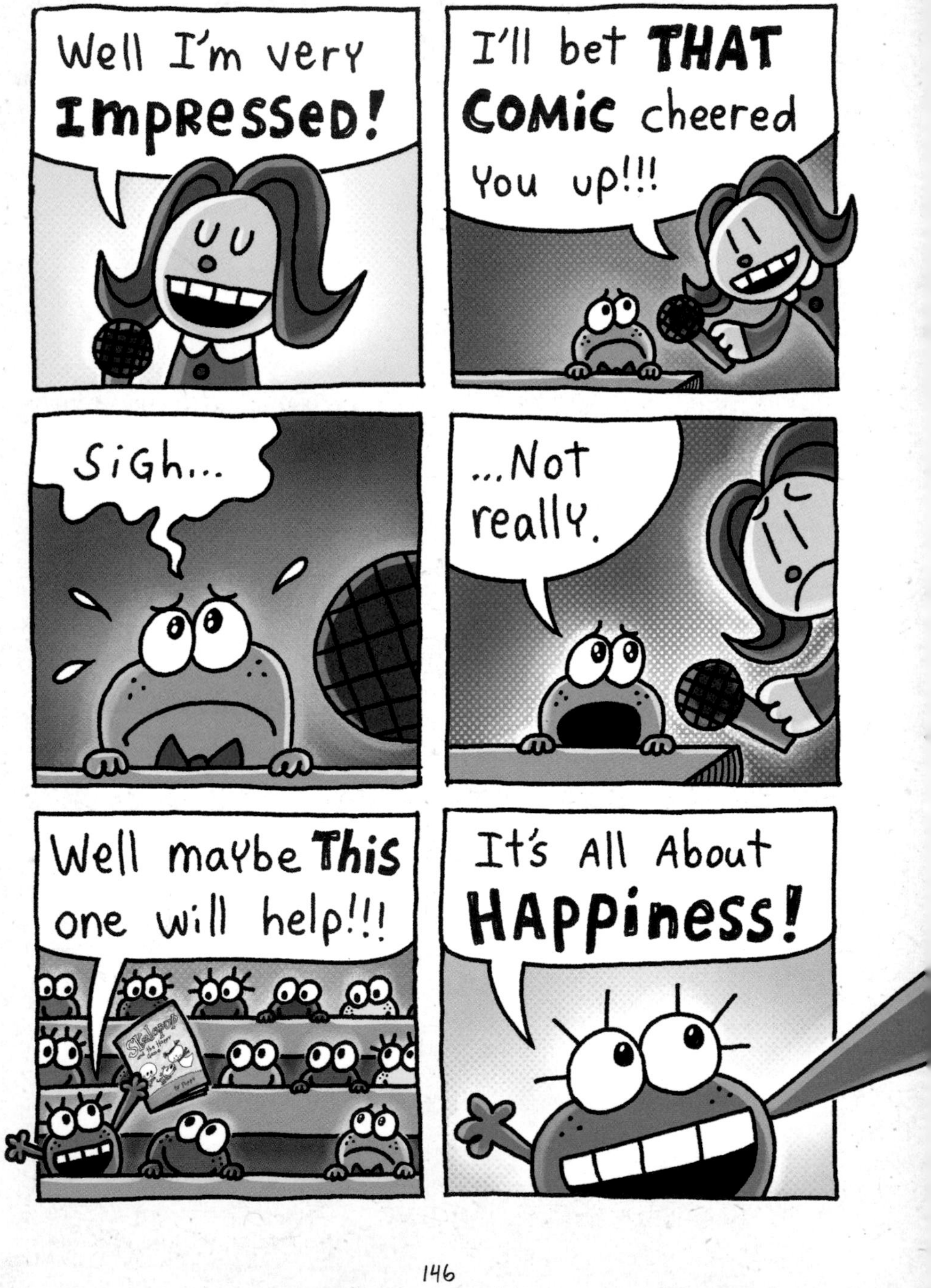
Well I'm very IMPRESSED!
I'll bet THAT COMIC cheered you up!!!
SiGh...
...Not really.
Well maybe This one will help!!!
It's All About HAPPiness!

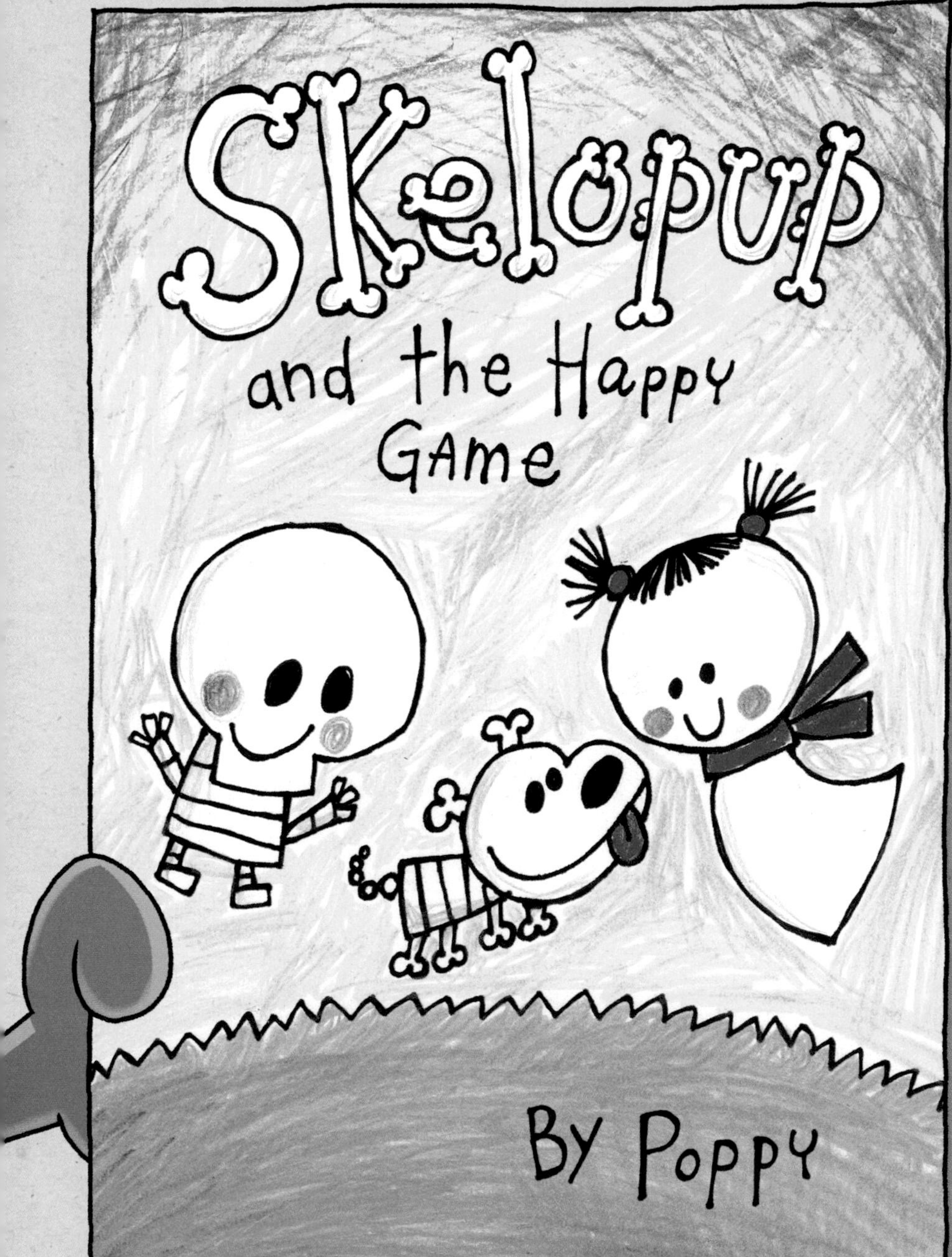
Skelopup
and the Happy Game
By Poppy

Everyone was worried...

...because Ghost Girl was so sad.

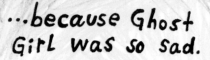

She missed her old cat very much...

...And everything she did...

...made her feel sadder...

...and sadder.

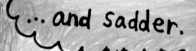

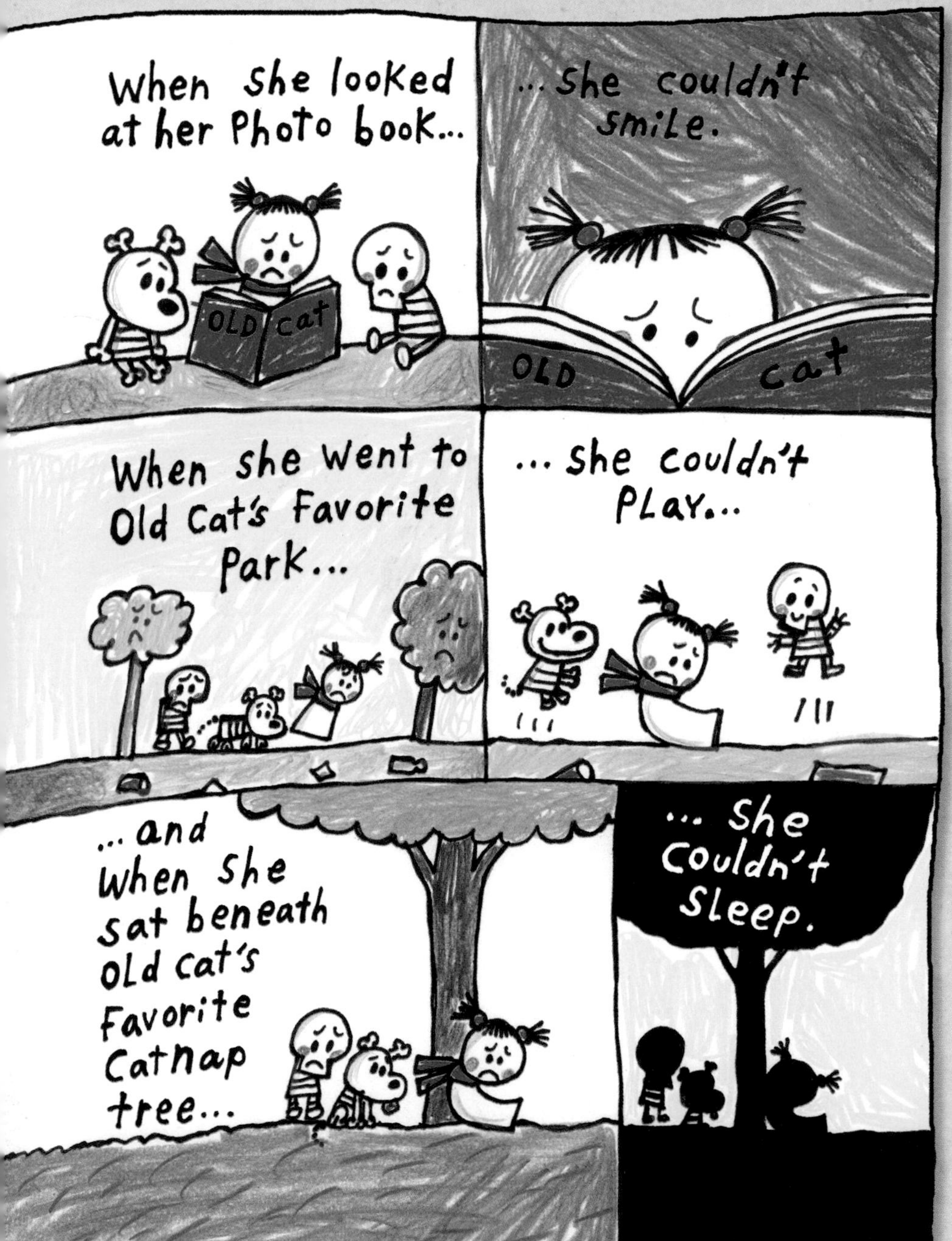
When she looked at her photo book...
OLD cat
...she couldn't smile.
OLD cat
When she went to Old Cat's Favorite park...
...she couldn't play...
...and when she sat beneath Old Cat's Favorite Catnap tree...
...She Couldn't Sleep.

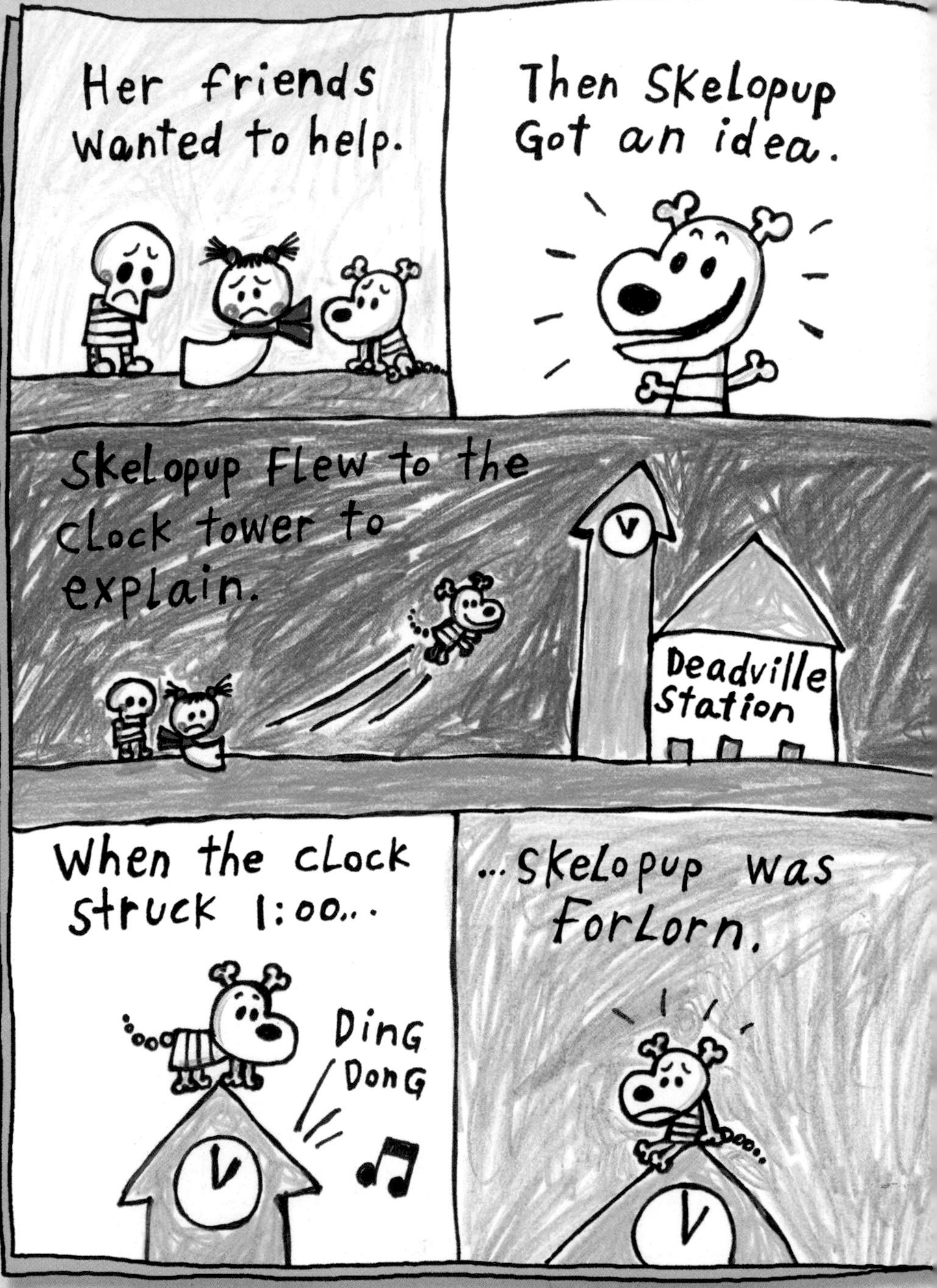
Her friends wanted to help.
Then Skelopup Got an idea.
Skelopup Flew to the clock tower to explain.
Deadville Station
When the clock struck 1:00...
DinG DonG
...Skelopup was Forlorn.

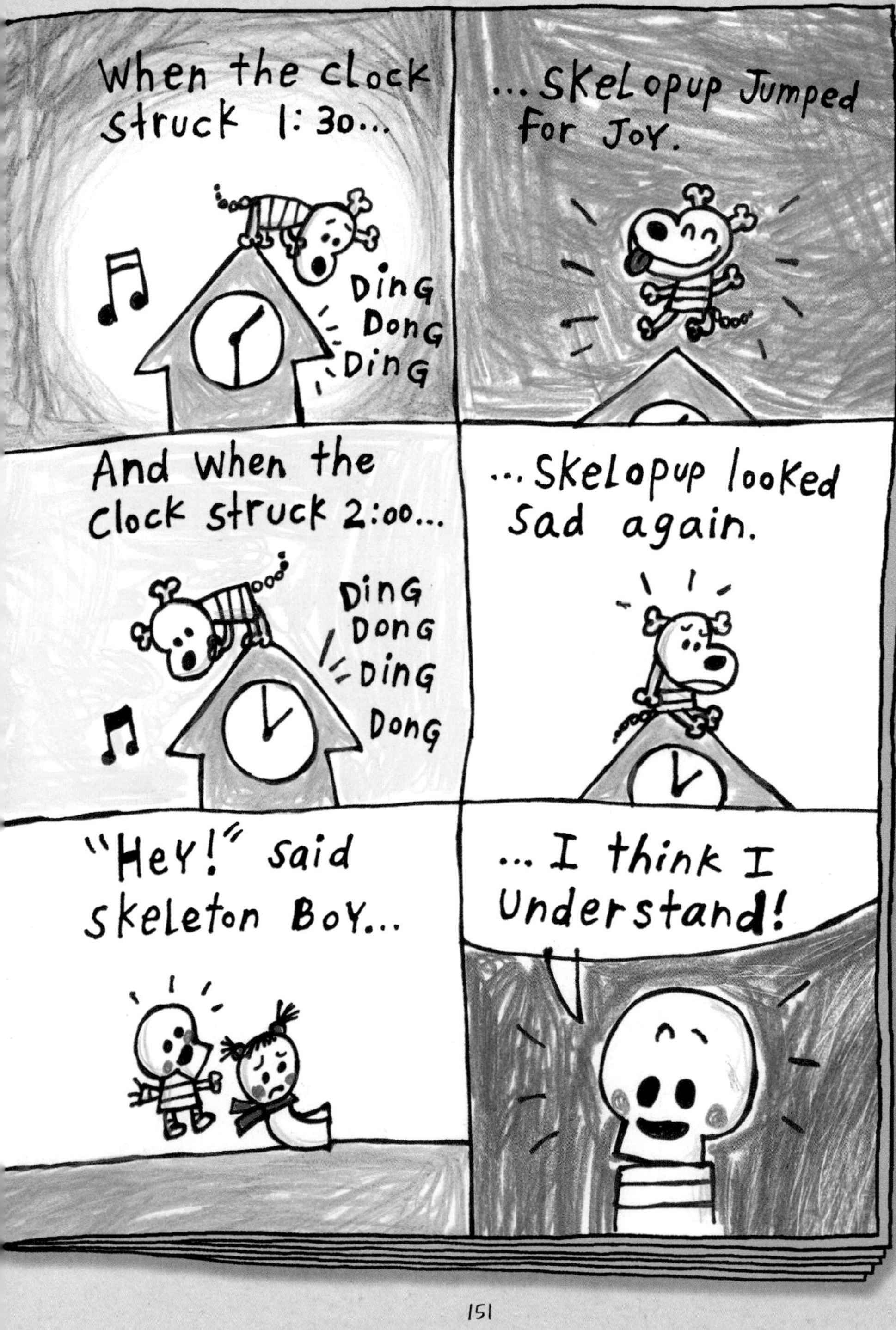

When the clock struck 1:30...
DinG
DonG
DinG
...SkeLopup Jumped for Joy.
And when the clock struck 2:00...
DinG
DonG
DinG
DonG
...SkeLopup looked sad again.
"Hey!" said skeleton Boy...
...I think I Understand!

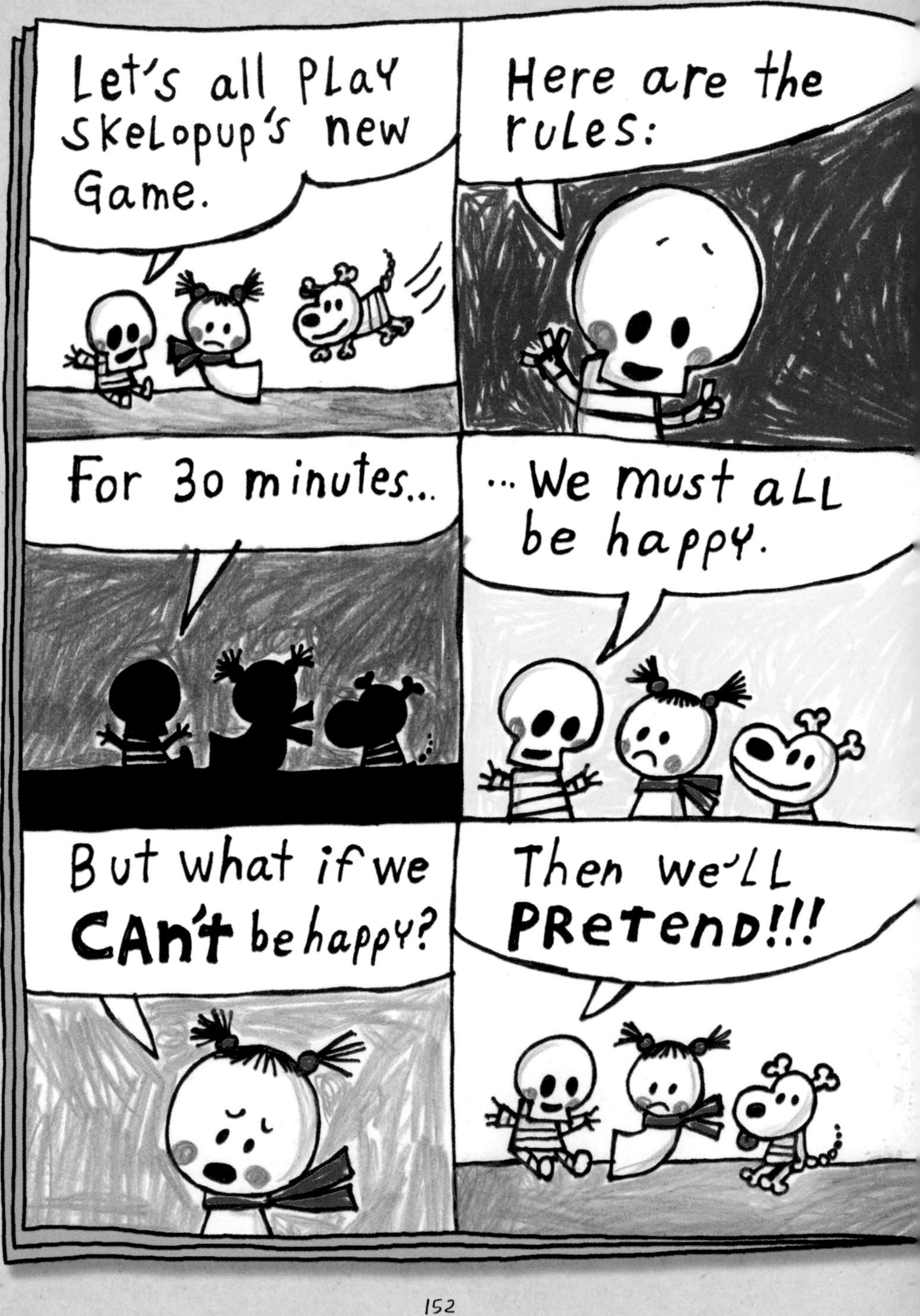
Let's all play Skelopup's new Game.
Here are the rules:
For 30 minutes...
...We must all be happy.
But what if we CAN'T be happy?
Then we'll PRETEND!!!

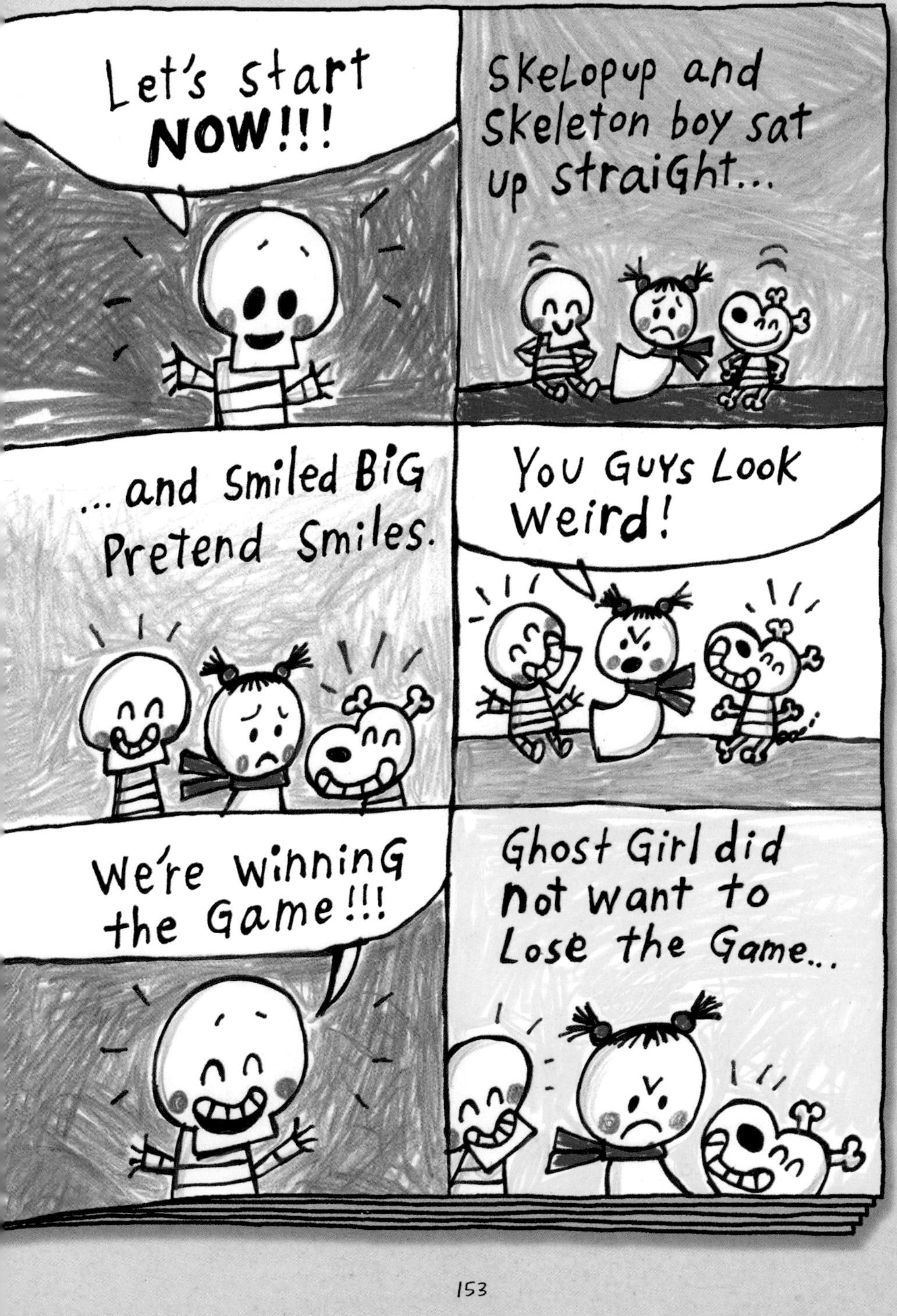
Let's start NOW!!!
Skelopup and Skeleton boy sat up straight...
...and smiled BIG pretend smiles.
You guys look weird!
We're winning the game!!!
Ghost Girl did not want to lose the game...

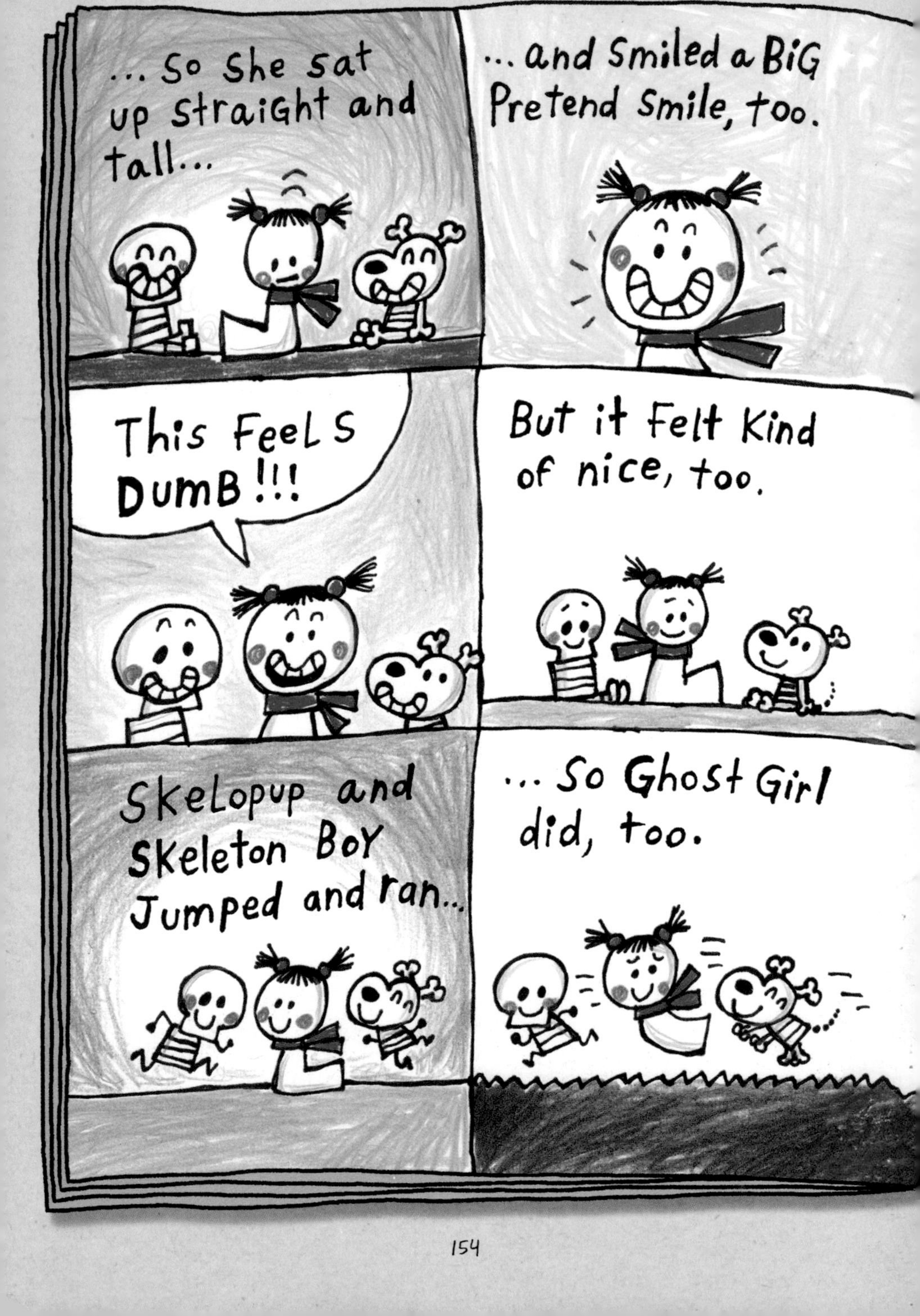
... So She sat up Straight and tall...
... and Smiled a BiG Pretend Smile, too.
This FeeLS DUMB!!!
But it Felt Kind of nice, too.
SkeLopup and Skeleton BoY Jumped and ran...
... So Ghost Girl did, too.

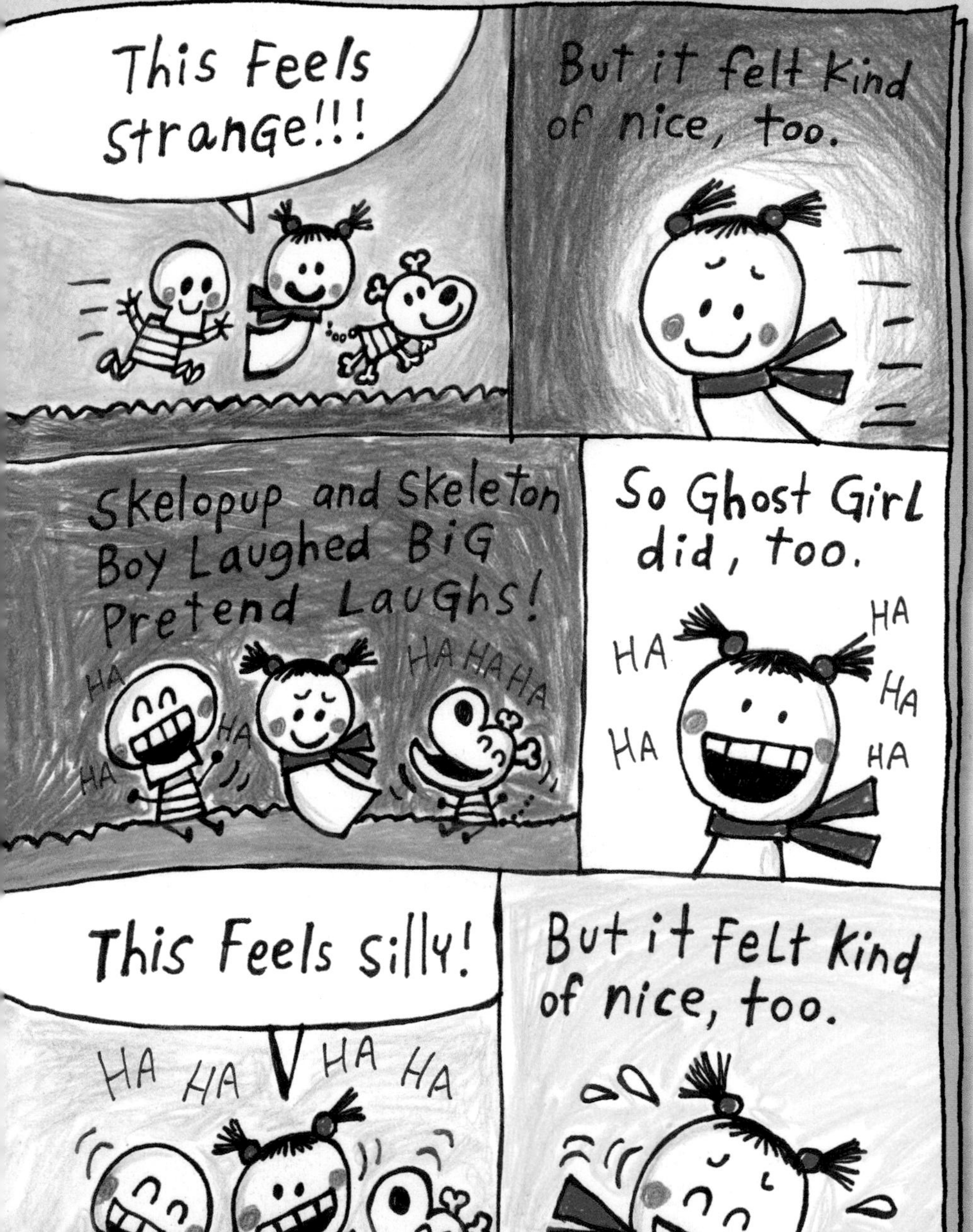
This Feels Strange!!!
But it felt kind of nice, too.
Skelopup and Skeleton Boy Laughed BIG Pretend Laughs!
HA
HA
HA
HA HA HA HA
So Ghost Girl did, too.
HA
HA
HA
HA
HA
HA
This Feels silly!
HA HA HA HA
But it felt kind of nice, too.

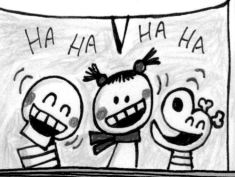

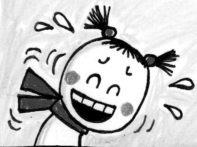

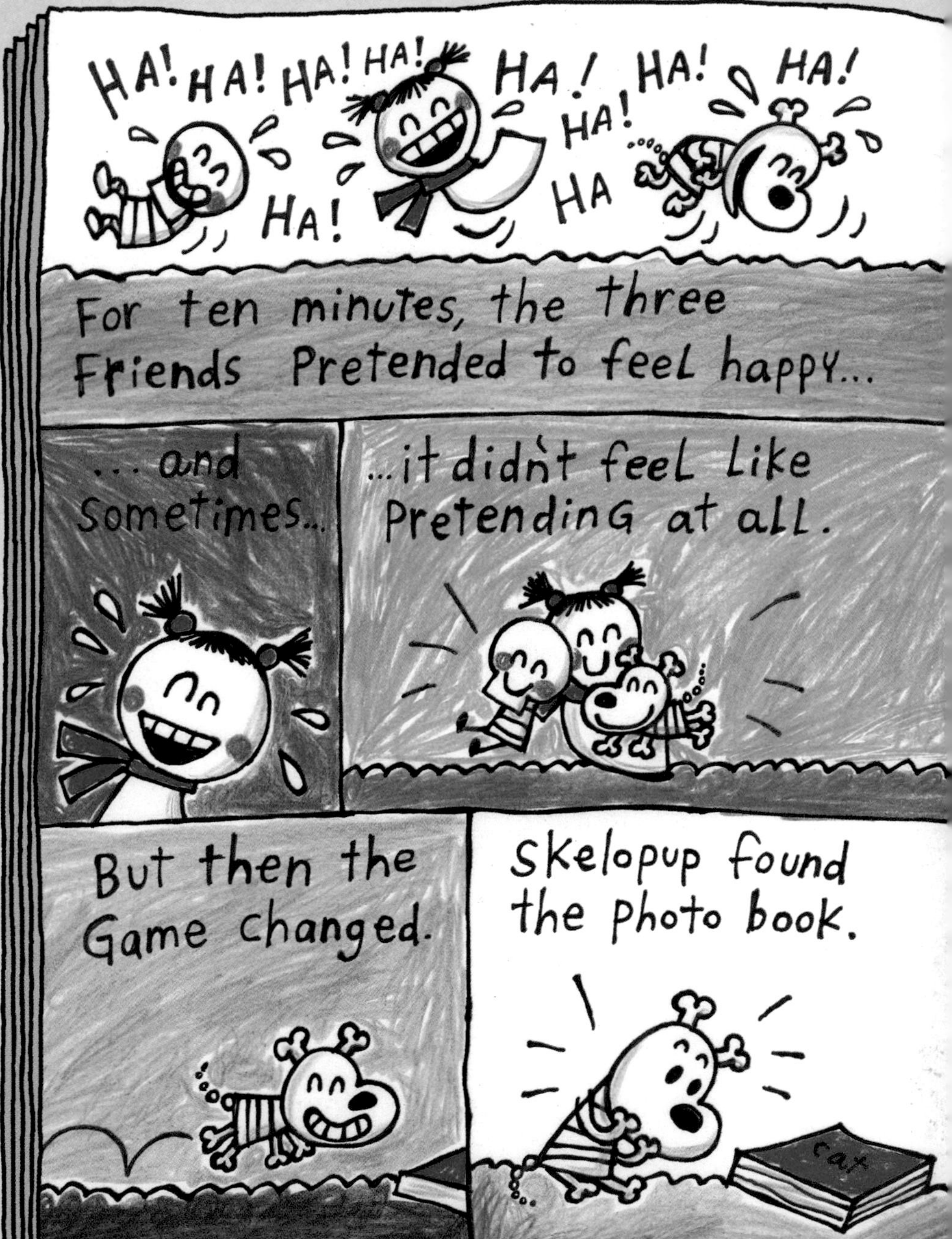

HA! HA! HA! HA! HA! HA! HA! HA! HA! HA
For ten minutes, the three Friends Pretended to feel happy...
... and Sometimes...
...it didn't feel Like Pretending at all.
But then the Game changed.
Skelopup found the photo book.
cat

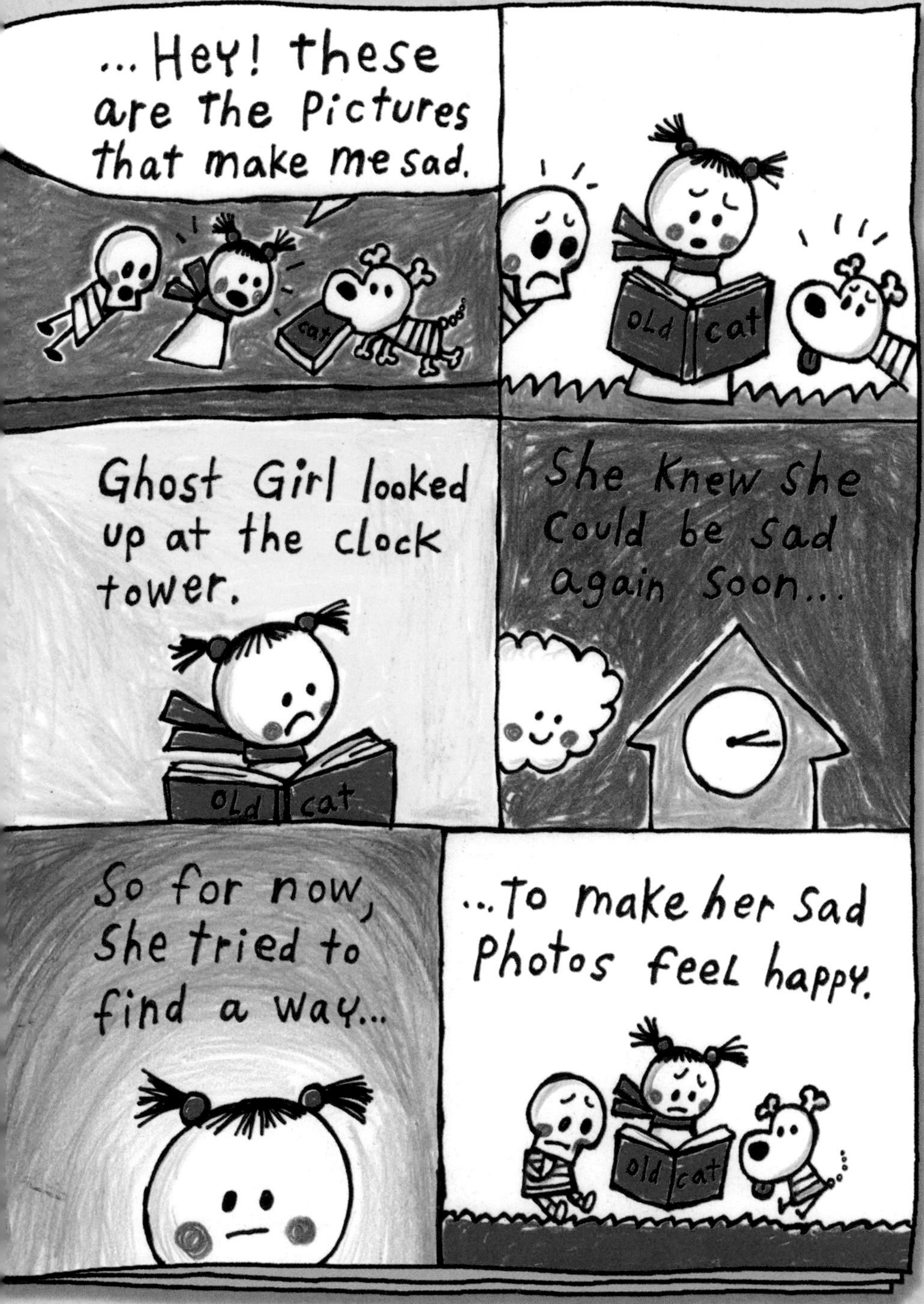

...Hey! these are the Pictures that make me sad.
OLD cat
Ghost Girl looked up at the clock tower.
OLD cat
She knew she Could be Sad again Soon...
So for now, She tried to find a way...
...To make her Sad Photos feel happy.
old cat

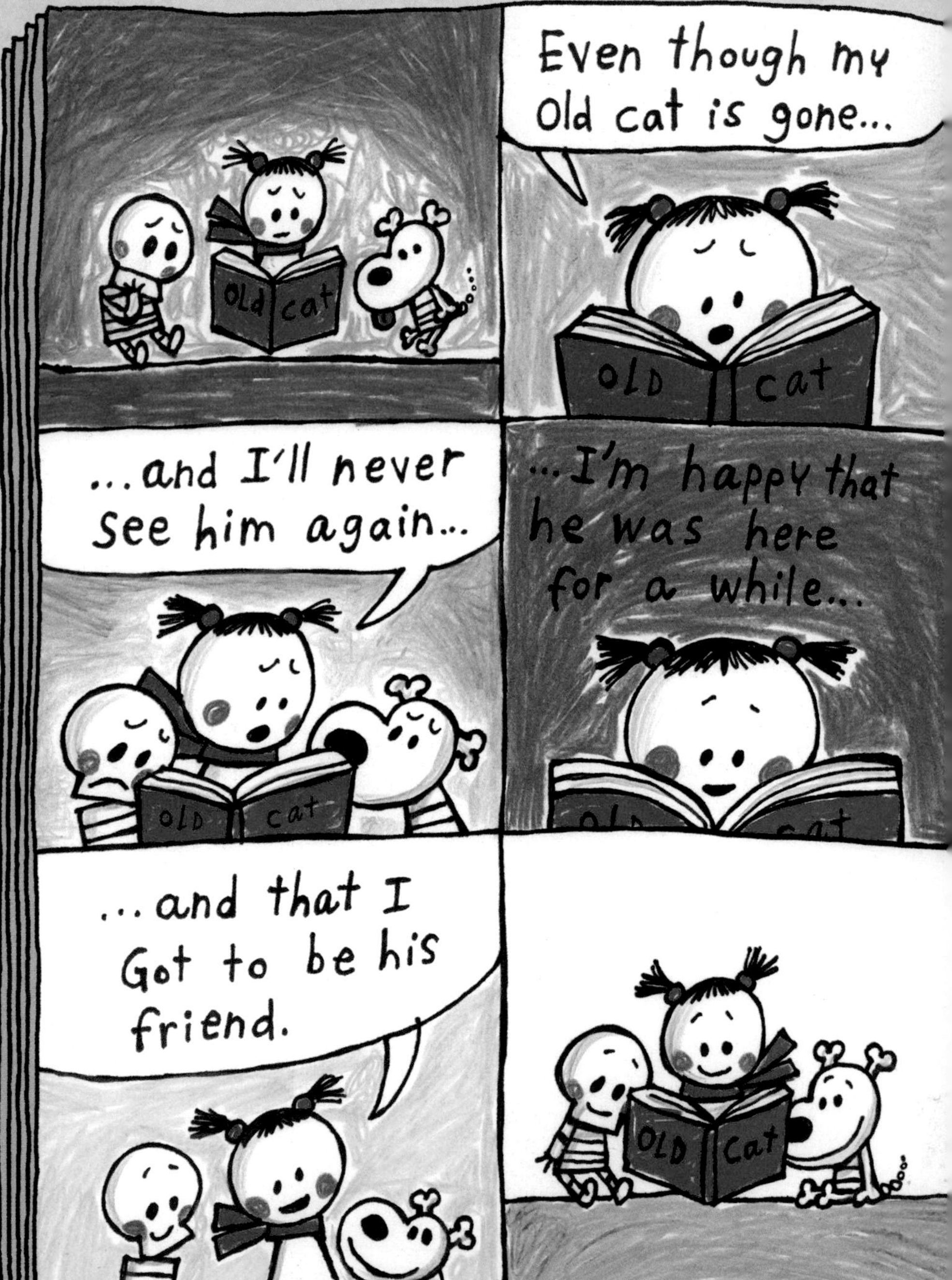
OLD cat
Even though my Old cat is gone...
OLD cat
...and I'll never see him again...
OLD cat
...I'm happy that he was here for a while...
...and that I Got to be his friend.
OLD Cat

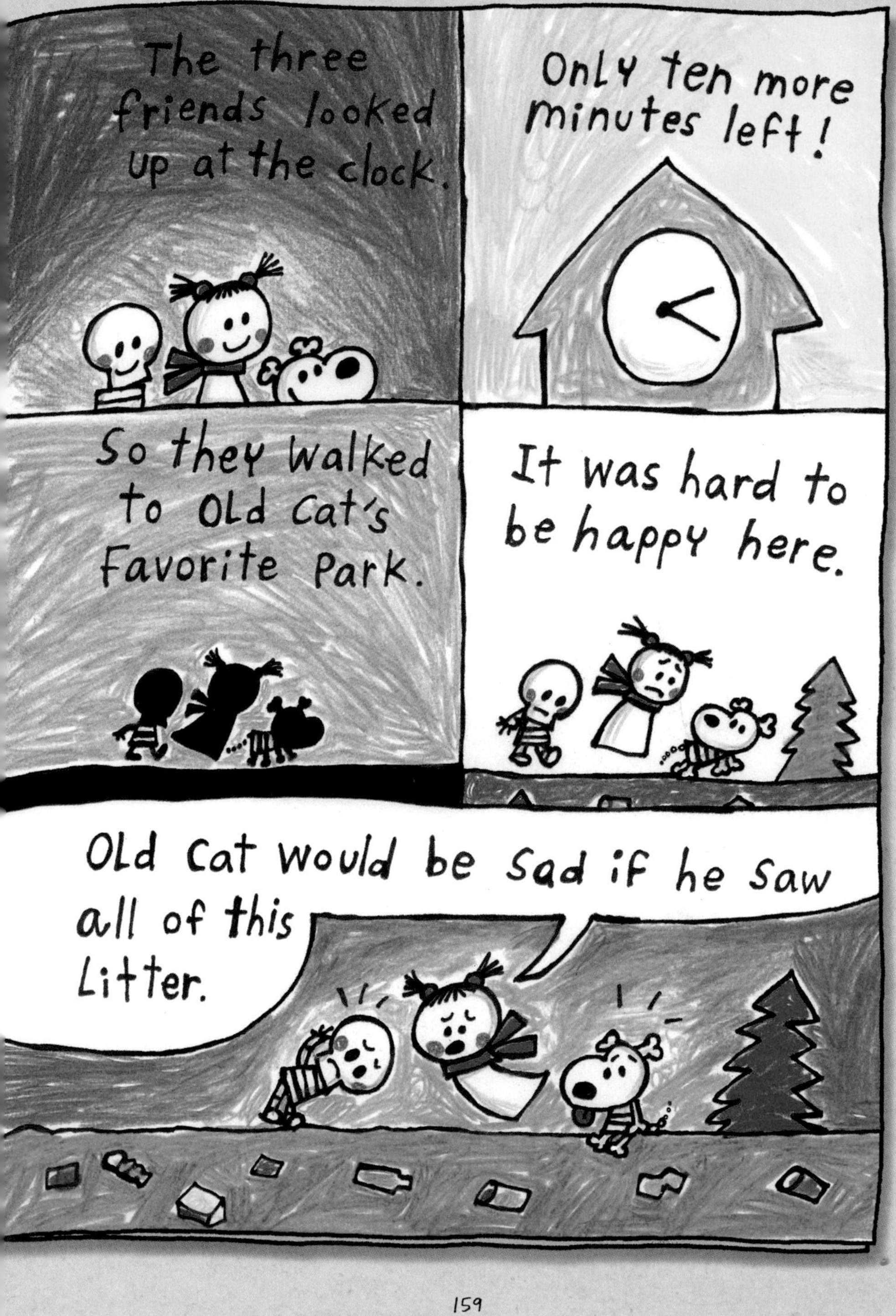
The three friends looked up at the clock.
Only ten more minutes left!
So they walked to Old Cat's Favorite Park.
It was hard to be happy here.
Old Cat would be sad if he saw all of this Litter.

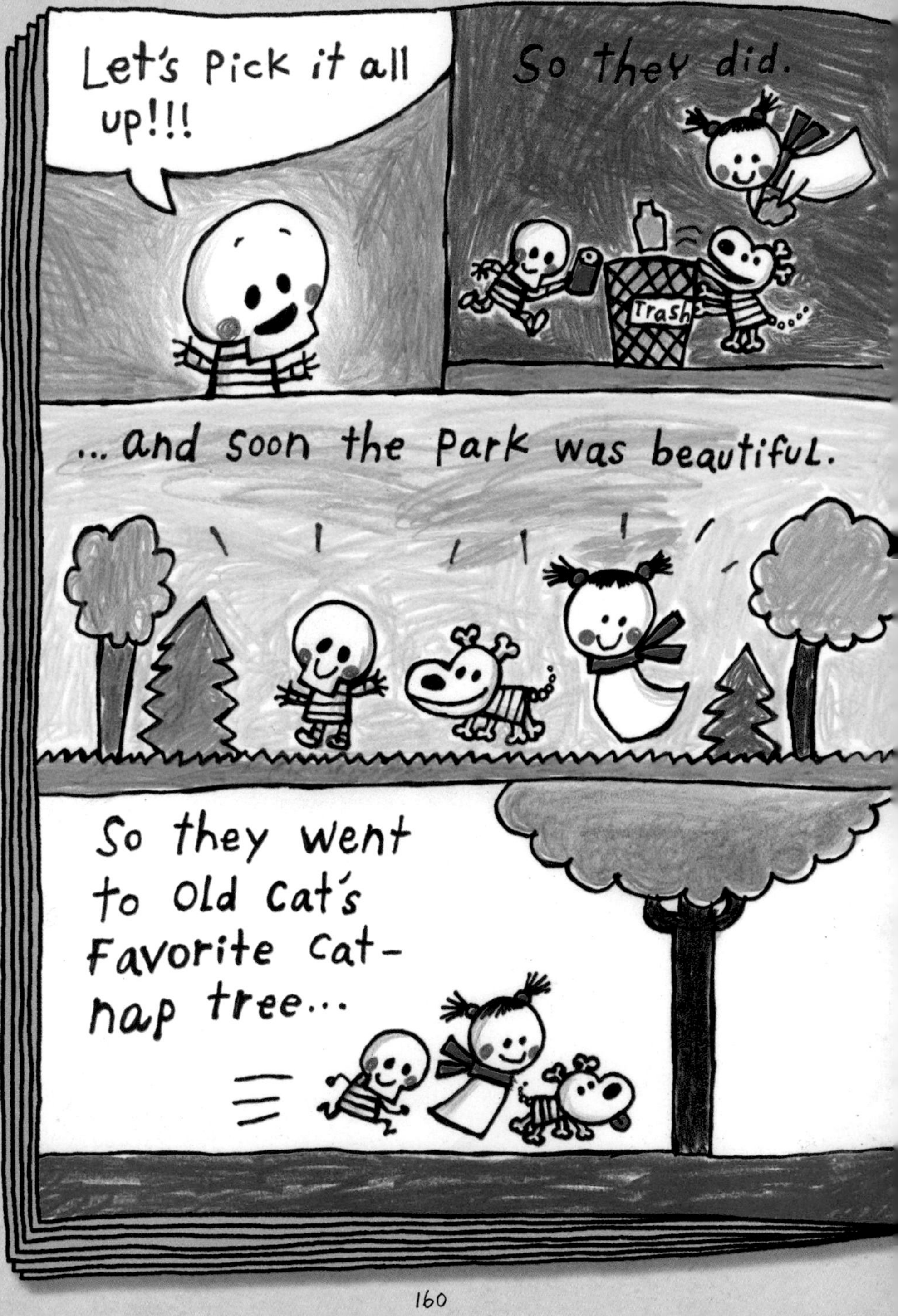

Let's Pick it all up!!!
So they did.
Trash
...and soon the Park was beautiful.
So they went to Old Cat's Favorite Cat-nap tree...

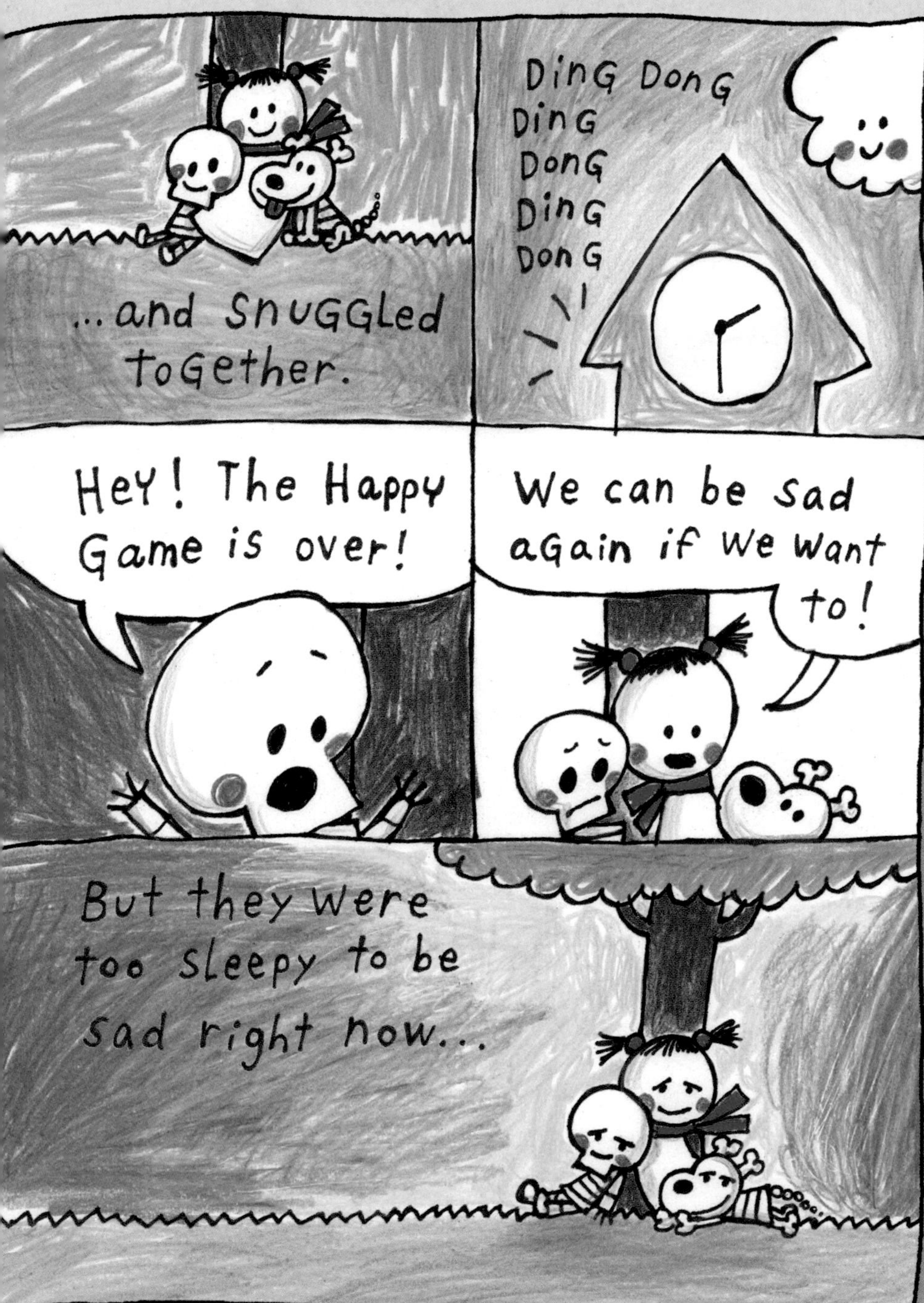
...and SNUGGLed toGether.
DinG DonG
DinG
DonG
DinG
DonG
Hey! The Happy Game is over!
We can be sad again if we want to!
But they were too sleepy to be sad right now...

...So they slept and slept and slept.

THE END

ABOut the Author/ILLustrator:

POPPY

Poppy Likes to draw and ~~tell~~ make up Ghost Stories and think about StuFF. she hopes we can still Get a ice cream machine even thouGh she is Lactose intolerant because it will be worth it if everybody else can be happy. Maybe it can make sorbet, too, which is good if you get used to it. But not Lemon which is gross.

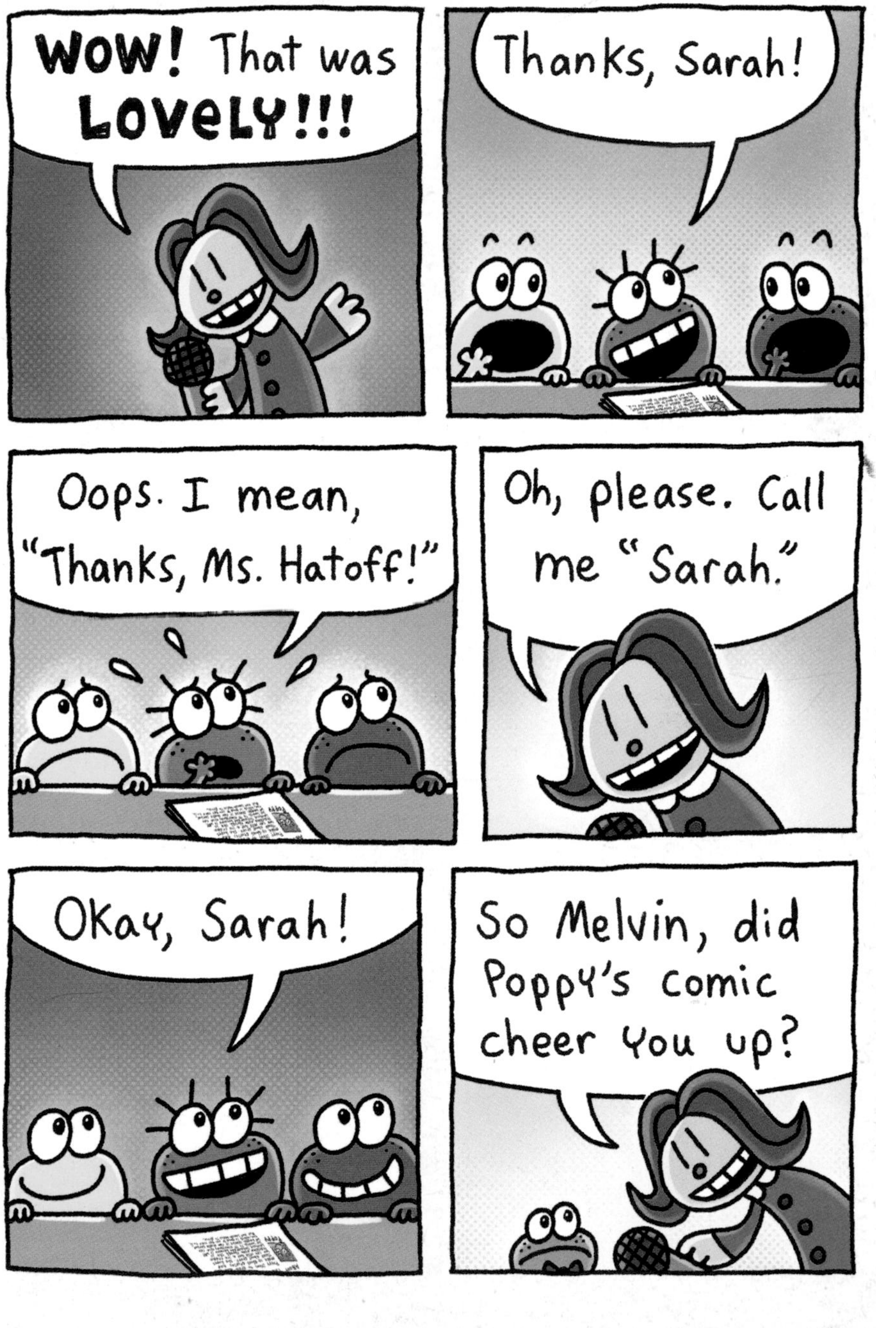
WOW! That was LOVELY!!!
Thanks, Sarah!
Oops. I mean, "Thanks, Ms. Hatoff!"
Oh, please. Call me "Sarah."
Okay, Sarah!
So Melvin, did Poppy's comic cheer you up?

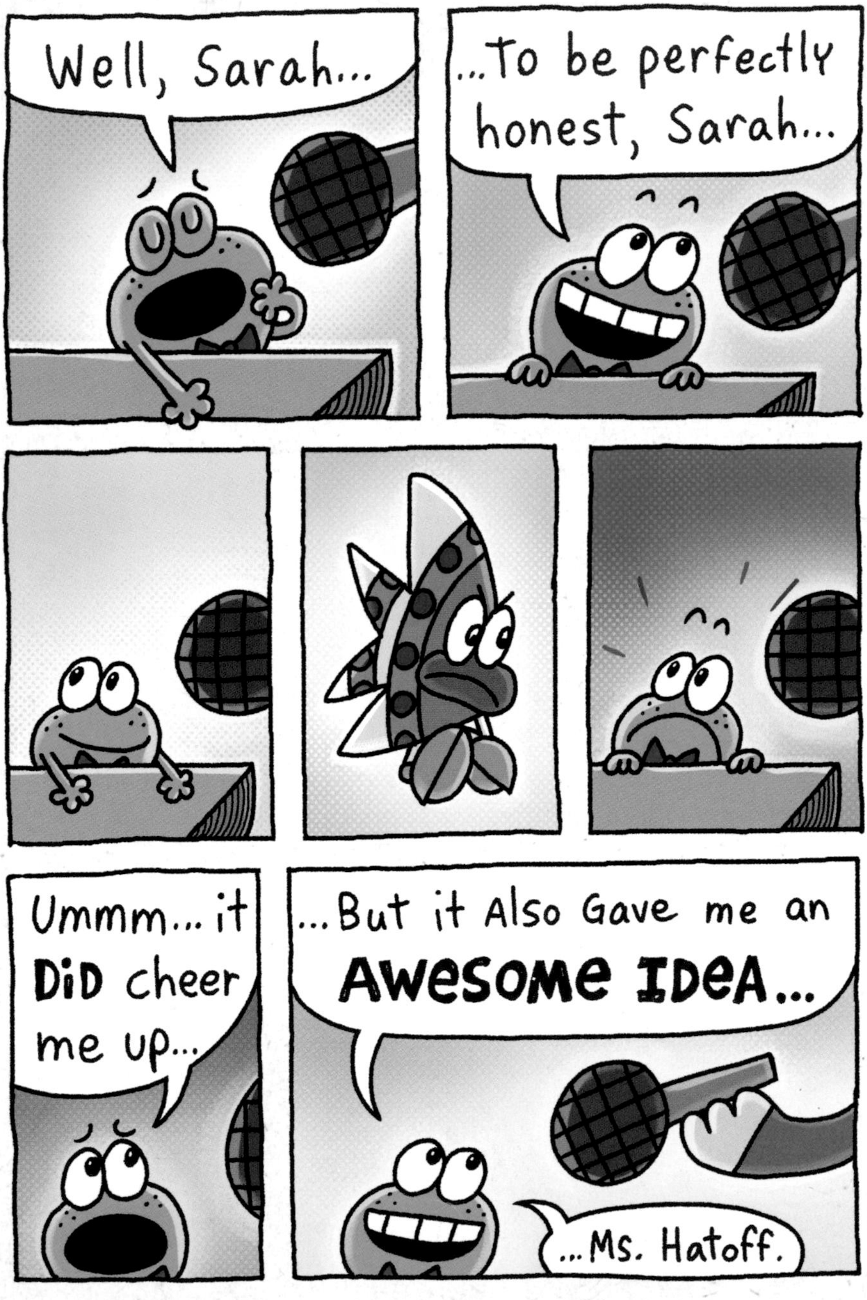
Well, Sarah...
...To be perfectly honest, Sarah...
Ummm... it DiD cheer me up...
...But it Also Gave me an AWESOME IDEA...
...Ms. Hatoff.

CHAPTER 11

Melvin's Awesome Idea

BABY FROG SQUAD
TRANSFROGGERS
Skelepup and the Happy Game
By Poppy

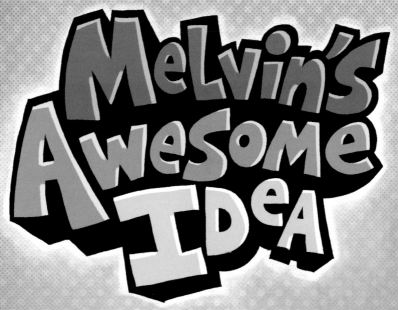

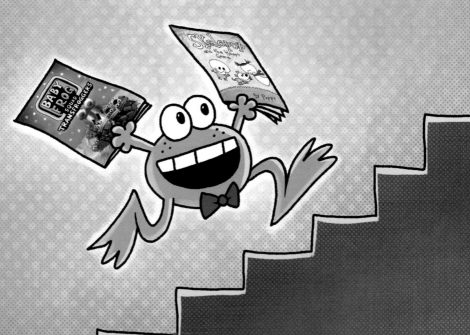

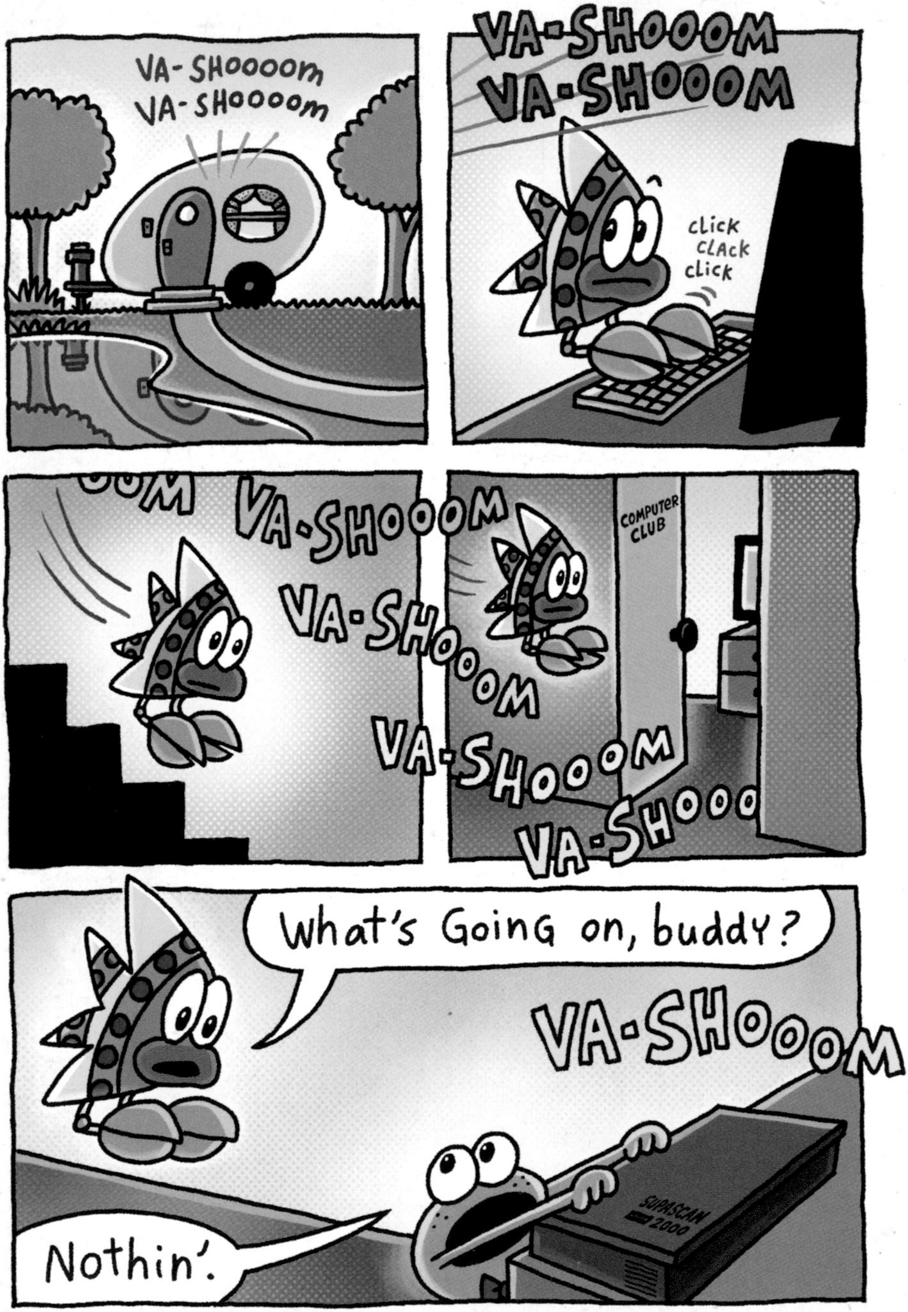
VA-SHOOOOM
VA-SHOOOOM
VA-SHOOOM
VA-SHOOOM
CLICK
CLACK
CLICK
OOM
VA-SHOOOM
VA-SHOOOM
COMPUTER CLUB
VA-SHOOOM
VA-SHOOO
What's Going on, buddy?
VA-SHOOOM
SUPASCAN 2000
Nothin'.

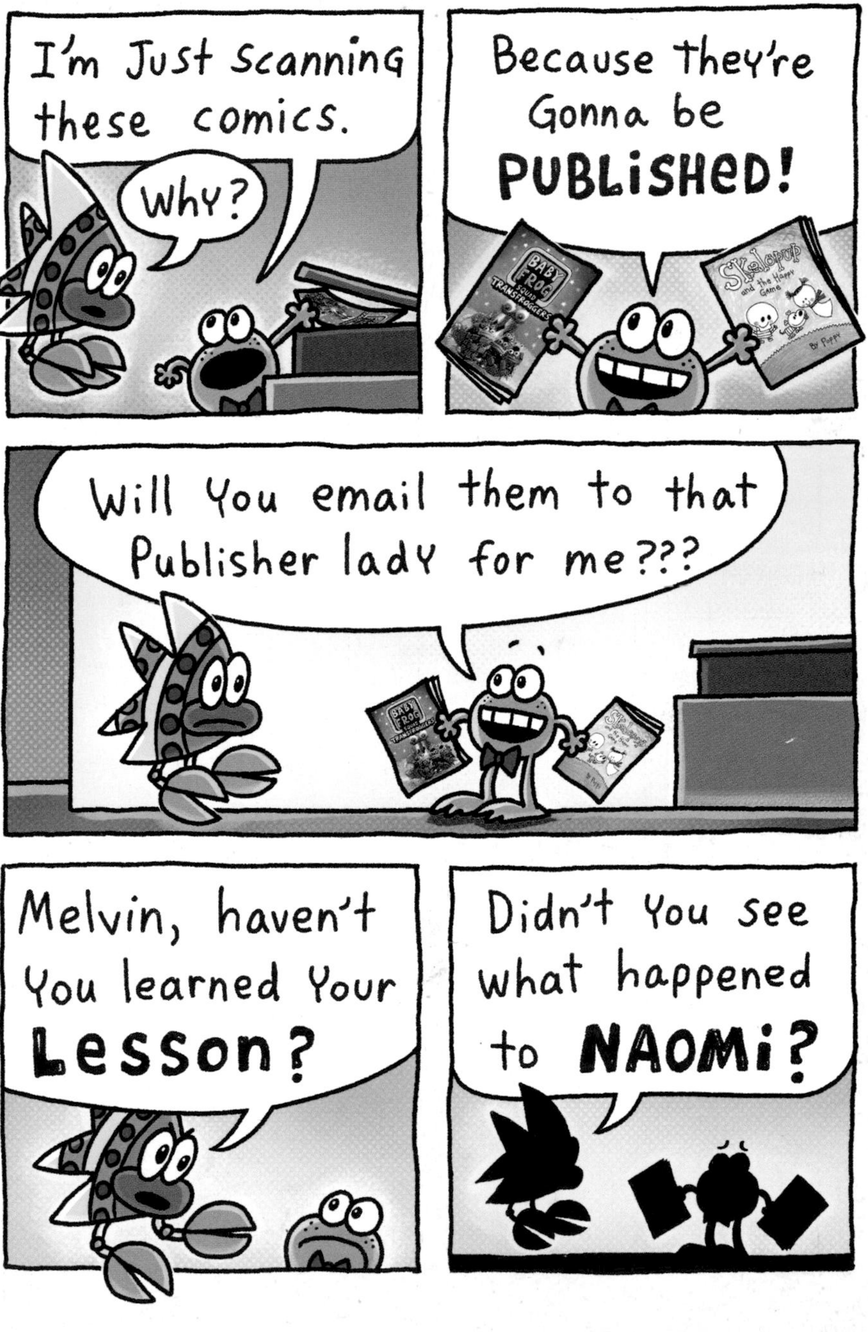
I'm Just Scanning these comics.
Why?
Because they're Gonna be PUBLISHED!
BABY FROG SQUAD TRANSFROGGERS
Skelopup and the Happy Game
By Poppy
Will You email them to that Publisher lady for me???
Melvin, haven't You learned Your Lesson?
Didn't You see what happened to NAOMi?

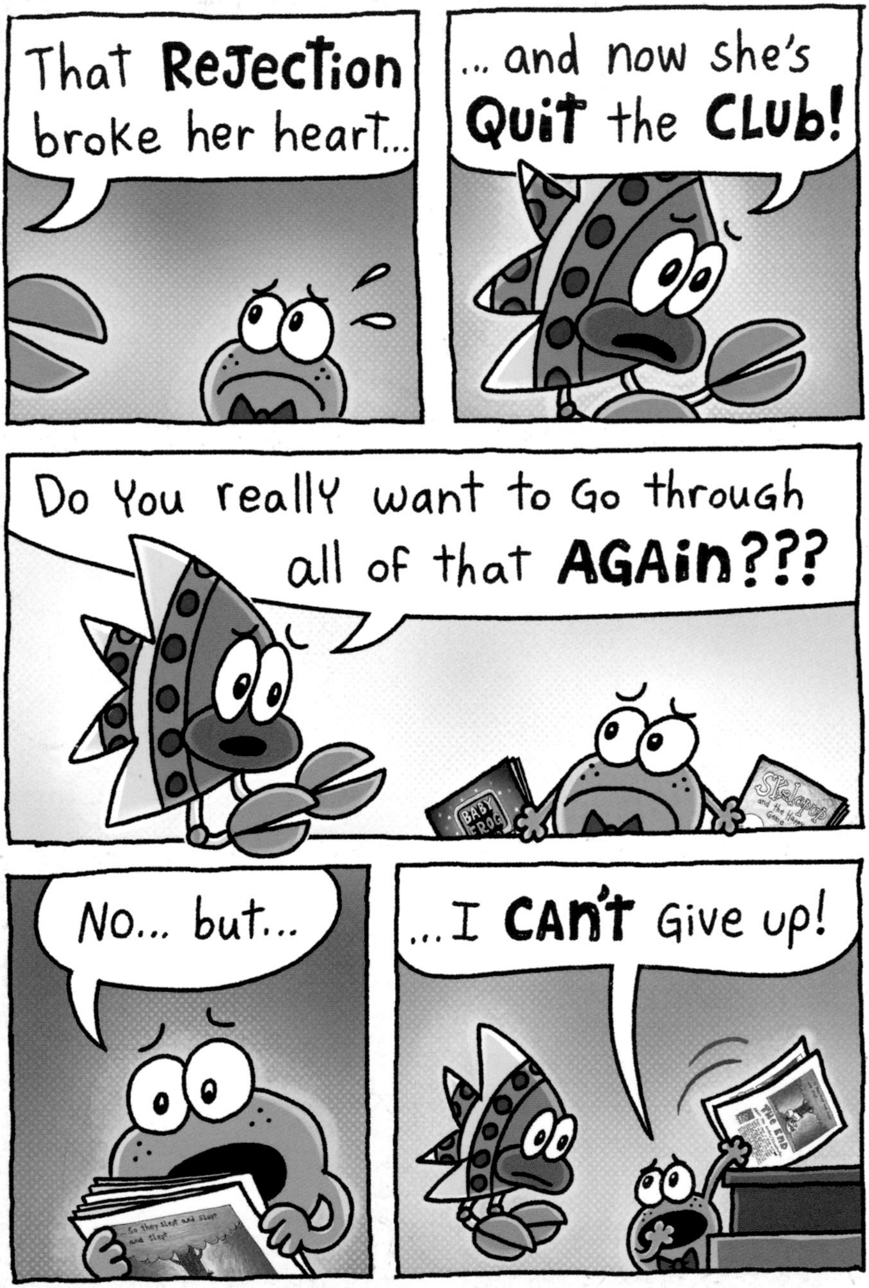
That REJECTION broke her heart...
... and now she's QUIT the CLUB!
Do You really want to Go through all of that AGAIN???
BABY FROG
NO... but...
...I CAN'T Give up!

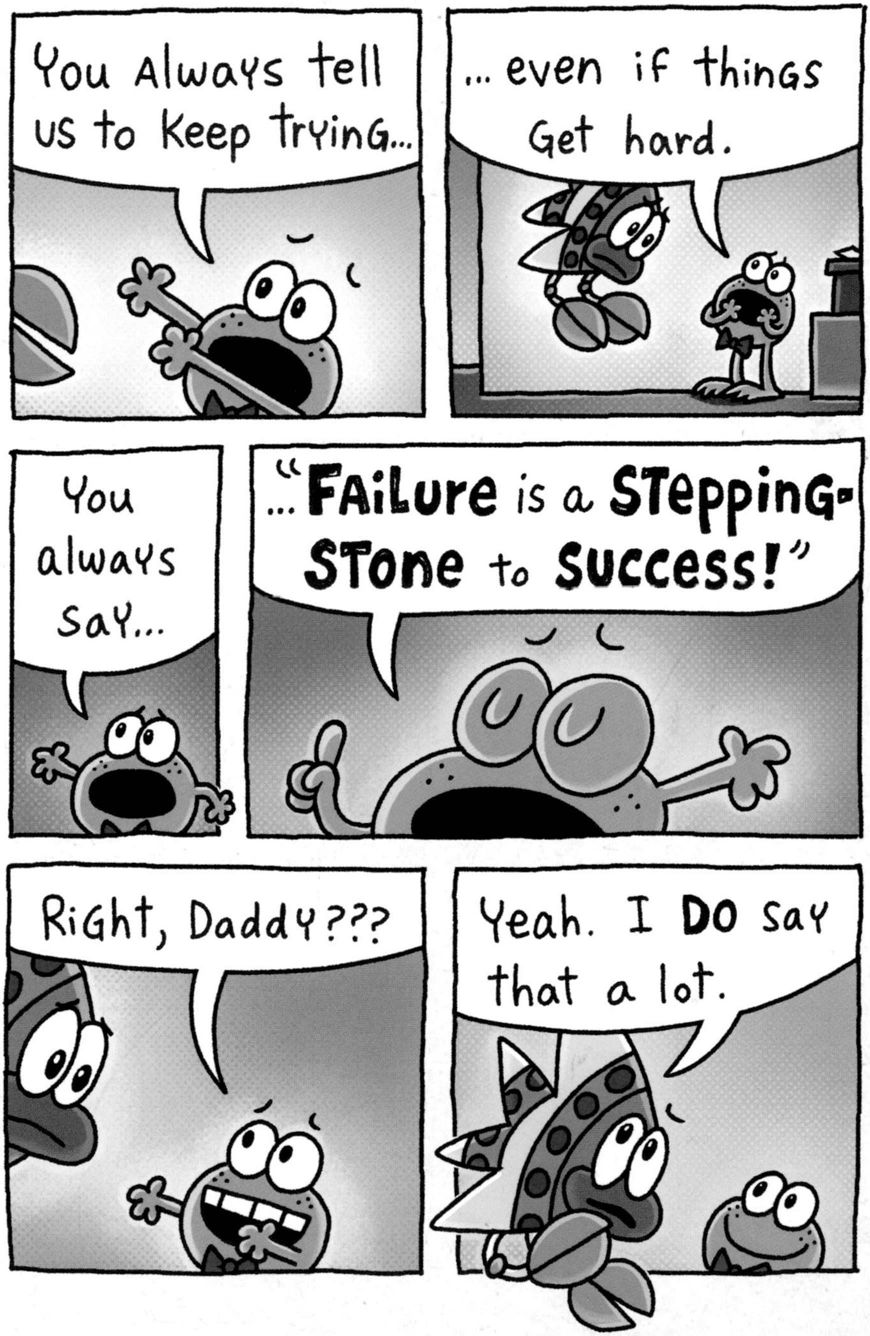
You Always tell us to Keep trying...
... even if things Get hard.
You always say...
..."FAILure is a STeppinG-STone to SUCCESS!"
RiGht, Daddy???
Yeah. I DO say that a lot.

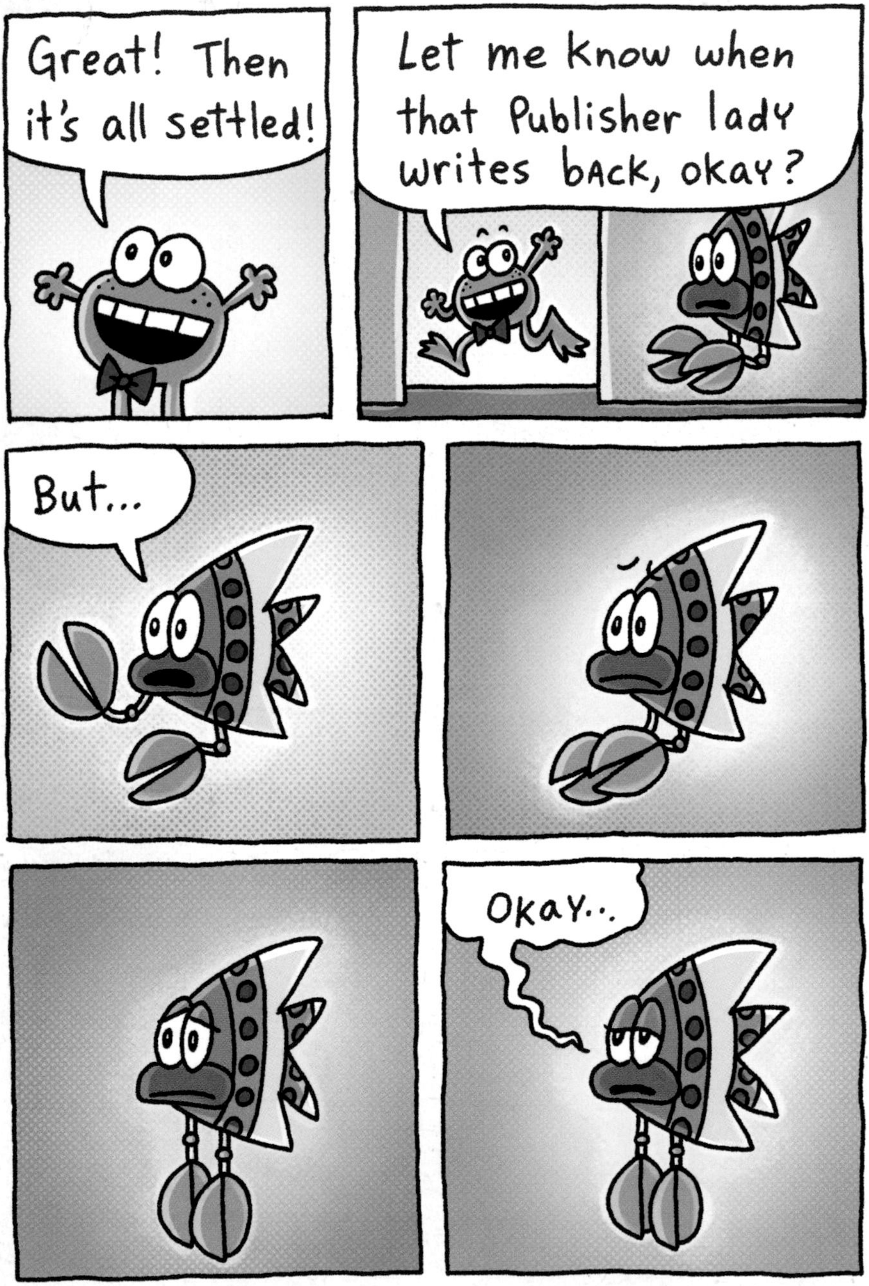
Great! Then it's all settled!
Let me know when that Publisher lady writes back, okay?
But...
Okay...

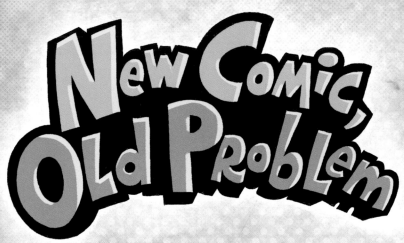

CHAPTER 12

New Comic, Old Problem

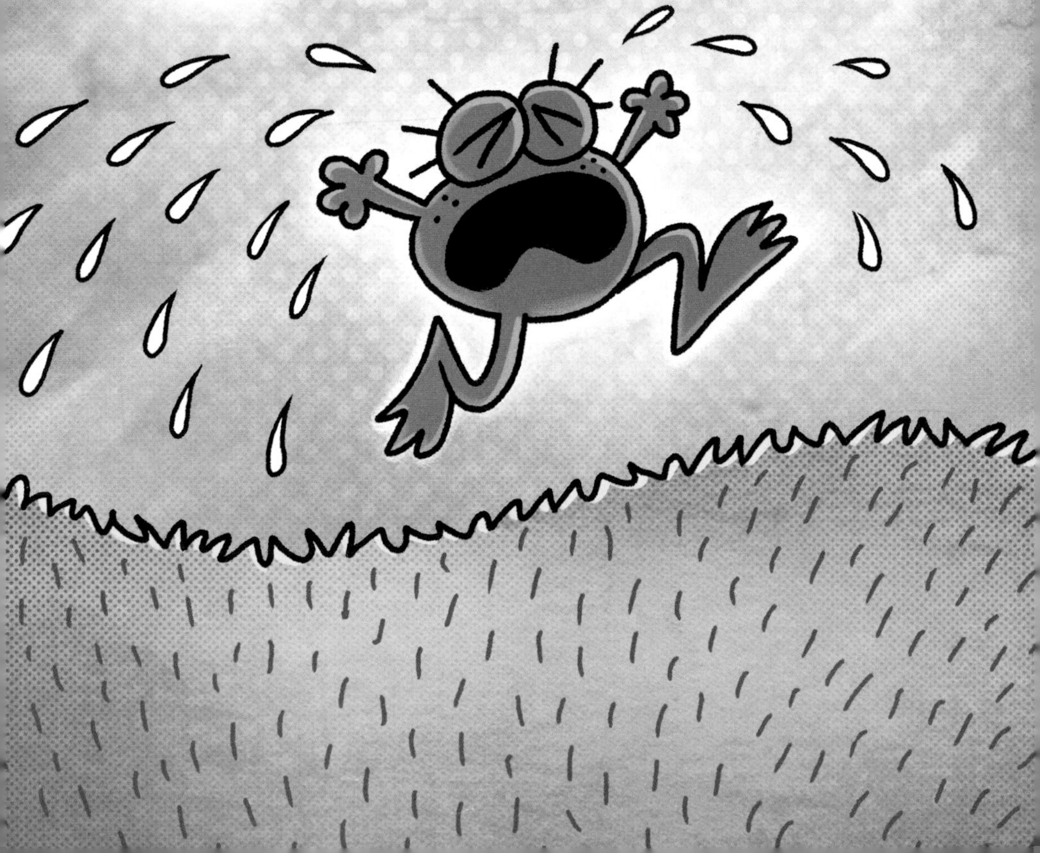

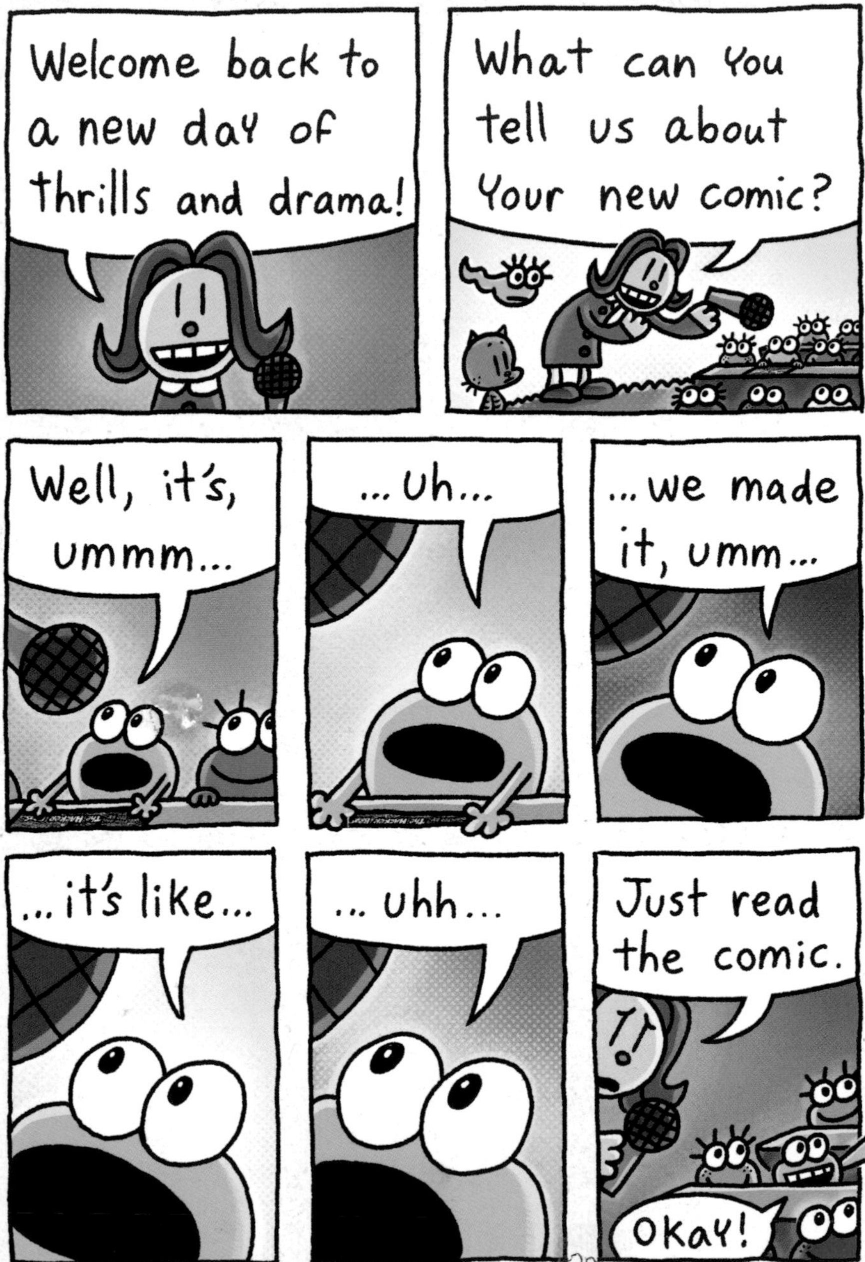
Welcome back to a new day of thrills and drama!
What can you tell us about your new comic?
Well, it's, ummm...
...uh...
...we made it, umm...
...it's like...
...uhh...
Just read the comic.
Okay!

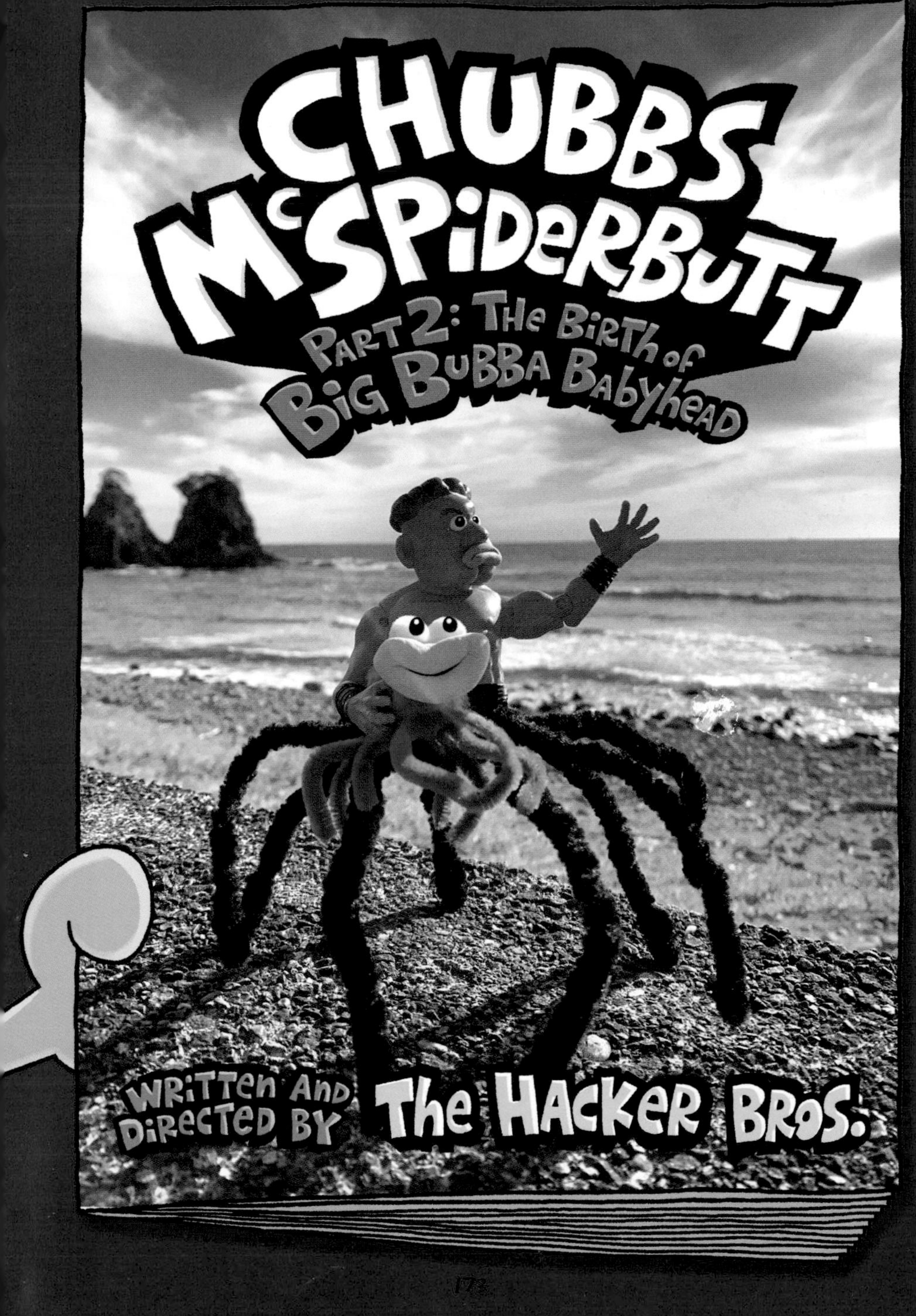
CHUBBS McSPIDERBUTT
PART 2: THE BIRTH of BIG BUBBA BABYHEAD
WRITTEN AND DIRECTED BY
THE HACKER BROS.

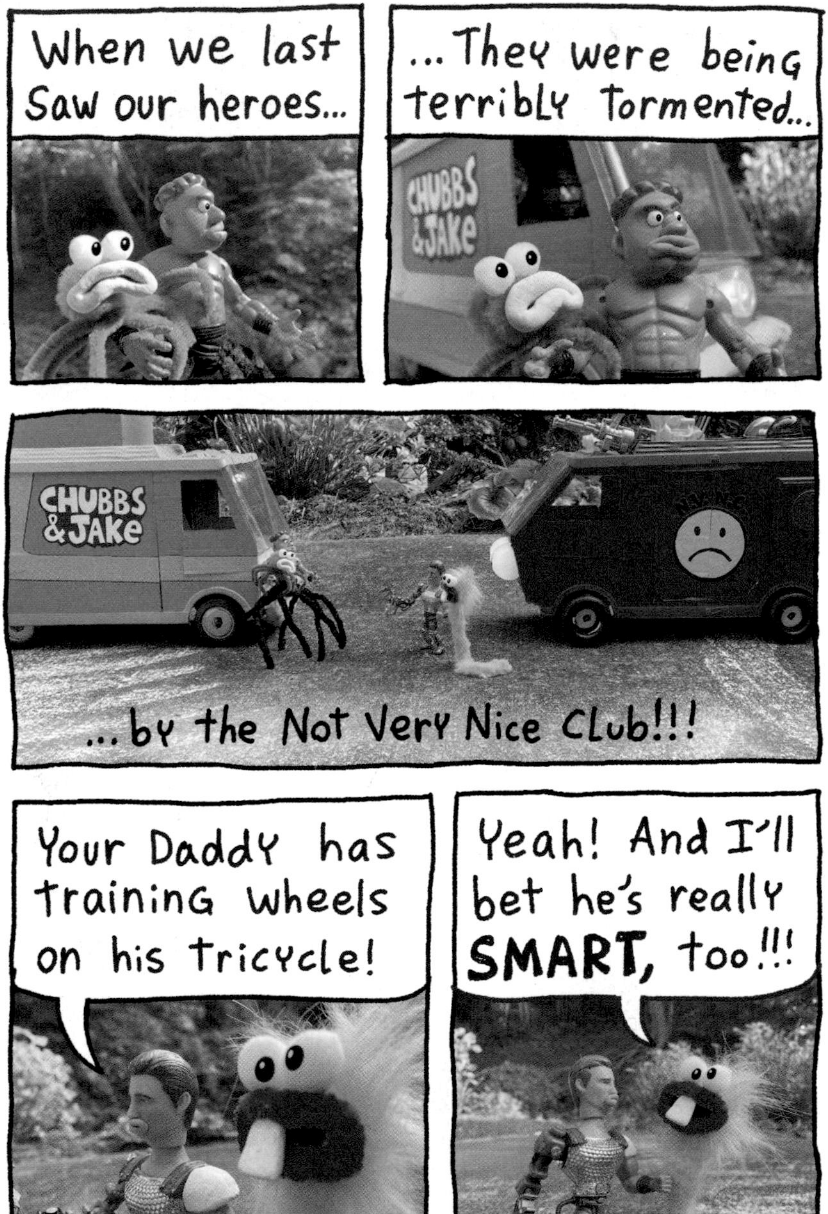
When we last Saw our heroes...
...They were being terribly tormented...
CHUBBS & JAKE
CHUBBS & JAKE
...by the Not Very Nice Club!!!
Your Daddy has training wheels on his tricycle!
Yeah! And I'll bet he's really **SMART,** too!!!

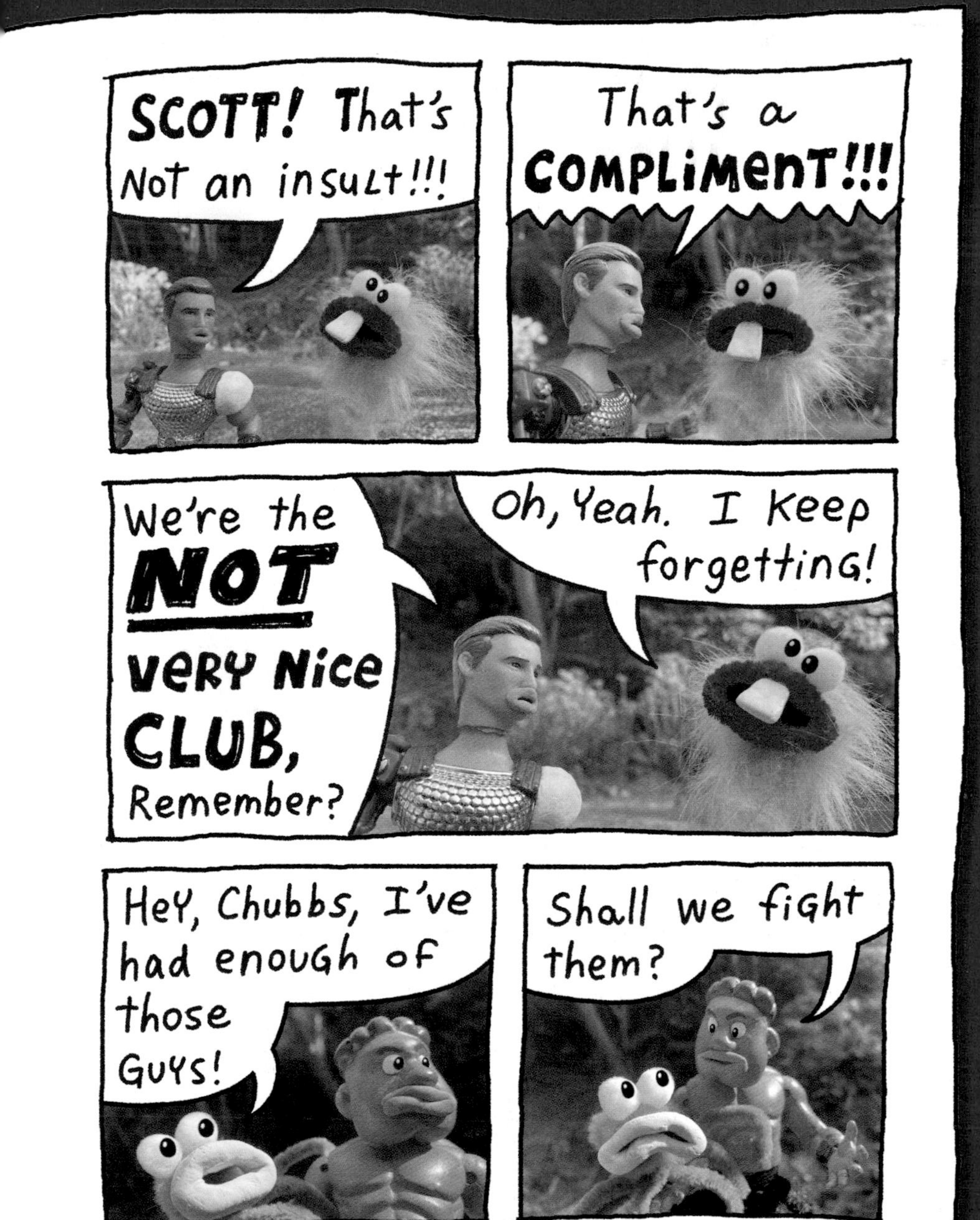
SCOTT! That's Not an insult!!!
That's a COMPLIMENT!!!
We're the NOT very Nice CLUB, Remember?
Oh, Yeah. I Keep forgetting!
Hey, Chubbs, I've had enough of those Guys!
Shall we fight them?

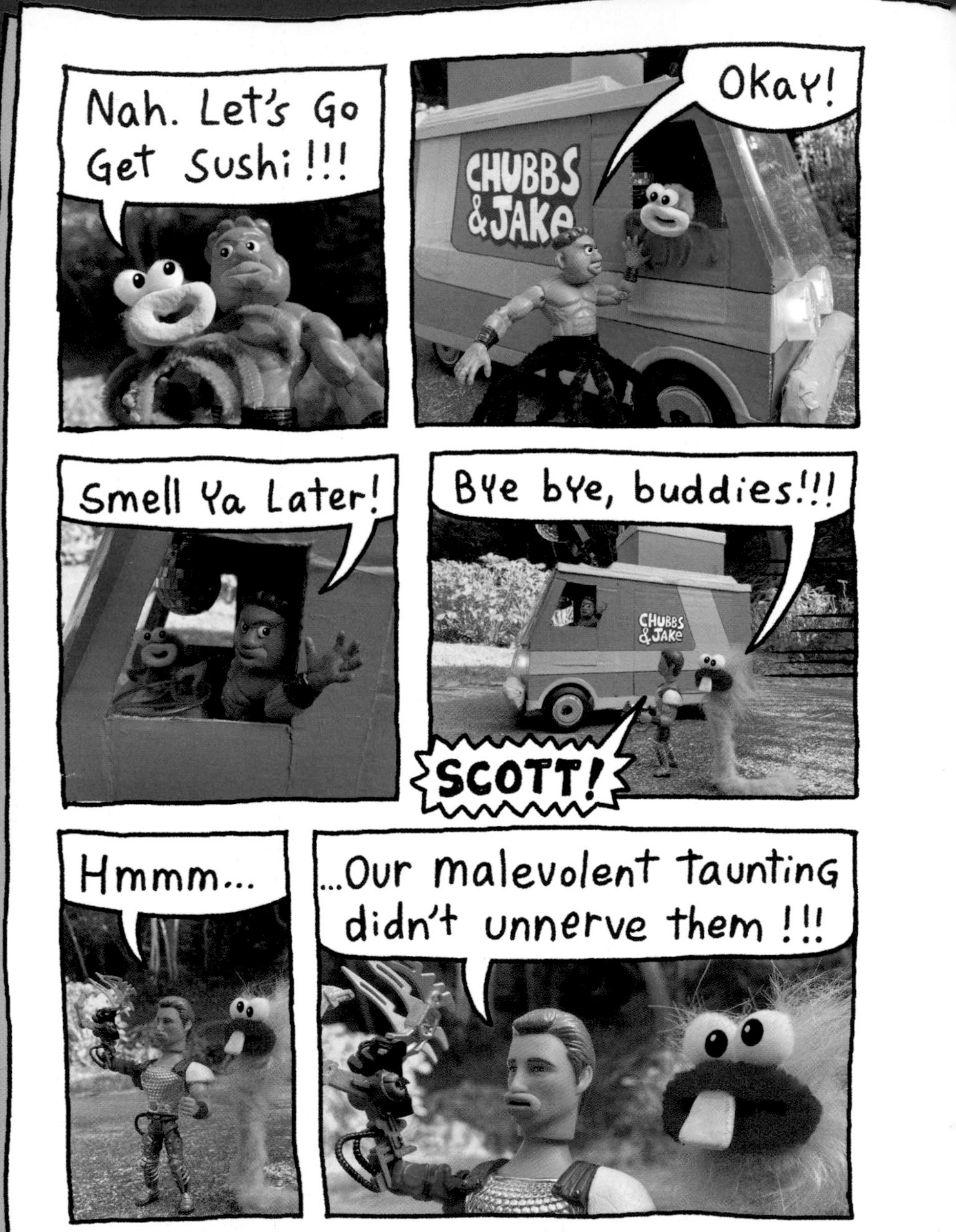

Nah. Let's Go Get Sushi!!!
Okay!
CHUBBS & JAKE
Smell Ya Later!
Bye bye, buddies!!!
CHUBBS & JAKE
SCOTT!
Hmmm...
...Our malevolent taunting didn't unnerve them!!!

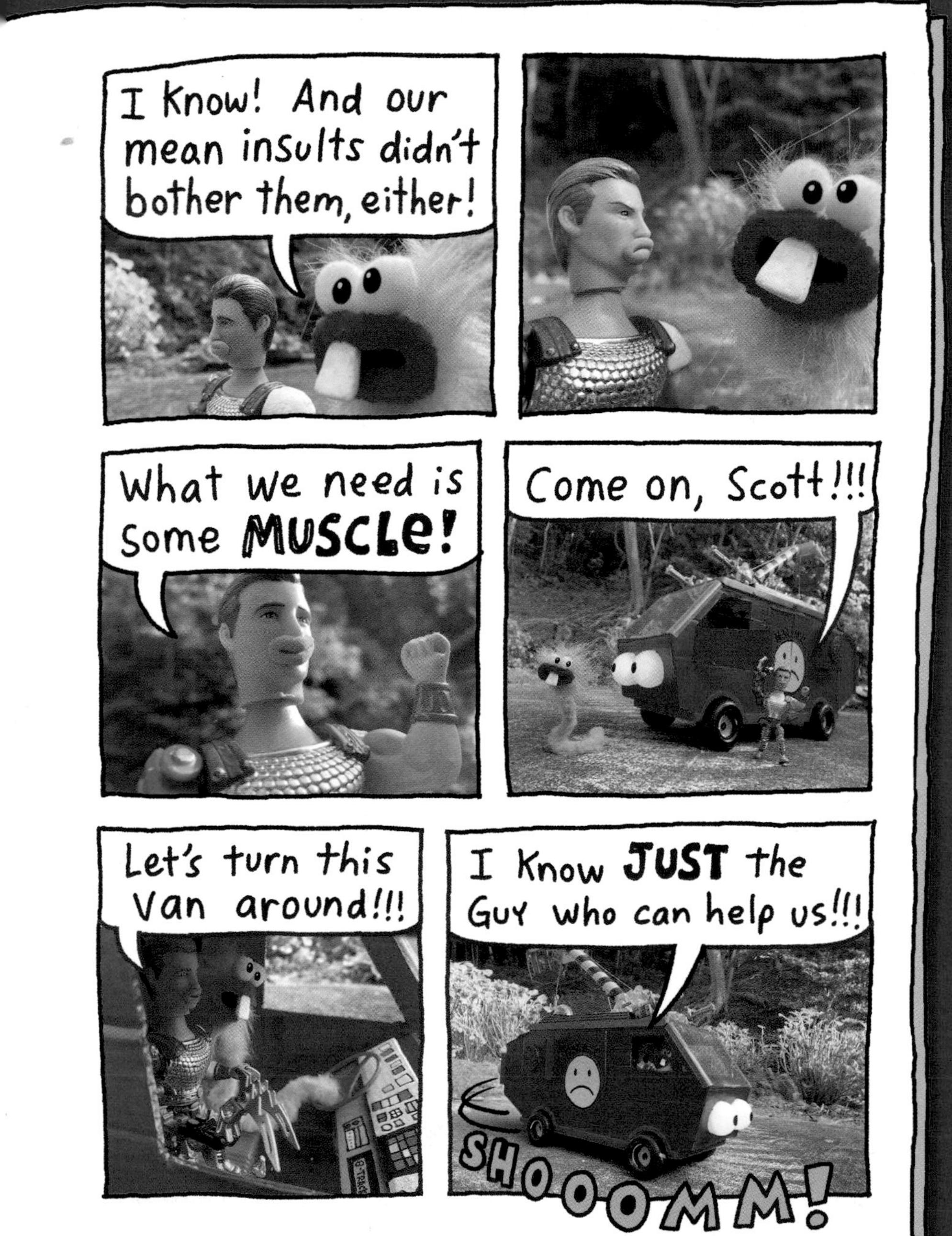
I Know! And our mean insults didn't bother them, either!
What we need is some MUSCLE!
Come on, Scott!!!
Let's turn this Van around!!!
I Know JUST the Guy who can help us!!!
SHOOOMM!

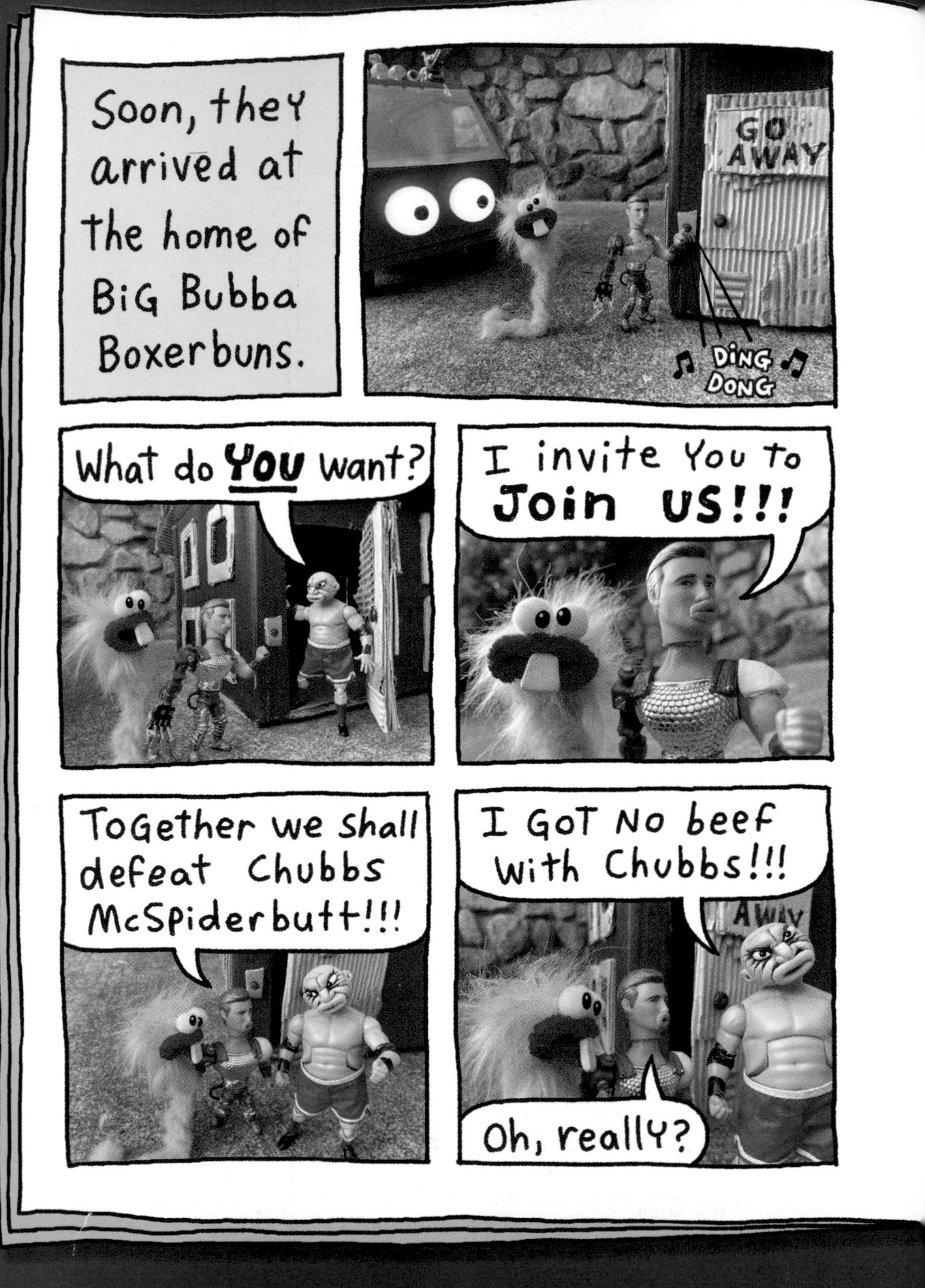
Soon, they arrived at the home of Big Bubba Boxerbuns.
GO AWAY
DING DONG
What do YOU want?
I invite You to Join US!!!
Together we shall defeat Chubbs McSpiderbutt!!!
I GOT No beef With Chubbs!!!
AWAY
Oh, really?

Well he said Your Gym shorts and dress shoes look silly together.

No he didn't!

Shhh!

Oh, he **Did**, did he?

So Chubbs McSpiderbutt thinks he can insult MY Fashion Sense...

...and Get AWAY with it ?????

CHUBBS iS Goin' Down!

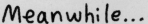

Meanwhile...

Mmm! This sushi is GOOD!!!

Are You Gonna eat Your uni?

It's all Yours, Little buddy!

Thanks!

Hey Jake, do You think we will ever be **FAMOUS?**

You mean like Spider-Man?

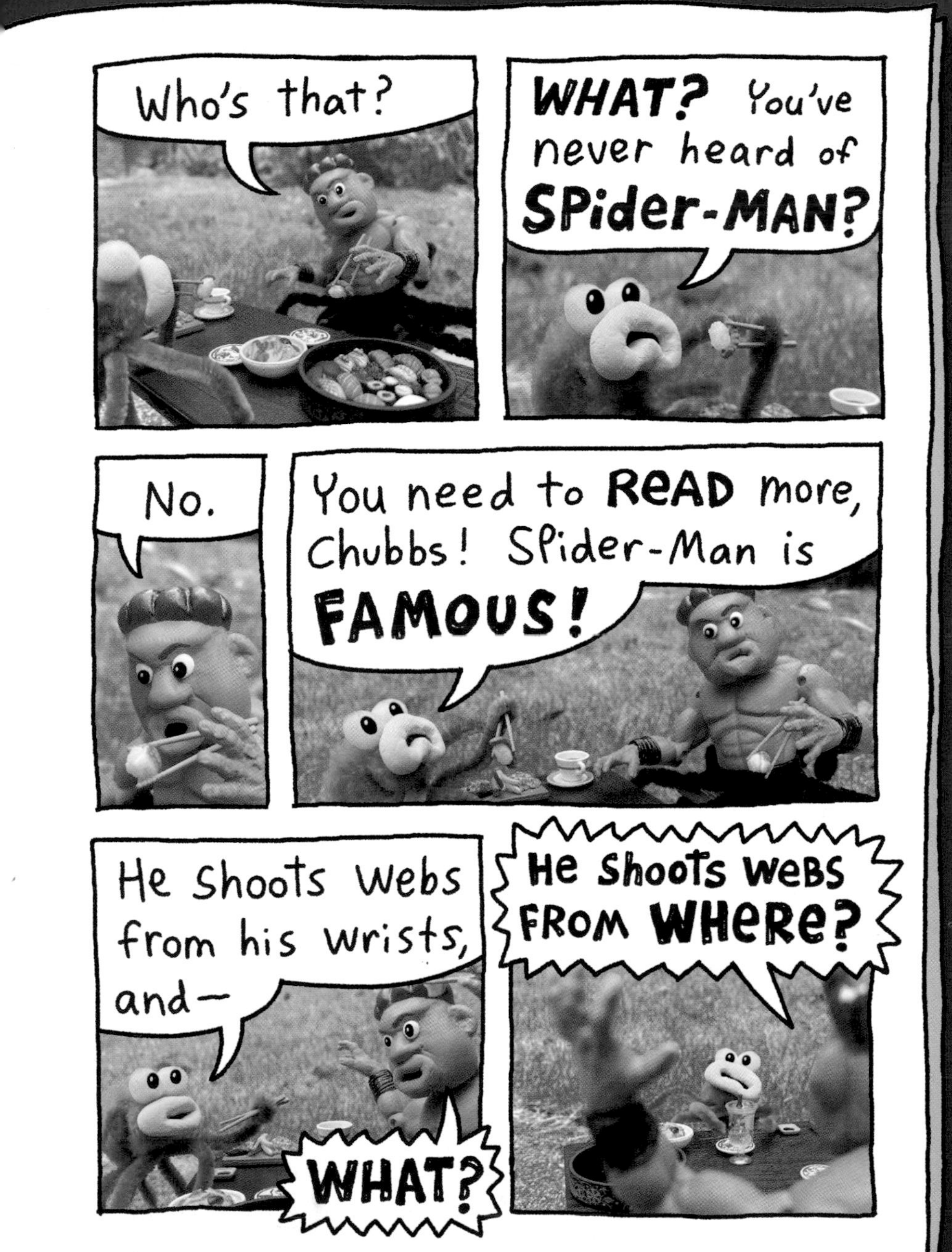
Who's that?
WHAT? You've never heard of SPIDER-MAN?
No.
You need to READ more, Chubbs! Spider-Man is FAMOUS!
He shoots webs from his wrists, and—
WHAT?
HE SHOOTS WEBS FROM WHERE?

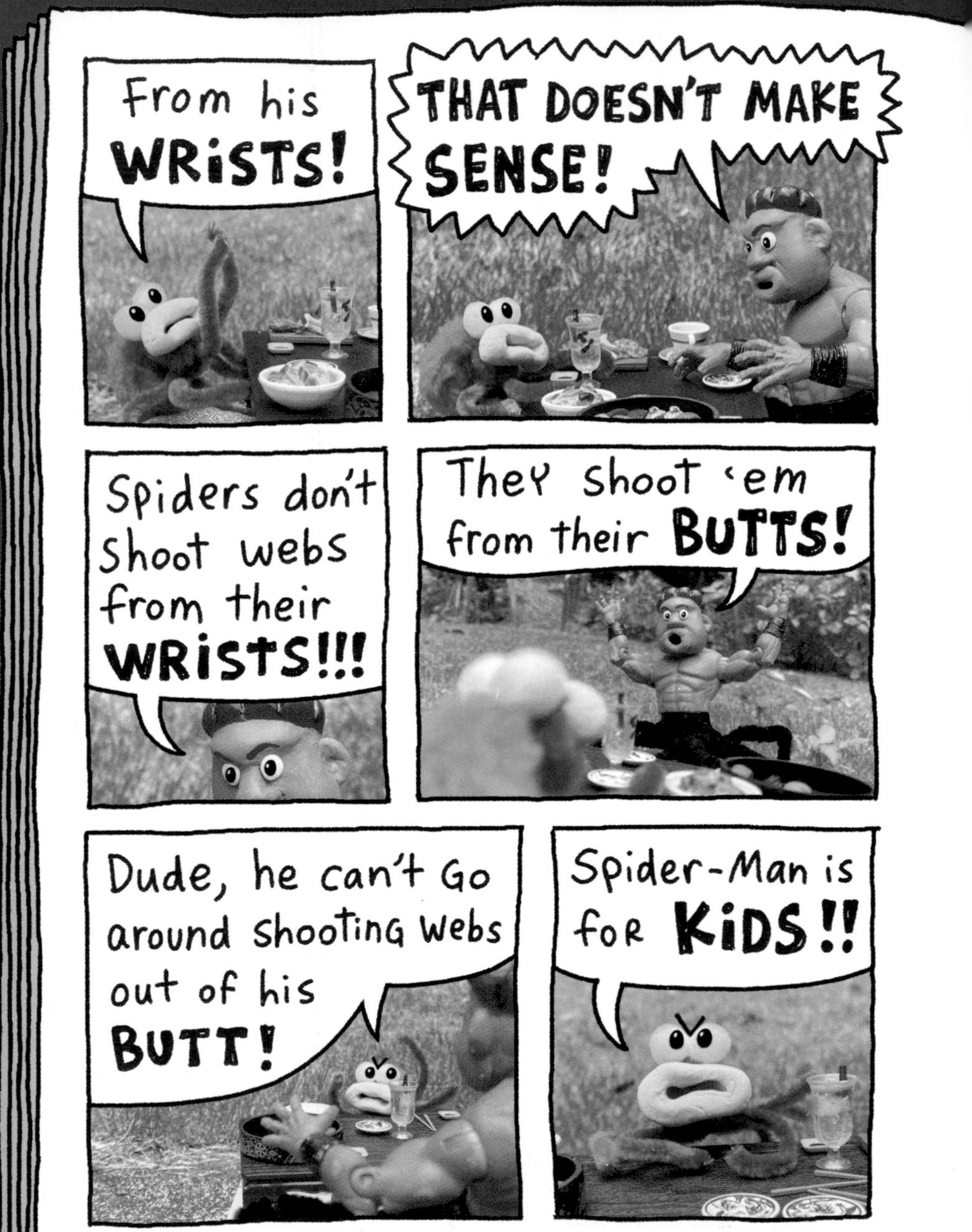
From his WRiSTS!
THAT DOESN'T MAKE SENSE!
Spiders don't shoot webs from their WRiSTS!!!
They shoot 'em from their BUTTS!
Dude, he can't Go around shooting webs out of his BUTT!
Spider-Man is for KiDS!!

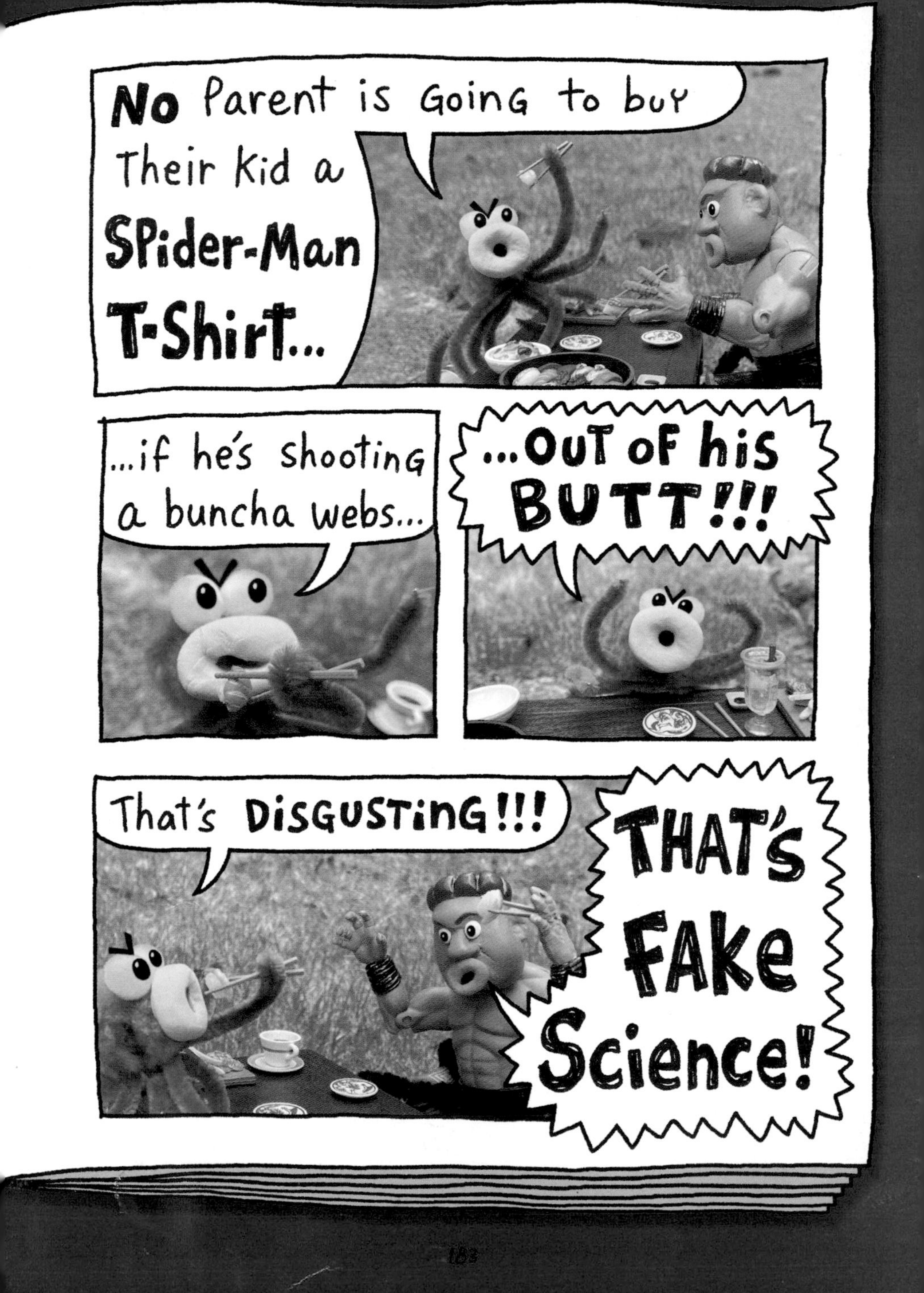
No Parent is Going to buy Their Kid a Spider-Man T-Shirt...
...if he's shooting a buncha webs...
...OUT OF his BUTT!!!
That's DISGUSTING!!!
THAT'S Fake Science!

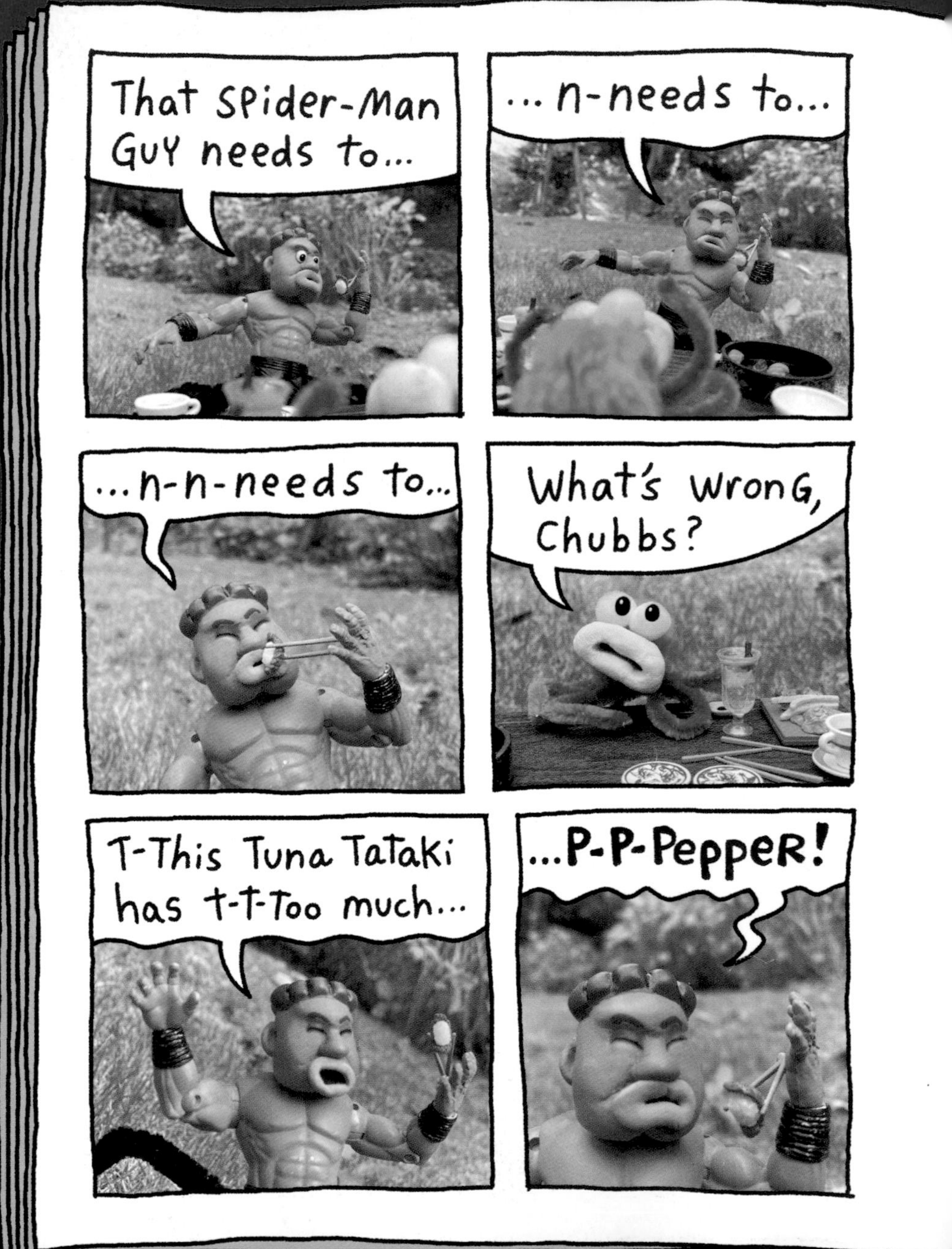
That Spider-Man Guy needs to...
...n-needs to...
...n-n-needs to...
What's wrong, Chubbs?
T-This Tuna Tataki has t-t-Too much...
...P-P-Pepper!

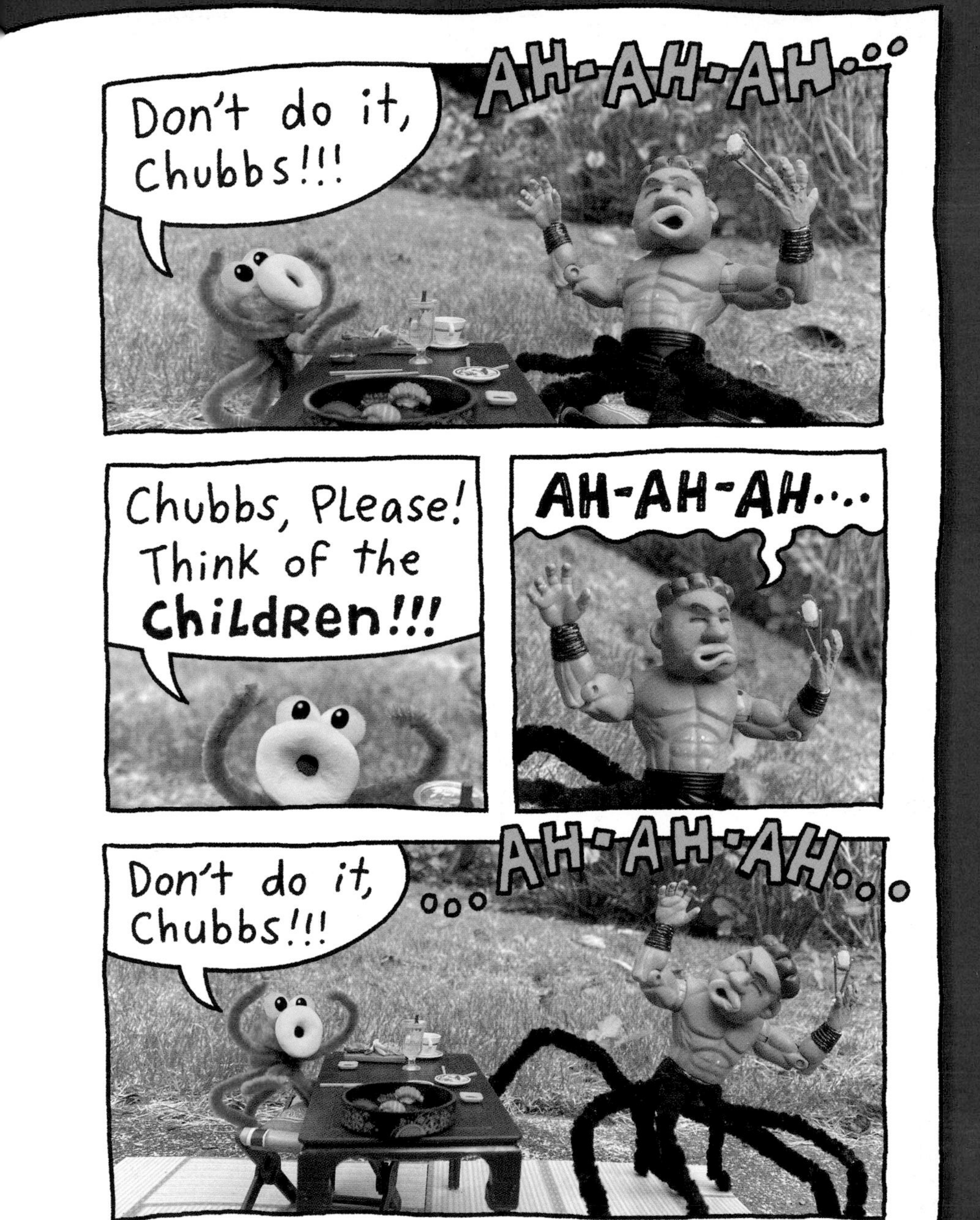
Don't do it, Chubbs!!!
AH-AH-AH...
Chubbs, Please! Think of the CHILDREN!!!
AH-AH-AH...
Don't do it, Chubbs!!!
ooo AH-AH-AH...

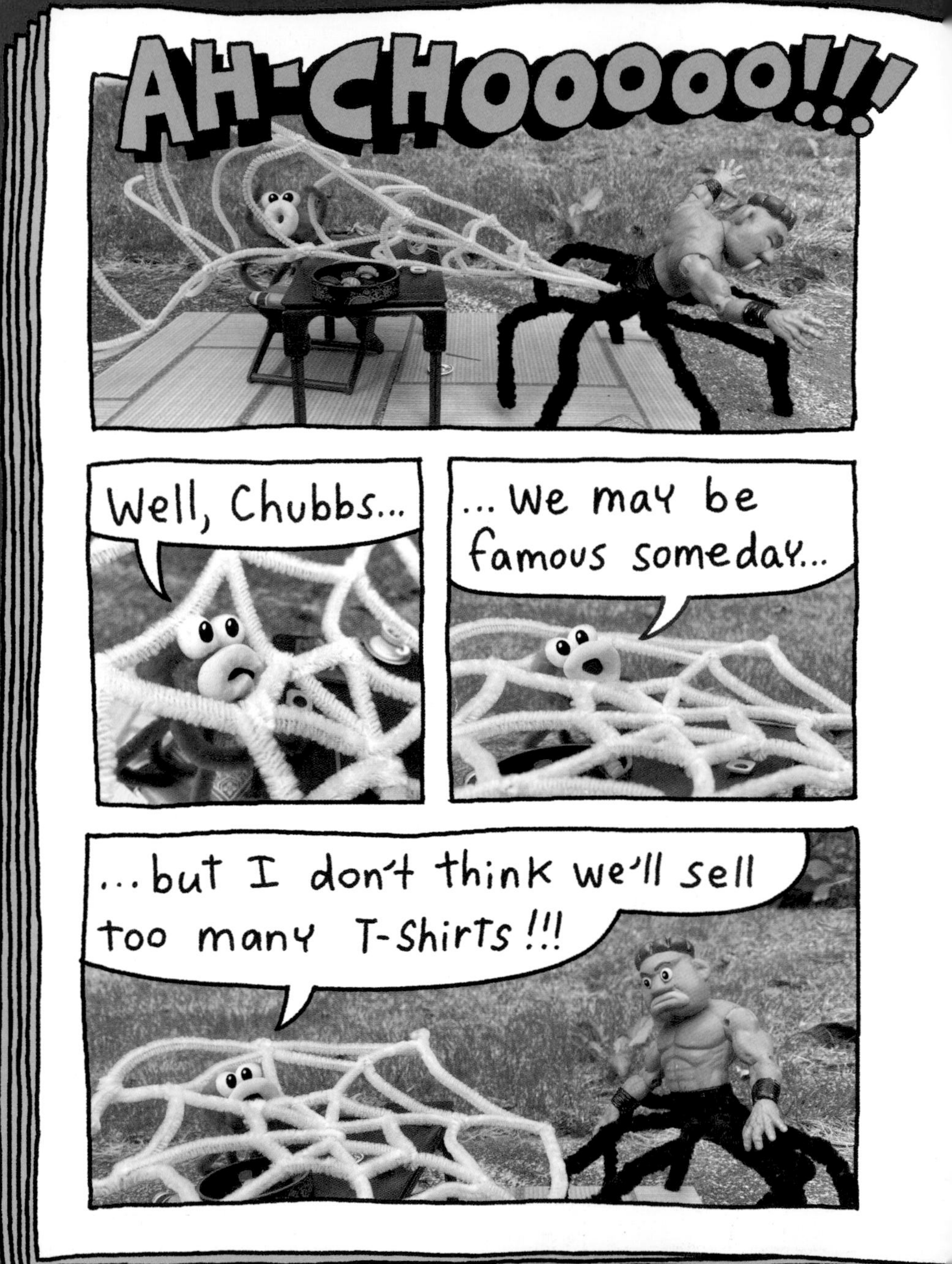
AH-CHOOOOOO!!!
Well, Chubbs...
...we may be famous someday...
...but I don't think we'll sell too many T-Shirts!!!

Meanwhile...

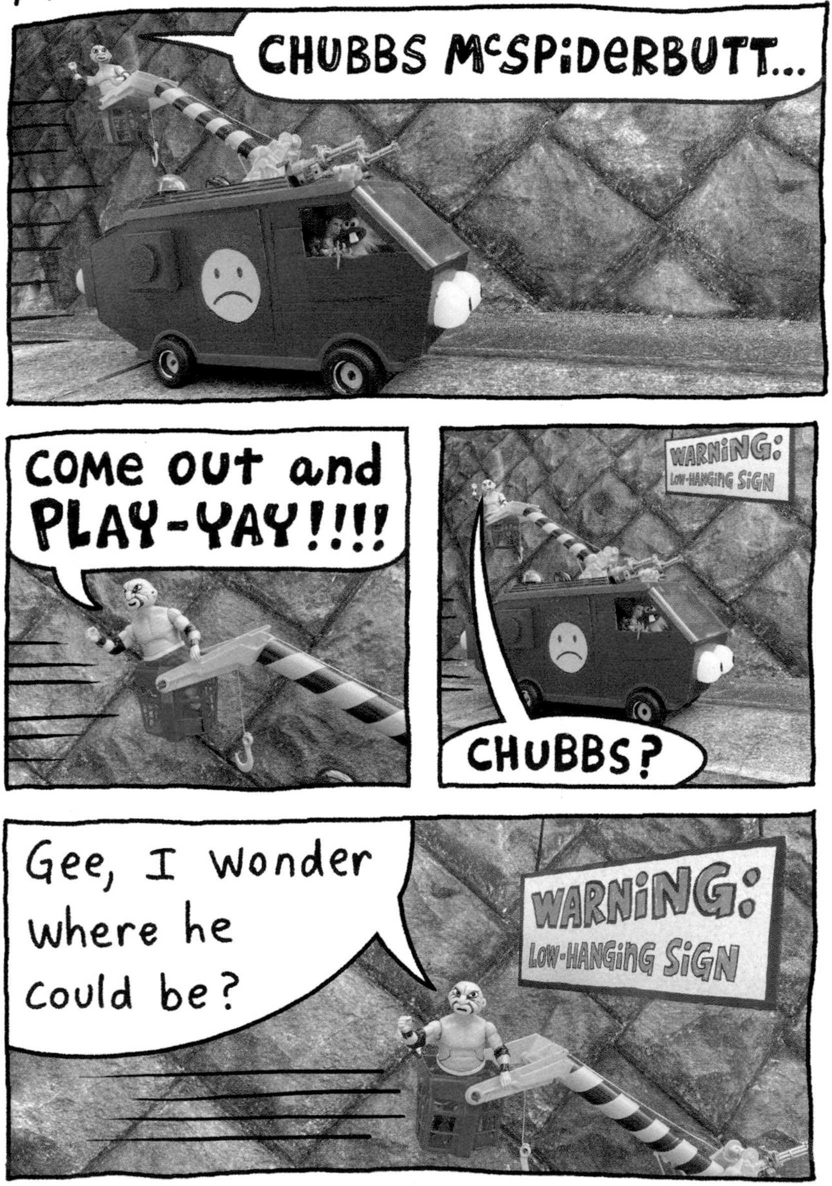

CHUBBS McSPiDeRBUTT...
COMe OUT and PLAY-YAY!!!!
WARNiNG: LOW-HANGiNG SiGN
CHUBBS?
Gee, I wonder where he could be?
WARNiNG: LOW-HANGiNG SiGN

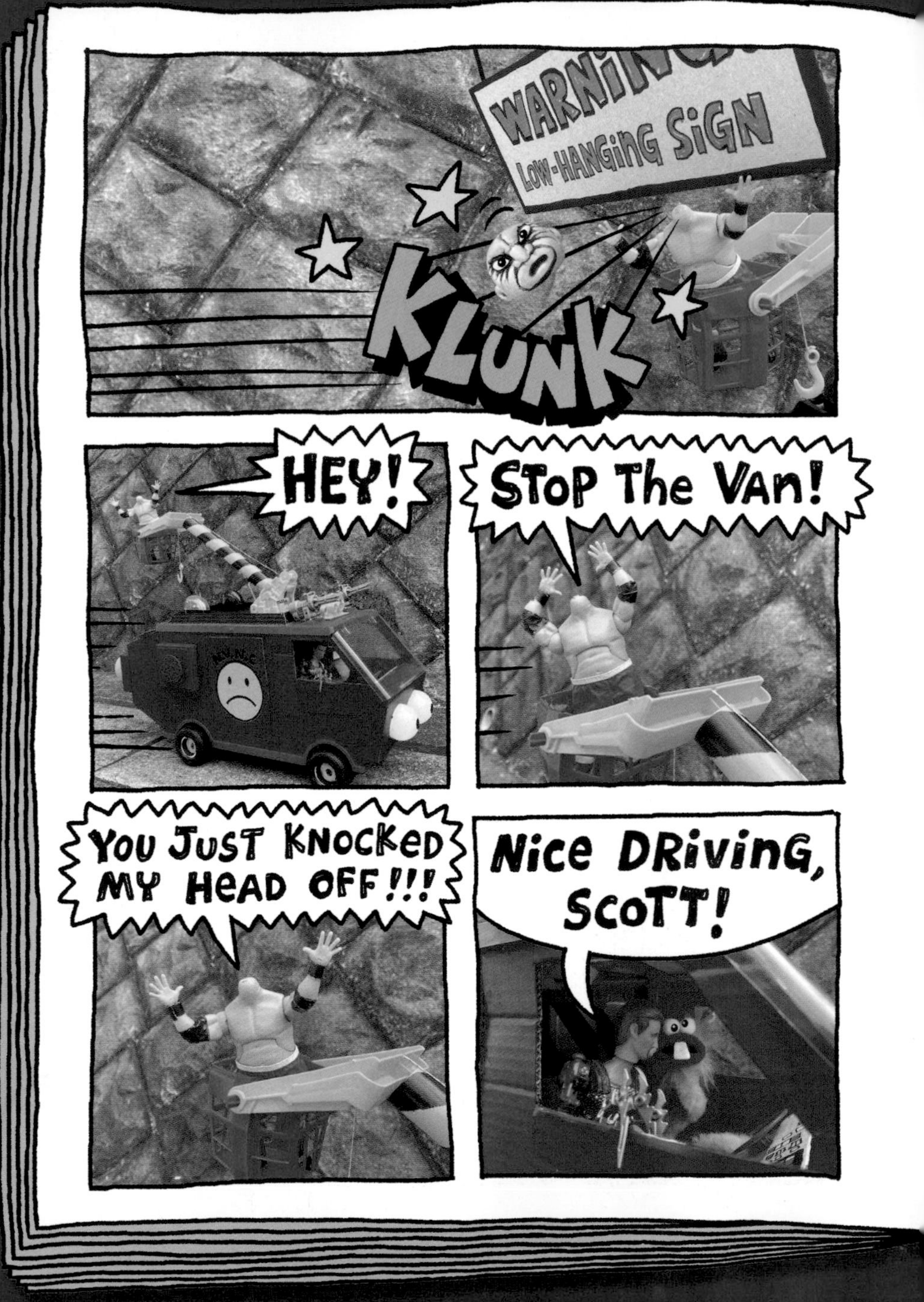
LOW-HANGING SIGN
KLUNK
HEY!
STOP The VAN!
YOU JUST KNOCKED MY HEAD OFF!!!
NICE DRIVING, SCOTT!

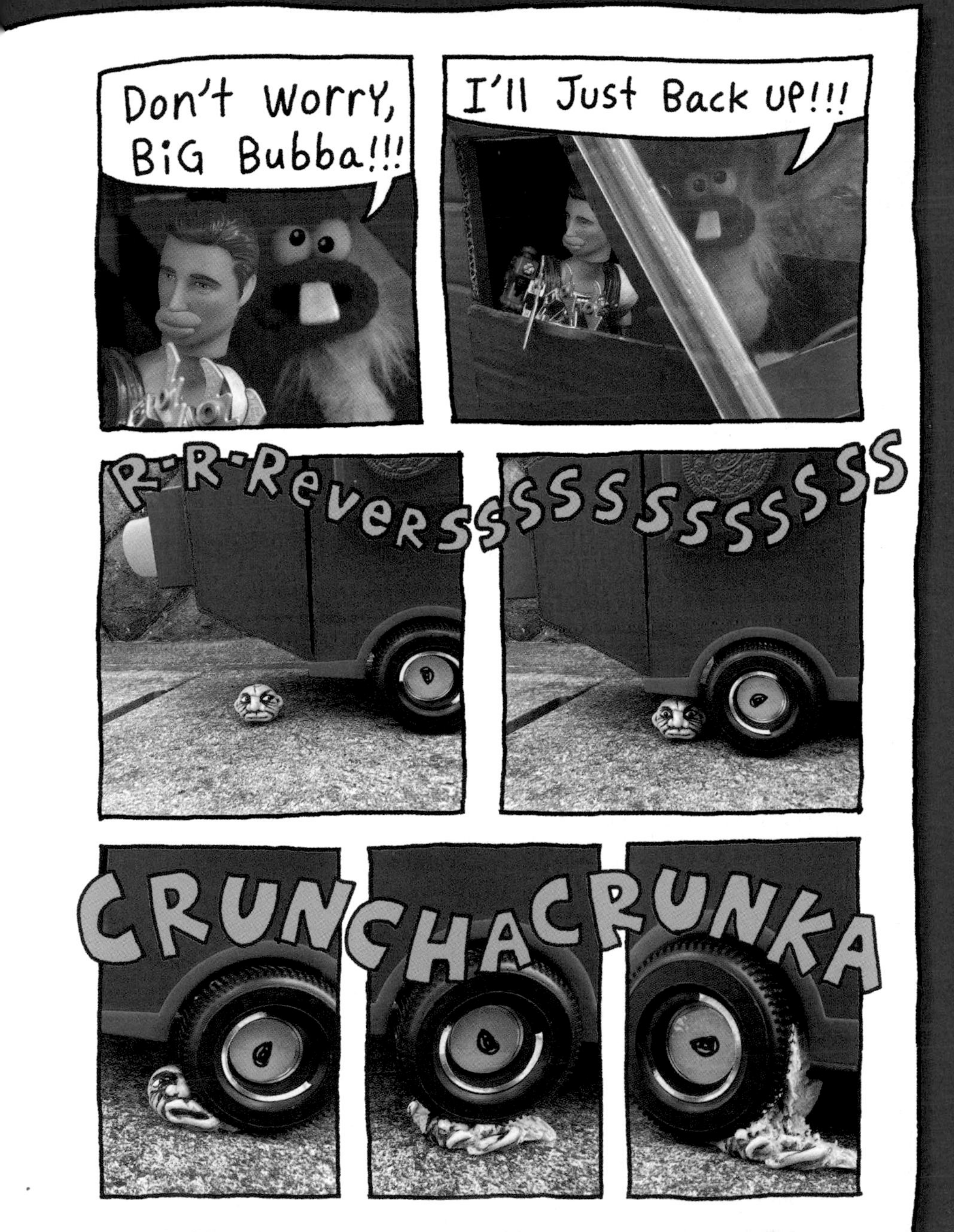

Don't WorrY, BiG Bubba!!!
I'll Just Back UP!!!
R-R-ReverSSSSSSSSSSS
CRUNCHACRUNKA

And so...

THANKS A LOT, SCOTT!

KA-CLICK

YOU RAN OVER MY HEAD!

I CAN'T GO AROUND LOOKING LIKE THIS!

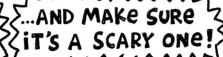

GO BUY ME A NEW HEAD!!!

...AND MAKE SURE IT'S A SCARY ONE!

OKAY!

Here I Go!!!

Dum-dee-dum-dee dumm...

This Must be the Place!!!

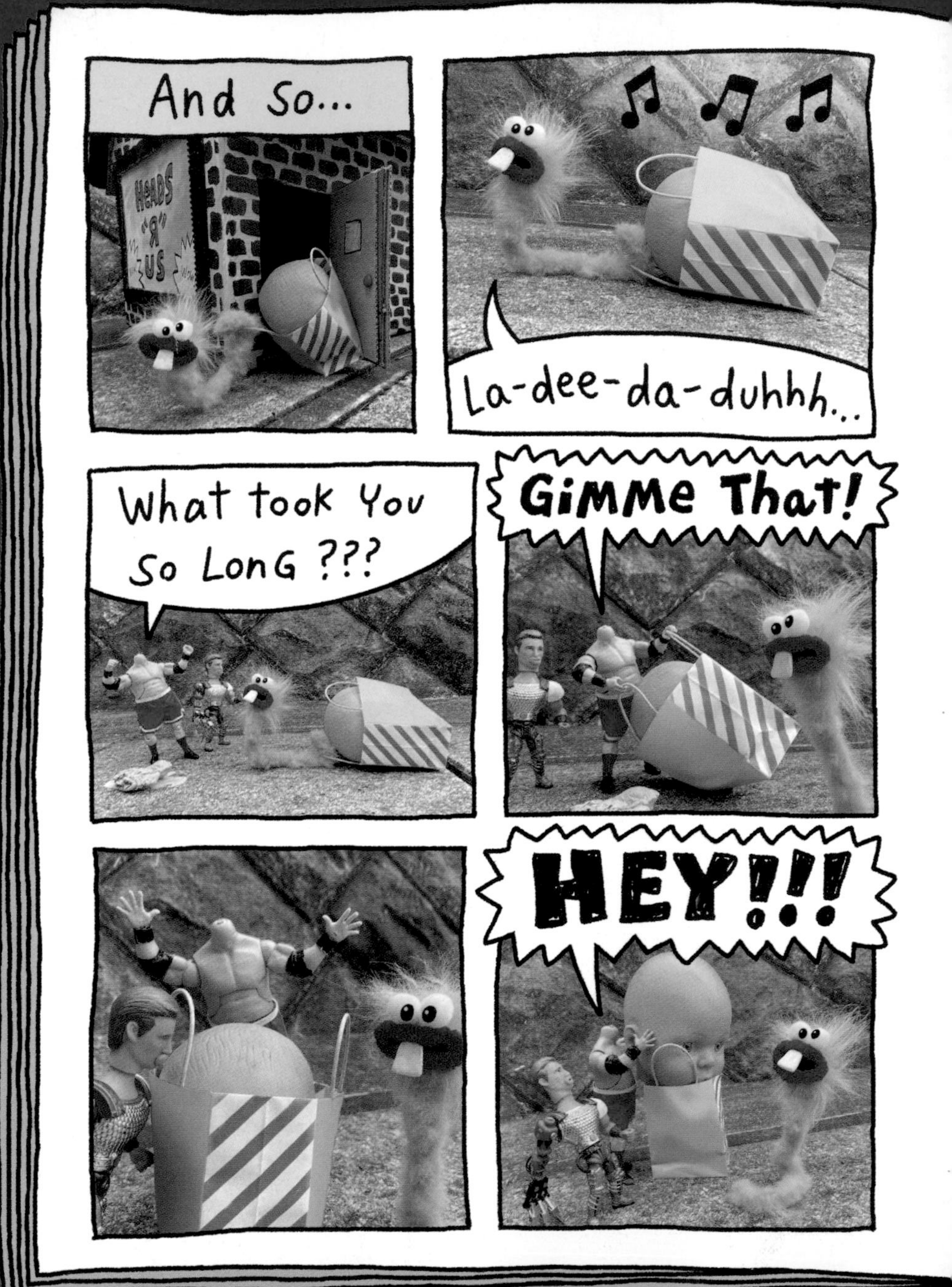
And So...
HEADS "R" US
La-dee-da-duhhh...
What took You So LonG ???
GiMMe That!
HEY!!!

WHAT THE HECK IS THIS?

WHY?

I TOLD YOU TO BUY ME A SCARY HEAD!!!

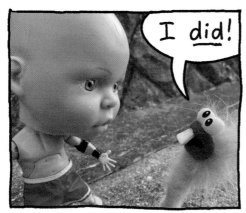

I did!

I'm terrified of Babies!!!

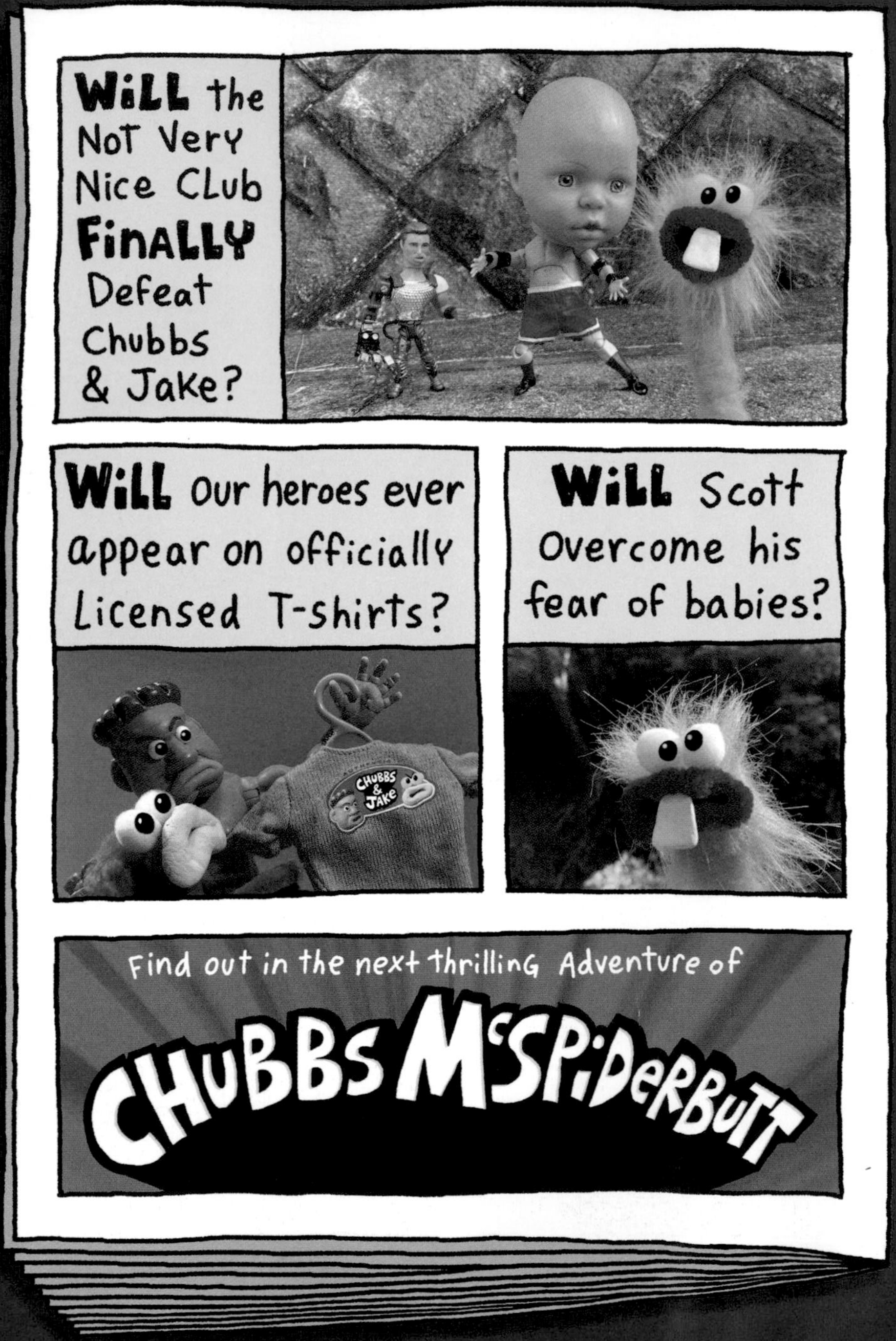

WiLL the NoT Very Nice CLub FinALLY Defeat Chubbs & Jake?
WiLL Our heroes ever appear on officially Licensed T-shirts?
CHUBBS & JAKE
WiLL Scott Overcome his fear of babies?
Find out in the next thrilling Adventure of
CHUBBS McSPiDERBUTT

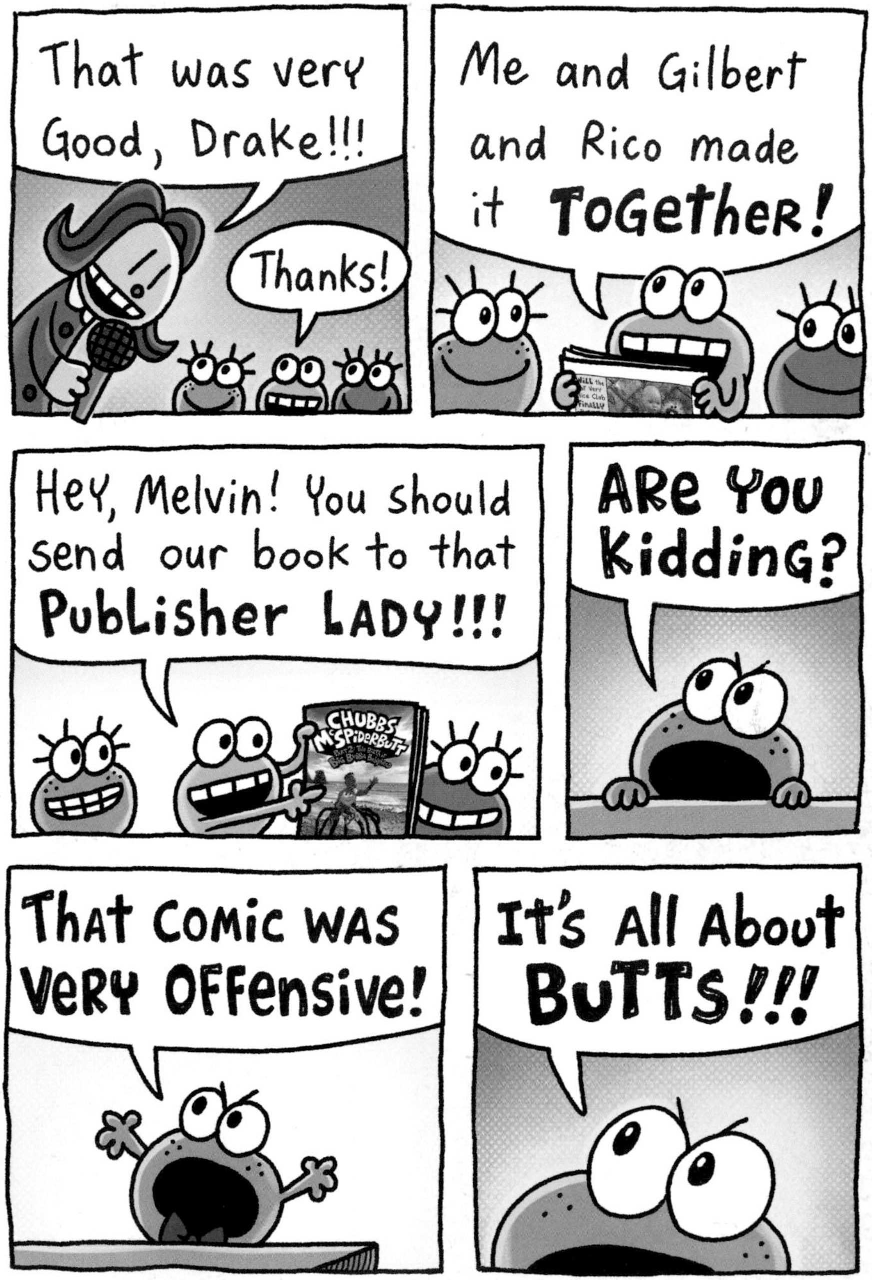
That was very Good, Drake!!!
Thanks!
Me and Gilbert and Rico made it TOGETHER!
Hey, Melvin! You should send our book to that Publisher LADY!!!
CHUBBS McSPIDERBUTT
ARE YOU Kidding?
That COMIC WAS VERY OFFensive!
It's All About BUTTS!!!

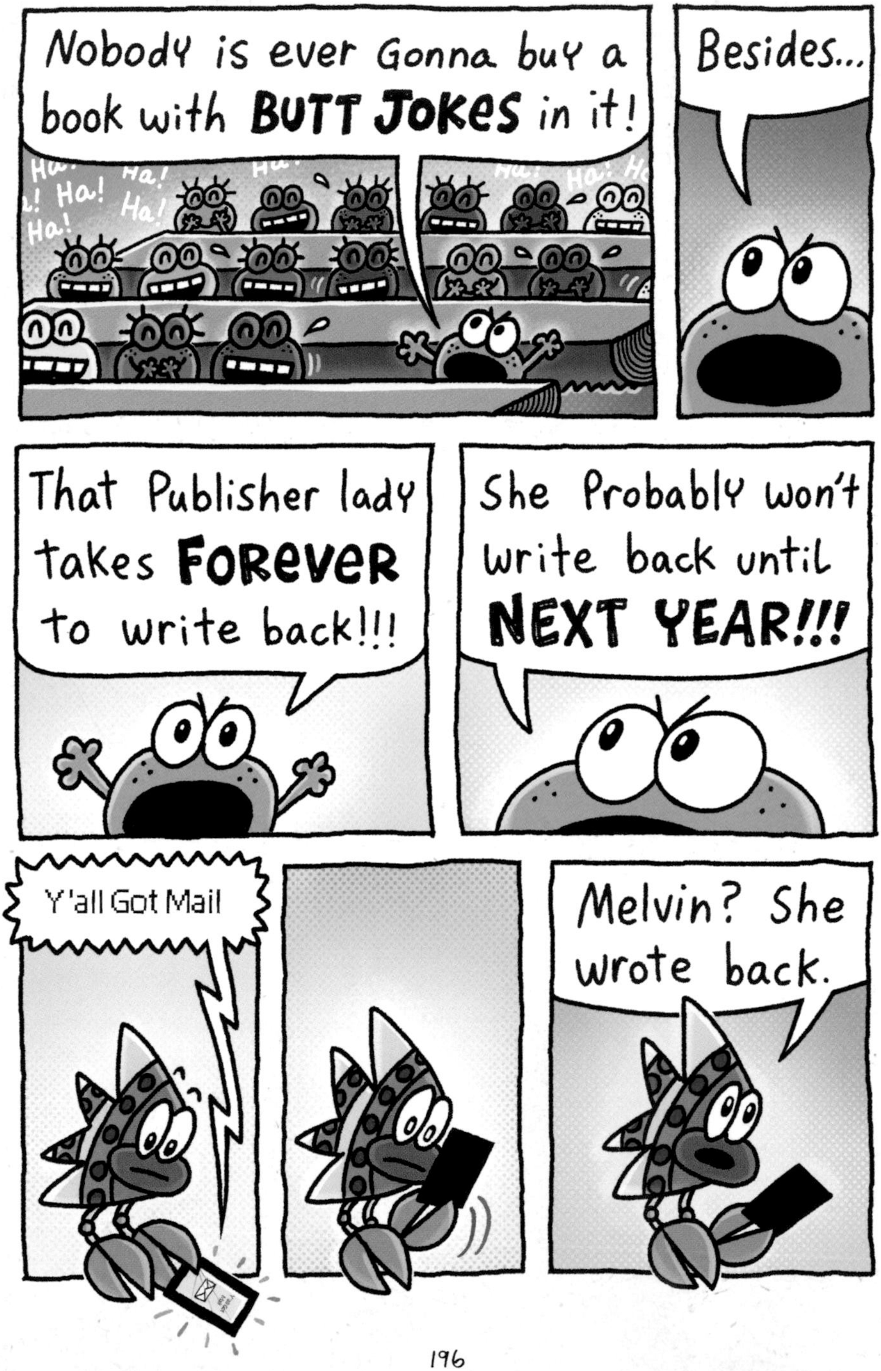
Nobody is ever Gonna buy a book with BUTT JOKES in it!
Ha! Ha! Ha! Ha! Ha! Ha! Ha!
Besides...
That Publisher lady takes FOREVER to write back!!!
She Probably won't write back until NEXT YEAR!!!
Y'all Got Mail
Melvin? She wrote back.

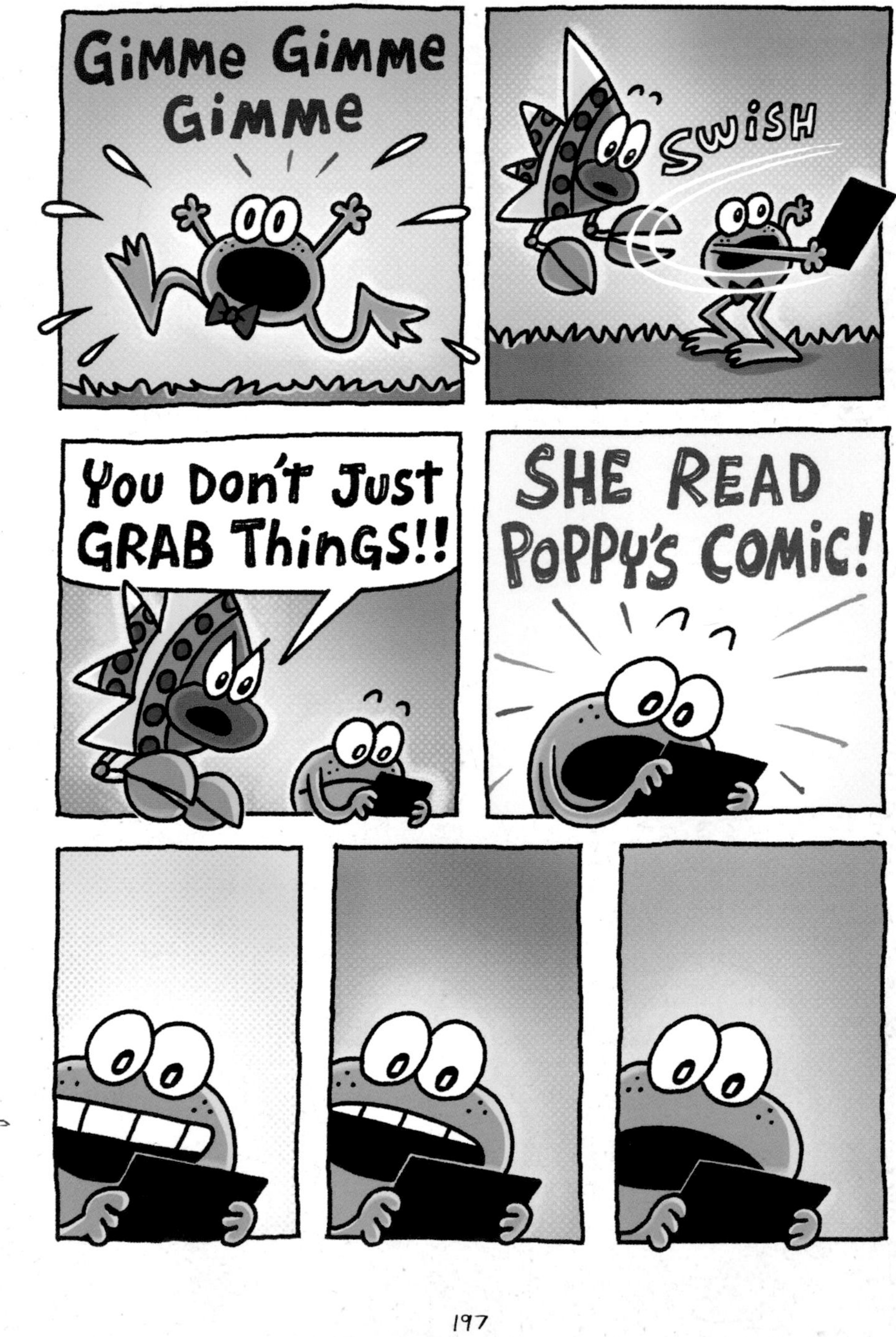
Gimme Gimme Gimme
SWISH
You Don't Just GRAB Things!!
SHE READ POPPY'S COMIC!

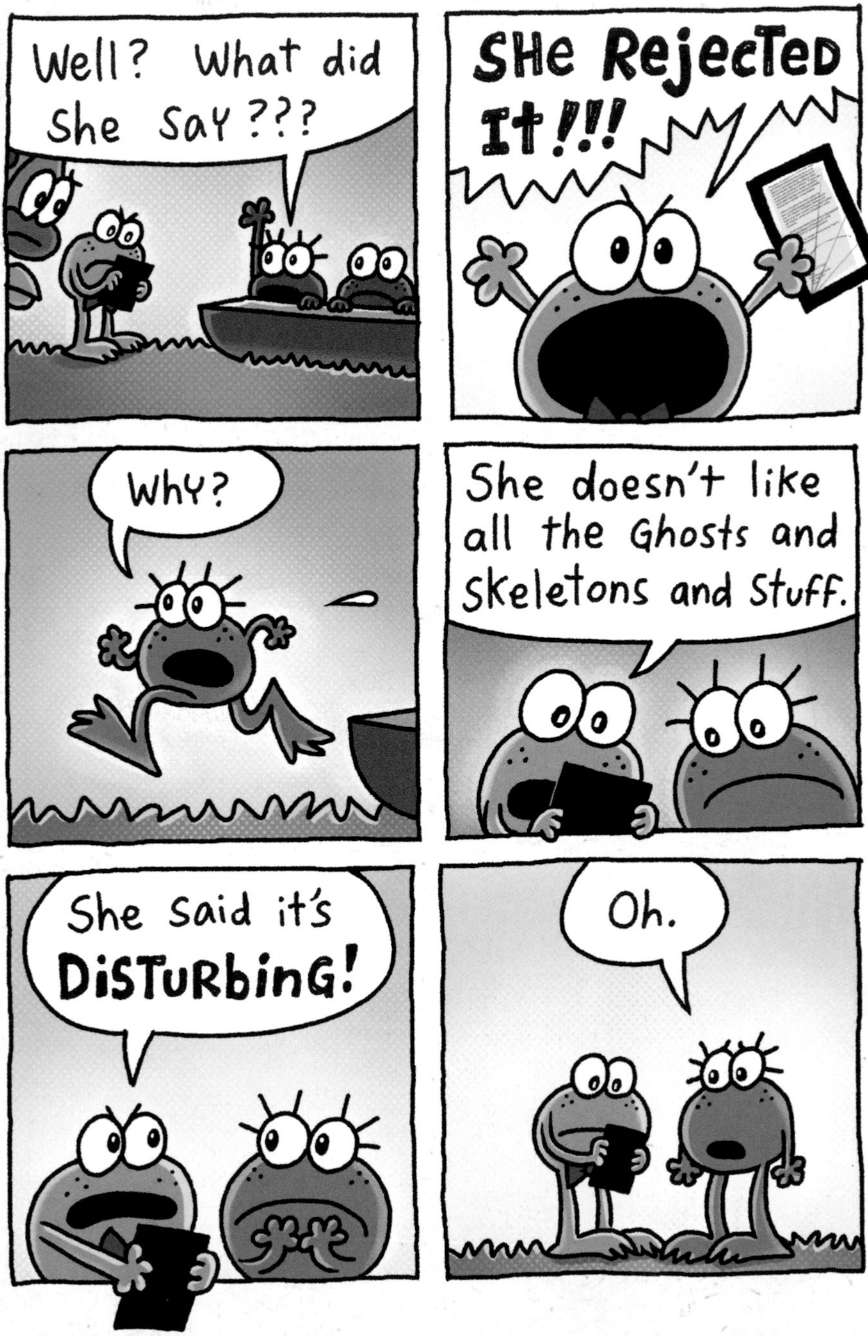
Well? What did She Say???
SHe RejecTED It!!!
WhY?
She doesn't like all the Ghosts and Skeletons and Stuff.
She Said it's DiSTURbinG!
Oh.

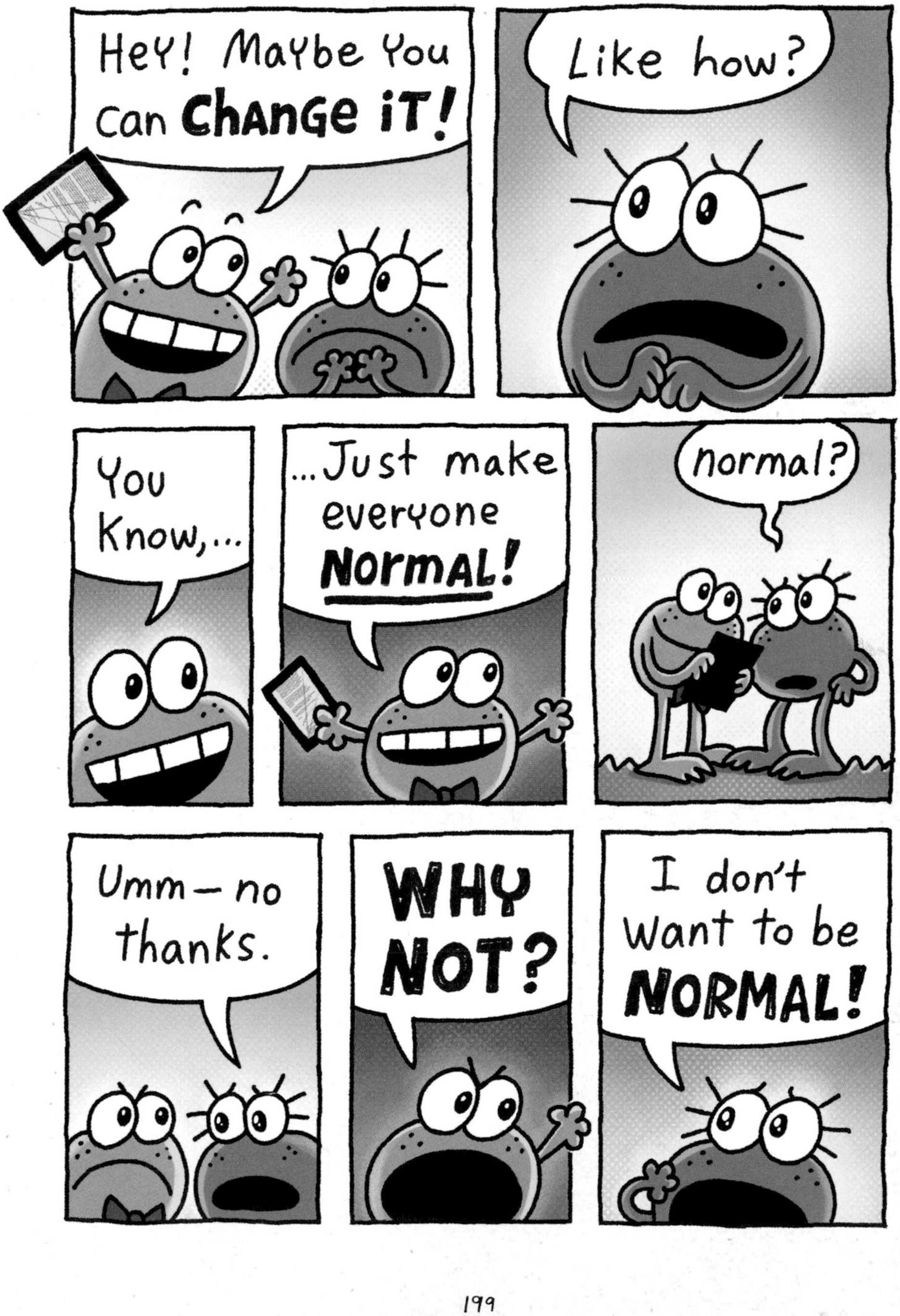
Hey! Maybe You can CHANGE iT!
Like how?
You Know,...
...Just make everyone NORMAL!
normal?
Umm—no thanks.
WHY NOT?
I don't want to be NORMAL!

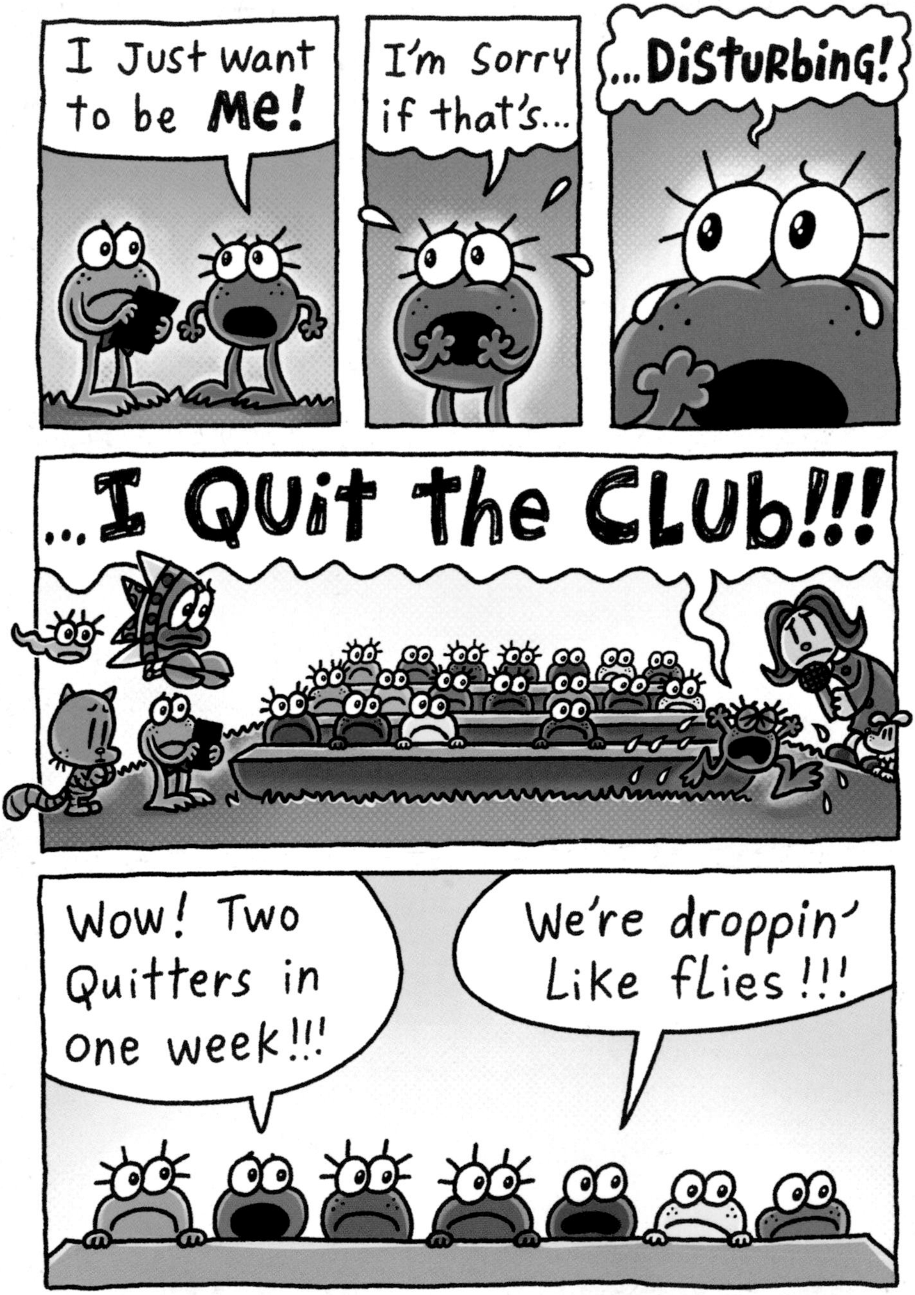
I Just want to be Me!
I'm Sorry if that's...
...DiSTURbinG!
...I QUit the CLUb!!!
Wow! Two Quitters in one week!!!
We're droppin' Like fLies!!!

CHAPTER 13

Just be You

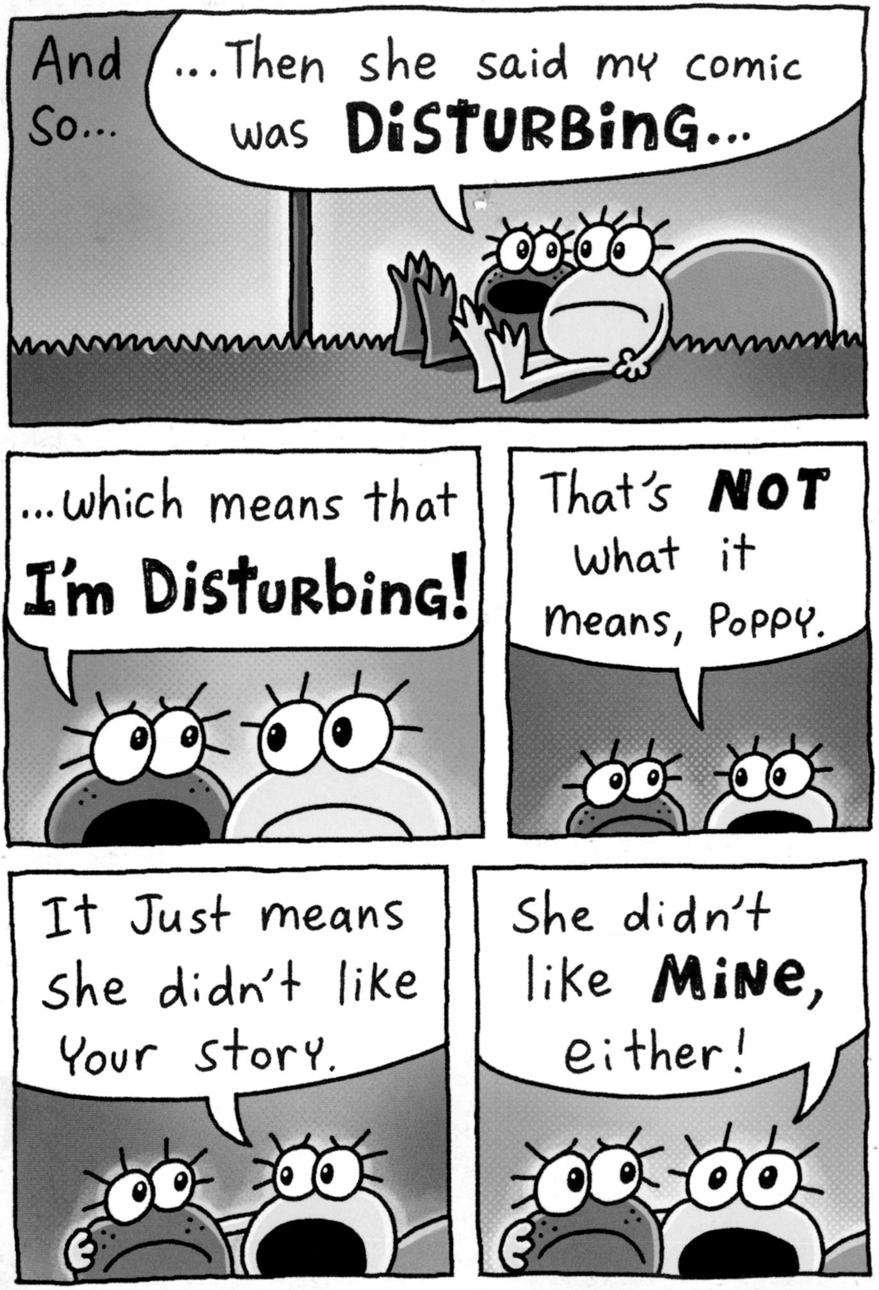

And So...
...Then she said my comic was DISTURBING...
...which means that I'm DISTURBING!
That's NOT what it means, Poppy.
It Just means she didn't like Your story.
She didn't like MINE, either!

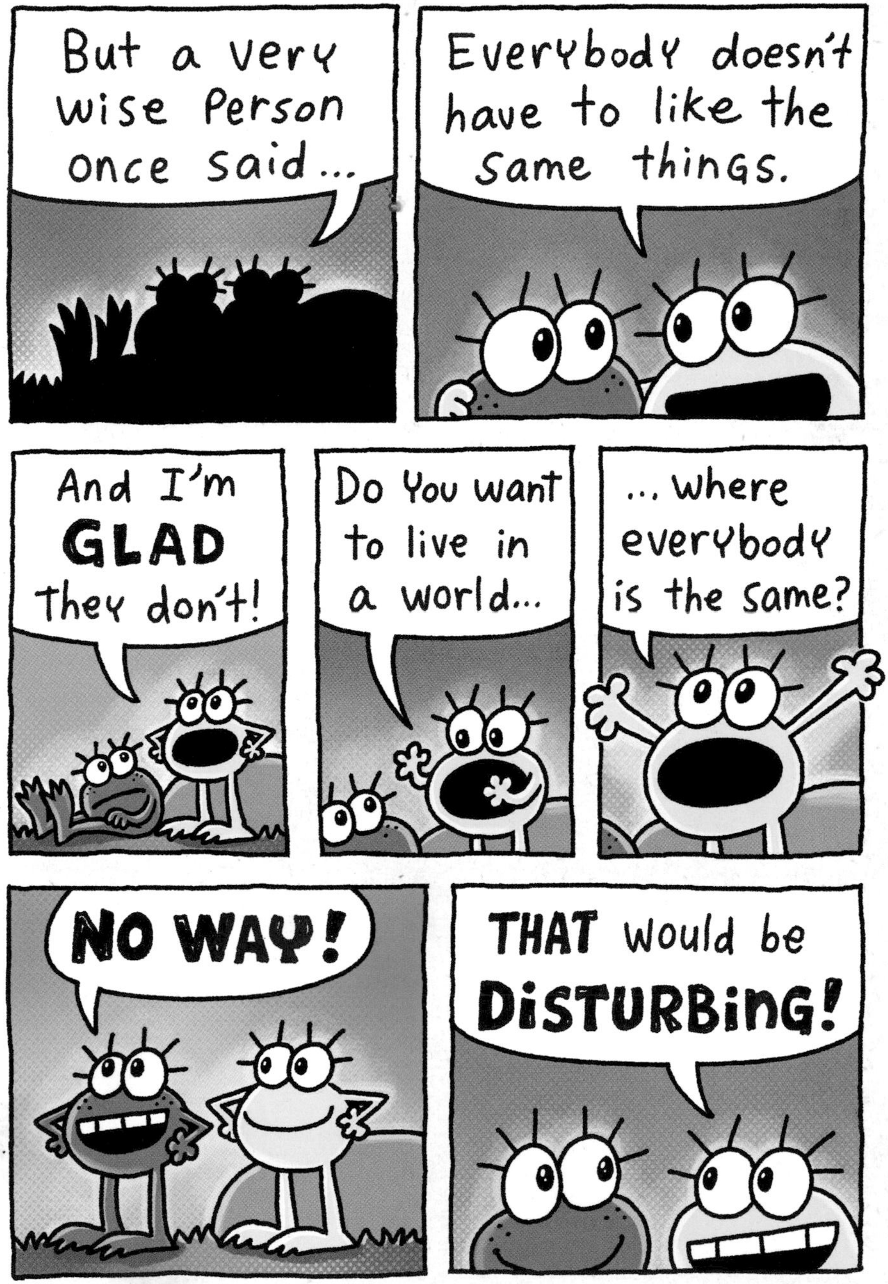
But a very wise person once said...
Everybody doesn't have to like the same things.
And I'm GLAD they don't!
Do you want to live in a world...
...where everybody is the same?
NO WAY!
THAT would be DISTURBING!

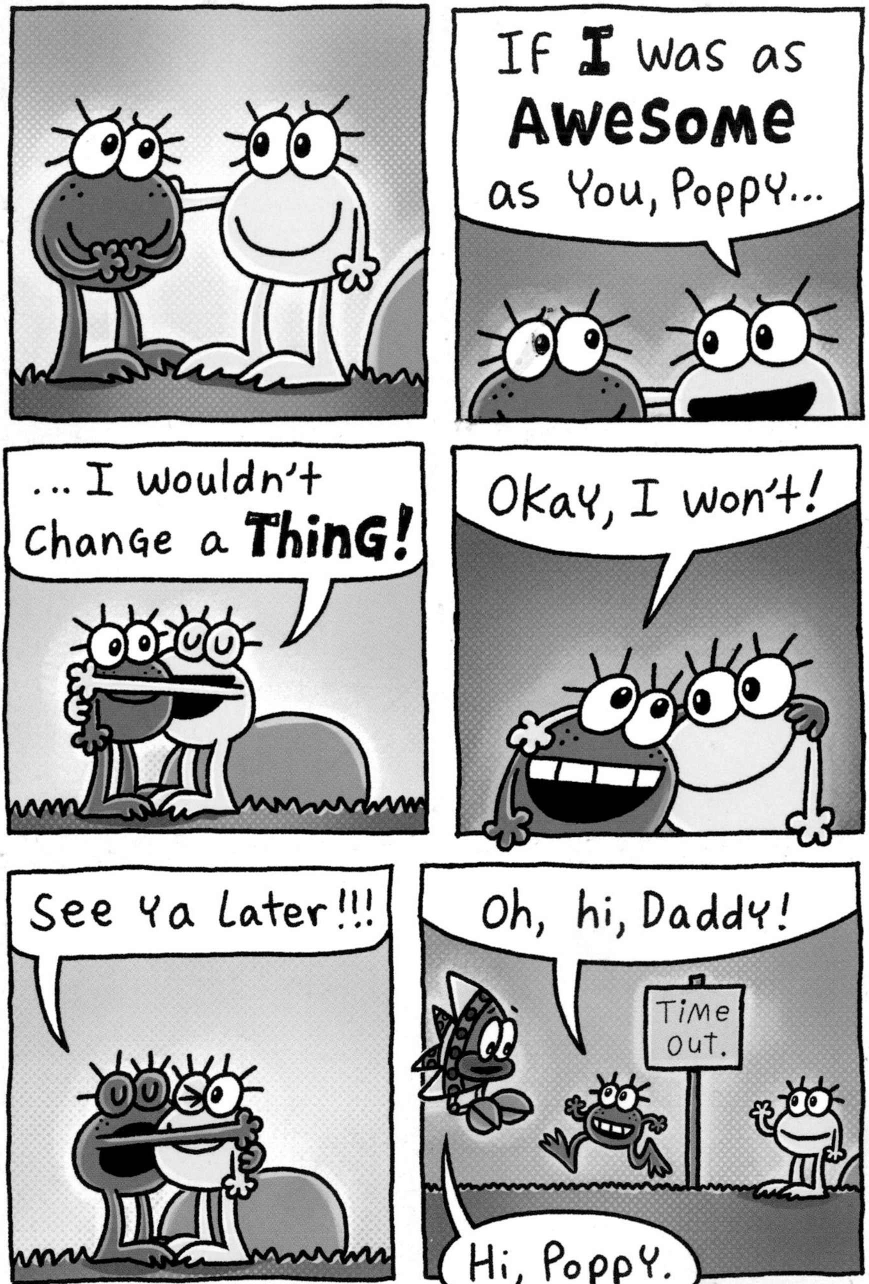
If I was as AWESOME as You, Poppy...
... I wouldn't change a THING!
Okay, I won't!
See ya later!!!
Oh, hi, Daddy!
Time out.
Hi, Poppy.

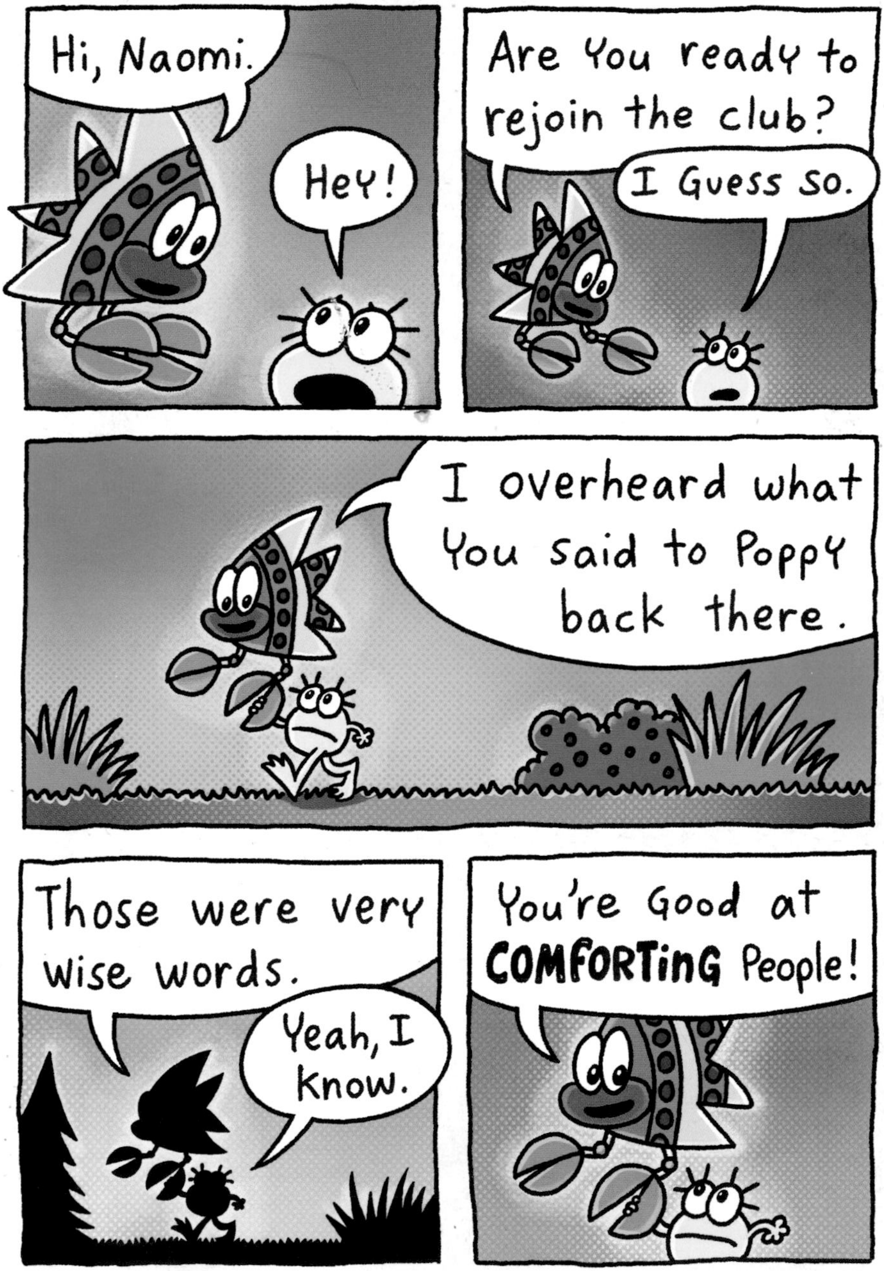
Hi, Naomi.
Hey!
Are you ready to rejoin the club?
I Guess so.
I overheard what you said to Poppy back there.
Those were very wise words.
Yeah, I know.
You're Good at COMFORTING People!

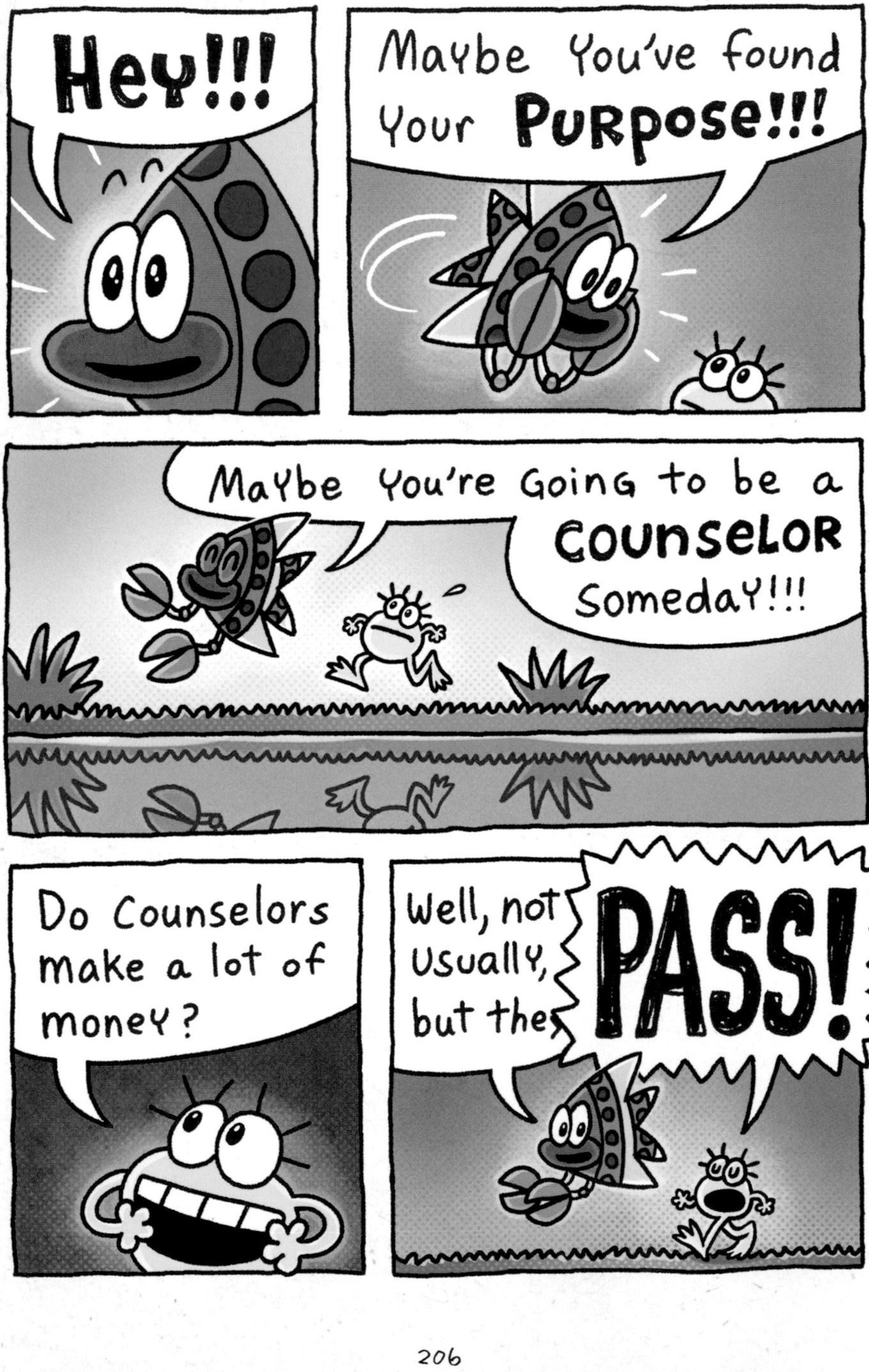
Hey!!!
Maybe You've found Your PURPOSE!!!
Maybe You're Going to be a COUNSELOR Someday!!!
Do Counselors make a lot of money?
Well, not Usually, but the
PASS!

CHAPTER 14

A Buncha Stuff That Changed Everything

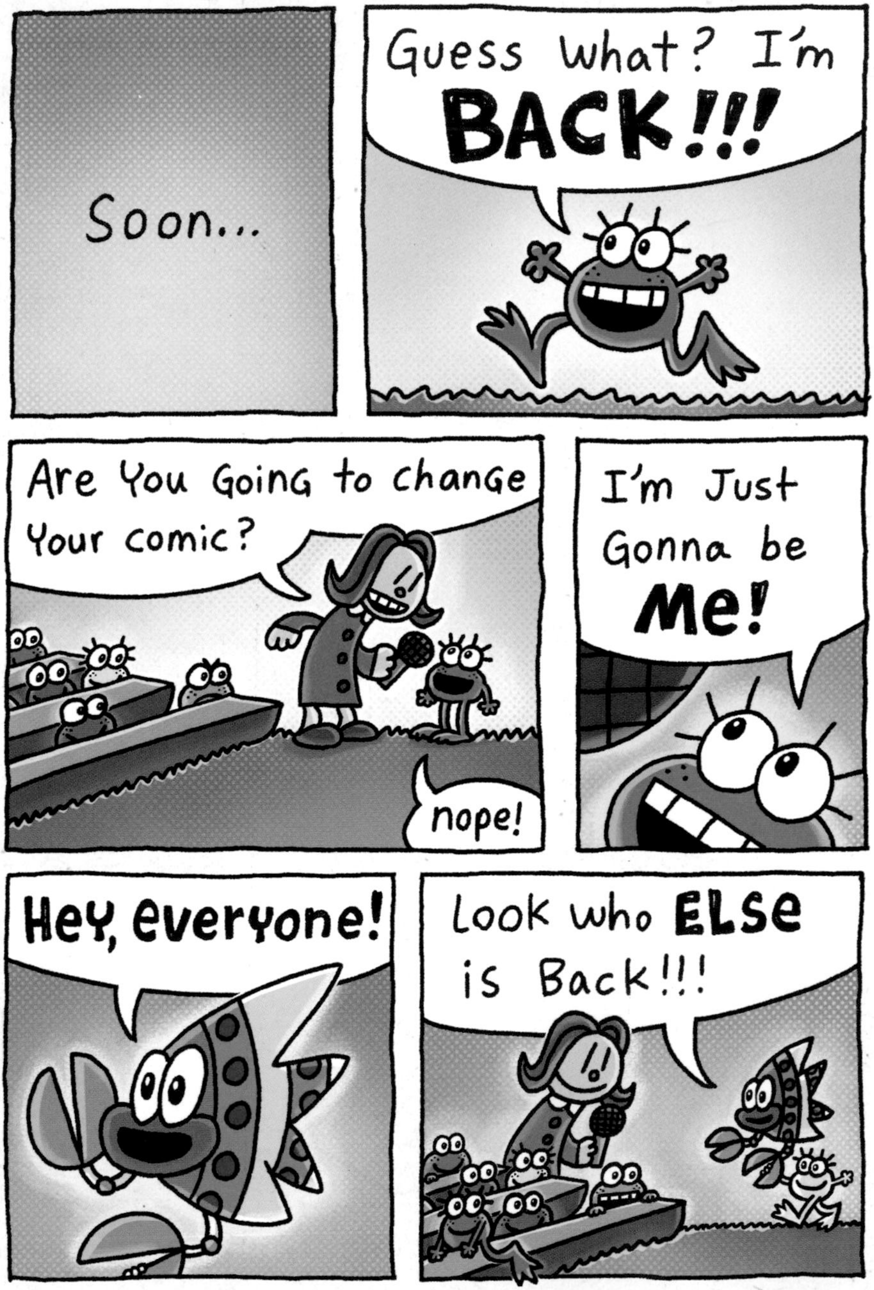
Soon...
Guess What? I'm BACK!!!
Are You Going to change Your comic?
nope!
I'm Just Gonna be Me!
Hey, everyone!
Look who ELSE is Back!!!

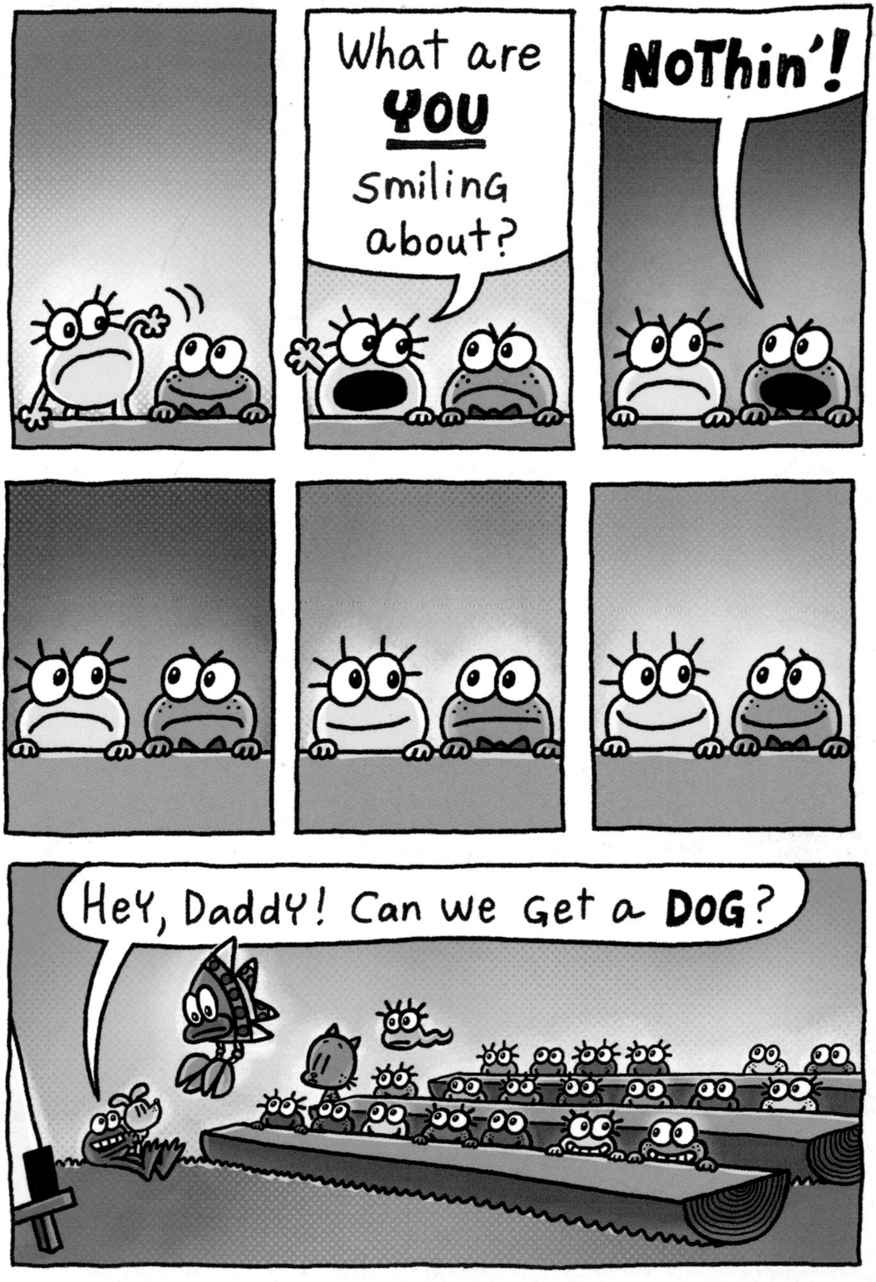
What are YOU smiling about?
NOThin'!
Hey, Daddy! Can we Get a DOG?

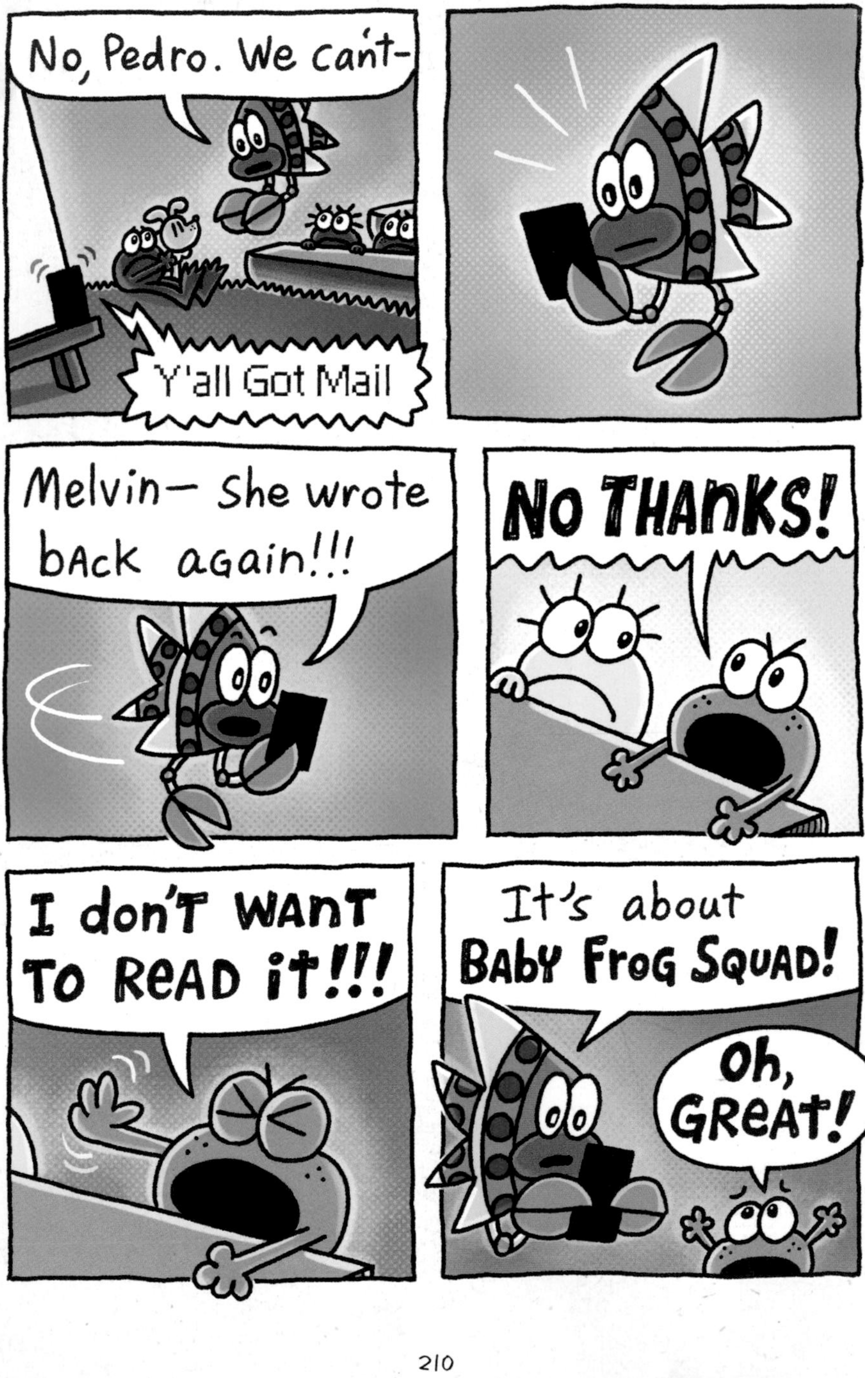
No, Pedro. We can't-
Y'all Got Mail
Melvin- She wrote back again!!!
NO THANKS!
I don't WANT TO READ it!!!
It's about BABY FROG SQUAD!
Oh, GREAT!

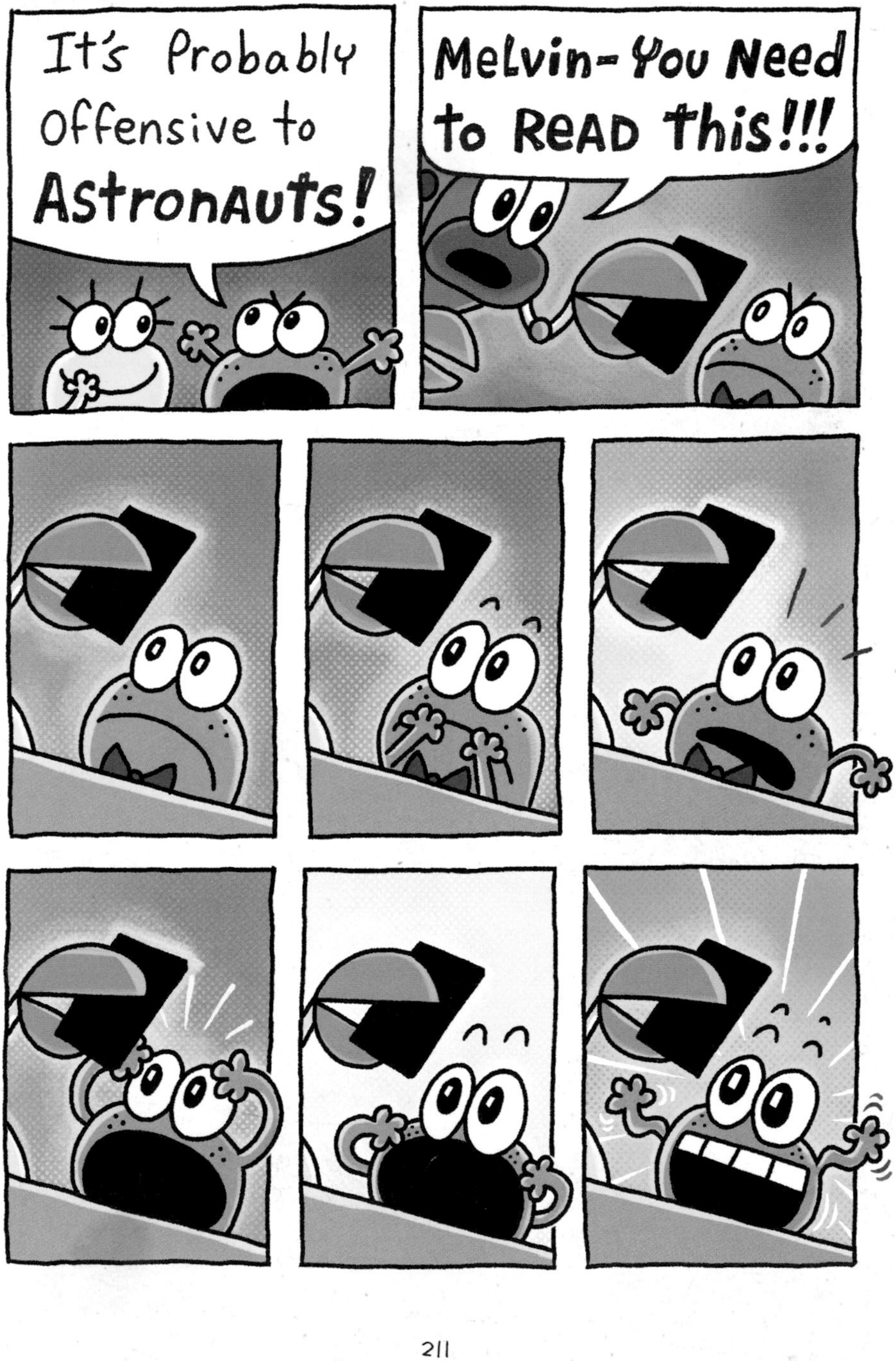
It's Probably Offensive to ASTRONAUTS!
Melvin– You Need to READ This!!!

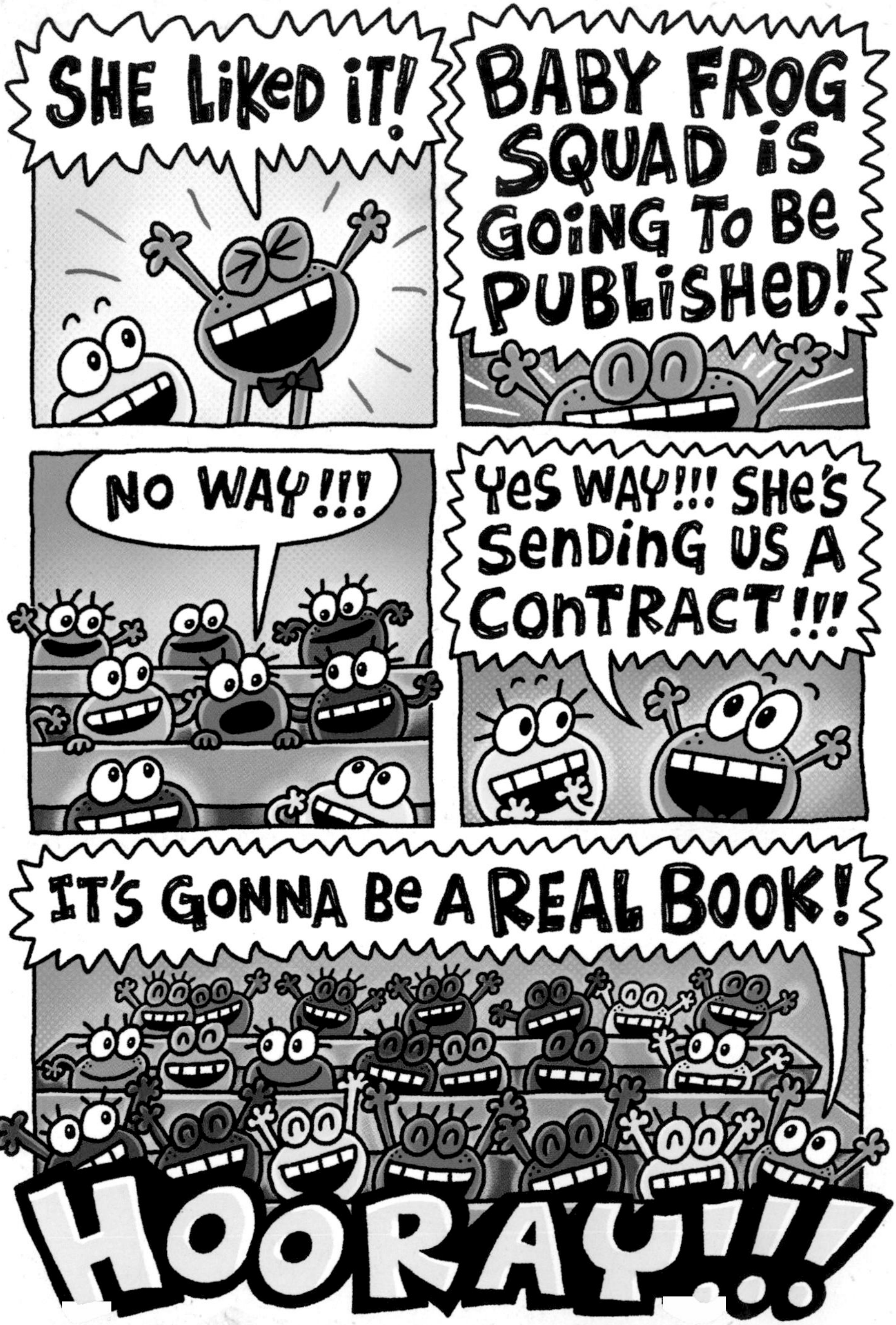
SHE LIKED IT!
BABY FROG SQUAD IS GOING TO BE PUBLISHED!
NO WAY!!!
YES WAY!!! SHE'S SENDING US A CONTRACT!!!
IT'S GONNA BE A REAL BOOK!
HOORAY!!!

ALL YOU have to do is make **TWO HUNDRED MORE PAGES**, And—

Wait, what?

It has to be **224** Pages!!!

224 PAGES?

WE CAN'T MAKE **224 PAGES**!!

THAT'S **WAY** TOO MANY PAGES!!!

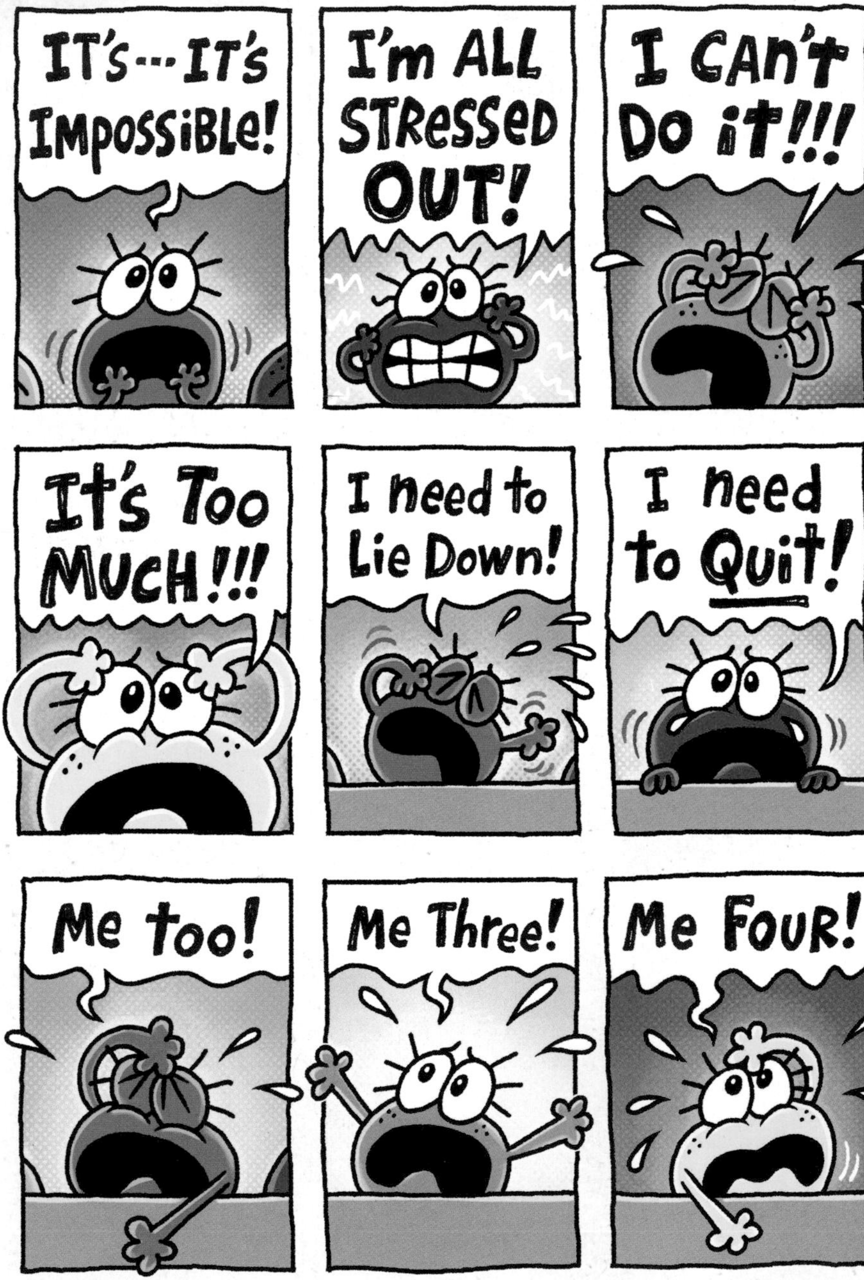
IT'S... IT'S IMPOSSIBLE!
I'm ALL STRESSED OUT!
I CAN'T DO it!!!
IT'S TOO MUCH!!!
I need to Lie Down!
I need to Quit!
Me too!
Me Three!
Me FOUR!

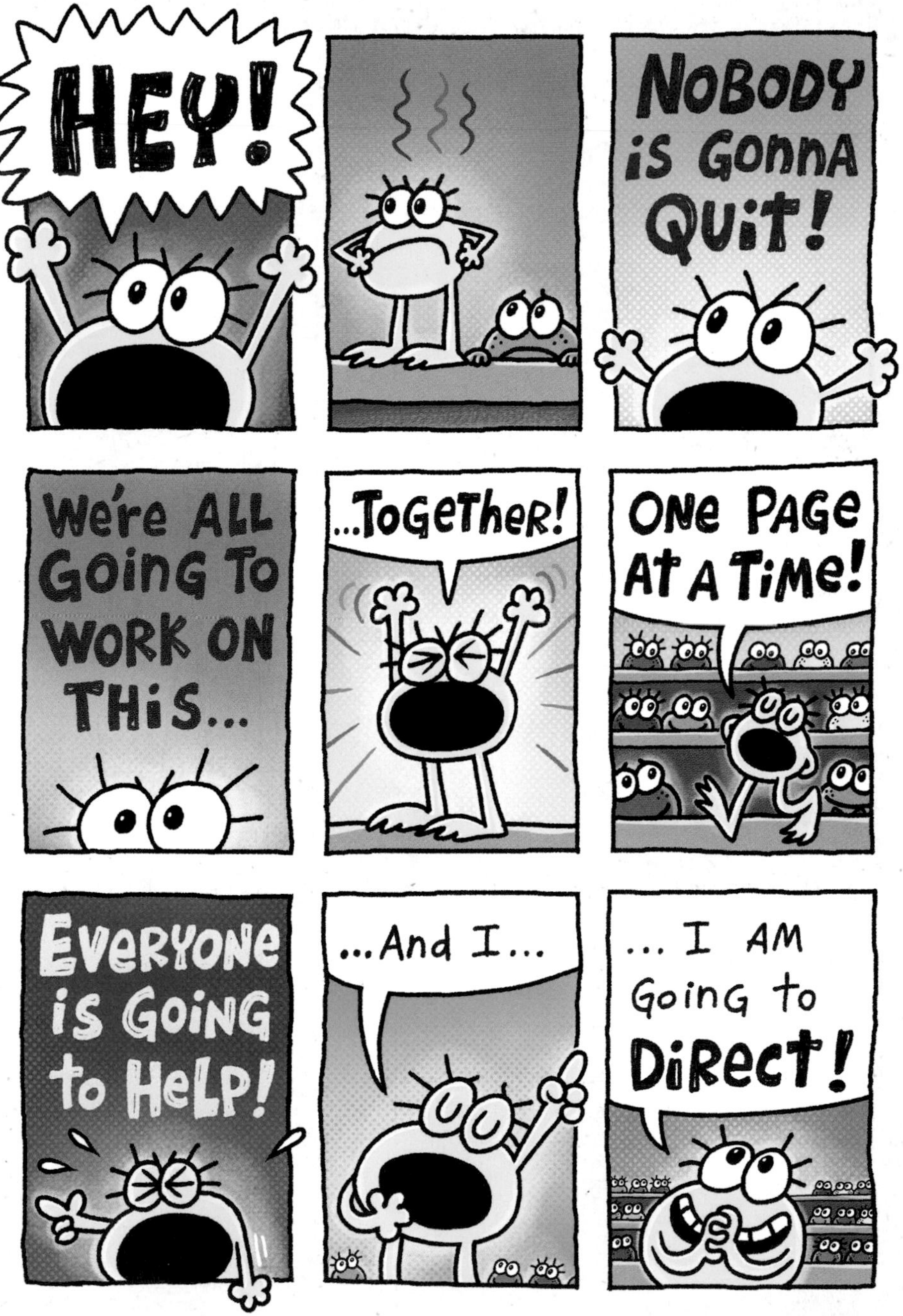
HEY!
NOBODY is GONNA QUIT!
We're ALL GOING TO WORK ON THIS...
...TOGETHER!
ONE PAGE AT A TIME!
EVERYONE is GOING to HELP!
...And I...
... I AM Going to DIRECT!

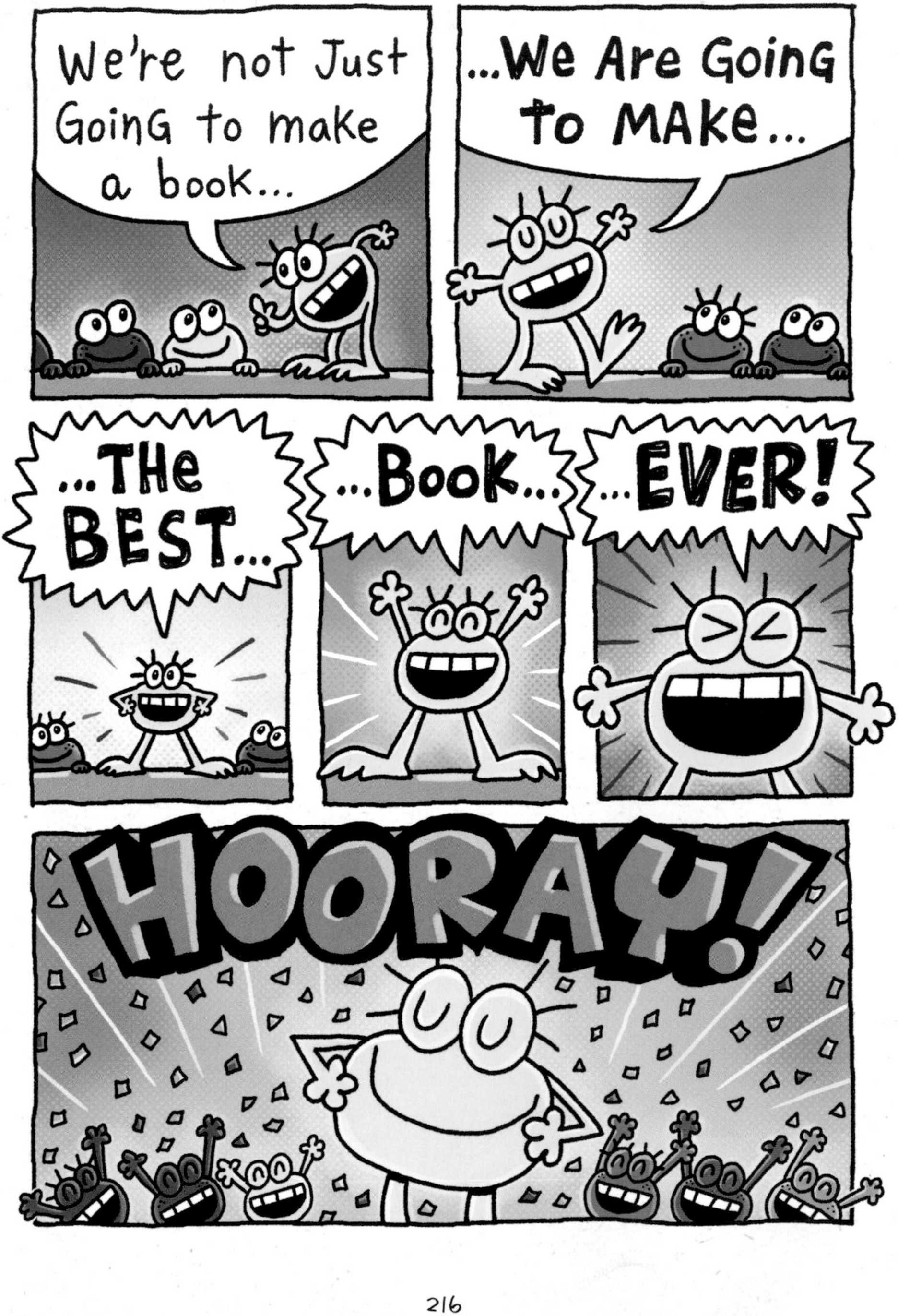
We're not Just Going to make a book...
...We Are Going To MAKE...
...The BEST...
...Book...
...EVER!
HOORAY!

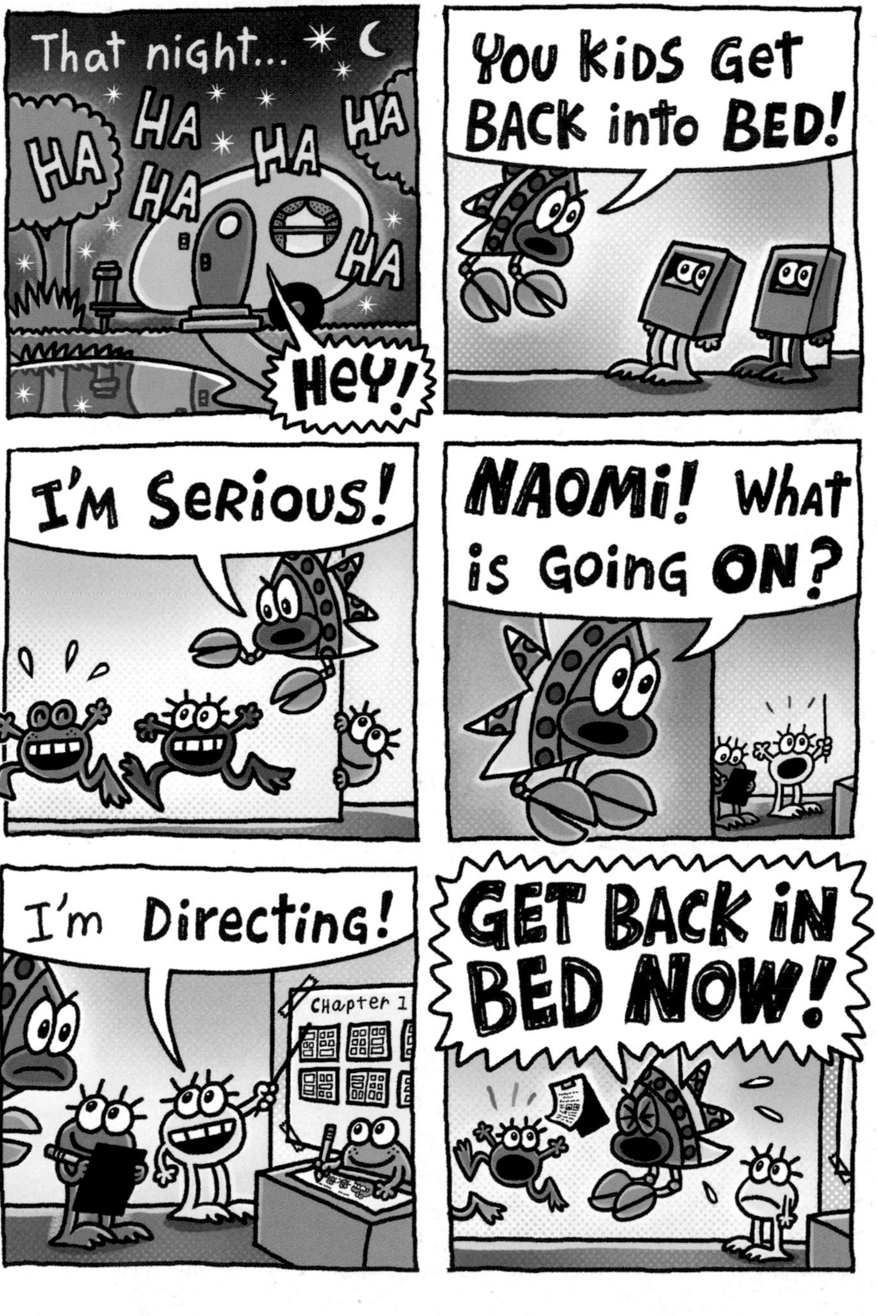
That night...
HA
HA
HA
HA
HA
HA
HEY!
YOU KIDS GET BACK into BED!
I'M SERIOUS!
NAOMI! WHAT is GOING ON?
I'm DIRECTING!
CHAPTER 1
GET BACK IN BED NOW!

Go on, Get in there!

Pat Pat Pat

I **Love** being a Director, Daddy!

It's the **Perfect** Job for me!!!

I'm Good at **STorytelling**...

...I'm Good at **Bossing People Around**...

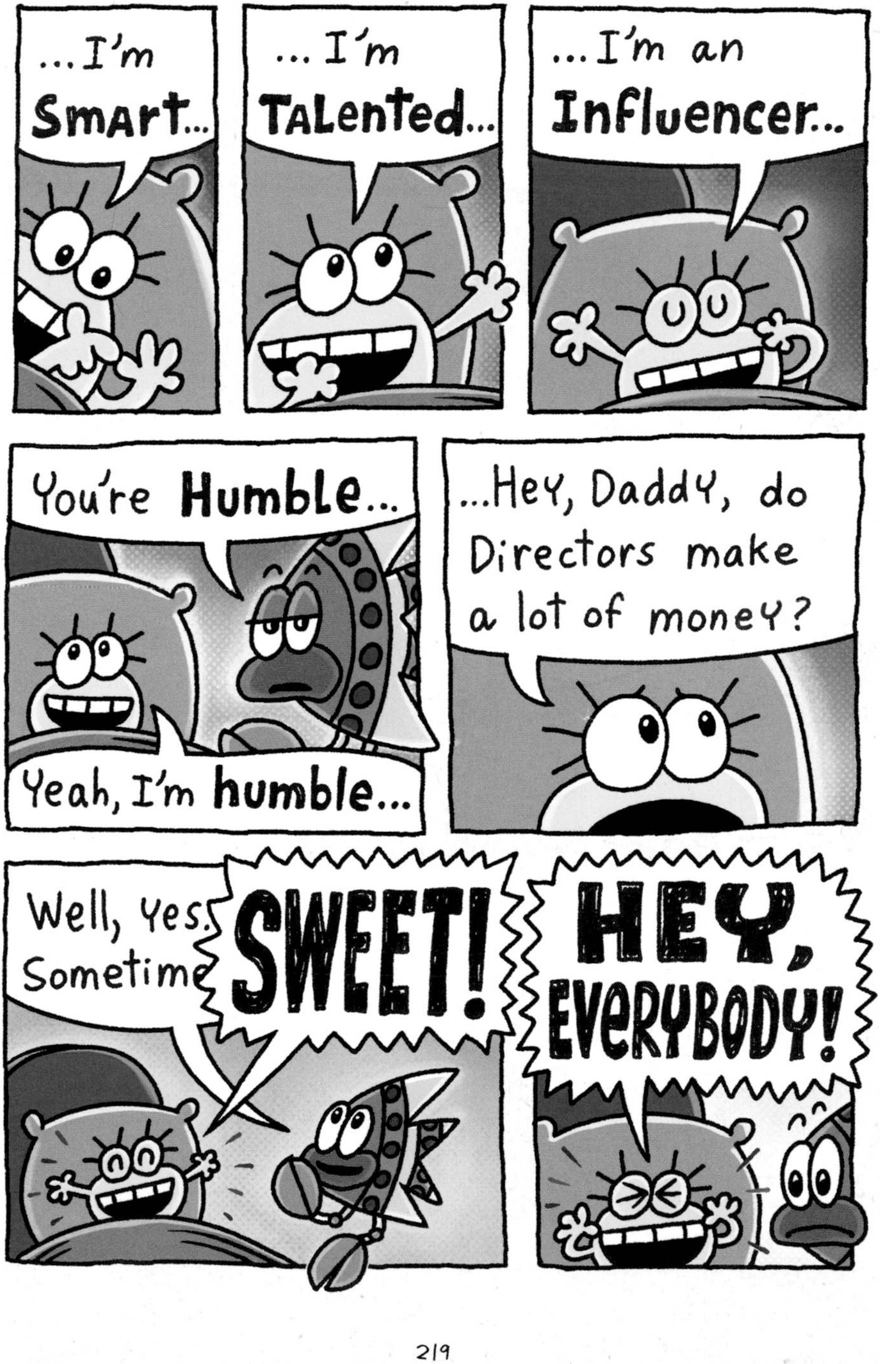
...I'm Smart...
...I'm TALented...
...I'm an Influencer...
You're Humble...
Yeah, I'm humble...
...Hey, Daddy, do Directors make a lot of money?
Well, yes. Sometime
SWEET!
HEY, EVERYBODY!

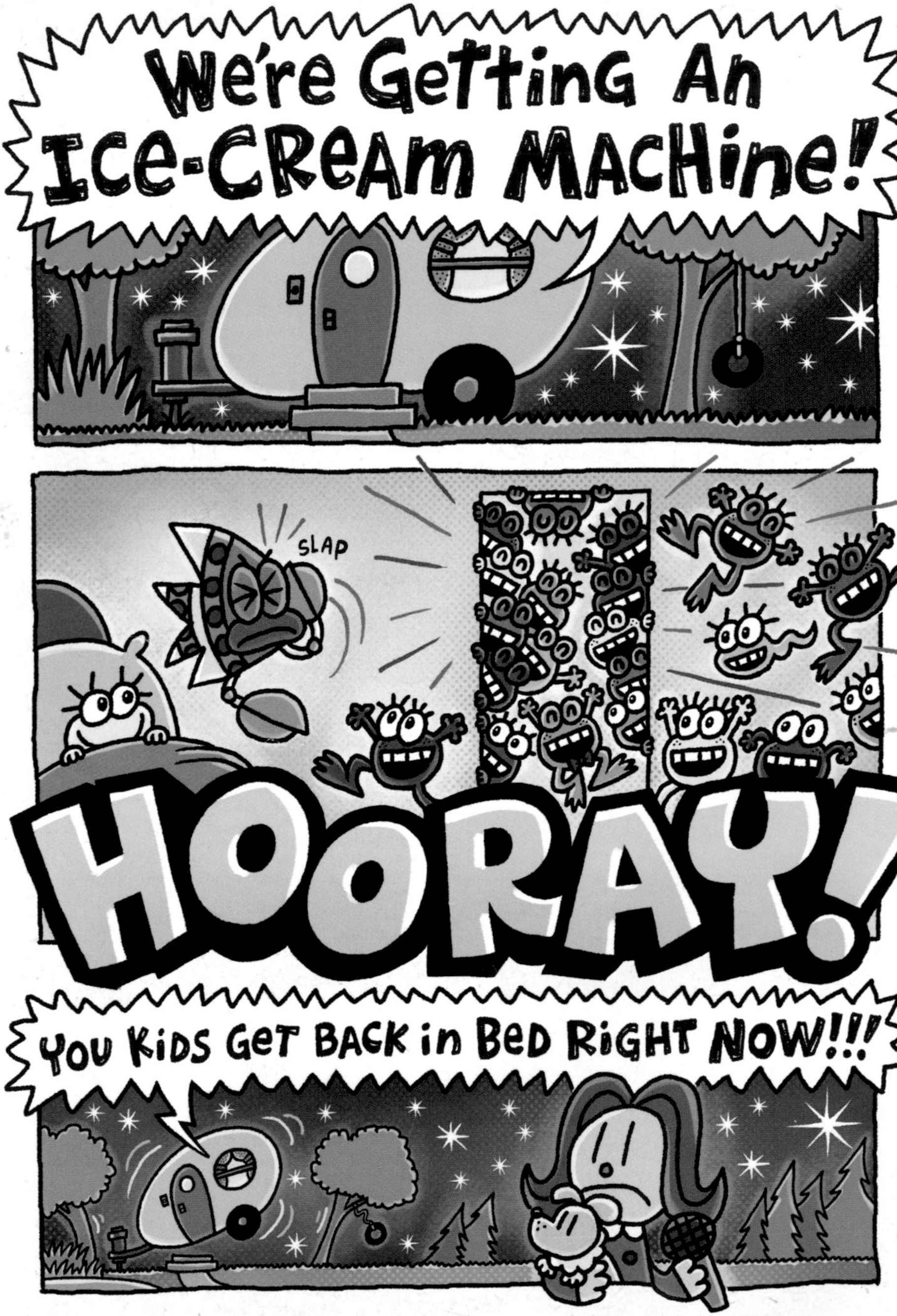
We're Getting An Ice-Cream Machine!
SLAP
HOORAY!
You Kids Get Back in Bed Right Now!!!

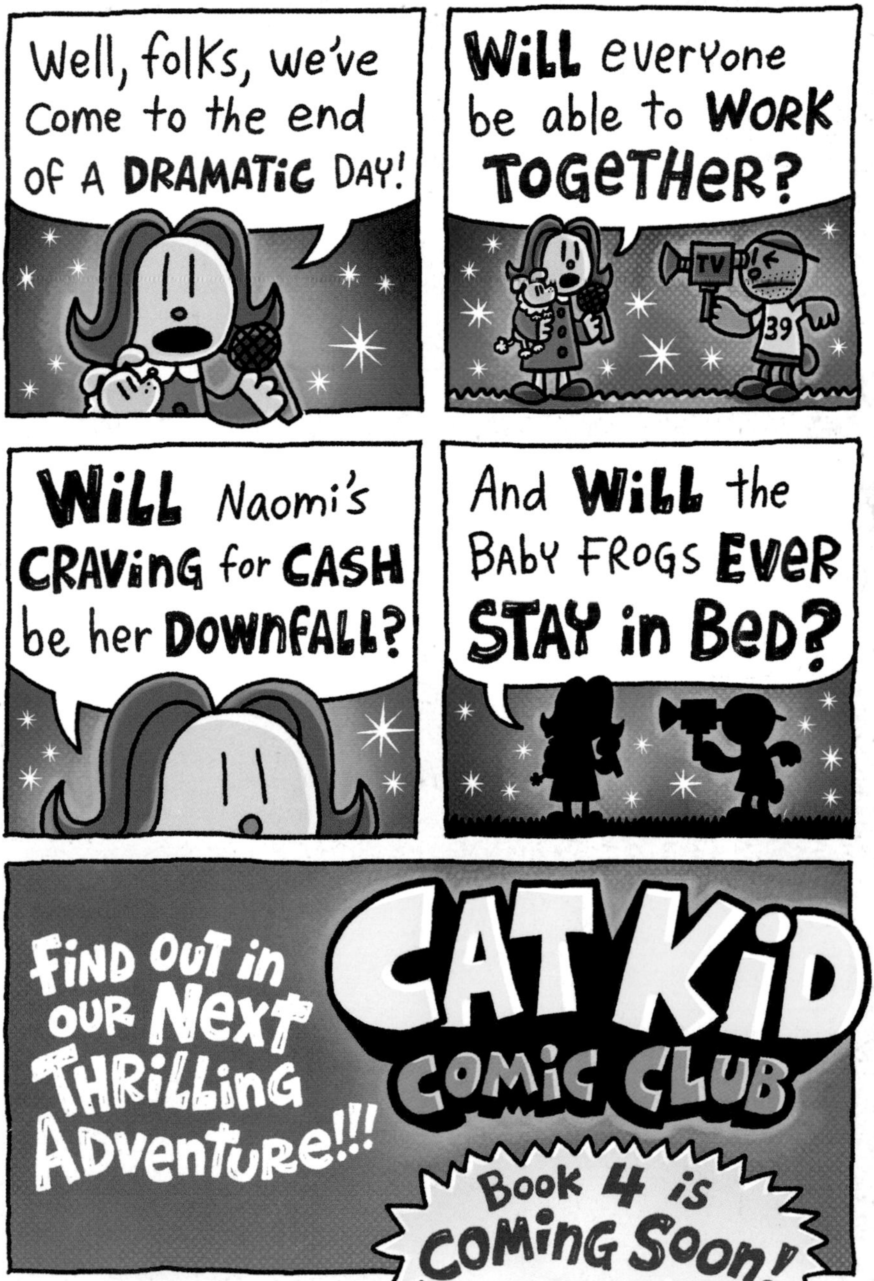
Well, folks, we've come to the end of A DRAMATIC DAY!
WILL everyone be able to WORK TOGETHER?
TV
39
WILL Naomi's CRAVING for CASH be her DOWNFALL?
And WILL the Baby Frogs EVER STAY in Bed?
FIND OUT in OUR NEXT THRILLING ADVENTURE!!!
CAT KID COMIC CLUB
Book 4 is COMING Soon!

NOTES & FUN FACTS

☆ The cover artwork for this book was made from cardboard, wire, crumpled-up construction paper, putty, acrylic paints, glue, and a small sheet of fake grass.

☆ Most of the planets in BABY FROG SQUAD are balloons, airbrushed with markers, that were photographed in front of a light bulb. The planet that looks like a melon is a close-up photo of the plastic lid of a fruit cup.

☆ The Baby Frog Squad's bunk beds were made out of matchboxes glued to bamboo shish-kebab skewers.

☆ Over 2,000 photographs were taken for the Chubbs McSpiderbutt mini comic, but only 111 were used.

☆ Chubbs is correct on page 182. Spiders DO produce webs from their spinnerets, located at the tips of their abdomens (their butts). Most spiders don't "shoot" webs, but a few do. The Darwin's bark spider can "shoot" a web up to 82 feet (25 meters) long. Sweeeet!!!

☆ Big Bubba Babyhead's gym shorts came from a 1972 action figure called "Big Jim." This action figure also inspired a character in the Dog Man series.

☆ The Ethel Merman Disco Album really DOES exist, although it is rarely used to frighten baby frogs.

☆ Melvin's words on page 169 were inspired by the following quote:

"Discouragement and failure are two of the surest stepping-stones to success."

— Dale Carnegie

KEEP READING WITH DAV PILKEY!

DOG MAN
DOG MAN UNLEASHED
DOG MAN A Tale of Two Kitties
DOG MAN AND CAT KID
DOG MAN LORD OF THE FLEAS
DOG MAN BRAWL of the WILD
DOG MAN FOR WHOM THE BALL ROLLS
DOG MAN FETCH-22
DOG MAN GRIME AND PUNISHMENT
DOG MAN MOTHERING HEIGHTS
DAV PILKEY

CAT KID COMIC CLUB
CAT KID COMIC CLUB PERSPECTIVES
DAV PILKEY

DOG MAN The Musical
Original Cast Recording

The epic musical adventure is now available from Broadway Records!

PLANET PILKEY

Go to planetpilkey.com to read chapters, make comics, watch videos, play games, and download supa fun stuff!

Download on the App Store

HOME BASE

SCHOLASTIC

GET IT ON Google Play

ABOUT THE
AUTHOR-ILLUSTRATOR

When Dav Pilkey was a kid, he was diagnosed with ADHD and dyslexia. Dav was so disruptive in class that his teachers made him sit out in the hallway every day. Luckily, Dav loved to draw and make up stories. He spent his time in the hallway creating his own original comic books — the very first adventures of Dog Man and Captain Underpants.

In college, Dav met a teacher who encouraged him to write and illustrate for kids. He took her advice and created his first book, WORLD WAR WON, which won a national competition in 1986. Dav made many other books before being awarded the California Young Reader Medal for DOG BREATH (1994) and the Caldecott Honor for THE PAPERBOY (1996).

In 2002, Dav published his first full-length graphic novel for kids, called THE ADVENTURES OF SUPER DIAPER BABY. It was both a USA Today and New York Times bestseller. Since then, he has published more than a dozen full-length graphic novels for kids, including the bestselling Dog Man and Cat Kid Comic Club series.

Dav's stories are semi-autobiographical and explore universal themes that celebrate friendship, empathy, and the triumph of the good-hearted.

When he is not making books for kids, Dav loves to kayak with his wife in the Pacific Northwest.

Learn more at Pilkey.com.